BY CHARLES BOCK

Alice & Oliver
Beautiful Children

ALICE & OLIVER

ALICE & OLIVER

A NOVEL

Charles Bock

 RANDOM HOUSE · New York

Published in the United States by Random House, an imprint and division of Penguin Random House LLC, New York.

RANDOM HOUSE and the HOUSE colophon are registered trademarks of Penguin Random House LLC.

Grateful acknowledgment is made to Mark Arm for permission to reprint two stanzas from "Flat Out Fucked," written by Mudhoney, copyright © 1989 by Better Than Your Music (ASCAP). Reprinted by permission.

LIBRARY OF CONGRESS CATALOGING-IN-PUBLICATION DATA
Bock, Charles.
Alice & Oliver: a novel / Charles Bock.
pages cm
ISBN 978-1-4000-6838-8
eBook ISBN 978-0-8129-8847-5
1. Cancer—Patients—Fiction. 2. Married women—Fiction.
3. Terminally ill—Fiction. 4. Domestic fiction. I. Title. II. Title: Alice and Oliver.
PS3602.O3255A79 2016
813'.6—dc23 2015022303

Printed in the United States of America on acid-free paper

randomhousebooks.com

9 8 7 6 5 4 3 2 1

FIRST EDITION

Book design by Simon M. Sullivan

For Diana Joy Colbert. For Lily Bock.

PART I

Induction

THERE SHE WAS, Alice Culvert, a little taller than most, her figure fuller than she would have liked. This brisk morning, the fourth Wednesday of November, Alice was making her way down West Thirteenth. Her infant was strapped to her chest; her backpack was overloaded and pulling at her shoulders. The Buddhist skull beads around her wrist kept a rattling time. She drank coffee from a paper cup. Sweat bubbled from her neck. Her scarf kept unraveling. She was rocking knee-high boots—sensuous leather, complicated buckles. Her gaze remained arrow straight, focused on some unseen goal. But she was slowing. A businessman only had a moment to avoid running into her. Alice bent over, coughing now, a coughing fit, bringing forth something phlegmy, bloody.

This couldn't happen. Thanksgiving plans in Vermont had been set for too long; her mother was *insane* to see the Blueberry. And an extended weekend at Mom's, with pecan cobbler and free round-the-clock childcare, trumped whatever bug she'd caught this time. She'd just have to swallow it, pretend her usual zazz hadn't been absent for the last week, throbs weren't emanating from her temples. This was adulthood, honeysuckle. You soldiered on. She was going to be on time, meeting Oliver at the rental car place. Alice regularly picked up winter coughs like they were sample swatches;

she'd spent all afternoon batting that lozenge back and forth between her cheeks (the ground strokes lazy, the rally unending), hacking through the last of her chores (folding T-shirts into her knapsack, making sure the baby bag was loaded with Wet-Naps). Out of their apartment, down the front steps, everything had been ginger. Right until the coughing, three increasingly violent retches. The jewel of phlegm—its hue the light pink of a rose pearl—was probably nothing but saliva and coloring dye number five. Just goopy residue from the cherry cough drop.

The rental agency was on the rim of the West Village, usually a five-minute walk, ten with the baby strapped to her. It took Alice half an hour. A rust-colored Taurus was waiting out in front, its driver's door open. Oliver stood on the side, making sure the suited agent documented every last ding. "Jesus," he said. "Honey." He felt her forehead. "You all right?" She answered: "Can you take Doe?"

Then they were emerging from the scrum of the city, into the bumper-to-bumper hell clogging every inch from Bridgeport to New Haven. Oliver kept blasting heat through the front compartment. No matter how many blankets Alice wrapped around herself, those weird cold sweats wouldn't stop. If anything, she felt worse, the chill deep inside her bones. Now, nearing the western border of Massachusetts, they sped down one of those empty rural interstates, tall barren trees looming dark on either side. Alice's voice quivered: "Could you pull over please?" Oliver veered into the first roadside rest area he saw, the lights of its parking lot distended and spooky. *It's nothing,* she assured herself, again. She lowered her seat all the way down, her body following the tight collapse as if her own internal gears and stopgaps had also received permission to give way. The sensation went beyond a mental or physical recognition of her exhaustion: she fell back and lay still in the collapsed seat and shut her eyes.

For a time, inside the house that was her body, it was as if she were walking out of every room and turning off the lights behind her, one by one.

Dimly, Alice was aware of tiny limbs readjusting inside the baby seat, the Blueberry letting out a contented, somnolent breath. She was aware of her husband forcing himself to sound calm, asking: *"Favorito?"*

Instead of answering, Alice recalibrated, focusing on the pulse behind her eyes, the labored rise and fall of her chest, how much effort it was taking her to inhale. Her weariness so intense now it *ached*.

"It's okay," she was told, the sweetest whisper. Alice moved toward its kiss.

It was not encouraging that her lips were a light purple. "Could be an early indicator of anemia. Could be something else." Dr. Glenn trailed off. Instead of indicating what that something else might be, he continued with the task at hand, shifting the small steel disc along the upper part of Alice's back, his concentration resolute, his movements precise, as if placing the stethoscope piece in the wrong location might set off an explosion.

"Deep breaths," he said. "Whatever you can do is fine."

She kept looking at the pink goo (wrapped in tissue paper, sealed inside a plastic sandwich bag, ignored on the instrument table).

The doctor wrote something in his folder, removed the stethoscope buds from his ears. Alice'd known him since girlhood, but, in the years since she'd last visited his family practice, he'd gone almost bald, just a few white cottony tufts left sprouting around his ears. A crescent of mustard from his lunch still smeared the corner of his mouth. He used to enter this same exam room and point his finger at her as if it were a gun—Alice was barely a teen when she'd first dismissed him: the kind of lightweight who knew he was being an ass but still acted that way. Who actually *chose* to spend his life

flirting with middle-aged earth mothers, jamming rectal thermom-
eters into their entitled kids? Life of the party in a small hippie
town.

Presently he looked up from Alice's folder. "I don't like your
temperature and blood pressure so low. Not with this lip color. And
what you were telling me about no appetite, the lack of energy." At
once serious as a Protestant but trying to be kind, the doctor leveled his gaze, made sure he conveyed a point.

"We're going to X-ray your lungs." To his nurse he added, "I'll
want some blood."

"What's going on?" Alice said. Fear rushed through her; she felt
her chin collapsing. "What's wrong?"

Minutes dragged, then disappeared, time flushing itself into a black
hole. Finally, that nice old doctor reappeared, but when he entered
the room, he moved with purpose, heading directly to Alice, kneeling in front of her. He touched her knee, looked into her eyes. His
face was already in mourning. "We have to get you to a hospital
right now."

Next to the exam table, Oliver Culvert had the baby cradled
against his chest. He kept rocking the little one—babies sensed tension, Alice must have told him this a zillion times. Oliver was not
one for sentiment—the saccharine of pop songs and greeting cards
repulsed him, demonstrative emotional reactions making him
freeze like a scared lizard. His natural response to most things was
self-consciousness: *How am I supposed to feel?*

Now he watched his wife's eyes enlarging, saw the fear across her
face.

The doctor continued, saying one awful phrase after another: you
are very ill, this is a grave danger, your white blood cell count . . .

Sick recognition spread through Oliver's stomach. He had one
thought: *No.*

Then he did his best to get beyond himself, and asked the doctor if he could slow down, could he please explain this again. Bureaucrats and medical personnel were shuffling in and out of the room. Oliver had the presence of mind to back away, giving them space to work. His back grazed the far wall, he made sure to hold Doe properly—protecting his child.

That was the least he could do. Take care of the small things.

Except the small things didn't turn out to be simple.

Just putting Alice in the rental car and hightailing her to the nearest hospital wasn't an option, it so happened.

"Do you understand," Doc Glenn said to Alice, "you are in the thrall of a neutropenic fever?"

Tearing eyes looked at the doctor like he was insane. "Of course I don't understand," Alice answered.

"For all practical purposes," the doctor said, "your body can't protect itself from anything right now."

She urged Oliver to ignore the old man, "drive us straight back to the city—our people are there, they can help with whatever needs helping." In response the doctor let Oliver know that, in his professional opinion, Alice would not make it back to Manhattan alive. "We have to have an ambulance anyway," Oliver thought out loud. "Can't the same paramedic just stand over and care for Alice all the way back to the city?" Oliver volunteered to foot the bill for the mileage costs, then nodded through the doctor's administrative blarney—the drive being a nonemergency, elective use of an ambulance probably not covered by insurance as an in-network cost. Like he knew or cared what any of it meant.

Oliver pressed further. Calls were made. But even if one of the Manhattan hospitals covered by Alice's insurance plan had an available bed—which they didn't, but even if they had—none of those wards would accept a body with almost no white blood cells after six straight hours on the road.

Frustrating as this clusterfuck was, Oliver—like many of his programming peers and former grad school classmates—had spent huge swaths of his adult life devoted to logical progressions, the evolutionary dances of trial and error that went into problem solving. So, yes, he felt the urge to lash out, punch something solid. But he also understood that every reason something couldn't work provided more information, another small jigsaw piece, the borders and edges gradually filling, a cumulative suggestion developing.

This is happening, he told himself. *Whether it feels surreal, or melodramatic, or whatever, this is happening.*

Now two men in dark uniforms angled the stretcher, making sure Alice's legs were raised higher than her head so that the blood would flow toward her brain. "Precautionary measure," explained the bulkier paramedic, whose responsibilities seemed to include talking to Alice. "Keeps patients from going into pulmonary shock."

That's really a possibility? Oliver started to ask. The question stalled in his throat. Its answer was apparent in the black stabilizing straps being buckled tight across his wife's chest, the secondary set constricting her thighs, the exam room now crowded and jostling and serious. The paramedics were counting to one another, one two tres; Alice was looking up, searching, her face pale, waxy. Her eyes were red and brimmed with tears. Now she locked in on him.

He would never forget those contractions, Alice taken by pain so encompassing as to be frightening, this highly functioning adult— this woman he loved so much (he felt his love throbbing inside each of his heart's four chambers)—reverting back to her mammalian origins, making horrible, primal sounds, the totality of her being committed, shrieking. Oliver was freaked, admittedly, and self-conscious to the extreme, but he absorbed the shooting pain from his wife's grip, and squeezed her hand in return; he breathed in tandem with her, and the contractions continued, and, on count, she pushed with all she had (*pushpushpush, breathe, pushpushpush*), and his gaze remained trained on her spread legs, making for damned sure that he was watching every second. Why had nobody told him he needed to watch and stay trained, why had he needed to figure this out for himself? Only after each contraction receded, when the baby was that much closer but not yet crowned, when they had a minute or whatever to recover and get ready for the next push, only then had Oliver looked back up at his wife's face; still continuing to count, still breathing in tandem, he'd used his free hand to pat her sweaty brow, repeating just how beautiful she was, how great she was doing.

This time her grip wasn't crushing the long bones of his fingers. Rather, she was clasping his fingertips. When this became too difficult, she was hanging on to the edge of his coat, holding its seam between her thumb and pinkie. Oliver still had the warm bundle of their daughter on his chest. He leaned down. Alice had just begun losing the pregnancy weight from her cheeks and chin. "I can't believe how much I want to fuck you right now," he whispered.

She coughed out the laugh he wanted. But by then the paramedics were lifting her, she had to let go of his sleeve. For an instant her arm remained hanging, outstretched. She looked back at him, her eyes huge.

Shielding his daughter from the sight of Mommy being wheeled out of the room, Oliver shouted, "Don't worry about anything." He rocked the baby to his chest, promised, "We're right behind you. We're with you."

His wife was receding, down the hall, toward an ambulance, away from him. "We're in your heart," Oliver shouted. "We'll beat you there, I bet," his screams almost gleeful. "We love you so much. I LOVE YOU SO MUCH."

Flakes of snow, random and swirling, drifted through the darkness of the small twin windows. She followed a single flake: it flipped along a gust of wind, ricocheting off the glass. Alice couldn't guess how long she'd been in here, how long they'd been driving. She couldn't hear the sirens, but from the way any pothole jostled her, the ambulance had to be going pretty fast. If she concentrated enough she could block out the beeping updates of her vital signs, the itching down the middle of her torso from this thin cheap blanket. What couldn't be ignored was the weight. Settling atop her chest. She imagined it so clearly. Light but firm. The black box with that black ribbon, tied in a huge, sagging black bow.

"I know this is overwhelming," Doc Glenn had said. Deep rivulets were etched in the skin around his eyes. "But whatever you are about to go through, you'll be able to get through it a lot better if you can learn to live with not knowing the answers. It's the patients who can handle uncertainty. They're the ones who deal with these situations better."

The ambulance came out of a turn and slowed, its vibrations lowering an octave. Arriving felt important: one part ending, a new one beginning. This was the transition. These moments were moving her into the part where she found out what was happening inside her body. The engine cut; the ambulance went still; for long seconds Alice looked up through the two long square windows, into the gloom, alone with the darkness and the black box and the anticipation. Then the doors opened; night flowed into the chasm, the chilled air stinging her cheeks. A few orange bulbs scattered light across the loading dock. As the paramedics set Alice down onto the cement landing, cascading flakes landed on their knit hats and thick winter parkas and gloves and thermal masks. She noticed the far wall of the parking area was cushioned: rubber bumpers for when the ambulance couldn't afford to slow down.

Alice's stretcher rotated, turning at an angle; she was rolled over rough asphalt. Beyond the boxy silhouette of hospital buildings, she could see the layering of dark mountains, a smear of charcoal sky. Inside swaths of the dock's streetlamp and tower light, the snowfall seemed like fireflies and stardust and the refractions off untold tiny spinning diamonds. It seemed to her the scene could have been manufactured on a Hollywood soundstage, or was part of an odd dream. She raised her head from the stretcher; snow stung her cheeks. For long moments she almost believed some peculiar form of magic was indeed waiting for her. Alice could not help herself: she extended her tongue.

If she hadn't pulled it together at the rest stop, found a second wind, and recovered enough to convince Oliver to get them to her mom's, so they could all have one nice goddamn holiday weekend, please. If her mom hadn't looked at her daughter in the bedroom that morning and ignored Alice's protests and placed that call. If good old Doc Glenn had been hosting his children and grandkids for Thanksgiving like he did during even years, and had been occupied with all that, instead of just waiting to board a flight, his mind not quite engaged by that newsweekly magazine. If the pay phone hadn't been free, and the doctor hadn't checked his service, heard that panicked call from a longtime patient, and followed up. If what might have been some dinky country office hadn't actually been fairly up-to-date, with modern equipment including a gizmo that could take lung X-rays. If the very same doctor whom Alice had considered a cornball bozo when she was growing up, with such little mental firepower, had indeed been a cornball, and had been satisfied with the X-ray's discovery of pneumonia, and hadn't ordered a round of blood tests, just to be sure. If that same little office hadn't had access to a blood lab that *not only* turned around results on the same day but also remained open for business on all days, including legal holidays. If pretty much everyone in the area code with anything resembling a normal life hadn't taken a proverbial hike on the day before Thanksgiving, and if local junkies hadn't had their veins full of a particularly average batch delivered down from Montreal, and if there'd even been a smattering of crazy accidents or family disagreements involving carving knives, so that the skeleton staff working at the laboratory, as often is the case with commercial medical labs, had been dealing with something other than a clear and cloudless docket, and had been forced to wait an afternoon, or even into the evening, before processing Alice's samples. If too much time had passed before the discovery that Alice possessed zero white blood cells, *zero*. If that same lab had discovered that slightly *above* fifty percent of Alice's blood cells were cancerous, rather than the number they found, which was just barely below. If one of the top cancer hospitals in the Northeast hadn't been available less than two hours away via ambulance—close enough that its doctors could apply their considerable expertise and equipment before more of those infected blood cells had replicated past the point of no return. If Alice hadn't been isolated and her treatments hadn't started before some random nearby person let loose with a stray sneeze whose germs had landed inside of her ridiculously compromised system, or before her pneumonia or fever had finished her off. Any individual clause in the list. Any offshoot of who knew how many other improbabilities. Any of the uncountable possibilities that happened to break her way when they could have easily broken the other way instead. If Alice spent a moment reflecting on any one of these, let alone all of them; if she so much as considered how lucky she'd been to make it to this moment, especially when she couldn't allow herself to conceive of what she still had to go through—the ifs were enough to stop her cold.

Do not pursue the past, she reminded herself. *Do not lose yourself in the future.*

She needed to appreciate the now.

Day three: her nose swollen outward from the nostrils, her cheeks inflated. A deep crimson discoloration had started behind her ears and now covered the underside of her jaw, the top of her neck. "Not all that unusual for daunorubicin," said the disheveled resident. "I don't think anything for concern about," added the visiting fellow (Mongolian, an emerging star, he'd been called in for a consultation).

The next morning, on rounds, the attending physician addressed those students who'd followed him into Alice's room. Exclaiming his pleasure about Alice's lack of a fever, he offered similar talking points about her newest rash (not at all unusual, no cause for concern). This one was a purplish shade, creeping out from under her pits, spilling in all directions. The attending possessed the good sense to keep his mouth shut about the possibility of the two rashes joining in a superrash. And no student doctor was brazen enough to broach the subject.

Alice took solace in the attending's air of authority but also had a flash of sorrow for all the years she'd dismissed Dr. Glenn. "Ointments should take care of the burning," continued the attending physician. He acknowledged the difficulty of keeping her hands still. Then, as if talking to a child, added, "Staying away from the rash is how we keep it from spreading or getting infected."

"I'll be good," Alice answered. "Scout's honor."

Still she scratched. She picked. Oliver also noticed her running her hand over her hair. More and more she did it, like one of those poker tells. This concerned him—he wondered if a catheter had wriggled free from a weak or wandering vein in the crook of Alice's right arm; if the IV drip was going into her biceps instead of her bloodstream. The resident, the fellow, and the attending were all sanguine. The infiltrating medicine was not a lethal mix; the swelling would recede. However, they also insisted: she had to keep that swollen arm stationary. And *still* she skimmed. Incessant, straight swipes with that same fucked-up arm, her fingers combing backward. To Oliver it now appeared as if his wife's face was in the middle of transforming into a mutant boar's; and watching her— ridiculously bloated, garishly discolored, frail, weak, covered in blankets, hooked up to all those goddamn tubes—all of that was bad enough. But here she was, *willfully and continually* disobeying doctors' orders, running her hand over her skull, checking yet again, displaying each new wisp that clung to her finger.

"Nothing like the handfuls you'd expect," she said. Her voice was hopeful, maybe even convincing. "I've heard stories—women who survived all sorts of chemo and kept a decent head of hair."

The attending physician let Alice get it out of her system. Then he answered, plain as white bread: "It's all going to fall out."

Of course, Alice's mom checked herself in to the nearby hospice. The white-haired woman who'd combed out Alice's tangles, apologizing, always, for the pain she caused; who'd asked that Alice hold still, wrapped her hair into untold ponytails, and taught her girl how to braid, ending each lesson with a kiss on the top of the head. The hospice was available for loved ones of long-terms and potentially terminal cases, and charged twenty dollars a night, more than reasonable, thought Alice's mom, especially with the lodgings being so homey: hand-stitched quilts and Americana on the walls, lace tablecloth and fresh flowers on the common table. Alice's mother was calm and rational and not a complainer in any way, and she quickly proved indispensable, each morning finishing her grapefruit, cornflakes, and strong black coffee, then exchanging best wishes with the sad married couple whose son had been in a hunting accident, and then changing and re-dressing her grandchild.

Whenever she and Doe found their way back to the hospital, Oliver's shift on guard ended, and it became his turn to ride the complimentary shuttle downtown, into four blocks of brick buildings that had been renovated to look historically quaint. This luxury, these few hours to himself, was mainly full of errands: sending necessary insurance faxes from the cluttered rear of the office supply store; settling into the phone booth of the nearby university library's lobby, where he used his long-distance calling card to update friends and family on the latest; concocting plans for how the biz would deal with things while he was stuck here.

That afternoon, the sky was heavy-handed in its grayness, the wind blowing the hail sideways in unending sheets. By the time Oliver found the weathered woodcut pole that the nurses had told him to watch out for, his clothes had long gone damp, his face and hands turned numb. None of the old men turned from their shaving chairs. Oliver picked through the newspaper's meager sections, not daring to interrupt banter about the weather.

The wind's bluster had eased into a mild, overcast evening. The baby dozing, Grandma as well. Visitors to the room were supposed to wear surgical mask and gloves. But in the recliner, Grandma's head was unadorned, tilted back, her mouth open wide enough to reveal gold fillings. Alice responded to the door's creak but appeared groggy, confused. Then her eyes went wide, her swollen jaw dropped as if unhinged.

"I wanted you to see it's just hair," Oliver said.

Her hands went over her heart. It seemed she would bawl.

"It'll grow out or it won't," Oliver continued. "Who gives a fuck."

"The most wonderful thing anybody's done in the history of time," Alice said. She threw both arms outward, set the IV machine jiggling. "Get over here, silly man. Let me feel, already."

That night he would borrow the electric shears kept at the nurses' station. Alice's hair was more than ready, releasing easily, some clumps falling from vibrations alone. His wife had a long-standing fondness for brightly colored streaks, exotic highlights, any tweak that might lend a bit of glamour. For important gallery openings, industry parties, or runway shows, it was assumed that a chunk of her afternoon would be devoted to some complexly pinned arrangement, be it chopsticks, feathery wisps, or exotic braiding, whatever the most stylish magazines would be cooing over in six months. Less than three minutes it took now to shave her skull.

Afterward they perched the baby between them in the crowded bed, her head its own pink planet, practically the size of the rest of her body. What few hairs she had were still short and translucent, their swirling growth pattern forming an almost imperceptible crop circle on the top of her head. Alice's mom fetched an overpriced disposable camera from the gift shop. Oliver pulled his little surgical mask down around his neck. He and Alice leaned their shoulders into one another. Doe gurgled, cooed, kicked out chubby legs.

"There they are." The nurse counted backward toward the flash. "The perfect, bald family."

Some things, however, were Alice's alone: the way those tiny lips attached themselves to her areola; how the ridge of those gums wrapped around her nipple; holding the baby's head to her and listening to the soft gurgles, feeling the sensation of her pull and suckle. Through the first five months of her life, Doe had known only her mother's milk. But the cells in Alice's bloodstream changed that. The chemo made her milk toxic.

Obstetrics sent a machine that looked like something out of fifties sci-fi, and when Alice's breasts got too full, she applied the ancient vacuum's suction attachment and performed a distorted version of her normal routine. A nurse in a blue mask, gloves, and lead-lined radiation gown carried away the results for hermetic disposal.

Without much fuss, Alice's mother went out and purchased formula from the Olde Town Apothecary. A tenth-grade English teacher for more than thirty years, Alice's mother was a pragmatic, thoughtful woman. Her daughter insisted, so she had to venture out a second time, scouring the few health food stores for something more natural. It took four days until Alice was sure Doe smelled different. Chemical-y. This new smell made Alice weep, and her body was weak enough that these jags became their own sources of pain. She couldn't help herself. She wept because Doe hadn't ever had a diaper rash before and would now. She wept because her baby still reached for Mommy's chest, and began her own bawling when she wasn't allowed to attach. She wept remembering how raw her nipples used to get, and she wept because, with every passing minute, they were getting less raw. At three in the morning, when a nurse came around to take her vital signs, Alice wept with the memory of the body weight of her girl by her side—rustling, half-awakening—the memory of plopping a breast into the little one's mouth. Whipping out the feeding curtain at Dean & DeLuca. Leakage spreading through silk-screened maternity blouses. Those nursing bras that she knew her husband so despised.

The visiting doctor from Eastern Europe had a habit of snacking on junk food in the hallways, and this was humanizing to Oliver, especially seeing that the man consistently seemed gracious toward other hospital staffers, so catching up with him outside the nurses' station, using words and mannerisms that included everything short of falling onto his knees and pulling down the guy's pants, Oliver pretty much begged for a promising survival rate, some crack of light, a taste that would help them get through this. "I mean, she's stabilizing, and we started the chemo, so . . . ."

With the same flat tone that his esteemed colleague had used to tell Alice that her hair was going to fall out, the attending told Oliver these words: "Cancer is hell of disease."

Teen years: lonely Bakersfield afternoons, his dad pounding dents out of cars all day in a glorified salvage yard, Mom making copies for an accountant, the stink of fertilizer constant, industrial farmland as far as the eye could see. His escape was a home computer store in a strip mall, Oliver learning code from his cousin's dad, who needed to distract himself from the paucity of people who were shelling out money for Commodore PETs and Atari home systems. Even before partial scholarships had gotten Oliver out of that cow town and across the country, allowing him to bust his ass through college and graduate school, his intellectual life—even his understanding of himself—had begun maturing, in no small part, because of his relationship with complexity. Those tedious hours he spent with infinitesimal units, information strings of code, copying the program for another adventure game, whose line progressions were listed in the back pages of *Byte* magazine. This, Oliver learned, was how massive, elegant structures were constructed. And, gradually, he became accustomed to converting the theoretical into something practical and sturdy and cleanly perfect.

It was gut-churning to hear that man say, *Cancer is hell of disease.* What felt worse, however—wrong in a way that betrayed everything Oliver believed about the cosmos—was the recognition. A doctor involved with his wife's treatment was openly admiring the elegant complexity eating at her bones and blood.

Comrade Doctor put his hands up. "I try again—" he said.

Damaged English followed. "As personal, I try avoid telling person news he cannot take." The doctor continued, sharing his belief that *honest assessment represent measure of respect,* as well as *importance give loving ones information so to be prepare selves.*

"You're telling me . . ." Oliver began, petered out.

"First hundred days," the man answered.

"What?"

"We see how she doing. Get sense how things going. Know more." He patted Oliver's shoulder. "Hundred days."

**Whitman Memorial, 1220 York Ave., 4th floor, Hematology/Oncology
(follow-up appointment: patient background/personal history)**

He couldn't afford one of the office supply company's high-end jobbers, so he'd sprung for your solid, middle-of-the-road, basic ergonomic desk chair. This was what he sat in. As for his diet, he tried, he really did, loading up on greens and boiled chicken, although he still snuck in red meats and fried calamari, more than he'd care to admit. Ever since kids had come into the picture, he'd been lucky to get to the gym once a fortnight. Admittedly he could have dropped fifteen pounds. Twenty pounds. So, basically he was a middle-aged somewhat-overweight white-collar dad going through the rite of manly passage known as chronic back pain. Maybe not a human interest feature in the local paper. But his spasms sure felt newsworthy. Had to pile throw cushions on that desk chair just to sit; pop Advils like they were candies just to get through the day. And rolling around on the carpet with Timothy and Suzy Jo? Please. Then his wife had heard about this acupuncturist from another mom at playgroup. And he wasn't exactly thrilled about it, but he let them put those pins into both sides of his neck, his shoulders, his elbows, his kidneys, his sacrum, the bottom of each foot, the space between each pair of toes. Afterward, he defecated for the first time in four days. Went home and slept like a stone at the bottom of the ocean.

Four weeks and twice as many visits to the acupuncturist later, the man received a shot of cortisone from his family physician to take care of the discomfort in his back. He got a script for ciprofloxacin to address his urination problems. The physician discussed whether the man needed an ammonium laxative to deal with his constipation and advised the man he needed to exercise more, and could stand to drop fifty pounds. The man followed the little taped instructions on his plastic pill bottles. He found religion when it came to his dietary habits, more or less, and made an effort to shut down his workstation an hour early in the evenings and get to the gym. Stretched his back for ten minutes before and after. But that belt of electric pain remained, strapped across his lower back. His stomach had gone bloated and light, as if hands were constantly pressing onto his abdomen. And he had unsettling stretches of numbness through his pelvis and lower spine. The man was getting night sweats, and at his office he sometimes wrapped himself in this frayed old beach blanket to warm himself, plus he scratched himself all the time, just couldn't stop. It was frustrating beyond words: he was doing everything he was supposed to do, then lapping those efforts by half. Was it so goddamn much to find out what was wrong with him?

The gastroenterologist explained that lymphoma was a particularly difficult disease to diagnose, especially when the lymph node beneath the pectoral hadn't yet swollen, as all indications seemed to be in this man's case. All the symptoms were pretty much right down the checklist. A biopsy would provide answers. They'd also find out if the disease had spread.

That was the bitch in cases like this, explained the doctor: the time it took for the disease to advance enough to diagnose was also the time it took for the disease to spread.

The now

T TOOK MORE than a month: her absolute neutrophil counts finally exceeding five hundred, the magic number necessary to spring her from Dartmouth-Hitchcock; the quiet rental car carrying them out of the Granite State, bringing them home, finally surrounded by what was theirs: hanging rolls of Chinese paper acting as curtains along the storm windows that filled the western windows; morning light oozing around the paper's tight borders. Now was bed, consumed by a comforter. Alice stared, without focus, at the large industrial fan above the bed, its blades dappled with brown rust. Lush carpets stretched across the walls for sound-proofing. Thanks to them, and the churn of white noise from the air purifier, she barely heard the clatter from outside, some six floors below—forklifts humming and shrilly backing up; workers groaning and cursing as they unloaded frozen sides of beef from semis that had fallen behind their normal delivery schedules, now downshifting into gear, hitting the road. Even these sounds were part of the comfort of what was known, part of what allowed her fear to recede.

The big questions were too much. But she and Oliver could handle logistics—couldn't they?

True, she hadn't yet found a suitable nanny. She had to make calls later about that, yes. But hadn't she, by herself, negotiated a matter of exponentially larger importance—the transfer of her care to Whitman Memorial (a well-regarded, smallish hospital on the Upper East Side)? Hadn't she put out feelers to friends, and hadn't they completed arrangements, scheduled appointments, procured an expert oncologist—*an impeccable genius,* according to Betsey Johnson's operations officer, *best reputation in the city*—now locked in, scheduled to take over Alice's treatment. All Alice had to do was bring her slides to that first meeting.

And during what she thought would be that routine call, when the nurse in New Hampshire had informed Alice about the hospital policy against sending blood slides to a residential address, hadn't Alice handled the little complication? Hadn't she gotten them sent straight to Whitman?

The memory infused her with a rickety confidence, reminding her of the competent professional she'd taken for granted not all that long ago, the woman she hardly still felt herself to be.

Except here it was, nine fifteen on a Friday morning, and Whitman *still* hadn't received their slides. Oliver had lost patience and commandeered control of the cordless. He wouldn't allow shoe wearing inside their loft, and she could hear him pacing in his gray gym socks, coming closer, floorboards creaking. She could hear him confirming that the slides had been sent, asking for the name of the person at Whitman who'd signed for them.

"Thanks a bunch." Oliver punched a button on the cordless.

His naturally curly hair had already grown back enough to be making that first twist, small tight rings sprouting neatly in every direction. His flannel was unbuttoned and untucked, his chest bare and concave, a slight paunch evident, a faint trail of fuzz running toward his pubes. Corduroy pants were slipping halfway down fleshy hips. On anyone else the look would have meant: *late riser, barely awake, struggling to get up to speed.* But Oliver seemed at home in his dishevelment, as if he reveled in the chaos, was invigorated by the challenge. A glance toward the crib; he ran his hand over the meat and fuzz of his jaw. He kept pacing the length of their loft. Their fat tabby scurried out of his path, and he punched at the phone. He gave the new oncologist's secretary at Whitman the name of the guilty party, the one who'd signed that delivery slip. And promptly learned it was her day off. Then a click.

Alice's skull—pallid and smooth—peeked out above the edge of the comforter.

Oliver pressed the flat pin of the phone antenna against his chin.

From behind her downy shield, she murmured, "You tried."

The phone went back into the cradle.

She said, "The hospital's on top of it."

Oliver stared at the sliver of work space through the partway opened door. Though he couldn't see the computer stations in the main room, he sensed their internal fans whirring, felt their dormant screens waiting to go bright with his first keystroke.

"It's Friday morning," he said. "We get to Friday afternoon, they haven't found the things, that office is empty all weekend. You get there Monday and they won't have squat. Doctor doesn't have anything to read? Why even show up?"

Her face emerged from behind the comforter: she didn't seem impressed by his logic. Instead, her movements measured, she propped herself onto pillows, let herself be supported by the wall. Alice let herself enjoy the chill of the white bricks against the silk of her pajama blouse. When her lids opened, she checked the corner, locking in on the crib.

Other than the usual three tries it took to get her down, and the de rigueur 4:00 A.M. screaming fit, Doe had had a restful night. Was still asleep.

Watching her breathe, Alice telepathically warned Oliver to keep his voice low. She massaged a dollop of coconut cream into the back of her palm. Skin that used to be soft now felt dry as chalk, and couldn't absorb moisture quickly enough. Alice straightened her back. She took three deep breaths, each coming up through her diaphragm. With every inhalation, the scent of her coconut cream was overpowering. Everywhere at once. Alice chanted a silent mantra, asking for calm, praying for peace. Her mind returned to the magnetized message she'd placed on the refrigerator door, long-ago-memorized words: *Before you speak, ask yourself: Does it improve on the silence?*

Alice did not open her eyes but whispered: "If you even possessed the *slightest* hint how many times I've talked to that receptionist in the past three days—"

Her index finger preempted, destroying Oliver's answer in its larval stage. "Can't you just *believe* that dear intrepid Beth will do her job?"

Oliver sat down next to Alice and stroked her hand. He had a flash memory, from not long after they'd started dating, back during a different reality: Alice at her sewing table, cutting the pattern for the pajamas she wore now. Forklifts beeped with faint accusations from the distance below. Alice's oversize Edwardian cuff wasn't buttoned. A black roach of a bruise sat along the thumb side of her wrist. Oliver's eyes followed the faded purple, the sickly green, the eggish yellow. He peered down the sallow length of her arm, recalling the morning when the skin around her port had gotten infected, when an air bubble had inflated, brown and transparent, in the middle of her biceps.

Mister Blister Alice had labeled that balloon. But it had deflated. Her piggish bloat had also receded, her recognizable features returning, so that she looked like herself, thank fucking hell. Oliver stared at the close pattern—small blue-and-silver chevrons and fleur-de-lis—which covered the former blister's location. For an instant he felt as furious as he'd been when the catheter's slippage had been discovered. Those nurses should've caught the infiltration earlier, should've known better than to go into a weak vein.

"That receptionist," Oliver said. "Figure she checks in how many patients an hour?"

"You're not—"

"Humor me, Alice."

"Oliver—"

"Figure a patient's showing up to see each doctor in the office every fifteen—"

She cut him off, exhausted, barely a whisper: "Then call again."

"You think sweet Beth isn't going to be hightailing it out of work on a Friday afternoon? In a goddamn *snowstorm*?"

"You just called. Look how well that worked."

"We have to stay on top of them."

"Oliver." Her chin quivered. "I'm going to be dealing with this doctor for at least six months." Her face flushed. "If the reception-ist hates me before I've even stepped through the door—"

"It's too much to ask you to make sure your *doctors have your GODDAMN LEUKEMIA SLIDES*?"

For a fraction of a moment things on the other side of the room were still. But then it began, a shift in molecules, a stirring, a con-sciousness turning on, confused. The baby gathered, then belted, at the seismic peak of her infant lungs.

"Wonderful." Alice rushed, struggling to rise, moving as quickly as her body would allow. "My hero."

When they'd gotten engaged and first started looking for their own place, Oliver had assured her that it was a steal—this tiny trapezoi-dal industrial area, just north of the West Village, by far the best value for their buck. He was, to put it tactfully, insane. The Meat-packing District's every daylight hour was dominated by dock thugs and frozen slabs; after dark, rotted zombie addicts held court with leather-collar sex club slaves and transvestite streetwalkers— the type of neighborhood that was superb for a night of slummy fun, Alice had no problem admitting that much, ordering the first round of shots, or shaming Oliver into doing the same. If the mood struck her, she'd be the first to hop on a bar and start dancing, and had no problems donating her bra (so long as it wasn't one of her fancier wire-support ones) to some hole's wall of fame. But as far as *bringing a child into the world,* as far as *raising their infant,* they'd have been better off if the area had been radioactive. Hell, for all Alice knew, it *was*.

Oliver felt differently. And this was tricky because he was one of those rare specimens: he actually followed up on ideas, possessing a special, almost preternatural talent for blocking out distractions, isolating a problem and breaking it down into smaller, solvable units. On a daily basis this could be annoying, it most definitely had killed more than a few date nights. But how else could he have successfully built a software and technical support start-up out of little more than underarm sweat and gum wrappers? Applying that same bulldog tenacity, Oliver came to her with a flowchart that showed distances to nearby gourmet grocery shopping and restaurants; he researched school districts, pinpointed the excellent zone they'd be in. Oliver went so far as to present her with a spreadsheet detailing possible upgrades to the apartment, options for what could be done with the rent money they'd save by living here. Equally unfortunate for Alice was that Oliver also had spent more than a bit of his childhood assisting his dad in odd jobs around the house. Meaning he was precise and crisp with a slide rule, knew the purpose of a flathead screw, how to find the load-bearing part of a wall for a shelving unit, even the dangers inherent in an industrial-size power sander. It also surely wasn't a coincidence that he'd scoped out the Upper East Side location where skilled nonunion day laborers hung around mornings, waiting for someone to offer them work. Yes, with his piercing intelligence, his formidable collection of technical skills, and his nonstop hustling attitude, Oliver created his own black magic, a momentum that turned feasible what should have been idle banter—daydreams the two of them mulled over while in bed, lying there satisfied, one of them idly tracing a finger up and down the other's inner leg.

Naturally, Oliver also *happened* to cross paths with some guy at a management company who needed quick revenue, and was willing to look the other way about a few pesky residential zoning requirements. Oliver had cajoled Alice, he'd harangued, promising to resand and refinish the wooden floors, install a fully operating kitchen with lots of counter space, erect one of those huge walk-in closets. Any demand she could imagine, he acquiesced, vowing to oversee or take care of it himself. And since the scraps of savings they had were basically his anyway, since Alice was already getting the wedding and going full-speed-ahead with her plans for a baby, if Alice hadn't exactly given in on this front, neither had she stood in his way. What she'd done, she'd allowed herself to see what would happen.

Editorial assistants at glossy fashion magazines; assistant editors at midtown publishing houses; junior publicists; gallery clerks; massage school graduates; yoginis; gofers; photographers' personal peons; retail sluts; the same neurotic, cooler-than-thou trailblazers who'd originally made hilarious and cutting remarks about the wisdom of buying a place in this neighborhood; who'd had first-rate original excuses why they hadn't visited, or who'd conversely finished their last bites of brunch and gotten down to brass tacks, expressing their heartfelt concern about what Alice and Oliver were doing; time and again they'd stepped carefully, decamping from the warehouse's freight elevator, always holding their breath so they didn't get a full blast of the dried cow blood stench from downstairs, pulling at the collapsing security gate—and then they'd be hit smack-dab by that first, full gander: the obscene expanse of square footage, the cavernously high ceilings, the exposed bricks at once dilapidated and futuristic. They gasped, gaped, craned their necks for a better look. They were blown away, these friends who still commuted from outer boroughs where they crammed into shithole apartments with roommates they could hardly stand; who'd spent years fighting like savages to establish their professional and personal lives; who made a point of being impressed by absolutely nothing and positively nobody. They held slack the ten-dollar bottles of wine and five-dollar bouquets they'd brought as housewarming gifts. Friends that Alice had originally bonded with during orientation week at fashion school clucked their reserved approval for the thick steel cookware that hung from the rack in the center of the kitchen space. Plucked brows narrowed when they saw Alice's pool-size designing and sketch table, her vintage sewing table from the nineteen twenties, the female mannequin form next to it. Tilda showed no compunction whatsoever about walking straight into Alice's personal closet and letting fly with gutter curses. No better were the boyfriends, the husbands, and Oliver's pals—junior traders from Wall Street, junior partners at midtown law firms, graduate assistants, PhD candidates, bookish band geeks, and/or dudes who were still figuring things out and working by day at bakeries or frame shops. Once they saw Oliver's row of workstation terminals, once they found out how little Oliver'd stolen this place for, and how comparatively little the renovations had cost—palms smacked against foreheads. There had been more than one real live spit take. As if to rub it in, Oliver would roll up the Chinese screens to show off that wall of windows, the panoramic view, only faintly filmed with soot: the abandoned train track, the dilapidated piers, the shimmering expanse of the Hudson.

Ego was a small thing. Its pleasures were shallow and venal. Alice had bathed in them anyway. *If my friends are jealous,* she told Oliver, at the end of more than one such soiree, *you know we're onto something.*

Still. When she was at her worst, when she needed to blame Oliver for something, for anything, she returned to the promise she couldn't forget, high on his list of guarantees: they'd be insulated; the smells from the warehouses, frozen beef and lingering death, wouldn't reach them. But they did.

Just a get-to-know-you visit

AND THEN THEY were on their way. Or something close to it.
The cabbie kept glancing over his shoulder, through the scratched bulletproof divider, getting his fill of the crazy woman in the blue wig and the surgical mask.

Well, let him enjoy himself.

Ignoring the driver, she asked: "Don't we deserve a treat? After everything we've been through?"

"Believe me." Oliver stared out the side window. "I want a treat just as much as you."

"And it's not like Thursday night reservations at the Black Tide are *easy* to get." Alice paused. "Honestly. I'm amazed we're discussing this."

Oliver checked his watch, the third time in maybe five minutes.

"I'm not just going to give in and play the martyr," she continued. "Just stay at home and be frail and wear a caftan—"

"No one's saying—"

"Friends will visit and I'll flutter my eyes and everyone comes away saying, *She's so noble, it's so sad*. That may be later. But for now—"

He released a breath that Alice knew meant he was trying to hold his temper. "If you could just walk me through it," Oliver asked. "Reservations or not, it's still the middle of one of the coldest winters in who knows. If I'm a freshwater crab swimming in the vicinity of the East Coast, I've got to be freezing my balls off."

"Actually," Alice answered, "I think those are the blue crabs."

There wasn't time to enjoy the right corner of Oliver's mouth rising, his grudging smirk. Perched in her lap, Doe had become fascinated with the string and fabric of Alice's mask. Her dimpled mitts grabbed. Alice began the delicate task of distracting her before those elastic bands hurtled, with extra momentum, back into her face. "Okay. Very good, sweetie. That's right."

Oliver had been up late, she knew, *entering Lynx into the UNIX*, which could mean entering code, or secretly masturbating, just enjoying some male alone time. Alice didn't begrudge him. She'd been asleep long before he'd come to bed. It was only when the Blueberry needed formula that Alice had stirred, enough to watch her husband clomp in from his work space. Seeing that she already had a bottle prepared, Oliver had been more than happy to get back to work.

Presently, Alice admired her husband's perfect nose; she appreciated him having shaven during the night, was impressed by the egg-blue silk scarf he'd chosen, surprised at how well it matched with the deeper blue of his cashmere topcoat. Usually Oliver displayed a willful disregard for his looks. He often wore the swag she got him through his four-day programming benders, unchanged. Alice suspected he actually *enjoyed* fine garments—not so much wearing them, but putting them through the wringer. As if he wanted to show they weren't so special. Not today. Today, he was immaculate. Groomed and ready to make nice.

Still, his eyes were puffy. He didn't just seem worn out, or preoccupied in his usual way, enmeshed in some logic loop or technical quandary. This was different. Since hitting this stretch of traffic, he'd avoided any sustained eye contact, and instead had sat hunched over his splayed legs, looking out the near window. Alice knew he was itching to tell her they should've taken the FDR instead of going up First. She also knew that he knew that, if he opened his mouth, she'd remind him about Beth calling from Whitman, chirpily informing Oliver the slides had been found, all crises averted.

Oliver checked his watch yet again.

"It's going to be fine," Alice said.

From her leather shoulder bag she coaxed an oversize plastic key ring, prompting a high squeak from Doe, who bounced in place and quickly occupied herself with the task of devouring the toy. Each landing of compact weight on Alice's thighs brought white pain. Alice winced, and followed her husband's line of sight out the window, for a time gazing at the fugue: a bus stop advertisement featuring a muscled white hip-hop star in sexy briefs; small red neon Hebrew letters blinking from a glatt kosher diner.

"Late or not, we have an appointment. It's not like they're going to *refuse* to see me."

"Oh, *that*?" he answered. "I forgot all about that. I'm still stuck on, if there's no way crabs are in season, how can that place be having mondo crab nights?"

She could have screamed. What did he expect her to do? She hadn't found the right nanny yet, and Monday morning was a nuclear waste zone for sitters, and his parents sure weren't about to hightail it across the country from Bakersfield to help. Which meant there wasn't any choice but to bring the infant, was there? Since they didn't have a baby car seat, she'd asked the driver to go slow. Was it her fault he made a beeline for the far right lane, or idled behind each double-parked delivery truck, every fourth dry cleaning van? Yes, blame her because progress up First Avenue no longer seemed the result of an engine, wheels, and unleaded gasoline. Osmosis was more like it. Magnets, maybe.

"My sweet lummox," Alice said. "The reason Crab Fest is a sensation is *because* nobody can figure out how the restaurant can be getting fresh crabs off the East Coast during the third week of January. They've had inspectors, government regulators. *New York* magazine literally staked out the restaurant. One shift of reporters in a van with a telephoto lens focused on the delivery dock. Another crew watching the front entrance through a telescope from a ninth-floor office across the street—"

"*New York* magazine doesn't have anything better to do?"

"*Nobody* has anything better to do." She laughed. "It's turned into this whole *thing*. I'm telling you, every know-it-all in the tristate area wants to partake in these magical mystery crab boils. Apparently people are *crammed* into these long public tables covered in newspapers. All kinds of hoi polloi and celebrities are in with you, cracking shells with their hands and thwapping claws with little hammers. Shards and crab goo flying hither and yon, the only thing anybody's talking about is whether they're all being played for fools."

Oliver's grunt suggested a grudging curiosity, even bemusement. "I bet they just flew them in from Australia."

Between Sixty-seventh and Sixty-eighth, the west side of York was nothing but sandstone, limestone, and marble. Remnants of the building's previous incarnation were apparent: Gothic stained-glass windows, a central cathedral, a rectory spire, parallel statues of the Virgin Mary with her arms out, accepting all in need. Where turrets guarded each building corner, however, the baroque ended, gleaming steel and glass blocking out the dishwater sky.

Alice reminded herself to breathe. So long as she kept breathing, the time would pass, she would get through this. Every day brought more humblings, she told herself. It was up to her to accept them.

She patted the sprouts of hair atop Doe's skull. The follicles were silky on her fingertips. Pressing lightly, Alice made an effort to absorb each single sensation. Appreciate each stroke. In the puffy pink winter coat Oliver's mother had bought, the little girl was a living doll. Alice kissed the center point on Doe's crown. She raised the miniature hood and its pink fringe over the child's head, and did not rush in passing her girl to Oliver, who was already out of the cab, waiting with the shoulder bag.

On the curb now, reeling from a blast of wind from off the East River, Alice burrowed into her own coat, watched her exhaled breath vanish. *Keep doing the simple things,* she reminded herself. She made sure to plant her feet, took steady steps toward the back of the cab, where the driver was lifting the stroller out of the trunk. Alice thanked him, saying, "I can use all the help I can get." His eyes returned a kindness that shocked her; she wasn't prepared for such dazzling pity. The wind whistled, truly *foul,* blue tendrils of Alice's wig swirling into her line of sight. Alice knelt, busying herself with the collapsed metal bars. Two well-placed yanks and the carriage came alive, straightening, its alacrity almost justifying the ridiculous price. Instinct told Alice to grab her daughter back, but Oliver was already setting Doe into the buggy. Watching her husband's ministrations—at once unskilled and suffused with care—relaxed Alice, a bit. "Settle up with the cabbie," she said. "I didn't bring any cash."

Leaving his answer behind, she commandeered the buggy's driving position—it was selfish, fine, and she'd need all her energy today. Still, Alice began pushing toward the sliding doors. She was halfway beyond a mulling cluster of doctors on their cigarette breaks. A security guard came out—to offer a wheelchair?

"I just love seeing moms work them baby contraptions," he said. Hands jerked, kung fu motions. "BAM BAM."

The foundry stone carved with SANTA MARIA RECTORY 1896; the ornate marble archway with small carved nun; the large letters of modernist font and industrial steel, appearing without any context, spelling out WALT WHITMAN MEMORIAL. Marble walls yellowed by age appeared that much more decrepit thanks to institutional lighting. With them came the warmth ubiquitous to certain types of lobbies, large rooms open and busy as the waiting area of a train station. A man and woman were inside the entranceway, guiding a dowager so old as to be mummified, all three visitors searching for the location of a certain bank of elevators. People in scrubs zipped past, carrying their morning bagels and coffees. Near the escalator row, scattered commuters paused long enough to grab one of the morning tabloids from the nearby blind guy, make change from out of his Knicks cap.

Alice noticed, near one of the saggy ferns, the man in light blue jammies—he was expectant, tracking comings and goings from the front entrance. He had no lower jaw. Instead of staring at his deformity, she forced her attention elsewhere, to the nearby gentleman wearing that season's nattiest three-piece suit, who was pushing a little boy in a wheelchair. The boy's hair was piecemeal, patchy, almost like Alice's had been before Oliver had plugged in those shears.

Her grip around the baby carriage handles tightened. Memories assaulted her now, visceral and consuming: the pungent, liquid-plastic odor of surgical gloves; the sensation of ice chips rattling around inside her mouth—a recollection so strong she could almost feel the ice against her teeth. In her mind's eye she saw the postcard with the ballerina that Oliver had taped onto the wall across from her bed. She remembered feeling so weak that the act of lying in bed was a chore, so weak that keeping her eyes open was itself exhausting, but also staring for what felt like long stretches, centering her thoughts on that gorgeous ballerina, her poise, her strength. Now Alice remembered the middle of the afternoon when she woke from a nap, and her eyes focused, and inside that hospital room in New Hampshire, she saw Tilda, and her mother, and Doe, each of them peaceful and asleep, slouched in a chair or lying on the foldout bed. Alice remembered thinking that she had to watch them sleep, she had to appreciate the sight of these three astounding women, she had to stay in this moment and soak in this experience, because she had no idea how many more times she might have it, or if it would come her way again.

There were other memories: yanking on the plug of her IV tower battery, pushing the tower toward the bathroom and yanking down her mesh hospital underwear; squatting just in time and releasing yet another diarrhea blast into the little plastic hat they kept over the toilet and feeling relief, she'd made it, she wouldn't be shitting herself this time, and feeling emptied out, too, because nothing was left inside, and she felt herself bleeding from her vagina, and bleeding from her behind, and then, her body unclenched once more, shitting out another burst.

Inconceivable. It was starting up again. She was back in this.

"It's just a get-to-know-you visit," Oliver said.

Alice nodded. "We're just going to get on the same page."

"No reason to worry about anything except what's in right front of us."

Her hand was clutching his. She welled up, swallowed, and said: "*Tu esta mi favorito.*"

"*Tu esta mi favorito,*" he said.

And in this way, they kept going, following the directions Alice had written in her to-do notebook, muddling through the lobby, their hands together on that stroller, the sick woman in the blue wig, and her dapper, stubble-headed husband, and their baby, too, a small, quiet family, shrinking, moving forward.

Yes, Everything Was Moving Forward

THE LIGHT HUE commonly associated with Creole heritage. Tiny and pretty, dark hair pulled back and away from her face, further highlighting bone structure that was delicate as a bird skeleton's, placing attention on eyes that were small and brown and entirely empty. She had the faint makings of a mustache. She took in Alice's wig and smiled in a manner that was either polite or perfunctory. Introducing herself, she asked, boy or girl, and how old Doe was, and the whole time reminded Alice of a little girl playing dress-up in her mother's clothes.

Alice had to make sure her hands did not tremble, but she managed to write a legible *Culpepper* in her notepad. Small letters followed: *"intern?"* Without fuss, Miss Culpepper led the family beyond the registration desk, into a short corridor. On the walls were framed, yellowing pictures from bygone eras—wimpled nuns tending to immigrants, beehived nurses aiding the bedridden. An obese woman stood just inside the hallway and was using a rolling chair as her support crutch while she placed manila folders into a filing cabinet.

"Before you can proceed to your appointment," Miss Culpepper said, her voice high, "I just need to make sure that all your paperwork is in order." Entering a low-ceilinged cubicle area, she pulled out a chair. The desk surface empty save for a boxy desktop computer (its plastic faded to the color of curdled milk), an opened carton of orange juice, and a series of elaborately framed photos, the same child: smiling in a tutu, smiling with her dollies.

"She has your lovely skin," Alice said.

Miss Culpepper blinked, a few times, as if figuring out how to respond. Allowing herself another minor grin, she sat, smoothed out the front of her skirt. A few taps at the desktop brought a pair of fresh pages from a printer the size of a minifridge, at rest on the floor behind her. "Review these. If the information on these pages is accurate, the hospital asks you to sign on two individual pages. This first one authorizes us to bill and share the information with your health insurance. Next to the Post-it, please."

Alice gripped the pen. *Keep doing the simple things.*

Miss Culpepper kept typing. A new page arrived. "This form, in case your health insurance doesn't cover the costs, or refuses payment. You acknowledge responsibility for the outstanding charges."

"I don't understand," Alice said. "Our policy covered most of New Hampshire, my chemo induction. There's no reason to think this should be different?"

The baby rattled and chirped inside the carriage. Three of the lines on the desk phone were blinking.

"By the Post-it," said Miss Culpepper.

As if this was his cue, Oliver shifted, jutting halfway across the desk. "We signed a proxy that authorizes me to talk about these matters—I faxed it at least three times. I'm sure a copy got to you." He unfurled a smile designed to be charming. "Miss Culpepper? My wife's dealing with enough on her plate. I'm sure you and I can discuss this separately?"

Miss Culpepper's eyes were large, but not engaged, or particularly interested. She nibbled her lip. "We here at Whitman do offer significant financial aid, available for those patients that qualify." She cleared her throat. "If and when the time comes that you should feel you need help, I can provide you with that paperwork."

"So nothing's necessarily wrong with our insurance?" Alice asked her.

"Hospital policy is, we can't let you see the doctor unless you sign this form."

"You're not answering my question," Alice said.

"Just let me worry about that," Oliver said. "Okay?"

Yes, everything was moving forward. Alice was even remembering to breathe. Even now she was breathing, releasing her worries as if they were doves outside an elaborate wedding. For the third time since her arrival at the check-in desk, Alice apologized for the confusion in getting her slides transferred from Dartmouth. Alice told Beth there had never been a doubt the mess would get straightened out, and she thanked Beth yet again for her patience and competence, and, Alice agreed, it *was* nice to see someone in person after so much time on the phone—she felt like she knew Beth already.

Squarely in her line of sight were placards informing of the high risk of infection among patients, and asking that any registering patient let the staff know about cold symptoms, and if you had any kind of rash. Holding the sheet with her orders for blood work, Alice turned her torso away from the desk, and began scribbling in her little pad, two lines beneath her notes about Culpepper, reminders for how to identify Beth.

Everything will be fine.

One of the other receptionists was occupied by the task of training a new hire, and the morning's backlog of patients was lined up behind Alice, with two elderly ladies bonding over the horrible traffic and how worried each had been about missing her appointment. Pushing herself upright, Alice eased between them, apologizing with a deference one normally reserves for royalty. She felt a lightheadedness, as if billions of carbonated bubbles were dancing and popping inside her brain. *Way to sabotage yourself, pushing that carriage all over the hospital.*

She leaned on a chair for support, wiped her brow, adjusted the pinch of the mask on her nose, and took her good sweet time, unzipping, removing, and folding her winter coat.

Your body can only do what it can do.

Over a long thermal shirt, she was wearing a tight, bright yellow tee. Across her chest, black iron-on letters screamed: **GOOD GIRLS GO TO HEAVEN. BLONDES GO EVERYWHERE.** She was wearing Thierry Mugler jeans strategically shredded with a straightedge razor. She was wearing combat boots with three-inch black rubber soles that were laced to the middles of her calves. She made sure the metallic-blue bob was secure on her head. She straightened her back, though not too straight, and lifted her chin, though not too high—she knew better from being behind the scenes at runway shows, altering and sewing up dresses at the last second while designers barked instructions at models. Alice swallowed the bile that had accumulated in the back of her throat, and, with the poofy jacket a black octopus bulging out from beneath her arm, she returned her focus to nailing each landed step, assuring firm balance. In this way she started back into the waiting room's garden party color scheme, pastels and soft greens, its walls adorned with Impressionists' landscapes.

The blood cancer waiting room is how she thought of it.

Golf shirts and elastic waistbands and old-lady Afros and blue surgical gloves, paunches and waddle necks, and oxygen masks and IV stands with clear plastic tubing; elderly people, mostly, reclining or sitting stiffly on comfy couches, their liver-spotted or gloved hands fidgeting, their eyes darting or downcast. They sat in small groupings, usually pairs. Who wanted to go through this alone?

On the nearest couch, a scarf of bright colors was wrapped around the head of a plump woman. A glance showed her to be a fright—swollen forehead, red rashy skin, a huge gauze patch where her left eye should have been, and that ubiquitous egg-blue bandit mask covering her nose and mouth. As Alice passed, the woman's good eye rose from her paperback copy of *A Time to Kill*. Her mask widened, scarcely containing an obvious grin. She nudged her husband: his white brush of hair rose from a hardback copy of *The Firm;* he took in the sight, and broke out as well, his face going joyful.

Alice walked past a patient strapped onto a stretcher; the bored EMT gave Alice a wink.

Past a doctor leaning over and talking softly with two pear-shaped seniors, telling them it would be at least a half hour before results came in. "Maybe you want to get some breakfast? When you get back, just tell the desk to let me know."

A man looked up: thin as a twig, gnarled, with a grotesquely humped back. His skin so gray it was almost green, his sunken eyes lively, almost joyful as they tracked her.

She noticed an immaculately attired Japanese couple watching her—how excellent the woman's boots were; Alice would have killed for those boots.

If these people took something from her defiance, she was happy to be able to provide it. In spades and clovers she could provide defiance. *God bless them all,* she thought.

Oliver had set up an outpost in a corner alcove, and, by the time Alice arrived, she was exhausted, and exhilarated, and deeply emotional, ready to cry, vomit, scream. "I have to remember that we all have our own times and journeys," she said. "Their situation is not my situation. I'm young and I'm strong and I have every reason in the world to get past this."

"Of course you do," he said. "You will."

She snatched her baby from Oliver's arms: the Blueberry was squirmy—exposure to day after day of passing nurses and doctors had turned her into an expert flirter, with an advanced degree in seeking out strangers, but this waiting room was proving to be too much, the child was overstimulated, turning cranky. Mommy. She needed Mommy.

Alice's hand went behind her daughter's head. She brought Doe in toward her bosom, the infant's eyes widening. Doe spread open her mouth, revealing the pink mountain ridges that were her toothless gums. Instinct taking over, she went straight for Mommy's breast.

Alice veered her off and rocked her in place and made clucking sweet sounds. In the child's lumpy potato of a face, Alice still got a thrill from recognizing Oliver's nose, his hard, dramatic brow, his protruding ears. She also felt chagrin, the child had not escaped the curse of Mommy's weak chin. Nonetheless, Doe was clearly her own self, this evident even as she satisfied another textbook baby cliché: her baldish head, wondrous eyes, and pink visage belonging to infancy, yes, but also to the ancients. Indeed, Doe's resemblance to so many of the seniors in the blood cancer waiting room was unmooring, and took Alice to a dark place, one deep inside her, a place of fathomless horrors.

Behind Oliver, just over his shoulder, a bronze plaque memorialized a beloved patriarch whose family had donated a wing. The air was cool and dry, which Alice knew was to prevent any germs from carrying. On the side table, a half-filled blue coffee cup was leaving ring stains. The table was covered with back issues of *Schlep*—"For Jewish Seniors on the Go." Oliver had been trying without success to get Doe to take her formula. He also had bottled water ready for Alice; all she had to do was glance a certain way. Alice crammed her fears back down into their deep dark resting place, and guided the plastic bottle toward Doe's open mouth.

"Instead of fighting being here"—she sniffed—"probably it would be helpful if I told myself, *This is where I'm going to get better.*"

Oliver ran a hand along Alice's arm. "If *New York* magazine spent all that time staking out the Black Tide," he said, "they must have found an answer about the crabs."

His face was blank, waiting for a response, which confused her. She easily could have fallen apart. Instead Alice swallowed a laugh.

"I couldn't get through this without you." She wiped at the corners of her eyes. "You know that? You know, *tu esta*?"

He kissed her hand. He whispered: *"Tu esta."*

"Really though," he said. "All those reporters? They had to find out something."

What they found was that the three fresh, polite young people working behind the front desk were backed up to Duluth, and that the exam rooms were all occupied, and that whenever one of those doctors with the bright white lab coats and the expensive ties popped up from the back area, he'd grab a nurse for a quick consultation and scurry off somewhere else. One didn't need a Ouija board to deduce it was going to be a while before Alice would get called for her bloods, let alone her appointment. She and Oliver filled the lag with hangman—Alice cruised in the first game thanks to *blueberry* (Oliver praising the word choice as excellent), to which Oliver responded with a feeble *plop* (Alice sussed it in a snap, a lonely oval marking her single misstep). Alice lifted and turned Doe around and smelled her rear. She wondered if they should try to hold out on changing the baby until they got into an examination room (one of those radioactive waste containers then could get put to good use, most likely). Oliver got up and used a hallway sink to wash his hands, as he'd been doing every nine minutes, even though he hadn't touched anything since the last rinse except his own pen. He asked a nurse for some medical gloves and blew them up into balloons with protruding blue fingers. In New Hampshire this had worked to distract the baby, but here, the hypnotic effects wore off after a few minutes. In New Hampshire, Oliver and Alice had passed untold amounts of time lying together in her hospital bed and playing rummy; they would remember to bring cards from now on.

Between Oliver's cleansing jaunts and parlor tricks, while he was getting his ass handed to him at hangman, he and Alice delighted in the sight of their little wonder charming everyone on the fourth floor's eastern wing, and they further procrastinated about the diaper now sagging with a green slush that Oliver liked to call *chana saag,* and they reminisced about their shenanigans back in their room in New Hampshire, and they proclaimed themselves incredulous at having nostalgia for that insane time, and they proclaimed themselves thankful for even having the chance to look back, and they proclaimed themselves fortunate for this astounding relationship of theirs, having as much fun in that stupid room as they had, under such ridiculous conditions; and proclaimed they would get through this mess as well, they would survive and look back at all this. Alice also held up a spare issue of *New York* magazine she'd been leafing through in the waiting room. She told Oliver that the magazine's spies had indeed learned about a special underground, speakeasy-era, trapdoor entrance to the Black Tide. Instead of printing the origins of those crabs, however, Alice reported, the journalists refused to reveal the answer.

"Hype for hype's sake?" Oliver made a yanking motion. "The real issue's whether the Black Tide purchased ad space from the magazine as a trade-off."

"You honestly think anybody gives a rat's rear if they flew those things in from Timbuktu?" Alice answered. "People *want* the mystery. It's better that way."

A man was limping—Alice had noticed him earlier, gnarled, with a small mountain rising from his right shoulder. He stopped in front of them. The gray skin covering his skull was stretched, all exterior layers of flesh having been burned away, so that it looked like the angles of his cheekbones threatened to break through. His eyes were freakish, hazel marbles sunken deep into their sockets. He focused on Doe. "What a beautiful, wondrous child you are," he said. To Alice now: "She's what—five months?"

"Six, yes."

"You look at one at this age, it rushes up all the good memories from your own."

The man said Alice looked *superb,* her attitude would make the difference. He thanked Oliver for his offer to scoot over on the couch but declined, explaining that couches were murder on his spine, he had a special ergonomic desk chair that he couldn't sit in without discomfort. Volunteering his name as Cael, he asked which doctor Alice was seeing. "The staff here is excellent. They do everything they possibly can."

Alice did her best to smile, but Cael picked up on her discomfort.

"Yeah. I know. I'm sorry. It's a shitty thing being here. Six years now, on and off, I'm in twice a week from Syosset. They've done chemo. Radiation. Experimental drugs. Seed implants. Special magical beans." He chuckled, grimaced. "Every time I was sure they'd got it. They tell you the treatment's going well. You go into remission, start to get stronger, brick by brick, start to rebuild your life. Then something isn't right. They do them tests. You get that call. Oh, the spot is back. The spot has spread. Stage four." He caught himself. "You're new, Jesus, the last thing you need is to be hearing my shit. I know better, I'm sorry—"

"Don't be absurd." Alice tried to smile, her stomach knotting on itself.

"It'll be different for you, I can tell. You've got that beautiful child."

His smile was trying to be generous, failing. This was a man who knew better than to keep talking, and could not stop himself. "Tumor's wrapped itself around my kidneys. Who knew cancer could even do that? It's ridiculous. You wish you could reason with it, explain that the more it grows the quicker that both of us are done. It can't live and be a happy tumor without me. My only option left is this special surgery. Doc doesn't even want to try. Honestly, I can't blame the man. He'd have to remove one kidney, take out the part of the tumor that's wrapped around that side of my body, and then use a vacuum to suck out the rest. He says surgery would kill me on the operating table. But if they don't go in—"

Cael took a rolled paper from his back pocket, tapped it out in front of them. "I signed the waiver, absolved the hospital, whatever they want. With any luck today I can convince them . . ."

He was failing in his effort to be brave, and Alice felt her own failure as well. She breathed in, released outward. She willed herself still. Did her best to stare at this man, to meet him.

Cael swallowed. No longer smiling, his pupils black, fathomless.

This treatment we're discussing

REQUISITE KNOCKS ACTED as both interrogative (*Is it okay?*) and warning (*Because I'm coming in*). The oncologist made sure the door was shut behind him, and joined the already crowded room. Where Alice's New Hampshire physician had looked as if he'd been ordered from a doctor's catalogue, this new one, the doctor now taking over her care and treatment, seemed to have been ordered from a more expensive catalogue, one with a glossy sheen and higher price points. A bit taller than six feet and robust, with a thick black field of hair slickly parted to one side, looking lightly wet or gelled, Howard Eisenstatt, MD, was neither as old nor as musty as his name suggested. His face oblong and pale, with a thin layer of baby fat; small brown eyes deeply set and hard with intelligence, his nose long and thin.

Acknowledging neither the nurses nor the other doctors in the room, he focused his attention on Alice, smiling in a manner neither welcoming nor insincere, his handshake strong without being warm. At the end of his lab coat's sleeve, peeking out from beneath an ivory-white French cuff, half of a chunky, high-end titanium watch was conspicuous. The doctor moved toward Oliver and similarly introduced himself. He completed the formality of washing his hands and stepped toward the office desk, stiffly taking in the dormant baby stroller, the folding chair overflowing with coats and shoulder bags and hanging sweater arms and that single, tiny yellow unicorn.

Adjacent to that pile, perched on what Alice realized was the doctor's prize—the sought-after stool—Oliver was using his toes for leverage, spinning himself and the little one in slow half circles, the child gurgling, holding her blanky, sucking with great affection on her pacifier; now aware of attention on her, she turned away from her father, checked out the nice new man in the lab coat.

Howard Eisenstatt, MD, once more extended those thin lips, revealing that tight smile. Scooting himself upward, he sat on the edge of the desk, stretched his pressed slacks diagonally out in front of him, revealing thin fine socks, perfectly matching his pants' gray shade. A glance toward his clipboard; Eisenstatt removed a ballpoint from the chest pocket of his lab coat. Repeated pressing didn't get the pen going. Licking the end was no help. The doctor looked down; fleshy folds of a double chin revealed themselves. Eisenstatt blinked at his pen, as if blinking were an expression of disappointment, as if expressing disappointment to a pen would somehow motivate the ink.

"We couldn't get a sitter," Alice said.

She sat, rigid, against the raised slab of the examination table, her left arm hanging straight down between dangling legs. A catheter was plugged in the soft of her elbow, and layers of clear plastic tubing were taped to her forearm. A quiet, head-scarfed woman down the hall was employed solely for the brutally tedious task of starting IV lines and getting blood from cancer patients, and she'd needed three sticks in order to penetrate Alice's vein. The number remained unsettling to Alice for reasons she would not allow herself to think about (*the vein had been found, onward*). The catheter had been installed, Fatima had explained, "in case doctors want plasma transfusion. Line ready to go. No problem."

Watching the doctor mess with his pen, Alice felt the urge to swing her feet, kick up her hot pink socks. Her boots were off so that a second nurse—Requita?—had been able to get an accurate weight. Her socks remained on so Alice's bare feet wouldn't come into contact with anything germish. Besides, the exam room was chilly.

"Are you okay?" asked Eisenstatt. "I know it's been a long day. Maybe some water?"

A rustling behind them, Requita began searching for a paper cup. Now the nurse left the room. At the same time a new woman entered, middle-aged, frizzy-haired Hispanic, unfortunately jammed into a tightly fitting, generic-looking blouse and slack set. She handed Eisenstatt a functional and spiffy-looking felt-tipped pen from her own overcrowded breast pocket. Alice double-checked the laminated hospital ID dangling from that bright purple strap—Dantelle? Yes, Dantelle. She'd come in before. A nurse-practitioner, a kind of cross between doctor and nurse. She'd gone over Alice's history, sympathized with Alice about childcare, hadn't been condescending or overboard.

"Water would be wonderful," Alice said. "Thank you, Doctor."

Near the elevated cupboards and shelves in the back of the room the final member of this gathering lingered: an attractive Indian woman, almost as tall as Eisenstatt, but willowy in a manner common to Alice's world, with lustrous long hair, hot-ironed to fashionable straightness, and cords in her neck from too much working out. Dr. Bhakti was a visiting fellow, training to specialize in cancer treatment. She'd been in earlier, introducing herself and going over cursory bone marrow transplant information. She'd also sized up Alice's outfit. Her glance might have been innocuous; still, Alice had noticed.

At the moment, Bhakti was sitting on the edge of a counter, filing her nails. Her boots were the second pair to capture Alice's fancy this morning—confirmation that *someone* needed to get herself new boots.

"We straightened out the problem with your slides." Eisenstatt read with medium interest from Alice's file. "So that's progress."

He flipped a page on the clipboard. "Everything indicates Dartmouth-Hitchcock did an excellent job. Getting you here to this stage was no small achievement. But there are still a few matters that I'd like to review. Can we go back and begin with the first symptoms, before you—"

"The nurse didn't write that down?" Oliver asked. "None of the three other people who took her history got what you want?"

"I don't mean to be difficult," Alice said. "We're grateful to be here. But we seem to keep going over information your staff asked me ages ago."

Eisenstatt tipped his forehead, the nineteenth-century gentleman conceding a thorny point. "It's maddening. You're going to get a lot of it. Standard medical procedure. We go over things repeatedly. This is our thinking: it's possible you'll remember something that deviates from what the nurse heard. You might add a detail that adds to Dr. Bhakti's understanding of this case. Each time a staff member or doctor hears your story, it gives us a chance to consult with one another, and hear everything fresh in our own ears. It's an inconvenience for you, I know—"

Dating back to the night of her admission to Dartmouth-Hitchcock, continuing all the way through the morning of her release, Alice had tracked her blood cell counts; she'd made it her business to memorize the names of the nurses, personalize herself to the nursing assistants. Here at Whitman, for the umpteenth time, she was more than capable of verifying that, upon her admittance to DHMC, she'd been given two drugs, Zithromax and ceftazidime, for her pneumonia. ("Lower left lobe," Alice remembered. "I'm fairly sure that's what they told me about the pneumonia.") She had no problem naming which antibiotics she'd been given upon her admission (acyclovir, and also some sort of azole antifungal), or "cytarabine," the first of her induction chemotherapy drugs, or following up with "the other one. The red drip. Dana Rubenson."

"Daunorubicin," the cancer fellow corrected.

"Dana Rubenson makes it easy to remember," Alice said.

She was counting the days until all this was over and Tilda and a bunch of other girlfriends formed a shopping mob with Alice and made it their personal mission to liberate every sexy pair of boots being held in the clutches of SoHo's boutiques. Accepting a paper cup—"Thank you, Dantelle"—Alice let herself soak in the relief of sipping lukewarm tap water. She allowed herself to enjoy watching visiting fellow Bhakti retreat back into her little corner.

The moment she answered the next question, Alice knew letting her guard down had been a mistake; she'd confused desonide—the ointment for the facial rash she'd gotten as a side effect of a platelet infusion—with triamcinolone—the ointment she'd been given for her postchemo chest rash.

By then Dr. Bhakti was alert, the nurse-practitioner was having her say, Eisenstatt, too—everyone correcting her.

"It can get confusing sometimes," Dantelle said.

"You're doing great"—Bhakti's voice dripped with honey—"remembering all this."

Alice half-expected a lollipop. Her own fault. "You are kind," she said.

Then the vancomycin she'd been given for that nasty blister and skin infection following her IV infiltration. The catheter-port contraption that had required minor surgery to install in her jugular, so they could run the IVs. The heparin drip into the catheter-port thing for the blood clot in the infiltrated arm. The transition from heparin drip to Lovenox pills, which had changed to Coumadin shots, after it turned out her insurance would not cover the Lovenox. Plus her platelet transfusions. And how long it had been since she last had a fever, her ordeal distilled into a connect-the-dots trail of pharmaceuticals and procedures. As if she were speaking about the intricacies and design specs of a blouse collar that she had been struggling with, Alice was as specific as possible about how many minutes after eating two spoonfuls of wheat flakes with sliced bananas she'd felt the cramping along the side of her stomach. She pointed to the right side of her abdomen, explained the shifting, cramps becoming something else, a rush both sudden and desperate, the consistency of her stool becoming *watery.*

Howard Eisenstatt and the nurse-practitioner shared a look. Eisenstatt speed-read a note from off her chart reporting that, after her induction chemo, traces of a stomach virus had been present in cultures taken from high inside her nose and deep in her throat. "Normally the virus goes away with time and antibiotics," he said. "I imagine that's been the case here." He ordered the nurse-practitioner to take more cultures. "If the virus *has* reappeared," Eisenstatt continued, "we need to make sure it just stayed in your stomach. I don't want you to worry. If it comes to that, we have a drug that eliminates the bug. You can take it through an IV."

"Even if the bug did get in your bloodstream," Dr. Bhakti said, stepping up. "There's an experimental form of the drug that's been testing to encouraging results." She crinkled her nose. "Only one potential problem. A number of patients have had some side effects." Realizing what she was saying, "The, ah, most problematic . . . being"—her voice slowed—"well . . . diarrhea." She waited. Then, for emphasis, added, "Dangerously explosive diarrhea."

Oliver snorted, looked at her as if she was crazy. "You're going to cure my wife's diarrhea with a drug that causes dangerously explosive diarrhea? *If it comes to that?*"

Almost as a reflex, he checked with Alice, meeting her eyes, anticipating unhappiness with his flippancy.

"We're not letting them do that to you," he said.

She emanated gratefulness, relief.

"We'll try with what we have," Eisenstatt answered, "if it comes to that." The doctor leveled a gaze at Bhakti, his irritation obvious. "And you're still taking the Coumadin shots every day?"

"Mmm. Oliver—my husband—gives them to me."

"Cancer in your family history?"

Alice's hands joined and webbed; she flexed them in her lap, pursed her lips. "My father died from pancreatic cancer when I was eleven." *Be calm. Release.* "And his mother as well—she was older by then, and two packs a day her whole life, a fiend. So I'm not sure how that affects the family tree, if you include . . ."

Closing her eyes, keeping them shut, she did a short breathing thing, unlocking her hands, putting them back on her knees, feeling the pointed jags beneath the denim. "Doctor, this whole day, being back in this . . . it's already—I feel very . . ."

"Take your time."

She held off her emotions. "I'm sorry. I'll do better. Keep going."

"There's no solid reason why people get leukemia. I wish I had something more definitive to tell you."

"What about heredity?" She jerked forward. "It's not genetic?"

"Very few cases of acute myeloid leukemia are passed down," Eisenstatt said. "If I had to guess—and it would only be a guess— I'd say chances are rare."

Alice grimaced, snorted, gasped for air, "She's safe?" Her chin crumpled. "My baby's going to be all right? She can't get this?"

The nurse-practitioner was at her side with tissues. Alice blew her nose, became aware of a disturbance. Her daughter's eyes, huge white saucers; Doe's little face uncertain, turning flush, light orange, now a deep crimson. Infant features scrunched around the meeting point of her nose; her mouth widened. That juncture, intimately familiar to a parent, right before the screaming starts. Horrible as your child's misery might be, when you'd been through it enough, the building process toward eruption could actually be endearing. Through her tears Alice made eye contact with an equally entertained Oliver. She motioned for him to bring over Doe.

The baby was inches from her mother's bosom when the inevitable finally took place, those tonsorial sirens blaring, their noise resonant, inclusive, the royal and imperial we: *We are all going to plummet to the depths of my unhappiness.*

Alice bounced Doe, made placating noises, grimaced.

Next to her, Dr. Eisenstatt pinched the bridge of his nose with his right hand. Bereft of a wedding band, an adult single childless male doctor, with how many patients waiting for him, he looked as if he'd gotten a wedgie in his ears.

"It runs in the family," Alice said. "We're criers."

She smiled at her girl, made more cuddly sounds. The nurse-practitioner came over and added a soft *"It's all right."*

Once Doe calmed, Alice began. "It's why we started early. One of the reasons anyway. I knew the disease was part of my family history. When you're a child, that absence defines you. You form around it, you know? Then, you get older, you don't know how long you have. Every friend—everyone we know, is busy trying to establish themselves, get their professional life going. I have ambition, too, I'm not Miss Merry Homemaker." She sniffed, motioned with her hand, an absent gesture. "I wanted to make sure I had the chance. To— to be a mommy. I wanted kids while I'm young and can care for them and chase them. I get colds, all the time, but nothing of consequence, my entire life I've been healthy. So I thought, *Okay, honeysuckle—*"

Her voice cracked. "And now, this."

She stared at the rack next to the door, cardboard boxes of light blue plastic gloves, surgical masks, hand sanitizer. Reaching around, so her child was still wrapped in her arms, Alice used the sleeve of her thermal, wiped at her eyes. Oliver was poised, ready with a slender stick of cheese wrapped in plastic.

"As I said, we really don't know why leukemia appears in most patients." Eisenstatt's face was pink with health and closely shaven, but also had a shadow, stubble coming in. "This says you don't have any brothers and sisters?"

"Correct." She lightly rocked Doe. "I'm an only child."

A pager in the room was vibrating on someone's belt loop. Someone was laughing and walking down the hall outside the door.

A doctorish thought formed across the doctor's face. Eisenstatt digested whatever he was thinking. When he said, *"Okay,"* his tone was more authoritative, the *okay* acting as a switch. Oliver withdrew a spiral school notebook from their bag. The doctor blinked and swallowed, tics that Alice would come to recognize as indicators he was preparing to speak at length.

"You're on top of your treatments, that's impressive. It'll be helpful down the road. If you have any questions, make sure to ask. If I'm telling you things you know, I apologize, but I'd rather we're all on the same page."

Medical personnel, doctors and nurses alike, talked in this clipped manner: short sentences, quick back-and-forth exchanges. It was the same way in the design world, or dealing with magazine people, anyone who seemed to straddle the lines between corporate and creative worlds. Time was at a premium. Unless someone was above you on the hierarchical ladder, you didn't have a moment to spare, merely enough time to explain what you needed, or wanted, or had to get across—then you waited for the person to catch up, nod that they understood, or stare at you looking glazed. Once the supervisor left, it was up to whomever to sink or swim. In the medical realm, at least, in Alice's experiences there—all of which encompassed her pregnancy and these six weeks of insanity—doctors pretended it mattered if the patient understood, before continuing to the next thing.

"You have acute myeloid leukemia, or AML," began Eisenstatt. "What this means: inside your bones there is marrow, a spongy red tissue responsible for producing your blood cells. AML is a mutation, or disruption, inside that marrow. Instead of producing a normal blood cell, your marrow produces purplish cells called myeloblasts."

He checked to make sure she was with him, saw an eager student.

"Your red blood cell counts, your whites, your platelets— myeloblasts are what is produced instead, and when they replace your healthy blood cells, this causes a major disruption. Among what's disrupted is the production of neutrophils—the part of the immune system that helps fight infections. We think this is what happened with your pneumonia. It's why it was key for you to get diagnosed as quickly as you did."

The sounds of Oliver scribbling. The conspicuous scratch of Bhakti's nail file, now pausing. Alice gave Doe her forefinger. The baby's cheeks imploded, her brow furrowed, her sucking rhythmic, fervent.

"With you, Doctor," she said.

"Based on the genetic makeup of myeloblasts, AML has three possible courses of treatment. First: *simple*. The genetic makeup of the AML cells is, for lack of a better term, the most straightforward. Treatment: straight systematic chemotherapy. With simple AML we have a good—"

"You can spare us," Oliver said. "We know we have the complicated kind."

Eisenstatt nodded. "So you already know we're looking at a stem cell transplant. And you know this is a serious procedure. We have to find a bone marrow donor with a genetic match of your DNA. There are ten categories that have to match. The more we can line up, the better we are." He waited a count. "Since siblings have DNA from both parents, they often give us a chance at the best match. You're an only child, so—"

"That option is not available," Alice finished.

"We'll look to the National Donor Registry. If and when we do match you with a donor, the next step would be an aggressive regime, followed by a transplant. You'll be in the hospital for six to eight weeks, under a high-level quarantine."

"The rooms on the transplant floor are very nice," Dr. Bhakti said. She'd reemerged from whatever hole, her nail file no longer apparent.

Eisenstatt put down the clipboard next to him, picked it back up, tapped it against his upper thigh. "Transplants are a fairly recent development. And as far as the success rate—"

Alice cut him off. "Let me be as clear as I can make myself," she said. "Any numbers or information that might upset me, *I don't want to know*. I'm young. I've been healthy my whole life. I'm not another one of the seventy-year-olds in your waiting room, health and blessings to them all."

She felt the bones inside her fingers vibrating, felt herself power-less to stop them, felt herself pulsing with strength, ready to vomit. "Please, just let me know what I have to do each day. Just put it in front of me. Do that, I promise, I will work hard. Because I am going to watch my child grow."

Dr. Bhakti was looking at Alice in a manner that suggested, for the first time, she considered the possibility Alice might have legiti-mate thoughts and feelings. Dr. Eisenstatt was squinting lightly, his eyes considerate.

"I think your attitude is admirable," he said. "I'll only provide statistics if you ask."

"Blinders on," Oliver said. "That's how we've been getting through this."

"You should know," the doctor said, "right now things are going *extremely* well. The work in New Hampshire was first rate. And getting you to this point was a big step. My job is to shepherd you to the transplant. I take this responsibility seriously. My modus operandi, I always operate on a worst-case-scenario basis. I'm going to assume the worst, give you the most conservative and op-pressive possibilities. Consider me your new Jewish grandmother." He met her eyes, gave a bit of a smile. "That's my job. Get you to transplant. Once we find a donor, a transplant doctor will take over. You'll go forward from there and be happy to be rid of me."

Doe squirmed, kicking at Mommy's chest.

"As I said, BMT *is* a fairly recent procedure," Eisenstatt contin-ued. "We've been doing it at Whitman for about five years. And while it's no walk in the park, it can work: genetic matches *do* happen, people *do* find donors. People have this procedure and they get better. From what we've seen, new marrow acts as a cure."

His words were punctuated by the redolent smack of hands against knees, Oliver rocking in place. Alice watched him flexing his feet, pressing forward from the balls of his toes; she was aware of her own stillness, the fussing child against the front of her right shoulder, her hand weak on the back of the baby's head, supporting her. The child was sweating, her little fuzz of hair damp.

"I'm also legally obligated to tell you," said Eisenstatt, "for medical purposes, we define *cure* as the disease being in remission for at least five years."

An unhappy squeal, little hands pushing away from Alice's neck.

Oliver was respectful, if uncertain: "You said you've only been doing them for five years?"

"Exactly," piped Bhakti.

"Classifying remission as five years doesn't mean your leukemia will return in five years," Eisenstatt answered. "As you said, you're young. You have a history of being healthy, a daughter and a husband—you have every reason to live."

Early in the afternoon, on day forty-seven since Alice's diagnosis in New Hampshire, Oliver was standing in the back of the exam room, listening to a chunky-watch-wearing catalogue-looking motherfucker talking about some sort of irregularities with Alice's blood work. Alice's numbers weren't bad, the doctor was saying. But he was still concerned with the makeup of Alice's cells. In fact, Oliver was watching the guy push to do some procedure that Oliver had vaguely heard references to before. "I'd like to do it as soon as possible," he was saying to Alice, "if that's okay with you."

This procedure, this aspirate—this bone marrow aspirate— would allow Dr. Eisenstatt to find out what was going on with the closest person to Oliver on this stupid planet, Oliver was hearing. And usually, when Oliver heard something scary, his means of dealing with, or addressing his fears was to share them, only he couldn't, not now, because these worst-case scenarios all involved the person he wanted to share them with. So, the sharing option wasn't on the table. And this lovely woman, she was bereft, her body racked, tremorous. She was gulping through tears: *"I'm never going to get better."*

Some sort of levee inside Oliver was breached, and now tears stung, left hot trails down his cheeks. "You're not allowed to say that," he said, fighting to breathe, embracing his wife. His voice went sharp: "That can't be true."

Alice had a deep-rooted conviction that, as a means of expression, tears were just as valid as speaking, just as necessary as laughter. Anywhere, any time, no matter how uncomfortable it may have made people around her, Alice was fine with a good cry. If Oliver mocked her, if he derived pleasure from needling her, that didn't matter much, in the end—for after all his little quips went silent, he still put up with her waterworks. Meanwhile, Alice could count on one hand the number of times she'd seen him cry. Number one was easy: when he'd cut the umbilical cord on his baby girl and taken Doe in his arms for the first time. Two, also easy: their wedding, staring into Alice's eyes, slowly rocking to and fro while the Ramones blared around them and friends watched in silent joy, their first dance together as man and wife. Three: the call from his mother with news that Magoo, his beloved childhood dog, had finally been put down. Then when that power forward on the Knicks—who Oliver rooted for and insisted was underrated—had choked on consecutive point-blank layups during a key sequence of a deciding play-off game against Jordan and the Bulls. (The image fresh even now to her: the final buzzer sounding; Oliver walking numbly away from the television, shutting their bedroom door behind him; minutes later Alice entering to see him sitting on the edge of the bed, face in his hands.)

Six years together and she could count these four times—three legit, one ridiculous and endearing. Now number five.

In less time than it took her to blink the tears away, not two seconds after they'd begun, Alice decided that if one ramification of her tears was going to be the loss of her husband's equilibrium, if seeing her crying was going to get him crying, if he was going to worry that she wasn't going to be able to deal with what lay ahead, and this worry was going to mean *he* wouldn't be able to deal— then, she wouldn't be the one who let them down.

She disengaged from Oliver's arms, dabbed at her eyes.

Doe, still cradled in her arms, was looking up at her, the largest, most concerned eyes ever put on a baby.

"Just a tug," she said, "or the full regime?"

"Full aspirate," answered Eisenstatt.

Alice could tell the doctor was being careful, wanted to keep their conversation grounded. "You should know," he continued, "there are a lot of bone marrow biopsies."

"My third," Alice sniffed.

"It's a stretch to say you'll get used to having these procedures, but they should stop being foreign. Before we start a round of chemotherapy, we always confirm with an aspirate and biopsy. That's what this is for."

"Excuse me?" Alice asked, bouncing the child. "Another round?"

"We know more chemo is part of the regimen," Oliver said. "But you don't mean another round, *now*?"

"What kind of time frame *are* we dealing with, Doctor?"

"There's really no point in getting excited by hypotheticals," Eisenstatt said. "Let's just see what the aspirate tells us."

Alice managed to nod, while Oliver stared with murderous intent at the series of plugs and holes against the back wall. Alice was peripherally aware of a knock at the door; a nurse entering, sharing something with the nurse-practitioner. She was aware of Dr. Bhakti, watching her, projecting a concerned, or at least involved vibe, while at the same time running a hand through that luxurious and well-conditioned hair. If Alice looked at the visiting cancer fellow right now, she'd scratch out that bitch's eyes.

This was when the baby decided she'd been on best behavior long enough. Rubbing her eyes would no longer suffice. Rubbing her ears had become old hat. Even rediscovering how good her toes tasted didn't placate. Doe let everyone within the tristate area know her nappy time was long overdue. It was an affront that people were paying attention to everything but her. Knee bounces and a fresh pacifier weren't going to solve jack. And when it seemed like her cries couldn't become louder, they became louder. Alice focused on a spot directly across the room. Her world became that small spot. After two counts, the spot widened to include her fussing child.

"Is there a bottle?" she asked.

"I also have something in my notes about the insurance," said Howard Eisenstatt, MD.

"Actually, that's what I'm here about," Requita said. "Business office called. On your way out, you need to go see them. I know you already did. They have something more."

"Give her," Oliver said. "Give her to me."

Taking the baby, he said, *"You're a good girl, okay, there, there,"* and started away from Alice, away from Eisenstatt, along the empty side of the exam room. "I've been dealing with Unified." His voice was resigned, more than a little defensive. "It's not a big deal, a bunch of red tape, mostly. But trying to get people to read the facts that are right in front of them, don't ask me why—it's really not worth getting into here."

Eisenstatt had the expression of a judge who may have sympathized with the defendant but had been through the courtroom sob story more times than he could count. "By necessity there's a wall between medical and billing." His arms folded over his clipboard and held to the middle of his chest. "I hate insurance companies.

Hate them. We'll do what we can." He asked the nurse-practitioner to put Oliver and Alice in touch with the hospital's social services liaison. She could act as a mediator and help with financial aid forms, if it came to that. "Make no mistake," said Eisenstatt. "You have to get this settled. Getting you to a transplant is the only option here."

Whitman Memorial, 1220 York Ave., 4th floor, Hematology/Oncology (interview), N.

They'd been friends a long time now, living down the hall from one another for upwards of twenty years. This friend of hers, a single mom. She used to drop the boy off whenever, then she lucked out and got herself remarried. She scooted out of the city and up to the burbs, Rye: her and the new hubby and her son. Kid was a bright boy. Salutatorian of his high school, even earned a free ride to someplace down south, one of the those states with traditions of Confederate flags and really good barbecue. When that child got down there, something happened—his heart got smashed, or being away freshman year was too much, maybe he just straight bugged. It wasn't uncommon— a kid is alone, the year goes on and the pressure mounts, he burrows deep inside his own head. This young man became withdrawn, wouldn't come out of his dorm room. Got so bad he had to leave school and head north. His mom kept wanting to know what was wrong. All he said: *I had to get out of there.*

So he returned to Rye and shut the door to his room and wouldn't answer any more of her questions, he ignored his stepdad's knocks, even stopped using his phone, basically the kid shut himself down, retreating into the quiet of that room. The most he admitted, he always felt weak. Whatever was happening to him, it would stop. He told his parents this. Claimed to be sure of it. But the only thing that stopped was his eating. No appetite. Through his closed door, his mom would hear him moaning. Whenever she wanted to know what was going on, he complained: *stomach pains.* She couldn't figure out whether the boy was sick, if it was in his head, what. But she also knew her son had always been sensitive. Even from a toddling age, he'd been too smart for the rest of the neighborhood kids. The mother worried that her son's problems might be mental. His stepdad meanwhile was losing what little patience he had left. He pounded on the door, told the kid to snap out of it. Even the kid started thinking he might have been making shit up. The boy started questioning every single thing he knew about himself. Nobody had any clue what to do. And he'd lost sixty-five pounds in three months. He was weak, frail, hunched over when he walked, looking like an old man. But he was just nineteen years young. Doesn't happen with a boy that age.

Then he got a fever. Hundred and five. Parents hauled him to the local ER. The emergency room doctor in Rye gave him aspirin. Three days later the kid's at a hundred and six. After all this, her mom got an idea, finally went through her organizer, and looked up Carmen, her old friend from down the hall. Carmen'd been a nurse for twenty-plus years. Carmen told that boy's mother, *Get off your ass.* You get that child to a different emergency room. No small-town country bumpkin place. A serious emergency room at a big hospital. They ask what's wrong, act like it's the first time you're seeing any-body. Those triage emergency room folk find out a general practitioner's seen her kid, they hear he went to a different ER, they'll think it's under control, send his ass right back home. Carmen told Evelyne to make a ghetto stink: *No we can't take care of him. You have to treat him. We can't have this no more.* ER can't have no young man sick with his moms screaming bloody murder around all the other patients.

Carmen told her that God understands a white lie. Sometimes you have to do it. They can't kick him out—goes against the oath.

The mom and her boy ended up at Sinai ER, telling the admit staff his story, his symptoms, everything that Carmen said to tell them. And wouldn't you know, their story got the emergency doctors listening. The doctors adminis-tered all the tests his momma had hoped for. And those tests led the boy to a stomach specialist. Finally, after all this time, he got to deal with someone with expertise. When the specialist heard their story, he got concerned. *He did tests.* Boom—abscess lining his kidney. Monster size. All sorts of toxic bile in there. But before they could start doing anything about the abscess, they had to pump his belly. They put the kid on IVs. His third day in the hospital bed, he broke down. Tears streamed down his face. *I'm hungry,* he told his mom, *I'm actually hungry.*

Requisite Business

"LIE AS STILL as you can," Eisenstatt said.

"It's cold," answered Alice.

"Nurse, more blankets."

"Blankets, Doctor."

"Before we start," Alice said. "If you could please—could you explain to me what you are doing, during the procedure, what phase we're at?"

"I'll do what I can."

"Kindly appreciated."

"What we're going to do is start at the area near the top of the back of the hip bone, the posterior iliac crest. It's our entry point. Still, please."

"Mmm."

"This is lidocaine. A local anesthetic. You'll feel a little pinch."

"Nnn."

"More lidocaine," Eisenstatt said. "Now we're going deeper."

"Ah. Ah. Ah."

"There. Let's let that sit." The doctor waited. "Please, if you can remain still."

"I'm trying."

(Stray odd sounds; the click of a vial twisting and popping open.)

"I think these are extra."

"Yes, Doctor."

"Do you have yellow?" he said.

"I'll get some," answered the nurse.

"Great. Okay. Okay."

(Faint scratches. Metal objects impacting metal. Echoes in a pan.)

"Okay?" said the doctor. "How you doing, Mrs. Culvert? Are you doing okay?"

Her answer was a light sob, a whispered chant: *Shamalam. Accept.*

Oliver eventually found the M bank of elevators, the stroller wheels jiggling over the slightly raised grooves when the door slid open. His luck held and the child remained comatose in the lobby during the wait. He started perusing an unattended issue of *Schlep*, enjoyed the cover story ("Venice: You Mean I'm Supposed to Get Around in a Kayak?"), as well as the little gray sidebar infographic ("And the Smell!"). The office door opened. A woman in a heavy, formless coat came out, followed by a tallish young man. He was pale, moving creakily, and so skinny that his powder-blue sweater engulfed him, the letters of its white TAR HEELS logo folding onto one another. The woman was cursing the office, wondering how could they expect her to get this kind of money? When she saw Oliver and the carriage, she went silent. Her son took her hand. Which of them led the other away was unclear.

Within minutes, Oliver was summoned by the same youngish financial aid woman as earlier, Miss Culpepper, who smiled that same politely annoying smile, and casually guided him into that same sparse cubicle, where she informed Oliver that because of the low ceiling on their family insurance policy, a hold had been placed on his wife's patient status.

Oliver tamped down on his rage. He had a role—in doctor meetings, this meant asking follow-up questions about side effects, getting clarifications without being obnoxious. Keeping his opinions to himself. For Alice, he swallowed and shut up. So now he kept his voice low and respectful, and explained out a piece of first-grade math.

"I checked with Unified on Friday. Our policy cap is three hundred thousand. We're around one fifty, is what they told me."

A finger gracelessly hit what sounded to Oliver like the return key.

"Your wife has leukemia?" Miss Culpepper's voice was disinterested. She pounded the key a few more times. "We have here her needing a bone marrow transplant? Bone marrow transplant's a major procedure."

"That's months away. You can appreciate—we aren't close to that point."

"Transplant costs more than what your whole policy covers."

Taking a moment, giving his best, most apologetic, most adult, taking-you-in-my-confidence look, he explained to Miss Culpepper about the small policy they'd basically gotten for Alice's pregnancy, how they should be able to transfer to another policy without hitting any rigmarole about preexisting conditions. He'd checked into all this, he said. He wasn't looking for pity: "But while I'm figuring out our best next step, if we're months away from even approaching our cap, I guess what I'm asking is: Why can't we just keep using the policy we have?"

Her eyes had glazed. "I can respect your situation, Mr. Culverts. I hope you can respect ours."

Oliver squirmed in place, decided to not correct her about his last name.

"Hospital procedure," she continued. "Once you reach a certain level on your insurance coverage, we flag your status."

"We're *not even*—"

Yet again he caught himself. Behind him, though, damage had been done: the baby carriage stirring, minor tremors followed by calm, silence. A near miss. Oliver's panic about the child awakening receded. He jutted in his chair now, whispering across the desk with the fervor of a person whose spouse's life depended on him being understood: *"We still have one. Hundred and. Fifty. THOU-SAND dollars. Alice was in the hospital for thirty-four days in New Hampshire and we didn't spend that much."*

"I'm sure you can appreciate, billing rates are a little different here in the Upper East Side."

"Look, you really want to get into this, you want to get into spe-cifics? Okay, say Unified has their way, just say we lose the appeal—"

"Mr. Culverts—"

"More of that billing's going to be classified out-of-network. It'll be a hit for me, a massive hit, fine, but it actually comes OFF our policy total of spent insurance money. We'll end up being MORE under the cap."

"I'd appreciate it if you please didn't raise your voice at me, Mr. Culverts."

"I'm WHISPERING."

"I'm not raising my voice at you, am I, Mr. Culverts? *I'm not los-ing my temper at you.*"

"I'm not losing my temper at YOU, either, Miss Culpepper. If I'm upset, *which I'm not,* but if I am, my upset is *not* because I have anything against you, I don't. It's you as the de facto representative of a bureaucratic nightmare that's creating all this *BULLSHIT—*"

"So you're screaming now?"

"—instead of doing what it should be doing, which is to make sure my *wife* stays *alive.*"

"This hospital's run by a private management company, *okay?* This management company, they has they own policies, *okay?* End of the day, I don't make policy. My job, I make sure the hospital *gets paid* for the services it provide, okay? That ain't me, that's *policy.* If you need, we got all kinds of financial aid and payment options to our patients. I'll give you the form."

"Miss— Where . . . How do I . . ." Oliver reset himself. "I have a little software business. That's what I do, Miss Culpepper. It's not big, I'm the only full-timer. But when I hand in the tax forms for any financial aid papers, it looks like we're loaded, like that lump is the business's regular yearly income. Really, it's all the money to get through development and onto the market."

She did not seem to follow, but stayed silent until she was sure he'd finished. "Until you rectify this situation," Miss Culpepper said, "your wife's appointments have to be approved once at a time. There's a hold. On Mrs. Culverts's account. Hospital won't make appointments after first of May for her. So that's three months you have. You still under the cap come May we can revisit the situation. If I were you, though, I'd have this problem solved by then."

This is the only way we know to make you better

IT TOOK ANOTHER hour before they let him back inside, where electric light, bright and pitiless, beat down on the sight. His wife was curled on her side, protecting herself in a sad imitation of a cocoon. Her bright blue wig, now askew, looked ridiculous, and worse. Her eyes were shut, but she wasn't asleep, just recovering, breathing softly, a thin white sheet over her torso.

An unopened can of cranberry juice sat next to a plastic cup near her head. A spot of blood marred the plastic exam table paper, which was creased and crumpled and had been ripped along the top edge. Oliver softly kissed her raised cheek. She was fragrant with heat and sweat, her skin chalky on his lips. Oliver kissed one shut eyelid. Then the other one, half-pressed against the starched sheet. Alice lifted her hand to his cheek. Fluttering eyes were unfocused, her smile sleepy. She looked beyond his shoulder, to the carriage, checking.

"Dr. Howard Eisenstatt, MD, is upset at me." Alice sounded airy, girlish, a little drugged. "I wouldn't let him tell me any results until you came back."

A brain trust of physicians were right outside the room, gathered over the equipment tray, checking the same paperwork and looking at the same clipboard; Oliver hadn't noticed them, but now they began entering. Eisenstatt stepped forward, his forehead and cheeks still tinged with the flush of exertion, his expression uncertain. How was Alice doing? he asked. Indicating concern as to whether it was okay to talk, he glanced toward the carriage.

"Thanks for asking," Alice said. "It might be a good idea to use our indoor voices."

Eisenstatt helped himself to a cup of water, looked toward the nurse, who was prepared with a Magic Marker and then a dry-erase board the size of a lunch tray. "I know it's been a long day," he said.

The doctor uncorked his marker and started writing, first on the left, then the right side of the marker board, slanted, quick, and a little sloppy, forest-green capital letters appearing parallel to one another:

I   *T.*

Eisenstatt accentuated the *T* with a squeaky, tight checkmark. "We need to get you to the *transplant*," he said. Circling the *I*, he continued. "You've been through *induction*. That was big, and you came through with flying colors."

"Doctor?" Alice's head was lying on its side, resting atop her hands. "This is going to explain my aspirate results?"

"The board allows us to understand your results as they relate to the bigger—"

More knocking. An orderly entered with a carton of milk procured from a lunch tray. Alice thanked Miguel, then looked over to Dantelle, and mouthed *Thank you*. Oliver had already started toward the sink, where he began washing out the plastic nipple. Watching, the doctor seemed impressed, but also taken aback.

"I'm with you," Oliver said, still pouring milk into the plastic baby bottle liner.

Only when the nipple top had been screwed back onto the bottle did the doctor allow his lips to form that tight smile, by now recognizable as a sign of growing irritation. "We want to make sure the cancer stays in remission," Eisenstatt said. "The way to do that is to stay on top of things, be proactive—everyone with me? Standard plan of attack. Two months after induction, we bring you into the hospital, give you another dose of chemo. This time it's a high-impact dose of cytarabine. We call this *consolidation*."

On the chalkboard he scribbled:

$$I \rightarrow c \qquad T$$

"During consolidation, you'll stay in the hospital for five or six days. For another week or two, your counts will plummet, that's typical, and you'll need a fair amount of support. But we'll also do your HLA typing, and get searching for your donor. HLA takes about three weeks to process. Gold-plated, best-case scenario, one consolidation, we find a match while you're recovering, move right into the transplant."

$$I \rightarrow c \rightarrow T$$

"That happens?" Oliver asked.

"It does." The doctor's voice trained on Alice, making sure she'd heard him.

"You are white, American, of European descent," Eisenstatt continued, "so the numbers are as much in your corner as anyone could ask. If you were an Eastern European Jew, the history of pogroms and the decreased breeding pool complicates a lot of genetic structures. Or with African Americans, the donor pool isn't as deep as we'd prefer. I don't make a habit of predictions, and can't promise anything. But in the case of Mrs. Culvert, it's conceivable we'll find a match. I'd say finding one quickly is within the realm of possibility."

"And if not?" she inquired, from her little protective shell.

"We will," Oliver said.

"I know. But if not—"

"We keep searching," Eisenstatt said. "It's not ideal. Time *is* a factor. And the way to solve this *is* a transplant. But consecutive consolidations" $I \rightarrow c \rightarrow c \rightarrow T$ "are an available option."

"I've got to get on top of the insurance thing," Oliver said. "I'm going to get that taken care of."

The doctor was quick, kept the discussion focused. "Let's talk about time frame. It's been seven weeks since you were diagnosed and started with induction. The normal waiting period between chemotherapies is about eight. Seven weeks is a bit early, but still in the ballpark." With military precision, his marker tapped against the dry-erase board, two hard taps.

"There are issues with your blood work."

The doctor spoke with a tone as even as was possible. "I took a quick look at your aspirate slides. Probably ninety-five percent of the cells look clean. But that five percent, they're a question."

Alice's eyes were shut in a way that meant she'd retreated into a mantra, one of her private worlds, and the sight was both a relief to Oliver and a little scary. Eggs of worry had hatched through his stomach, spawning colonies at the base of his spine. Eisenstatt was saying that the structure of Alice's leukemia cells was particularly complex: it was possible the cancer could go dormant for a time, then reemerge. He was saying those five percent cells might just be regular, small, dead, noncancerous cells, in which case everything was fine. "The other possibility"—he spoke as if he had no choice—"these cells are, in fact, cancerous."

A skilled palm wiped the board clean. Eisenstatt waited, checking whether Alice wanted to watch. "We have to be vigilant. We wait a few days with these cells, see how they mature, what happens when they replicate." The doctor's cheeks ballooned, he let out a breath, glanced at Oliver.

"If the leukemia's started to replicate," he began, in Alice's direction, "we have no choice. We have to deal with this. We'd be at an advantage in that we're catching this early. Those first cells barely would have a chance to replicate. We go as aggressively as possible. I can't say I'd call it a setback for your treatment. It doesn't change any of our long-term goals. But what we'd need to do—" He raised the board. The marker tip squeaked on the slick surface:

$$I \rightarrow I$$

Alice had indeed opened her eyes and was looking at the board, at the doctor.

"Obviously, going through reinduction's not ideal," Eisenstatt continued. "The stress on your body is not something to take lightly. But if, *if* we have to go this route, we're fortunate in that, as we were saying, you're young, you're coming into this strong and healthy, you have your beautiful baby, a positive attitude toward your recovery. You'd be on the ward as an inpatient for at least four weeks. So what we'd shoot for:"

$$I \rightarrow I \rightarrow T$$

A small voice asked if she might see the board, please.

Alice held out an open palm. In two strides, Eisenstatt propped the dry-erase board against her sheet-covered thighs. Now he set the marker in her waiting palm. Without so much as a glance in response, Alice turned her attention to the board. One motion added a short, crooked line across the bottom of the T;

$$I \rightarrow I \rightarrow I$$

She kept writing:

$$I \rightarrow I \rightarrow I \rightarrow c \rightarrow c \rightarrow I$$

"That's not going to happen," Oliver said.

$$I \rightarrow I \rightarrow Ic \rightarrow c \rightarrow I \rightarrow c \rightarrow c \rightarrow c$$

"Blinders on, remember?" he pleaded.

$$I \rightarrow I \rightarrow Ic \rightarrow c \rightarrow I \rightarrow c \rightarrow c \rightarrow CCTCXXXRIPBYEBYEFUCKFUCK$$

"Let the record show, Mrs. Culvert, I'm not presenting what you wrote as a possibility."

"No, Doctor." Streams flowing fully down her face. "You are only proposing to pump toxic chemicals in me until I'm fluorescent."

"Alice—"

"I don't think anything is solved by heading down this road right now, Mrs.—"

"What other options do I have, Doctor? I mean, really now, wouldn't it be at least *humane* to tell me what else I can do?"

"Ali. We're going to find a donor. We are."

"You can seek a second opinion at other hospitals," Eisenstatt said. "It's your body. You have every right to decide what kind of treatment you do or do not want. Nobody is going to stop you. We'll help you get into contact with whichever hospital you choose. But let's be clear: time *is* a factor. And with that in mind, I'd like to focus on the situation in front of you right now. Because you have a decision to make, Mrs. Culvert."

He let the sentence sink in, gave her the chance to prepare herself. "One way or another, you need chemotherapy. If the results are clean, we want to keep you in remission. If they show up different, we need to get you back to remission. You're right on the cusp of the time frame where we'd start consolidation therapy anyway. You have to decide if you want to start treatment here, of course. But in a sense, we're just waiting on whether the treatment will be reinduction or consolidation, and when we need to start. Oh, and your green light, of course. Getting beds here has been a problem of late—at the moment, the ward's at a hundred and seven percent capacity."

"One ten," corrected Bhakti.

"Ten?" His eyes closed, a disbelieving beat. "With your permission, Mrs. Culvert, I'd like to put you on the admittance list, try and get you in here as soon as possible."

A flash of panic; Alice sought out her husband, began propping herself upright. "What about Thursday? Crab Fest?"

Howard Eisenstatt, MD, let out an airless gasp. "The Black Tide?" he sputtered. "You have reservations?" An amazed laugh; he shook his head, rubbed his chin. "Mrs. Culvert, you're obviously a resourceful woman. But this time it's my turn to be as clear as possible. Leukemia and induction have *severely* compromised your immune system. By severely, I mean to say: your immune system is *as close to nonexistent as is possible*. I'm telling you I'd rather you not go out in public *at all*. If and when you go out, it *must* be in a controlled environment. This means wearing the mask. The gloves. Antibacterial wash in your purse. No way you're going to a crab boil."

Alice absorbed his disapproval, her expression insisting, *What, you can't mean me?* However, it was also apparent: she knew she was in the wrong, knew she was caught.

"We'll go next year," Oliver said.

She spent a quiet moment looking into her lap, her jaws clenching, the tendons in their hinges flexing. When she spoke, her voice was a whisper. "I keep telling myself I need to accept this. It's a serious condition and I should treat it." Flicking her wrist, she gave an idle wave, as if shooing away a nuisance. "Part of me always knew I couldn't go. You knew it, too, didn't you, Oli? Humoring me like that, sweet." Her eyes wandered, back to the source, the place they always returned, the baby carriage. "If it's all right, Doctor, could my husband and I call you in the morning about the admittance?"

A careful nod, another tight grin. Eisenstatt tapped the marker on the clipboard, as if punctuating it, bringing the discussion to an official end. He started to turn, then waited. "There's something else. I hesitate to bring it up."

The nurse-practitioner stepped forward—she'd been quiet for so long that Alice had forgotten she was in the room. Now Dantelle (right, Dantelle) had an expression of patience and authority. "You told me the little one hasn't had her shots. When she's in the waiting room, there's a chance that she carries in germs. She might potentially transmit them to a patient. There's also a chance she picks up something from a patient. Hospitals are very dirty places. And her immune system is still unformed."

Oliver couldn't restrain himself. "Doe was with us in New Hampshire during induction."

"It's all right," Alice said.

"We can't take the risk," Dantelle said. "I'm sure you can appreciate—"

"Nurses *creamed* themselves when they saw her."

"Oliver." Alice forced an imitation of cheer. "It's fine, Dantelle. We'll just make my appointments for later in the day, when we have the sitter."

The practitioner looked embarrassed. "I'm not making myself clear. This would be encompassing your chemotherapy as well."

Eisenstatt patted Dantelle on the meaty part of her upper arm, taking back control of the room. "Hospital policy is clear."

The doctor did not sound as if he enjoyed relaying this information, nonetheless he was keeping a taut measure of just how much empathy he could dole out. "We don't worry about how things might be run at other hospitals. Our obligation is to our patients. On the chemo floor, we don't allow children under eleven. To make sure that everyone is safe—please, don't bring her."

"You'd be free to come down to the lobby of the first floor during the early parts of chemotherapy," added Dantelle. "Before your numbers drop, it should be more than fine for you to go downstairs. She could visit you in the lobby."

One part of Alice's practice involved an exercise that asked her to imagine digging into the black, cold earth. Hands dirty, caked with mud, she'd dig until she found a root, taking that imaginary root in her hands, cradling that root, pulling at it, dislodging the thing. Where that root had been, into the space she'd vacated, the exercise asked her to see light. It was time for her to dig. To pull.

"You want me in here for a month. You want to put me through all this *again,* and you say you're going to keep my child from me?"

She was holding her little girl, and the doctor was next to her now. "We want to cure you. We have to bring you in for chemotherapy. We have to find a donor. We have to do this transplant, and we have to start now. Time is a factor. None of this is fair. But we don't know any other way to keep you around so you can be a mother to your daughter. This is the only way."

PART II

Consolidation

What Life's Supposed to Be About

AROUND THE TIME Alice Culvert entered her third trimester, a software program known by the acronym Mosaic stepped out of the university computer labs and became commercially available for use with personal computing systems. This was its own, minor upheaval. Until Mosaic, computer users could only enter what was popularly called the Net via designated gatekeepers—America Online, Prodigy, and CompuServe—though there were also smaller, more specifically focused portals. ECHO was particularly popular in Manhattan (and had an added bonus: supposedly as many as forty percent of its members were women), as was the Well (whose membership was rumored at a whopping nine thousand), and MindVox (the go-to choice among cyberpunks, anarchists, and lesbians). With this new program, the dynamics changed. So long as your computer had a fairly consistent modem connection, you could bypass portals and directly access any corner or cranny of the sprawling and amorphous universe known as the worldwide information superhighway. Even *better,* this new software didn't charge fees based on the amount of time a user spent online.

Related to this development, or serendipitous with it, was Oliver Culvert's decision that he could no longer tolerate moving the phone cord from its wall jack into the side of his computer, then putting it back, a half a dozen times a day. To say nothing of the *massive* pain in the ass of incoming calls interrupting any decent connection. He had a second phone line installed in their new loft. He connected this line to his personal, boxy UNIX terminal. To Alice, he extolled, ad nauseam, the merits of this obscenely fast connection—42,800 *kilobytes per second*—how it would allow him to stay connected to the Net, make new contacts, and extend the scope of his consulting business. He believed his own deluded words, Alice knew, but from her vantage point, the shop still wasn't much more than a front for their illegally zoned living situation, with Ruggles—Oliver's sharpie of a best friend from undergrad— hustling up clients from the low-end brokerage houses where he had friends, while Oliver and that other unfortunate flunky, the Brow, handled tech support, all at discount prices. This quote un-quote *business* let Oliver fart around with those few stray grad school ideas to which he couldn't quite say goodbye (i.e., a questing-type computer game in which a college kid undergoes the travails of the *Odyssey* on his campus). To Alice it seemed like a safe place for her hard-driven husband to catch his breath, tread water, avoid the oncoming tsunami of real life.

Her view did not change as Oliver started spending more time with his new portal-toy-program-game-thing. Or when Ruggles, and the Brow, and Jonathan—Oliver's first cousin, whenever he stopped by, sweaty after one of his ten-mile runs—joined in. In between calls when some day trader got walked through basic tech support, and those rare projects where an algorithm got concocted on deadline, the group, somehow, she saw, had stumbled into a new useless obsession. This one entailed working in shifts, was fueled by liters of a cheap, overly caffeinated soda (available in bulk at the bottom of the back cooler of the lone nearby twenty-four-hour Ko-rean grocery), and fortified by bags of discount potato chips that weren't quite tasty but were very nearly digestible (overflowing from that grocery's dusty racks of chips). She recognized that her

husband's little group was on some sort of quest: tangibly imprac-
tical, yes; pragmatically unproductive, definitely. Epic nonetheless.

The constant raped-cat shrieking of the phone line connected
with the external modem. Seas of glowing text endlessly surfed
along, with backgrounds fluorescent enough to scar the retina; untold manifestly botched hyperlinks; that same goddamn graphic of
a seal spinning that same rotating ball on its nose. Each new bul-
letin board devoted to *Star Trek: The Next Generation* may have
been mundane, but it allowed them to push onward, to the next
page bemoaning the cancellation of *Mystery Science Theater 3000,*
the same audio outtakes of the famed radio host spitting curses
during *American Top Forty.* And toward quality stuff, too. The
best Telenet and FTP sites. Encyclopedic reference resources nobody even would have known existed. Most mind-boggling of all,
in less time than it took to microwave popcorn, pixilated pictures
came into focus. Naked women. All as easy as hitting F4.

Alice popped in every so often: dressed to kill in chic power garb;
her belly huge and exotic; hauling in the various portfolio folders
she'd needed for her meeting with that East Village shopkeeper
who sold her own clothes but needed sewing help; sloppy but
glowing in loose maternity sweats, having come back from some
sort of mommy-preparation-Buddhisty-new-age-yoga-crystal-tantric
thing. "My happy band of Orcs," she'd say. "What useless efflu-
vium have you uncovered today?" And would be answered with a
RealPlayer audio clip of a gay man in San Francisco screaming at
his roommate, *I will crush you, little man.* The looks she bestowed
upon Oliver were at once bemused and patronizing, and, more and
more, toward the end, aghast. *This is how the man I love chooses
to spend his life instead of preparing to be a dad.*

Jaundiced faces went scraggly and oily. Scraggly hair turned oily
and tangled. An odd gray stink cloud formed around the workstation. By then, Alice was occupied by her newborn; what did she
care if those idiots had molded like fungus onto the furniture, if a

stack of pizza boxes had formed an installation art piece in the loft's far corner?

They'd visited somewhere like two hundred thousand pages when, out of nowhere, Ruggles brought back up a dilemma they'd had during sophomore year. That their loose circle of science-focused and business-heavy underclassmen could survive their requisite English and comp classes with a minimum of actual work, they'd wanted to read, compare, pool, and copy one another's essays. "Should have been simple," Ruggles remembered. When he paused to suck some stray potato chip flavoring dust from his fingers, he and Oliver recalled the writing programs they'd used way back when: Oliver loyal to WordStar, Ruggles swearing by Word-Perfect, the Brow with that piece-of-shit off brand, EditOre. *None* of which, they'd also remembered, had allowed you to load or share files from the other programs. When you shoved your hard square little disc into someone else's desktop, it wouldn't open, or the text came out as gibberish. No, the only way to get an essay that your friend had written on a different platform onto your computer would have been to install *both* software programs onto *each* desktop—although installing *any* of these programs would have required five different hard discs, one inserted immediately after another, in a specific ordered sequence, which was all but impossible: some of those discs always got corrupted, or had been lost, or their little metal clip-edge thingies had come loose.

When Ruggles or Jonathan stopped by to veg out and commandeer a terminal shift, the discussion continued. Soon enough, their bull session had turned serious. Soon enough, Oliver and even the Brow were taking breaks from their time-wasting, attention-suck of a Web-quest-thing. They were listing what functions a new program might need. Ruggles jumped on top of cost-benefit analyses. The result was pragmatic, somewhat optimistic, and fairly well thought through, replete with marketing, viability, and programming plans. All of them centered on a semigeneric text field that would act as an amnesty zone. A writing program that would accept alphabet, number, and formatting systems from any and all other writing software.

They'd just moved on to coding the thing when, miracle of miracles, that prodigal impossible quest, their original slacker dream, came to fruition. Only four months, seven days, and nine hours later, but still: the evidence was undeniable. Any page they visited, they'd seen before. Just south of one million websites. *They'd visited the entire Net.* The celebration was underwhelming, all things considered: exhausted head nods, numb smiles, a sense of *Thank God that's finally over. Can that really be all there is?* At any moment more sites were being created, they knew as much. However, in this fixed time frame, in this moment, their journey was comprehensive. *We did something, but what?*

Before the group had agreed upon any kind of answer, they were back inside their programming project, taking care of its attendant affairs, for instance, settling on both the company's and the software's name, each one the same word: *Generii,* coming from the Latin, *sui generis.* In a nice little inside joke, this translated into *original* or *of its own.* (The second *i*, Ruggles explained, makes it ours.) Oliver threw in what scratch he'd managed from his other part-time job; Ruggles put the squeeze on some of his junior trader brethren to chip in a few nickels; Jonathan—unwilling to see his cousin take an absolute bath on this—also ponied up. There still wasn't quite enough to finance software development *and* pay licensing fees to the companies whose writing programs Generii was ripping off, so the official company line was *Fuck 'em.* Don't pay one shiny dime. Once Generii showed the coding was theirs and original, as opposed to just stolen from the other writing programs, once the software was up and running and didn't have any more problems with line breaks and format glitches and bugs and viruses, once they'd properly carpet-bombed the taste influencers of Manhattan with CD-Rs as if their program were America Online's sign-up discs, their product would get firmly ensconced on every important desktop in the midtown and downtown area. And when that happened, any cease and desist orders would be immaterial. The thing would be in the world.

Another foregone conclusion: her baby would be born naturally. No way Alice would consent to an epidural. And since she was the one carrying the little, ahem, *blessing*, seeing how the whole infant thing, basically, had been her deal, Oliver knew better than to do anything on this front besides tallyho: he'd followed Alice's lead (*as he should,* he could hear her saying).

Another shocker: she hadn't wanted to know the sex of the child beforehand. Once again, he'd acquiesced (*as he should have,* he could hear her, once again, this time getting impatient), agreeing it was better this way, more natural, they were going to love their child, what really mattered was their baby would be healthy, absolutely. For a few seconds, Alice held that little crimson bundle: no knowledge of gender, no knowledge of anything, just *her baby,* its physical presence, its cries of health, *her baby her baby,* and the waterworks had started, and she'd finally demanded, *what is it,* and had cried even harder, because the awful truth was, they didn't have anything for a boy, why, the two of them still had been *discussing* possible boy names while hoping to induce labor, slowly walking laps around the halls of St. Vincent's obstetrics ward, Alice's arm around his shoulder and Oliver's arm around her waist, Alice insisting on something Eastern or new-agey or fashionable, Oliver responding with a choice inspired by *Blade Runner.* For a boy's name they had uncertainty, a theoretical love but not a settled name. For a girl, however, porcelain perfection—or, rather, one of those self-serious and self-important and pretentious names, the kind that drew attention to how smart and open and giving and knowing the parents were, although, at the same time, this one had a purity to it, a lovely grace, just what Alice wanted—a little perfect lovely graceful Doe. As for Oliver, after eighteen hours of labor, he'd been exhausted—just the witness and supportive partner, he understood now why it was called labor.

Afterward, the nurse transferred that swaddled little crimson bean to him. Oliver collapsed in the cushions of the recliner chair next to Alice's bed. The infant actually fit inside the length of his forearm, her little smushed face so deeply darkly crimson, her eyes closed like those of an iguana or a weird pod creature, maybe. Holding his daughter for the first time, bringing her onto his chest, feeling her little warmth, her package weight, not ten minutes old, that had been what really did it. Reading a sonogram didn't count. Placing a hand or ear on Mommy's giant belly was not the same thing: the baby motionless, lying on him, absorbing his smell and his weight and heat, Doe's little neurons and cortical paths assimilating, learning and adjusting to and accepting, forming that bond that was deeper than blood. This had been the first true physical profundity between them, and Oliver had been impacted by the magnitude of what he would be to this little helpless bean, what was signified by her little fingers curled, moving just the weeist bit, toward him.

The next morning, the next lunch,
the next evening

IN THE MAN'S business, among people who did what the man did, there was this story. The man had not read it, but that didn't matter. The story was well known. The man knew it without having to read it. "A machine is invented," he told Oliver. "An amazing invention. It can tell a person when he's going to die—the precise time, the exact date. He can decide whether he should save his money or go bonkers on women and liquor. He can figure out how he wants to live with the time he has left. Who wouldn't want such information?"

The man on the other end of the phone paused, but not for long enough to allow an answer.

"Naturally, insurance agencies buy the patent. The business model doesn't work if customers know when they're going to get sick."

Phone jammed in the crook of his neck, head tilted to the side, Oliver set his coffee down a decent distance from his keyboard. He zipped down the menu list of file names. "Hold up. Okay, with you."

"It's why they don't want to let anyone with a partial or small policy—something with a low ceiling and higher deductibles, like you and your wife had—why they don't let you upgrade to a more expensive policy after getting diagnosed with something serious. Why should they let you cost them huge amounts of money when you haven't been paying in your fair share? In the biz, we call it apples to oranges.

"That's one thing you and your wife have to worry about."

Typing, grumbling into the phone, Oliver saying something in the neighborhood of: "Wait, fuck me, go ahead, sorry."

"Three hundred is a very low ceiling" came in response. "When the two of you hit your heads on that, one possibility is, switch to another apple. But even that's a short-term fix. It's not going to get your wife the transplant she needs. And from the way those Senate hearings are going, Hillarycare is running straight into a ditch. Ain't no relief coming that way, not anytime soon. How we upgrade your wife to a better policy, this is the question we have to address."

Ruggles had reached out and connected Oliver with an ambitious, prematurely balding counsel named Mr. Blauner, who specialized in health insurance law. Pro bono, Mr. Blauner was presently in the process of telling Oliver that absolutely positively not one thing from the financial end had happened. Account holds, flags, supersecret probations; nothing more than institutional language. The only difference between now and the day before that hospital visit, a definitive time frame had been placed on when Oliver needed to have that new policy. "That and the chick handling your account is not on your side."

"I'm telling you," said Oliver. "Lady might as well been the Christmas log channel. For all intents and purposes, I *was* talking with the Christmas log. I'm listening to her, thinking, *This empty little child is going to bring on my family's ruin.*"

"Boychick, that little girl wasn't hired to solve your problems," Blauner answered. "They don't train her to take care of your questions. Her deal is to get balances paid. No matter how supportive they are or how nice she sounds at first—"

"We didn't even get that."

"She's been given a script. She wants to keep the conversation focused on that hospital, her employer, getting paid. That little young lady lives in the Bronx or something. What she cares about is keeping her kid in that Montessori school. She cares about not pissing off her supervisor. So one more deadbeat, no offense intended, is not her problem."

Oliver mumbled something unintelligible, followed it up. "Yeah. I know."

"My young charge, no matter where you go, everyone thinks they're the one under assault. Both teams think that way. Get used to it."

"Chemo Barbie," Alice volunteered. "Barbie whose hair falls out. Her boobs are detachable. Her skin turns rashy."

"And when she's asleep, the doll versions of the nursing assistants can steal her clothes."

Alice gasped. She let out a guilty laugh. Tilda kept wiping the infant, straight from the front down to the back. "Fine, I'm racist," she admitted. "Against healthy and beautiful toys. Guilty as charged."

"Healthy. Beautiful. That's certainly not me."

Tilda paused from her application of Triple Paste. She looked Alice right in the eyes: they'd been friends for almost a decade; since orientation week of college, skipping out to get pastries at Veniero's. "Stop it. Do you even know how glamorous you are?"

"Yes, a regular Holly Golightly. Only with complex blood cell cancer."

Something was forced, self-serving, even small in her words. But Tilda didn't have a chance to respond to them: Alice's laughter led to coughing, which escalated into hacking, which, once started, she could not stop. Long woolen strings dangled at the ears of her ski cap; Alice's heaving was heavy enough to leave them swinging. The sounds coming from her throat were brutal. Then mucus, strings followed by a thick green globule. Finally a break. Taking the baby wipe offered by her friend, Alice dabbed. She caught her breath enough to say it was fine. She was fine.

On the side of the bed, Tilda remained perched and observant. Only after a period of silence, and with much hesitation, did she return to her assigned duty, and connect the Velcro straps, which sealed and signaled a successful diaper change. Blowing a raspberry into the dough of the baby's tummy, Tilda broke the room's thickness, was rewarded—Doe turning joyous as pie, squealing; her mom beaming as well.

Tilda had brought over a plastic high chair, bless her, as well as a bunch of onesies, which the two women had folded, organized, and cooed over. Tilda had mixed the baby's formula with three parts water from the Poland Spring jug (the Brita didn't make a dent against the old building's pipe sludge). Using the pages of Alice's leather organizer as a guide, she'd even started setting up a tree of friends who'd bring homemade food for Alice, help with babysitting, and call one another to coordinate and schedule. Tilda now folded the stained wipes inside the used diaper; she dropped the stinking package into the canvas sack that hung from the side of the bureau, put away the changing pad, and lifted the cooing baby. All the while, she updated Alice about interviews conducted over the course of three hours of her previous evening, the advantages and disadvantages of the various earnest college kids and actresses in need of cash, the Dominican and Haitian grandmothers who had generations of experience raising entitled Upper East Siders, the Thai teenager who'd spoken English with surprising precision and most likely had answered Tilda's classified while hidden in a supply closet in the back of some Chinese take-out joint.

Alice appeared thankful, if half-impressed. "I just don't comprehend. How hard can it be to find someone I don't mind spending my days around who understands she'll be entering a . . ."

"—delicate situation." Tilda picked up the phrase on rhythm, started repeating the words in a singsong. "With a number of unique demands—"

"—who can be trusted with my child's care—"

"—ten A.M. to six each afternoon—"

"—though, sometimes longer—"

"At a rate that isn't completely obnoxious," Tilda finished.

Alice was a grinning skull. "Precisely. Why is that so difficult?"

In the background, an album of contemplative Ghanian tribal music had run to completion. Alice extended her hand toward one of their CD towers (each: wavy, six feet tall, burnished steel). She grabbed a jewel case and opened the plastic cover as if it were a book—Oliver had a long-standing gripe about his wife's lazy habits, in particular her proclivity for putting compact discs in the wrong cases (inside cases showing plaid-shirted screaming guitar misfits, too often he'd find the meditative sea songs of humpback whales).

Tilda motioned without patience. "Here. Let me." She was a largish woman, but moved with coordination and an athletic grace, pulling out different jewel cases. Tilda wasn't about to pretend she didn't know Oliver referred to her as Matilda, let alone Hungry Hungry Hippo, and "a woman on whom every single piece and color of fabric magically turns to brown." Inserting a performance art monologue about female friendship during menopause into the prog rock slipcase, Tilda recounted her trip to that sketchy warehouse district under the Brooklyn Bridge.

It was the regular deal: the windows on the F train carved up to where they were impossible to see through, the station signs, once you got out of Manhattan, splattered with graffiti and unreadable, Tilda waiting for that first stop, paying attention so as not to miss her exit. "But here's the wrinkle. As soon as I arrived and came up from out that shit-ass station, *wild dogs* started chasing me. *Wild dogs chased me through DUMBO for four blocks.*" She laughed and updated Alice on her attempts at networking: "Oh, I dropped something off for the group show I told you about. The assistant said the curator'd get back to me, so, I mean, I know what that means, but who knows, right. . . ." Then moved on to the *gloriously sketchy* legal proofreading class she'd found in the back classifieds of the *NYPress:* "It's taught out of this woman's apartment, okay? It's enough to make me ashamed of myself. You take this class and instead of having to go through the official certification rigmarole, this woman gives you a list of phone numbers of *other people* who've taken the class. They're working at law offices and vouch for you. So long as you pass the official proofreading entry test, you're in. Then *you* vouch for other people from the apartment. Naturally, every name on my contact list is disconnected."

"There must be a way for me to see Doe during chemo," Alice said.

Tilda went quiet. Her puttylike features froze.

"Whether I need to talk with another hospital," Alice continued, "the transplant surgeon, whoever, there has to be someone. I mean, we don't have a choice about this consolidation, okay. But to not see my child?"

"She won't remember a thing," Tilda answered. "It's going to be harder on you."

"I can't do this and be separated from my baby. I won't."

Tilda took care in placing the debut album from Oliver's favorite noise band into Doe's little grip; she let the child slobber on the silver surface; she softly rubbed the length of Alice's calf. "Enjoy your time in the now. The treasure is right here."

"I don't trust Western medicine," Alice said. "If I didn't have Doe to consider, I could easily go up to some ashram, treat myself through meditation."

"Western medicine can be part of God, too. You just have to let it be."

Alice batted her head, as if swatting away the remarks. "The uncertainty is the hardest thing." She teared up. "Living with fear."

"People who go through something are interesting. They've lived. That's worth something. Believe me: writers, fashion, art, whatever, if it has no point of view, if it's entertaining but not profound, I always want to say: *Why do this?* How many guys have I met that are wastes of time like that—"

Alice leaned back, giving her weight to the headboard's wrought-iron curls and swirls. She closed her eyes. "In the winter, when a tree hibernates, all of its strength goes down to the roots." Feeling for Tilda's hand, Alice clasped. "I have to leave behind my smallness, my pettiness, all the things I don't like about myself. If I keep on doing things the same way"—a dismissive flick of the wrist—"this is a failure and a waste of time."

"You can't honestly believe there's some connection? *Habits* have nothing to do with this."

The sound of the noise machine. Then a sniffing.

"I'm giving it a year," Alice said. "In a year all will be better."

Tilda nodded, then became distracted, an awareness: dawning, taking over. Alice smelled it, too. Always that dry ice.

"Can we— Let's get out of here."

Tilda did not move.

"I'm up for it," Alice said. "Toesie-swear. Come on, honeysuckle. Don't be such a puss."

Legend had it that the owner and his pals used to ride their motorcycles around inside the biker bar. Behind the massive ornate wall mirror, bras hung like toilet paper from tree branches: some were lacy, worn, and supportive, others had underwire, still others were made for business. Each was deeply sexual. From behind the ancient oak bar, young men in expensive suits stood, four thick in the stacks, jostling for position, waiting for their turn to try for the attention of one of the hot little numbers plying drinks. One otherwise indistinguishable white young man waved his money. The brunette passed. Leaning toward his childhood friend, straining to be heard above the music and din, Ruggles screamed: "The science these people have now, fucking *nuts*. They have more answers, sahib. More *knowledge*. Telling you, best time in the *history of civilization* to get sick."

Every day was like this for Oliver. Another member of the inner circle getting in touch, another heart-to-heart. The next morning it was Jonathan, his older cousin, a survivor of three consecutive New York City Marathons, asking to meet him at the West Side Pier, where Jon ran in the mornings before heading in to the architecture firm (he was a junior junior something). Having just finished ten miles, Jonathan was bent over, taking deep breaths, his lightweight jogging hoodie open, his shirt soaked. What did the perennial voice of reason want to tell Oliver? "At least you're not referring to the baby as *it* anymore."

Friends, long out of touch, called as soon as they heard. "Unbelievable" was said, again and again, each pal heartfelt, having the best of intentions, wanting to know: "Can I do anything?"

Ruggles lifted his PBR, kicked his head back, took yet another swig. He loosened his tie and did not pretend to hide his appreciation of the cowboy-hatted college girl behind the bar. "Sahib, I'm telling you, fucking *way* more's being done to make sure Phase One and Two cancer drugs are available to patients these days. Serious, man. Cancer drugs are rainmakers. So much goddamn capital's invested in them. Don't let this shit get to you, understand?"

Going into a stretch of early afternoon. His dad barely waited for Oliver to pick up the phone. "Those insurance agencies," Dad began. "Buncha dirty whores. I say this 'cause they have sex for money and don't bathe after."

Ruggles slapped away Oliver's attempt to pay for a round. He smiled at the waitress, watched her withdraw and sashay past. "Jillian made me see *Angels in America*—you see it? Hell of a play. One of the main characters leaves his infected lover. I couldn't help think of your situation." Ruggles took a swig, swallowed. "That's cocksuckers, though. You're being a man.

"Plus no kid involved," Ruggles added.

Oliver returned a call from the previous day's seven in the morning. Blauner told him to hold on. After a few minutes, there was the sound of a door shutting. When he returned, Blauner was apologetic and asked where they were. Trying to keep medical costs from preventing his wife's lifesaving transplant, Oliver said. That was where they were.

All the good friends who showed up but were stunned and didn't know what to say or how to act, and Oliver had to get the hell away from, ASAP.

"And that motherfucking Speaker of the House. Bastard serves his wife with divorce papers *while she's in the hospital getting chemo*." Ruggles wiped his mouth with his sleeve, continued. "You tell me how that fat fuck looks at himself in the mirror."

"Help with the baby?" A chorus of inquiries. "Help with groceries?"

"Isn't a bone marrow transplant the modern equivalent of the iron lung? Oh, sorry, I didn't mean—"

"Where can I register to be a donor? Is there anything you need?"

"One thing you're going to learn," Blauner volunteered. "Doctors can be the best people on earth. They can be the worst. Sometimes you get both in the same."

Jonathan apologized to the nearby bum who asked for spare change. When the vagrant finished cursing them, Oliver's cousin motioned toward a bench by the water. Fog was thick but not impossibly so. Jonathan said, "I can't begin to imagine what you're going through."

Oliver felt the breeze on his face. "Honestly, I'm in it, and I can't imagine."

Ruggles stared into the dregs of beer number whatever. "Serious now, sahib, you've been screwed. You have every right to feel sorry for yourself. I mean, your wife's been royally screwed. And that poor kid. But my God. What's happening to you isn't fair. Isn't right. I know you know this, but fuck it, I'm drunk, you need to hear someone say it."

(Dumbfounded, swollen with appreciation, Oliver stared in return.)

The alarm clock showing six thirteen, the phone echoing, his dad calling from the deepest worst part of the night in Cowtown, California. "Sure you don't want a second opinion?"

"You're still the poor sonofabitch who's got to stand strong." Ruggles's tongue flared, licked the foam from his lip. "You have to strap up for battle and take care of your family. You're the one carrying the burden. It's bullshit and it sure ain't fair, but that's the deal. The shitty business of being a man."

During that most indulgent stretch of the eighties, in the wee hours of those wild nights, back when stockbrokers and club freaks had finished their cross-cultural tangles on the various dance floors of Limelight, or had tired of dry humping in the most impenetrable crannies of Tunnel, or had chopped out their final lines on Nell's glossy tables; after the go-go boys of the Paradise Garage, the strippers from Billy's Topless, the bears at Mineshaft, and drag queens of Jackie 60, to say nothing of the dominatrices from all those converted basements, and the chicks with dicks who were hooking for tricks on Little West Twelfth; once all of those beautifuls and their damneds had finished crawling through the darkness, done with their respective hobbies, predilections, and transgressions; when they were still strung out, still jittery, and needed a place to calm down, somewhere to hash out all those loose ends, relive the night, perform some more, or just grab some decaf, accepted wisdom—

among those who knew—had it that no matter where you'd been, no matter *whom* on the West Side you might have done, someone else from your particular locale of debauchery would have made *their* way toward that street of deep grooves and broken cobblestones. The aquamarine-blue metal panels from a different era. Oversize steel letters provided a stylish signature: R & L RESTAURANT, the name of some disappeared Hopperesque diner. This decrepit neighborhood's single safe haven for a fag to plop himself at such hours. The only place chic enough for a late-night countercultural epicurean to want to hang. The only open joint where there was passable coffee, let alone steak-frites, or the poached egg Caesar with goat cheese (legitimately *inspired*—you *had* to try it).

Breaking off a discussion with his liquor distributor, the restaurant owner hurried over, kissing Alice on each cheek of her mask. She looked radiant. How glorious it was to see her. His accent as glamorous as his dusty shag of hair. A moment of proper admiration for the *bébé,* then he hooked his arm in Alice's—at which point something clicked. He was horrified, and withdrew what he realized was not a sterile arm—an arm that had put her at risk for infection. His apology was both obvious and implicit, although in Alice's eyes no damage had been done, and nothing needed to be so much as implied; in this place there was only love.

Taking hold of the stroller handles, the wide-chested man Alice called Florent pushed the apparatus out ahead of them, thus allowing Tilda to guide Alice, the two friends progressing slowly, because Alice had to go slow (*Careful,* Tilda warned): down the gap of space between the lunch-counter stools and the row of square school-lunchroom-style tables; over linoleum slick with carried sludge and wet footprints. The above-the-fold, large-headline-famous artist, in his usual lunch seat beneath a map of the country that boasted his name, looked up at Alice; all the members of his lunch party did the same. The eyes of busboys consciously avoided Alice, as the owner had long ago ordered others to do with a generation of sickly patients.

. . .

"I pray every day for your wife to survive" came through the phone, Blauner pausing for effect. "And when she does get through this, in all candor, she's got a lot to deal with. One little gem: she's no longer going to be eligible for life insurance. So your parents, her parents, too—if they have any money—start putting it away for your daughter. Trust fund. College fund. Something."

"I hadn't even thought of that—"

"Right, why would you? Good I remembered. And when you file your joint return and itemize the deductions you're allowed to take for medical expenses—which you should do, and are allowed by the law—all the co-pays, prescriptions, out-of-network costs, anything not covered by your policy and that you have to pay, soon as you report them on your Schedule A, one hundred percent guarantee, that number's going to wave a red flag for the IRS."

"You mean—"

"Your business and personal returns get audited. So keep those receipts."

"You've got to be, *shit,* it's not enough that—"

"You've got a while until that happens, though, so there's more immediate problems. While we're working to land some good new insurance, the ceiling on what you have is low. Three, right? Let's do whatever we can to make sure your policy covers as much as possible, let's stay on top of costs—"

"I just, I mean—"

"Bubbie, you've *got* to be with it. Every time a doctor comes into a hospital room, that's a billed visit. Research doctors, no. Students on rounds, no. But each time the person in charge of your case comes in? Bill. Any test procedure? Different bill. People reading the results of that test?"

"Bill." Oliver was with the program, even if he wasn't happy about it.

"It gets nuts," the lawyer continued. "Doctor visits get processed in a department specifically for doctor costs. Hospital costs get processed somewhere else. Lab costs, somewhere else. You're going to get these different statements, all from different areas, sometimes different companies."

"That's already happening. Most say we don't have preapproval, which is just bullshit—"

"Boychick, the only way to handle this is calm. You've got at least a month before insurance processes and approves. Until then you're getting those bills. Don't overreact. Just confirm: the doctor's office sent insurance the precert."

"Got it. Okay. I've been trying to read the statement sheets, but there's no logic. It's to where I have no clue—"

"That's what I'm saying. And your doe-eyed case manager?"

"Culpepper."

"Go over her head. Deal with her supervisor. Soon as you can. Today. You write a letter to the hospital finance office. Let that supervisor know you're appealing everything with the insurance. Every single out-of-network charge. You request medical notes from the case, the case manager, the doctors. Date and sign that letter. Make copies for your file. You want that hospital financial office helping you. Right up until the second they have to start trying to get the balance of what your insurance didn't pay."

Oliver typed. "So pit the hospitals against the insurance companies?"

"Part of the process. You and your wife have to be in this for the long haul."

"Goddamn long-term ground war in Russia."

"It's up to you to use the time. Lengthen out how long it takes to settle each appeal. That's over, apply for financial aid—see if the hospital reduces the bill. Hospitals are like private schools in Manhattan: they have all kinds of money for aid; only the applications are huge, *specifically to discourage people from applying*. But, kid, you jump through hoops the right way, there's aid. Still, even afterward, you want to elongate out the payment period for what's left. Whitman's going to be in business, so don't you worry about them."

"I know we have enough insurance to get through that consolidation thing—five days of chemo, we stay under the cap. Another induction, though—I mean, if Alice agrees to try. . . . But thanks. What you're telling me helps."

"You've got to adjust how you deal with these people," Blauner said. "Every time you call your health insurance company, make sure you get name and number of each operator. Take complete notes. Repeat important info back to them for confirmation. When that phone-automation system tells you they're monitoring a phone call for quality control? Don't kid yourself—they're checking on employees to make sure they follow the company script. They're also monitoring your response. So no yelling at operators. Ever. Don't give anybody reason to claim you're unstable, you're violent, they can't work with you."

"Yeah, well . . . it may be too late for that, but it's good you told me."

"Kid, believe me, I understand. But cut that shit out, pronto. Any rep, you're as polite as with your sainted granny on her birthday. Soon as you wrap up a conversation, say the rep's been very helpful. Ask for her name—because you want to tell her supervisor. Then send a thank-you letter for the information you were given. Put that information very specifically in the letter. This way you create a paper trail of what you've been told, by whom, and when. Keep your own copy of everything."

"What's the worst they're going to do?" Oliver asked. "It's not like insurance companies can seize property."

"You're funny."

"What?"

"Boychick, you never heard of a court order to freeze accounts?"

"Fuck."

"That's down the road. But still—any way for you to hide assets? Do you *have* assets?"

"*Fawck*—"

"I had a client. She had cancer, is in for chemo. While recovering she gets pneumonia. They CAT scan her stomach before letting her come home. This at the start of the Christmas holiday weekend. Short staff, all senior docs away on vacation, residents and interns galore through the ward. Scan shows liquid around the gallbladder. Radiologist reads the pictures, sees the liquid, but also fuzz. He can't make a firm deduction. He writes the risks are significant and could be examples of serious problems. This is what goes into the official report."

Oliver started to ask what that meant.

"Attending reads the report, refuses to release the patient, naturally. My client complains to the daily resident. She wants to go home for Christmas."

"I know that scene."

"So the resident calls the radiologist. Off the record, the radiologist's willing to admit the scans don't look bad, whatever's happening around the gallbladder isn't such a kenahora. Besides, CAT scan results can be days behind what's really happening."

"So the radiologist's just covering his ass."

"Well—he can't afford to have the patient released, and not have a warning in the paper trail. That happens, the radiologist's legally liable. Client owns the hospital."

"Why not fucking unplug the tubes with your hands?" asked Oliver. "Just take yourself out. They can't keep her against her will."

Blauner laughed. "Leave a hospital against medical advice? Insurance doesn't pay for your stay, doesn't pay for any procedures during that stay."

A long breath outward.

"Exactly. There's all kinds of angles."

Another breath. Oliver said, "I just don't see how we're sup-posed to get through this."

Alice raved about how *scrumptious* the seared strip steak had been, even if she'd only been able to eat a few bites, it had been no less *divine;* and she told Monsieur Florent how much she appreciated being in such a welcoming and lovely space, and the restaurant owner responded by kissing Alice's hand as if the medically neces-sary rubber gloves were elbow-length silk, and he clasped into her palm a black business card, and told her that any time she needed anything, just call—didn't matter if it wasn't on the menu; they would have it for her, they could deliver to the loft. Bread baskets and water glasses were refilled; Florent told the women to take their time and he receded. Alice recounted for Tilda being in the blood cancer waiting room and meeting that man with the hump on his back, just what it had been like staring into his eyes, looking right at someone staring at his own death. Alice said she'd seen his death. She'd traveled into his void. Why should she get to live, she wanted to know, why should she get a chance, have everyone be so kind, all these people with their pity and their good wishes?

But staring at that man also allowed her to realize something. It was up to her to accept the void. She was the one who ultimately had to kill her God, kill her parents, kill herself, kill her identity, kill her personal narrative.

Interrupting, sheepish, apologetic, the creative director at a clothing house where Alice had never once set foot introduced him-self, and asked if she needed any clothes, if he could do anything for her, anything at all. Alice thanked him for his kindness and ac-cepted his hand in hers, and once he'd gone, she told Tilda that well before she'd ever fallen sick, she'd known about a form of Bud-dhism that prepared for death by having its practitioners chant: *Every day, I am getting older, my body is decomposing, I am closer to my end*. She used this chant while she was doing yoga, or chopping up celery and cleaning the sink.

Taking her time, catching her breath, in spurts and segments, with sips of cool lemon water now and then to refresh her, Alice told Tilda that she'd been reading, when she could, and there was another koan—this one about a mother monkey and her baby. The mother monkey swings through the forest, while the baby monkey clings to her. In this way the baby monkey is taken care of by her mother. "I'm supposed to be the mother and the baby. I'm supposed to let go of my worries, cling to the knowledge that the earth will take care of me. Which sounds all well and lovely. But maybe it's just giving myself an excuse to not fight?

"Theory is theory," Alice continued. "Every day I do try to believe there are all kinds of ways the earth can take care of me. But there's still this black box, always pressing on my chest: the possibility that I'll never know my child, that she'll never know her mother. I'll be leaving helpless little monkey alone in the world. I try to live by these—but I'm sorry. I'm sorry. I'm small. I'm selfish. I won't give up my husband. I won't give up my baby. I *can't*."

Tilda had risen from her seat, was on her way around the table, sitting next to Alice, visibly exhausted, ignoring her own tears. Tilda dabbed at the river flowing down Alice's face. Alice did not have to give up anything. They were going to find a donor. The transplant would happen.

Alice murmured, placed her head on Tilda's shoulder. Downy hairs were alight, standing along the length of her wan neck. Tilda stroked, down their side, pressing with a feather's pressure.

"We live in categories," she said. "You're a mother. A wife. A patient. Lots of things, right? But categories don't bring you to your soul, do they?"

Alice's breaths arrived—each lighter, softer.

"Religion doesn't have an answer for what's happening to you. Maybe you really will end up being one of those impenetrable Zeny paradoxes. What I know is this: we can be here for you. We can love you. That is all we can do. You still have to go through this. You're the one on the spiritual pilgrimage."

Spent, Alice murmured again, nestling further into the safety of her friend's bosom. Tilda kept stroking. Alice's eyes stayed shut. She made a blissful, dreamy sound. Dishes clattered in the background, table conversations carried on. Undisturbed, Alice nodded off to sleep.

How to Save the Day

T HE BATHROOM DOOR was ajar in case she needed to call for help. He could see plumes of steam, mirrors gone smoky. The effect was dreamy, almost mystical; a half-concealed, shimmering creature, her oval head ungainly, precariously balanced on the pale cord of her neck. She was looking down. Along the top of her head, nubs were nascent, rebirthed. No way she knew he was watching; otherwise she wouldn't have remained so exposed, naked, absorbed in her private ritual: two spiderish fingers scooping into a tin, emerging with a viscous cream.

Oliver had traversed the terrain of her body more times than he could count; presently it was almost unrecognizable—alien in the sense of foreign, but also otherworldly: smooth, oddly shaped, glowingly pale; broad shoulders gone hollow. In the wiped-away streak of an otherwise steamed mirror, her breasts were still impossibly gorgeous with poisoned milk, her nipples lipstick pink. And then her leftover pregnancy weight, still somehow unaffected by the chemo; her papoose of a stomach jiggling, just a bit, while she placed the cream below the jut of her clavicle, a bright white smear now covering the cigarette burn of a bruise, where her intravenous port had been.

The skin hung loose across her buttocks, sallow flour sacks—

he'd once loved spanking them, sinking his teeth into them. The sight unsettled him and he couldn't look for long. In the mirror's reflection, he caught her absence of pubic hair. Even after all this, he was shocked—both drawn to her cleft and repulsed by it.

She kept rubbing, smoothing the cream with her fingers until the white glop disappeared and her chest glowed. Flits of loose dead skin shed with her touch, flakes lifting into the steamy, wet air. Alice hardly noticed.

He came up behind her and nuzzled into the delicate architecture of her nape, resting his head on the safe side of her shoulder, where there had been no ports or surgery. Oliver planted a butterfly kiss on the middle of the back of her neck. Alice made a shocked, satisfied noise, let her head rest against his.

The phone kept ringing. She steeled herself, remembered that good old Doc Glenn *had* checked his service from the Burlington airport. She told herself her red-balloon-pig features *had* receded. For reasons logical and comprehensible and for no reasons whatsoever, every single time, improbabilities *had indeed* broken in her favor, a forged trail. Near and perilous misses. Improbable if minor successes.

Each ring was an opportunity; the chance to face that terror, to do something better than pee on herself. Alice exhaled, reached, and lifted the cool molded plastic. Bringing the receiver toward her ear, she managed a greeting, felt herself tensing, tried to relax her shoulders. Alice confirmed for the caller her date of birth. She then listened, and learned that her five percent mystery cells had come back decidedly clean. Her upcoming chemotherapy would *not* be reinduction.

The first molecules of air rushed into her lungs. Once again *if* became *had* became *will*. I will survive. We will find a way.

"There's more to it," Beth said. "Let me double-check the notes."

A tandem of pigeons had landed en masse on the sill across the way from the apartment's eastern windows. The wash of soot outside the window was substantial enough to make gray birds look mottled and filthy. Alice watched their little heads bob, their beaks peck; she listened.

Vintage board games dug up from obscurity; metal lunch boxes celebrating science-fiction shows; odd dolls manufactured to monetize a moment's quirky breakout star. Each item miraculous, preserved against time. Love Saves the Day. Alice and Oliver let the window display distract them. The passing sounds of the East Village vague behind them, the air thick and cold. She laid her head against the warmth of his shearling. From the stroller, the child reached toward the finger puppets and stuffed animals on the other side of the glass.

Doe would be every bit as entertained by the tumbling clothes in the dryers of the launderette next door, and the family would continue—meandering on the lightly frosted pavement of Second Avenue, passing into the junkies, hoodlums, and creative entrepreneurs who'd started laying out a veritable thieves' market. Oliver picked through record albums and cassettes that lay next to a disemboweled car stereo. Alice enjoyed guessing at the logic behind a tapered leather jacket with hugely padded shoulders, a lining of cowboy fringe. "The eighties," she said.

Their trek was incremental, but steady. Doctors' orders be damned, she wanted her last meal outside to be special. And no way Oliver was going to stop her from sitting at the common table at the vegetarian restaurant where she'd been ordering since freshman year. Soon, long deep breaths allowed Alice to ingest the steamy swirl of hot green tea. She managed to down the entire cup. For old times' sake, she and Oliver shared a dragon bowl of piping hot tofu, sea veggies, and rice.

Without prompting, she asked: "It's going to be all right, isn't it?"

. . .

One immediate way to provide an answer was to satiate an appetite. Another was to walk, unwind your thoughts along the way. And, too, there was home, wrapping yourself in the safety of dim conical lighting, the refuge of a boxy sofa sectional, designed with the elegance of fifties modernism. The little one may have been months away from possessing the balance to stand, but she was giving it her best shot, grabbing at the couch, using its far arm to pull herself vertical, wanting to get up there with Mommy and Daddy. Such a good sport.

Alice smiled toward her child. "I'd be crazy to think of this as a spa," she said. "But that doesn't mean I can't treat this stint as therapeutic, take care of things a more competent person would already have done."

She continued with her arrangements. First the small boxes of thank-you cards wrapped in plastic, then the calligraphy pens. Now those slips of paper and napkins with contact info that had to be added to her newest organizer; now a Moleskine notebook with virgin pages. Alice picked up the thick paperback of *Emma* she'd been meaning to read for a while. "Last time I read a book for pleasure?" She ignored Oliver's uninterested shrug, jammed the book into the secondary pouch of her Himalayan climbing backpack, and stretched herself across the length of the sofa. Resting on the breadth of Oliver's chest, Alice wondered if he'd seen her Discman.

And felt him flinch. And went cold herself.

The answer to her question lay where it had been since their return from New Hampshire: with all the other stuff from that room, untouched inside a backpack, thrown into the back of their closet.

Lifting Doe onto her chest still was effortless, Goddess be praised. Alice started with the opening letter of the alphabet. Oliver joined, a shaky harmony. The infant latched on to a strand of Mommy's wig. Alice's voice cracked, but she would not stop, even as the child dislodged her wig, ice-cream-orange hairs going askew.

"Next time won't you sing wii-iith mee-eeeeee?" The final vowel sounds stretched.

"That was nice." Alice shifted, dislodged herself from Oliver's shoulder, lifted her way back upright, and rocked her child, transporting herself again, heading now to a place where she could not hear Oliver's remarks about the hospital visiting schedule, how well prepared he felt they were.

"I don't want to lose my eyelashes," she said.

"Look at me," he answered.

"Being bald is horrid enough. And eyebrows don't matter so much. But I always had pretty eyelashes."

"Alice, just—please look at me."

"Your mommy's going to be a tree," Alice told Doe. "Or how about a smooth bald butterfly with no eyebrows?"

After a few more moments, she gave in, and turned toward him. His hand went to the underside of her chin.

"You still have your eyelashes," he began. "They're—"

"They're thinner. When I put on eye shadow I can tell."

"You are gorgeous beyond words."

"It's horrible to feel vain about these things, but I can't help it."

"With or without hair, with or without eyelashes, I still and completely want to bend you over this couch."

"A charming nondenial."

"We're going in there and we'll take care of this. All this shit's going to get behind us."

"I know." Her voice soft.

"We just have to go through it—"

"Yes."

"If there was any choice—"

"Yes."

Her plan was to read bedtime stories, feed her baby bottled formula, and lie with her in the darkness until Doe's restlessness stilled. Check-in was at six, in case she needed surgery for a central line. Then that would be at eight. Alice planned on listening to her child's breaths and snores for as long as she could bear, lying with her sleeping Doe and staring some more. Then Alice was going to come back out into the living room. Entwining on the couch with Oliver, she was going to finish packing, pick up their conversation again; talking deep into the night, confiding in Oliver and assuring him at once. She hated herself for how agitated her disease made him; she knew it was stupid, but nonetheless felt guilty. Before her physician-mandated moratorium on the digestion of food and drink kicked in at its mandated midnight hour, she planned on un-zipping his jeans, releasing from his underwear that gorgeous prick of his, and, even if it was all sweaty and smelly, even if Alice's body may have looked like something beamed down from a mothership, she planned on giving Oliver one hell of a reminder of her wom-anly charms. But her plan was even bigger, extended even longer, into the healthy life she planned on having. Whenever entitled young men and gorgeous women would not give way as she pushed her monstrosity of a stroller down the street, Alice planned on re-membering what it had been like to feel that young and beautiful and invulnerable. On Friday afternoons when the child was being impossible and the weekend was looming—all those empty hours with little childcare, few moments of rescue—Alice planned on re-calling *this* particular moment, how afraid she was. She planned on appreciating Doe's amazement at blue and red mixing into purple. On some freezing day in that kindergarten school yard, as Alice tried to halt Doe's supreme shitfit about not being able to *share* some other kid's toy, she planned on being that much more patient. She planned on soaking in the sight of her young little lady, all el-bows and knees and sparkly taffeta princess dress, Doe climbing brownstone steps, ringing doorbells, and letting loose: *Trick or treat*. Sneaking her growing child up the secret entrance that got you onto the roof of the Plaza hotel; telling her about the summer night she and Doe's father—back when they were first dating—had climbed up and sat with their feet hanging over the edge of the roof, and between bits of good cheese and sips from a bottle of cheap red, they'd leaned into each other and sweetly made out. The plan was to strike the right balance—sixty percent fury, forty compassion—when her teenaged daughter experimented with all the things a teenaged Alice had experimented with. For sure Alice planned on being in the front row with a camcorder when her child graduated from an Ivy, one of those good ones, where undergrads had majors that actually let them earn a living. It was a goddamn law of nature that she was going to walk that little girl down her matrimonial aisle.

Alice was the sun. A groggy sun, a sun who had just enjoyed an evening of walking and laughing and wonderful food, but who still had enough energy, she was sure, to enliven the thick blanket of darkness that covered the Meatpacking District. Enough light to fill the arid compartments of the yellow cabs parked along the side streets. Wake the drivers catching up on their needed sleep. And the ones waiting for relatives to get to the designated changeover spot and relieve them after a twelve-hour shift. She watched the men in industrial jumpsuits spraying water through the grooves between cobblestones on the street, washing away the blood and excess and pink slime. The sky wouldn't light up for a few more hours yet; this sun was justified in her sleepiness.

Oliver brusquely lifted the black boxy object out of the cab and set it to the ground. He pulled on the suitcase's roller handle. The rag doll that was their dozing offspring hung wanly from the straps around his pecs. Alice murmured another apology. She'd lasted as long as she could, hadn't meant to doze off, hadn't wanted it to be that way.

He did not make eye contact, said it was fine.

Pink hues crept along the high-rise silhouettes, the sides of the canyon that was Sixty-sixth Street. Thick clouds hung, low and heavy, over midtown. The night air thinned into a hue of tarnished silver.

On the sidewalk near the hospital, a dowdy figure was lumbering toward the revolving entrance doors with that recognizable, troubled gait. Alice welcomed the distraction. "Oh, Tilda," she said, allowing herself some distress and drama. "We bought that coat together. The most lovely, fine cream you ever saw. Like it'd been whipped to that shade."

Now the coat was the color of lentils. Oliver knew better than to respond. However Tilda's pheromones might transform wool and rayon and polyester, the woman had risen at this horrid hour, made her way from a one-bedroom, fifth-floor walk-up in Hoboken—a trip that had encompassed not just the PATH but across this city. None of her de rigueur grumbling, or her usual under-the-breath disagreements. Tilda had *volunteered* for this thankless task, out of simple goodness, because having a friend keep Alice company was *aeons* easier than finding a sitter at this hour, which otherwise would have been their task. (*Anything you need*, Tilda had said before the request was even finished.) A woman worth her weight in brown gold.

"Stay," Alice told him.

Obedient, Oliver allowed his wife to lean in, nuzzle, and kiss her child on the crown. Alice inhaled, Doe's vanilla scent expanding through her lungs.

"I just have to get on with it," she said, but sat awhile longer.

Somewhere a driver was pressing on his car horn, not letting up, right until the moment he surrendered. Alice remained motionless, holding her child. Oliver promised that as soon as Jonathan's wife came to take care of Doe, he'd be back. When Alice knew her schedule, they'd figure out the right time for the baby to visit. These were the confirmation numbers he'd gotten from the insurance people, the name Alice was supposed to use in case they gave her any problems.

He caught himself. "Everything's going to be great."

Now he put a hand on each of her cheeks and held her motion-less body. *"Tu est ma préférée."* And pressed his lips onto hers with the momentum of a rumbling train, until his fervency eased, his force subsiding, his lips strong but also patient, assuring, ice cream melting inside the scoop of a spoon, so soft, dissolving Alice with them.

Behind a desk stacked with files and folders, a largish woman had a phone jammed between her tilted head and raised shoulder. Chewing gum, sweating lightly, breathing through her nose in short whinnies, she stared without engagement in the direction of a computer screen. Her index and middle fingers kept pounding at her keyboard. Alice noticed the majority of her fingernails were formidably long, painted to form a fluorescent rainbow; but her two typing fingers were naked, their nails nubs, furiously pounding those small plastic squares.

Alice followed Tilda's directions and did a breathing exercise. She squeezed Tilda's hand, concentrated on the solidity and mass around her fingers, let herself be encompassed by that strength.

When a light started blinking on the desk phone's console, the woman rolled her eyes, punched at the light, and greeted whoever was on the other end—a throaty and doubting *"Mmmmn?"* that granted permission to speak. Receiver pressed up against an ear lined with tiny jewels, the engine of her jaw seeming to chew that much harder. The receptionist listened. Black braids—thick as electrical cables—remained coiled, cemented in place around her head, even as the large woman shifted in her seat. Her face suggested a profound understanding of the problems of this hospital. "What in sweet Jesus we doing have this lady check in at the early light if she going to wait till the middle of the afternoon for her room?" she wanted to know. "Oh, you going to do something about it, Geraldine. Come on down then. Bring your paltry ass on down and look at this lady the shape she in. You tell her she got to wait.

Geraldine—Geraldine. What orderlies on the shift? *Diaz?* Tell that lazy fool I'm on the phone. This woman ain't going through enough already and we can't get a bed cleaned? Go get Diaz for me. *Sí. Sí. Pronto. Pronto ahora.*"

In an exam room on the fourth floor, once the nurse put the thin layer of paper on the bottom of the scale—yet another unneeded reminder of Alice's delicate condition—the numbers showed that, since her last doctor's visit—four days ago, at her primary care physician's office—Alice had dropped three whole pounds.

"Wait until you read the book I'm going to do," Alice said. "*The Chemo Diet.* Women will be *lining up* for chemotherapy."

Behind large plastic eyewear, the nurse looked confused. In her line of work, three lost pounds were not reasons to celebrate.

"You know what I always say," Tilda broke in. "Cancer, schmancer. Long as you're healthy."

Beams of delight radiated from Alice's face. "I adore you."

Through the hallways and waiting rooms, word was spreading: the new IV expert lacked her predecessor's delicate touch. And maybe there *was* more than cultural jealousy and suspicion to the rumors, for during Alice's first awful visit here, Fatima had needed three sticks to find a vein. Beneath her thick head scarf, the demure lady now was visibly concentrating, ignoring Bhakti's suggestion to use a vein finder, kneading the inside of Alice's forearm. She tapped at a vein with two fingers, pressed with her thumbs. "Wrists and forearm look good only . . ." Her voice petered out; she kept rubbing.

"Dr. Eisenstatt's going to see you a little later." Dr. Bhakti's arms were crossed and she was grinding a fashionable heel—those same boots as at Alice's first visit. Was Alice just lucky enough to come in every day that Bhakti chose to wear those gorgeous things?

"And we have all sorts of positive news," Bhakti continued, her words traveling in a line over the scarved head of the concentrating nurse. "Your aspirate shows an absence of leukemic cells in your blastocysts. Meaning your remission is still strong. That's what we want going into consolidation."

Loose sleeves covered Fatima's arms to her wrists. She kneaded the soft skin in the crook of Alice's right arm. Her head shook. "Nothing worth going in for."

"Plus your counts are high enough that we can take you off the Coumadin. So no more blood thinners for you."

"Even this feels collapsed," Fatima mumbled.

Aware of the nurse now, Bhakti spoke politely. "You tried the cephalic?"

A glare in return: *What do you think?*

"Could someone go to the trouble of bringing me more blankets, please?" Alice asked. "It's chilly in here."

"Well, we have to get this line started." Bhakti tossed her hair behind her ear and was apparently oblivious to how such a maneuver might be taken by a bald chemo patient. Recrossing her arms, she lifted a pen to her mouth. "You've got a blood transfusion scheduled, then nutrition." She bit, gnawing at the pen's end, an action incongruous with everything Alice had assumed about her. Now Bhakti's voice sounded like someone consulting with a waitress about unfamiliar menu items. "The thing about the IV team, if we call, we're committed. Then add two hours to whatever time they estimate for arrival."

When Alice had been in New Hampshire, and it was time to remove the catheter from her clavicle area, the doctor had told her to hum. As soon as she started, he'd yanked. There had been a sting and it had been over, like that. "I had a central line the last time," Alice said. "I'm sure you both know that." She sought out Tilda, explaining. "First they tried to go into my wrist. This monstrous harpoon of a needle. I was horrified, but I don't think I even had the energy to start shaking, that's what kind of shape I was in. Oliver told me some stupid joke he loves—it doesn't matter what, trust me, it isn't funny."

"Shocker there," Tilda said.

"It makes him laugh," Alice continued, "and that always makes me laugh, and so I love the joke. He brought it up because he knew I enjoyed his pleasure. And at that moment, it was so ridiculous, I couldn't help be surprised. That helped me calm."

Tilda's eyes rolled upward; Alice recognized her skepticism. "I know you and he butt heads, Tilapia. But he's always showing me new forms of love. It's how we survived that horrid month."

The overhead lights kept humming.

"Let's just put in a central line and hook everything to that," Bhakti said, shrugging at Alice. "I mean, you're already scheduled for a port."

She was rising, propelling herself upward from the bottom of the ocean, kicking against gravity's pull, pressure on her face, her lungs burning, ascending through pockets of warmth, layers of freezing cold. Breaking out of the depths, into consciousness, awakening, gulping, taking deep breaths. Overhead light panels were graceless and harsh. Running across her clavicle, aftershocks were like electricity through thin aluminum bars.

It took some time, but, muddling through the thickest parts of her Percocet haze, she realized that the clear plastic tube was new, and this catheter was different, a new device had been placed in her body, but in the exact location as the one in New Hampshire.

"This one hurts more," Alice mumbled. "Lots more."

She still wasn't coherent when the familiar voice nagged, through her fugue, coming from some outpost: *They think they might not have used enough morphine.* Tilda, bless her. Wearing one of those infernal masks and a pair of gloves that would be de rigueur for as long as Alice was stuck here. Only something didn't make sense: Alice was accustomed to seeing the minty green accoutrements of New Hampshire. Tilda's mask was the soft yellow of light filtered through a picture window on a lazy morning—*aeons* more pleasing. Alice did not understand how Tilda had gotten to the hospital so fast—somehow she'd made it up to the Granite State before they'd even gotten off the phone, Alice terrified, sharing the news in a blubbering, hysterical conversation.

The deep part of another evening: Oliver had been snuggled next to her in the bed, on a break from watching whatever movie he'd rented from some video place near campus. He'd wanted to know if they'd get to watch the little scrap of mask go brown on Tilda's face.

Alice had smiled, blown a parched kiss.

More of her surroundings were recognizably mundane: intravenous glass bottles and plastic expanding fluid bags hanging above her, all of them connected to a large aluminum tree and a robotic battery pack; that orange plastic bin by the room's entrance, specifically there for needles and radioactive trash; Alice's patient folder open on a tan linoleum counter. Tilda sat in a cushioned seat beside her. Directly across from them, a wall of windows ran the length of the room. What was unexpected: about five yards away on Alice's right side, a mud-green curtain acted as a separating wall. From behind the curtain came the spreading applause of a studio audience, loud enough to shatter eardrums.

Tilda flipped open a notebook. While Alice was unconscious, she'd taken notes. Not much, she said. Then she let Alice get acclimated to the land of the living, poured and handed her some water, gave her some ice chips. And only then, not wanting to leave out any last detail, did Tilda unpack her list, anything that might be moderately worthwhile: that Dr. Eisenstatt apparently had been detained by some emergency, but was still hoping to visit this afternoon; that the sheets and pillowcases were indeed hypoallergenic, the nurse had double-checked. Also, Alice was scheduled for tests today—"an EKG, an echocardiogram to make sure your heart's okay, um, a CAT scan." Oh, pills. Alice was supposed to take her pills: the little red one, that was an antifungal, and the white one, right, ay-psych-lo-veer, that was an antiviral, which meant no STDs, which meant Tilda probably needed "to grab a few for myself."

They enjoyed one another's laughter, a nice break, before Tilda continued. The pills: Alice was overdue to take the bunch on the counter in a plastic cup. Alice recognized the third one—a yellow horse-looking number of thickly packed potassium. In New Hampshire she'd been assured it would help with digestion. "Only my diarrhea hit, and every time, that huge pill passed right out of the other end."

Tilda called it a koan worthy of the Buddha: *How does one digest a pill for diarrhea if the diarrhea forces the pill through you before it can be digested?* Alice was still enjoying the quandary when Tilda chugged forward again, this time to the little old woman on the other side of the curtain. Mrs. Woo. "She's pretty much trapped in bed. They've got a tube in her throat," Tilda said. Whenever any of the nurses came to talk to Mrs. Woo, they talked slowly and loudly, Tilda could not believe how bad, patronizing beyond words. Mrs. Woo had two full-grown grandchildren, and they came and went from the room at will, according to Tilda, apparently unable to speak English, but nevertheless possessing quite an endearing game show fetish, along with a preternatural aversion to turning off their television set.

"I asked about a private room. The nurse told me you could contact your insurance and see if they want to pay the extra fee. Five hundred and fifty more a night." Tilda snorted. "I can call if you want?"

Glowing appreciation in the direction of her friend, Alice wished she was clever enough, that her mind was working well enough, for a proper counter. She wished she could keep this banter going.

Then she recognized a sound—that beeping. She'd hoped she was done with it.

Congruent red light flashed from the top of the battery apparatus. Feeling around for the intercom system, Alice told the floor operator, "My IV's beeping."

In the window on the opposite wall, blankets of snow were coming down with speed and violence, falling so fast and hard that it was difficult to see the building just outside the window—a structure from some other century, stone and bricks worn down by time and the elements. She could barely recognize decorative flourishes on the marble window molding, a dancing cherub, its carved, curving belly. Fresh snow had accumulated into a thick pile on the ledge. It all looked close enough that if a person had a ladder, she might finagle it out the window, fight through the blizzard, and reach that other floor. She just might make her escape.

The Best of What Life's Supposed to Be About

His cousin's wife had sworn she would be at the apartment by eleven, *at the absolute latest*. Reliable, for the most part. Her fervor to help sure was genuine. Yet the absolute latest had come and gone, and still there was no word. Most likely she was stuck: in transit, on a subway, in a cab jammed in traffic. Jonathan also had stopped answering his phone, meaning he hadn't heard anything, either, or was in a meeting, or had nothing new to say, just didn't feel like answering.

Oliver lay in bed, feeding the kid a bottle, rocking her lightly, singing to her just a bit. Doe was overtired, wanting Mommy, not happy but responding anyway, moving less, getting quieter, one more stage closer to sleep. Oliver slowed his rocking. Being with the baby was fascinating. It was involving, necessary, rewarding, all the good shit that Alice—and every other woman he knew—had promised when she was pregnant and he'd been freaking out. Only there came that point; you reached a ceiling to all the Suzy Creamcheese homemaker blessing bullshit. Oliver could be making calls, like maybe to figure out how to save his goddamn wife's life. Just where the *fuck* his cousin's wife was, Oliver wanted to know.

Instead of the phone, he heard a muted clacking. Carrying from the loft's work area: terminal keyboards, that itch that he could not reach. His programmers, for sure, were keeping it down as much as they could, they were trying to be respectful, but Oliver could still hear them. And there you had it: his family, his old life, his company, the camaraderie of friends, and the mental involvement of a challenge, all of it was yards away, on the other side of a plasterboard wall. And whenever it seemed like he could join them, when the kid seemed ready to drop, or had passed into slumber, just when Oliver started disentangling himself, Doe. What looked like a tremor. A spasm. Rousing. Again reattaching her little arms around Oliver's neck. Clinging that much tighter.

Those first fleeting moments: his newly born daughter had been resting on his chest. Oliver told himself that, in the years ahead, he'd be looking back at *these* moments, trying to remember the soft warm exhalations of Doe's little lungs on his face right now, the way her little fingernails were digging into his jugular.

Finally he emerged onto Whitman's fourth floor, Alice's backpack dragging on his shoulders and smacking against the middle of his back, shitloads heavier than he would have guessed, especially considering the way she gallivanted all over the city with that thing. Oliver also was pulling her travel suitcase behind him. He was worrying about how pissed she'd be. The hallways perennial in their brightness, that constant tart, antiseptic smell of cleaning fluid. Rolling shelves were abandoned at random junctures, their uncovered trays of half-eaten lunches stacked in sloppy piles. Oliver passed blood vials left on some sort of lab rack. He flashed back to New Hampshire: he couldn't use the john in Alice's room because they were measuring her urine output, and it wasn't worth the risk to disturb the plastic pot that had been placed over the toilet's opening. One night, like always when he had late-night soda, Oliver's bladder had acted up. In the bathroom at the end of the hall, he'd heard the night security guard; locked behind a stall door he was quietly moaning and making sounds of quick friction, noises any man recognizes from his own fist-pumping episodes.

Oliver focused about two-thirds of the way down the hall, about where Alice's room number would be. The stylish Indian doctor stood, addressing an Asian man and woman as if directness would ensure understanding. "You really should talk to Eisenstatt about this," Bhakti said. "And we do need a decision on the DNR order." The Asian woman turned from the doctor and started speaking in some Asian language to the man, who was maybe ten years older. He answered, and the two began trading phrases. Oliver clearly heard the word *resuscitate*. He moved beyond them as quickly as possible.

Warning signs on the door served as yet another reminder of what they were dealing with, but Oliver didn't need their printed proscriptions. He'd donned the protective masks and gloves for fourteen hours a day, was well accustomed to that layer of sweat bubbling inside the glove latex so his finger pads were always squishy, his breath ricocheting off the insides of his paper masks, rising into steam.

The small rectangular window peering into the room was covered with black construction paper, he noticed. A trademark Alice maneuver—she hated people looking in on her, wouldn't want excess light if she was napping. Had to be a decent sign. He also knew she'd have the room like a sauna, and he removed his coat, followed by his sweater. Turning to the side vestibule, Oliver blopped pink fluid into his hands, which he washed and dried at the sink. Since it was easier to put on the mask before the gloves, he reached into the cardboard box and brought one of the little yellow guys to his face, its chemical smell immediately pungent. His last name was being called, *"Mr. Culvert. Good to see you."*

Coming toward him, Bhakti showed a controlled irritation. She was a handsome woman nonetheless, striking for her dark hair and skin, her long lashes and slim figure. She asked how he was doing, though he knew it was a formality.

"Well, we got to this point," Oliver answered. "Day fifty-one, that's pretty good."

"I'm sorry?"

"The first hundred days after diagnosis? They're key, right? We're on day fifty-one."

Bhakti softened, eyes widening enough that she looked embarrassed for him. "I'm not sure what you were told or read." Her mind was active, calibrating. "Those first hundred days after a diagnosis *are* key. Getting through these first six months *is* key." Lashes batted, emerald-green irises focusing on him. "Your wife will go through a number of risk periods. That's what happens. She gets past one marker, we look to the next. The first hundred days after the transplant. The first year."

Down the hallway the Asian brother and sister's discussion had turned heated. An orderly had stopped next to a nurse, and both were watching. Dr. Bhakti, meanwhile, had a shapely upper lip, one ripe with possibility. She told him that Dr. Eisenstatt was going to be in shortly. If Oliver needed to talk to him more . . .

Oliver stopped listening. Washing his hands for a second time, he left the faucet dripping, grabbed protective gloves from the box with the L sizes. He piled his jacket and sweater together, folded them under one arm. Pulling the travel suitcase behind him, he steeled himself, leaned his shoulder into the door.

Alice wore a tie-dyed motorcyclist's bandanna wrapped around her head and the white-framed cat's-eye granny glasses she favored whenever she was hand sewing. The purple and pink knits that she often described as *magical* were wrapped, twisted around her neck like a boa constrictor, or the scarf of an early aviator. Inside her fluffy, cotton-candy-colored robe, with her lower extremities covered by a multicolored quilt that had been knitted by her great-grandmother (then passed down through the generations of women in her family), Alice looked luxurious in her comfort. From beyond a fuzzy pink sleeve, she was waving three postcards.

The purpose of overhead lighting panels was to make evident to the medical staff all possible physical problems, but orange sheets of crepe paper had been taped over them, and the space had the muted vibe of a hospital room transformed into an opium den. A lovely melody, courtesy of Stevie Wonder, carried from the bedside CD player, where framed family photos faced the room. Oliver followed the arc of his wife's waving hand, across the room, to the imaginary line's logical end point. What had been a dull wall now boasted an oil spill: bright colors, body parts, ripped magazine pages.

At the near juncture where the long separating curtain met the wall of windows, Tilda stood on a chair. Responding to Alice's direction, she was lifting the end of a series of taped-together pages, stretching them so they were no longer sagging but taut. Running across half the partition, a thick-markered message read: **CANCER SCHMANCER SO LONG AS YOU'RE HEALTHY.**

Alice paused and acknowledged her husband. Mischief and delight danced across her face. "We're making headway, don't you think?"

He took three steps and reached her bedside. For the second time this day he placed a hand on each of Alice's cheeks. Once again he held his wife in place.

Every kiss had to let her know.

"Hello, my heart," he said.

Her expression was satiated and dreamy, and he tried to memorize that moment. "You two've been busy."

"I was going to call and ask if you could bring a rug." Alice's eyes danced again. "You know, something big and patterned. Tilda felt that might be a bit too, I don't know . . . arabesque."

"It's already quite arabesque up in here," Oliver answered. "Knowing you two, it's only going to get arabesquer."

Oliver accepted Tilda's remonstrations about making time in his busy schedule to grace them with his presence, and dutifully apologized for how long it had taken to make it back uptown. He assured Alice the baby was doing great, *really great,* and asked how she was, if the doctors had said anything (or even been in yet). He told Alice about the calls from her mother, ready either to come down to the city or to have the child come up to her (naturally). Lifting the mask back up to his nose, he said, "These things smell like baby poo."

"Oh, let me."

Her inhalation was that of junkie needing a hit; Oliver recognized he had to change the conversation, keep Alice from sulking.

"I like these yellow ones," he said. "They're jaunty, more . . . optimistic."

"We were talking about that." Tilda tried to hide a glance, checked her beeper.

The requisite knock of doom. Entering now, a lithe Dominican woman moved with efficiency and pep. Her hair was frizzy and reached in eight directions. A mole about the size of a quarter was conspicuous over her right brow. "Vitals time," she announced, then eyed the amount of water Alice had left untouched in her glass. The nurse made an unhappy sound. "You been through this already," she said, "so you know drinking water and sucking on ice chips is a major importance. And still I got to flog that dead cat." Her voice changed now, her words came quicker, as if she were recounting newly memorized facts before they disappeared: "We got four pillars for chemo patient recovery. Uno: hydration. Number two, protein. Then exercise. And mouth care."

"Oh, Carmen."

"Looking at that lunch tray, on one and two, you already off to a bad start."

"In the name of the Green Gay Goddess—"

"When you start up with that chemo, you going to lose your appetite something serious. How abouts we load up on the food while we can?"

"Look at that sad little gray chicken patty," Alice said.

"I want to be a team player," Tilda interjected. "But honestly, Meryl Streep couldn't convince the Donner party to bite into that thing."

"*Completely* through the looking glass." Converted to the mode Oliver referred to as her fashion voice, under the ostensible premise of speaking to Tilda, Alice performed for the room. "Do you know *the hospital* won't give me fresh fruits or vegetables? How can it possibly be in my best interest for them to shove *canned fruits* at me?"

"You want to do this again?" Carmen asked. "We can do this again."

"Every single bit of received wisdom about good food turns upside down."

"Your counts get low, and if there's a stray germ on a piece of fresh fruit—"

"I have Oliver throw the microwave out of our home, yet you insist on nuking anything that comes to me?"

"In a can, we control. What's so hard to understand 'bout that?"

"My counts are good, Carmen. They told me this morning."

"Your counts are good considering you got cancer."

"I do *not* have cancer," Alice stated. "I am *en remissyionne.*"

"You in here for a reason, mama—"

He used to stare at their door in Dartmouth-Hitchcock, counting the hours, then the minutes, until Alice's mother arrived, as if wanting hard enough would somehow will her presence. Some days he had more patience, managed the boredom, the procedural small talk with doctors, nurses explaining what the next test was, all the waiting, the begging Alice to eat, listening to her looping monologues (how could she do this, it was *all so hard*). Also the stretches when he had the opposite problem: getting through the quietude, Alice sleeping, red glowy numbers on the alarm clock ticking away their savings, their dreams.

But once Grandma and the baby arrived, then wham, the clock started eating into his holy and awaited break time. As if rushing out of a building's flaming wreckage, Oliver would hightail it for the parking lot's courtesy van, heading to one of the places downtown, grabbing a chicken sandwich from a sports bars near campus, some sad Chinese lunch from a buffet table of greased food rotting beneath heat lamps, maybe an Indian special that was as thick and spicy as cow dung. If the weather wasn't too foul, and he really needed to clear his head, he might just walk, away from the old gentrified district, out toward the town perimeter and the strip malls. Overprocessed, grease-fire-charred garbage: his official coping mechanism. He made sure to binge away from the hospital, out of sight of Alice; she'd disapprove big-time, and about the last thing he wanted was to have her see anything that revolted her, anything that even had a chance of teasing her for her lack of appetite. He wouldn't let her see anything that might cause her faith in him to waver.

When Alice's face had still been pretty swollen, and her counts were still in the shitter, and she'd barely had the strength to hold up a glass of water, and couldn't eat so much as a third of Dartmouth's version of scrambled eggs, Oliver had realized: *This is one way it could happen*. The fear that had followed was visionary. Whether or not her hunger strike was intentional or drug induced was beside the point. No matter how much the doctors, nurses, Tilda, Oliver, or even Alice's mom prompted her, no matter whether Alice understood their words, caught their implications, without eating, Oliver had realized, she'd keep fading: turning too weak to try and pick up a plastic fork, too weak to chew. At which point, her inability to put a piece of food into her mouth, the impossibility of her chewing, the momentum of her weariness and weakness and lack of appetite, they'd spur more weariness and weakness, furthering her lack of appetite. Liquid nutrition would not matter.

This was one way she could vanish.

"These eggs actually look pretty good," he'd said. "Why not go for one more bite?"

CASE STUDY # $\boxed{368}$

•Mt. Zion Cancer Center, 1200 York Ave., Hematology/Oncology, Rm. 820
•Whitman Memorial, 1220 York Ave., Hematology/Oncology, Rm. 412
(critical)

Two separate bouts of induction chemo. Six consolidations. Plus enough
radiation to create a mutant army. These along with *two* bone marrow
transplants—the first allogenic, then, when the cancer returned, a nonallo-
genic transplant, using a chemo drug approved for use on children, still experimental in adults. In short, every weapon they could think of. Still her
leukemia came back, its third and final stay. In the back of the exam room, the
doctor, damp in the eyes, continued with his responsibilities, explaining that
they'd continue the woman's regular appointments, keep monitoring her, administering her routine of blood transfusions; she'd come into the urgent care
center when necessary, and the hospital would of course admit her if and
when needed. If she was strong enough and was willing, they could even try
more chemo. But the most that could be expected was temporary easement.

The best thing to say about any day that followed was: she did not feel any
worse; at the same time there were no days when she felt an improvement.
No days when she felt stronger, or had sustained bursts of energy, when her
counts rose of their own accord, when her most cherished foods seemed
more appetizing than biting down on a cinder block. She regressed from
walking to needing a walker, from needing a walker to taking a wheelchair.
The woman could not take care of herself but was too proud to enter a home;
she felt that was giving up. But her insurance would not cover a home living
aide; so one of her grandchildren took a leave of absence from Columbia's
graduate program in nanophysics and moved into the old Queens brownstone; and since the old woman's thighs were too weak and the toilet too low,
five or six times a day she helped her grandmother—all wrinkles and skin and
noodle appendages—squat onto and rise from the bowl. The granddaughter
herself was spindly in the manner of a preteen boy, accustomed to huge science books and hours of reading, not even close to in shape to lift anybody,
even a shriveled old woman. She certainly had no experience transporting

invalid seniors back and forth to the hospital. But she purchased a heavy steel ramp, and convinced the super to let her store the thing in the ground-floor maintenance closet, so on the two days a week when it was time to get Granny out of the apartment for her transfusions (the only things the old woman left the apartment for anymore), the granddaughter could get her up and down the large front steps out in front of the stately prewar building. She ordered an expensive car service for each trip, paid the super to set up the heavy ramp over the front steps. Transferring the old woman out of the chair and into the car was one more slice of fresh hell; the super had been a Russian mob underling before coming to America and refused to get involved unless the granddaughter paid him more; usually the driver stood and watched.

In this joyless manner the two women moved from the beginning of the endgame to wherever this new place happened to be, and were summarily informed that the insurance company had determined that, in this new phase, they no longer needed care from an elite hospital. The granddaughter stayed up late reading policy manuals, she spent untold hours on the phone appeal ing the transfer of care, dealing with all the attendant paperwork that surrounded her appeals. The granddaughter conscripted very bright friends to do research, make calls, cast the proverbial wide net. She did not want her grandmother transferred to that city hospital. Her friends came up with a drug, not yet approved by the Food and Drug Administration, but undergoing testing at various hospitals in the Northeast. The tests were still in their early stages; some results were encouraging. The woman's eyes were gummy each morning; her left lid was red and inflamed; she saw things in double and triple, and was weak in a manner that made her previous states of weakness look like workouts by steroid freaks on Venice Beach. The city hospital was a dark and gloomy hull, a broken-down graveyard, especially in comparison to the gleam of new money that sharpened Mt. Zion's hallways. The city hospital's waiting rooms were like outclassed cousins whose attempts to keep up made them appear much more quaint and sad.

Her new doctor thought her vision problems might be from leukemia in the brain. He urged a kind of low-grade chemo, *immediately*, a syringe of it pushed in to linger in her brain fluid. Actually, he said, it's a lot better than it sounds. She refused: nothing till the tests came back.

Wouldn't you know, the numbers came back. Turned out she'd been drinking too much water, which had been clearing out her system, causing all kinds of imbalances, which may have played a role in her vision problems. It raised the possibility the woman's vision problems weren't caused by brain cancer. It also was eminently possible medicines had caused her muscle weakness and the problems with her gait, which was why she'd been so unsteady. The hospital corrected the problem by giving her different steroids. Instead of water, doctors had her drink Gatorade. She was released in four days.

And this, the woman being right about not getting the chemo injected into her brain, would indeed have been a nice little we-really-did-know-better-than-the-doctors type success story, high-fives all around—that is, if the cancer had indeed subsided after the woman had switched to Gatorade. But we all know, Gatorade does not cure cancer. When the woman got out of the hospital, she still needed her wheelchair and her ramp and her car service. She had to have someone bring her food and aid her up that little step into the bathroom and get her up from off the toilet. In a matter of weeks some other germ got to her and her lungs were filled with so much mucus she was back in the hospital, and in order to breathe, in order to save her life, she needed this thick tube jammed down her throat. Insurance wouldn't spring for a private room, they put her in with another sickie, apparently everyone would just have to cross their fingers and hope that a thick vinyl curtain would stop any germs. In the side counter of her small basement dry cleaner's, the woman used to have a boxy television set with shitty reception, lines of fuzz and white noise, the images going wavy whenever the 7 train passed nearby, and still, through the course of her days at work, she watched game shows. *Press Your Luck. Wheel of Fortune.* She used to rise every day at dawn and walk her two little Yorkies and do tai chi in the small cement park next to the expressway. She'd helped teach the granddaughter how to organize and alphabetize by using the numbers and names on laundry tickets, and that same granddaughter was now taking up very large chunks of her grad-school-insurance-paid-for fifty-minute therapy sessions complaining that she could not take any more of this, her own life shrinking, she was being forced into a cage, but she also *had* to take more of this, because the only way things looked like they were going to change was in the wrong direction, and she wasn't prepared to handle that.

Still. Rumbling around in her head, that fledgling idea.

Her older brother flew in from the West Coast after she shared her idea. And once they'd struck out with the Indian woman who followed around their grandmother's doctor as if she was his pet, they approached the real man in charge, cornering the doctor in the hallway outside the room their grandmother was sharing, and bringing him up to speed about this drug that hadn't been FDA approved for leukemia, but *had* been approved for other forms of cancer, and that even now was being tested in other hospitals. They gave the head doctor the experimental drug's clinical trial prospectus. The granddaughter pleaded for him to take it home over the weekend. Give it a read.

The doctor told her he knew what they were trying to do. It was admirable. But they were talking about a controlled trial being conducted by another hospital. The doctor had never worked with this drug, and the granddaughter wanted him to prescribe it on an outpatient basis, for a disease it was neither intended nor approved for?

The granddaughter's voice was steel as she reminded the doctor he sure didn't have a problem recommending the injection of chemotherapy drugs into an old woman's spinal fluid *before* tests had confirmed the cancer had spread there.

The doctor flinched and responded, with some ire, that he made a diagnosis; and the granddaughter did not flinch, and said she knew he did, and he should diagnose this. He should prescribe this for her.

People were openly gawking. Orderlies and nurse-practitioners had stopped in place to watch. The doctor's voice was searing now as he said the grandmother would take the drug and the odds were she would be dead in a week. Even today her condition was serious. He might need to perform a procedure to clear her lungs that was traumatic to say the least, and was going to require that the granddaughter and her dad finally make a decision on the do not resuscitate form.

The doctor then reminded the granddaughter that hospital policy was to do the most humane treatments for their patients. In reply he was told it was awfully big of him to consider this option so seriously and decide what was so humane.

The granddaughter could not make him prescribe that drug, said the doctor.

They locked eyes and the doctor maintained his gaze and purposefully slowed his words and said the hospital would do their best to get the grandmother stabilized and home to the granddaughter. He told the granddaughter that if the grandmother felt sick again, they could bring her in, or could choose not to. He said he was sorry, he could imagine how the granddaughter must feel.

"You can?" she answered. "You can understand, but still say no?"

Welcome to my body

HE BLUE OF cloudless skies. A woven mesh, lightweight metal, materials designed to ward away, to shield. Everyone who entered wore one. And of course the usual gloves. The masks.

Alice asked if she at least got a smock. Carmen gave a small laugh, made eye contact with the second nurse. Working as a pair, they made sure that the patient number on Alice's plastic bracelet corresponded to the numbers on each round glass bottle or plastic bag, asking Alice when her birthday was, then checking that item off their list. Carmen showed Alice each bottle, explaining: *This is an antibiotic drip of penicillin. This is Sapeptamonizene.*

In the two big windows the sky had darkened, the snowfall thickening even further, and between this and the colored crepe paper over the lights, the near side of the room was enveloped in gloom. Carmen asked if it was okay to take down the mood paper, they needed to be able to see everything. Alice looked disappointed but nodded, then mouthed out her recognition of the second nurse, the name emerging as a question. Requita winked back, kept on hooking up the glass bottles of cloudy drips, the transparent bags bloated with mucus-looking liquid. Above the battery pack, an almost ghostly tree formed, branches thick and limbs spreading, tubes running down toward Alice's port like so many vines. Carmen was using a red Magic Marker to write on Alice's skin the current military time and date, so the next nurses would know when to change dressings, replace catheters; Requita was casting evil eyes toward the battery pack's infernal beeping. Now she rolled back the sleeves of Alice's robe, began wrapping gauze around Alice's forearms; she wanted to ensure Alice's arms stayed warm. This would help the medicine circulate.

"We're putting you on a steroid," she said. "It'll run through the course of the consolidation. It makes you feel energetic, even a little high."

"With any luck," Carmen added, "you'll start that appetite."

Near the entrance, Dr. Eisenstatt began fitting his arms into his blue smock, leaving the strings that were supposed to go around his neck untied, giving the smock a looseness, a droopy scoop around his upper chest. When he stepped forward the nurses ceased jawing. The doctor's forehead was flushed; his eyes darted, wide, a bit wild, but disciplined. He acknowledged Oliver, checked that the nurses were properly subdued.

"Where have you been, *Howie*?" Alice called. "I thought you'd *abandoned* me."

It was evident Dr. Eisenstatt was not accustomed to being teased, especially not by patients. His already flushed face turned a deeper shade. The doctor seemed to stare through his chart. He did that thing where he pinched the bridge of his nose. Rubbing his eyelids with his thumbs, he murmured something unheard, took a few breaths. In the scoop of his undone smock, Alice recognized his starched and narrow pin collar, replete with gold bar running behind the raised tie knot—a flourish that defined custom-made, high-end dress shirts. Alice also noticed that his shirt was a bit too large, couldn't have been custom made. The thought flashed through her mind that the doctor's mother bought it for him at a Barneys Warehouse sale. Alice chided herself but also felt nourished—not merely by the doctor's brain freeze, his vulnerability, or even his confusion, but rather, by the vehemence of her own cattiness.

"Aside from your concerns with my tardiness," Eisenstatt said, "which I certainly understand and can sympathize with, and apologize for." Eisenstatt refocused and paused, gracious. "Now that I've finally managed to get here, from all indications, things appear to be going quite well, which is heartening." He stepped toward the bed. "It *also* came to my attention that you and the nurse had a meeting of the minds."

Breezing past the nurse to whom he'd just referred, and whose name apparently did not matter to him, Eisenstatt stopped at the side of the bed. "Mrs. Culvert, let me assure you. You are exactly where you need to be. If the cancer was present, you'd be back in reinduction, understand?" His intelligence added weight to each sentence, and his focus impacted this weight, landing smack between Alice's eyes "We want to keep your cancer in remission. This is the treatment."

Alice's silence conveyed acquiescence. Readying the late pages of a tattered notebook, she followed the doctor as best she could, scribbling along while Eisenstatt explained that her consolidation chemo cycle was scheduled to run over the course of six days. Alice would get her dose at 7:00 P.M. and 7:00 A.M. Would have a day of rest afterward, on-off, this the pattern through her six-day cycle.

"So before and after seven, Doe can come." She wrung out her writing hand.

"She misses you," Oliver said. "I'll have her here."

On her side, Requita was wrapping a blood pressure sleeve around the arm nearest her port.

"I don't think that's a good idea," Alice told her. "I'm not meaning to be difficult."

Eisenstatt watched the nurse undo the sleeve. "A lot of our patients take for granted that consolidation is routine," he said, a hint of the scolding father coming through. "Assuming things go according to plan, you'll feel fine for most of your stay. When you go home and your numbers start to drop, that's when you'll get weak and tired. Probably half my patients end up coming back to the hospital—not from the chemo but from infections. Consolidation chemo is actually more potent than the induction."

"Already you are bringing clouds of doom, O Jewish granny. Does this officially make you a yenta? Is that the term?" Motioning to the pictures on the bedside table, she spoke to Oliver. "Little kumquat."

"You've been through this already, I understand. But we don't want expectations working against you. It is not uncommon. After patients have been through chemotherapy once, they think they know what's coming."

"Doctor, is it possible for me to hold the drugs?"

Howard Eisenstatt, MD, looked at her as if she were from another planet.

"The chemotherapy drugs. Before we start?"

The ripple of confusion swelled, extending into uncertain looks. But he had no reason to refuse. The bottle itself was thick as a jelly jar, without a single contour: it came off the tree. Alice let it rest in her lap, then she pressed her palms until they were flat against each side. She shut her eyes, kept pressing her palms until the atoms of her flesh merged into the smoothness, until flesh and glass and medicine were one being, one thing. Inside the eye of her mind, Alice envisioned a smooth whiteness—flowing through her, pushing out stray thoughts, flattening worry. She inhaled up through her diaphragm, felt her chest rise, felt air swell through her, made her inner self as massive, as empty as possible. She took a long exhalation, pushing all of this gathered swelling energy out through her nose, feeling those flat stray worries push out of her body. Alice lingered on her child. Her friends. Her mother. Her passed father. Her husband. Her child. Love palpitated through her, and she channeled this love, harnessed it. "You have an important job,"

Alice told the clear contents of the jar between her palms. "Welcome to my body."

Exhaling again through her nose, Alice felt her skin alive and vibrating; and she was not scared. Handing back the bottle to Carmen, she gave thanks. Oliver was lowering himself with care onto the opposite side of the bed, making sure he did not land on her; he was lying sideways, at once next to her and on her, his chest warm on her arm and shoulder without being too heavy, his groin rubbing into her hip, the sensations wonderful, his leg now wrapping itself over hers, his touch tantalizing. Alice grabbed her husband's hand. He kissed her on the neck, nibbled her hanging lobe. The nurses could have used popcorn, gawking the way they were.

"I was thinking a little 'Captain Jack,'" Oliver said.

She laughed. "So hideous."

"Right to 'Piano Man' then?"

"At least that has ambition. The ambition is what makes it so perfect in its terribleness." She searched out Carmen's face, signaled it was fine to begin.

"You want it that way, we go to the heavyweights." Oliver put his arms around her, used the lower part of her eardrum as his microphone. *Love on the rocks. Ain't no surprise.* He paused. "Most self-pitying song in the history of the world."

Alice's face was luminous, basking. *Pour me a drink.* She rushed through the next sung phrase.

Perplexity; laughter from the cheap seats, one of the nurses complaining, she liked that song. Single drops were being released, in a maudlin and constant time signature, through the thumb-operated drip clamp, down into the tubing.

Their nightly crooning sessions had been neck and neck with the laps they walked together through Dartmouth-Hitchcock's hallways, the twin peak joys of their time in New Hampshire: eighties hair metal ballads; self-pitying alcoholic nightclub crooners; the worst tripe they could come up with.

They paused, Alice asking if Dr. Eisenstatt wanted to join them, and took more than a little joy in his demurring smile, his uncertainty about whether they were still making fun of him. She and Oliver kept belting, side by side, all but joined together and at the same time forgetting themselves, their joy palpable, emanating. *Contentedness? Love?* Whatever this feeling, Alice felt it: intangible, inviolable, invulnerable. At the same time, she recognized something else. This feeling had its underside, its darkness. However, the contrast allowed her to focus that much more, gave her access. For now she understood that this palpable feeling of hers was so very fragile, nothing more than glued together, the reconstructed shell of a once-shattered egg.

Evening

S
HE MANAGED TO eat almost a third of the black bean soup that he'd picked up from a Greek diner, and the food was sitting in her stomach without problems, so maybe the steroids were starting to work. Her blood pressure had normalized, one hundred over seventy. Her temp was stable. She was cleaning Oliver's clock at rummy pretty good, the two of them snug together in the bed, idly discussing movies Oliver could rent for the next day, whether they had enough time together to do her walking laps. Their inside hands were entwined, her left, his right, and this mingling had its own associations: Oliver coming to bed late after a programming jaunt, Alice, half-asleep, reaching for his hand; that white-knuckled delivery room and him counting out breaths for her while she all but crushed his fingers; the pleading need while the paramedics lifted her on the stretcher, Alice not wanting to let go.

From the television on the other side of the room the newscaster promised audiences that in two minutes they'd hear all about the trendy restaurant and the mystery of where in the world they could be getting fresh crabs. *Hear what the Department of Health and the ASPCA have to say about this shocking obscenity.* Oliver clapped and hooted. Alice said nothing, but her eye contact conveyed entertainment, delight.

Then the call. She'd been expecting it. But for once Winnie was early, confirming she'd brought Doe, the two of them were down-stairs, waiting. Only why was Oliver tensing? If things were what Alice wanted, his energy would have changed in a different manner, he'd have been devoted to preparing his wife to go to the lobby. So why was Oliver listening, agreeing, saying he understood, he'd be home as soon as he could? Alice gripped his palm, demanded, *"What?"*

Placing the room's phone back into its cradle, Oliver laid his free hand on the comforter, overturning an unimpressive run of cards. The baby was fine. Everything was okay. "I know you said we could rely on her. I know Winn's a nice friend and wants to help and all." Oliver assured Alice, as she removed herself from his side, "It's no biggie. Some scheduling thing with her dance troupe. The easiest thing is for me to go home and take over child duty."

Alice told him it was fine. There would be other adjustments as well. They'd deal with each as it arrived.

"We'll be here first thing in the morning," he said. "I promise."

She released his hand; Oliver looked for his shoes, began the pro-cess of gathering his wallet, his sweater. Alice thought he looked anxious to leave, and this struck a low chord. She said maybe she'd go and try a few laps. It made sense to move while she could. "Bet-ter than just sitting alone being disappointed."

Oliver returned to his wife and threw off the little paper rectan-gle. They held one another along the sides of their faces, Alice ran her hands down his jaw, felt his gristle. "I love your face," she told him, and he violated hospital policy, pressing his lips onto hers.

"Your first night with her alone," Alice said.

"If you need a nurse for those laps—"

"You should git."

He tore the strings holding together the back of his smock, rolled off his gloves, slam-dunking the garments in the trash bin near the door.

Through the windows on the other side of the room, the night was weirdly vivid, the snow still falling at a crazy pace, the flakes distinct, bright enough to glow. In the opposite building, most of the windows were dark. One window on the right side was lit, body outlines half-shredded by flimsy blinds, two men sitting like potato sacks, facing one another at a desk, one man rubbing his eyes, the other drinking coffee.

Alice could hear Mrs. Woo on the other side of the partition, breathing through that pipe, rhythmic bursts, *long in, wheeze out.* It occurred to her that she hadn't heard the television for a while, and for this she was thankful. She sat upright, shifted her legs to the side of the bed where Oliver had been, its safety bars still blessedly down. Easy to slip into her bunny slippers; Alice, however, searched out her knee-high boots, their leather so deliciously soft it did not stand upright. The million and eighth thing to be thankful for: that her feet had not swollen back up. Million and nine: she could still fit into the boots, Alice buckled, zipped, was surprised to feel the lack of a head rush as she rose, her balance natural, strong. She knotted her robe, reached for the wall, yanked with both hands, enjoying the exertion necessary to unplug her battery pack. How good it would feel to go on a looting, riotous rampage. Then she thought about the poor souls who'd have to clean up, and who'd have to pay for everything, and what about everyone who suffered because of the damage you caused?

Wrapping the thick cords once around her neck meant she wouldn't trip over them. Alice took her time, dragging the battery pack and its tree of fluids alongside her, the IV pole jiggling, which was fine, except being on alert, making sure that all was safe, was even more taxing. Where visitors wore the mask and gloves and bib so they wouldn't transmit anything, Alice wore them so she wouldn't pick anything up.

In New Hampshire, after her numbers had started to climb, and the doctors had given her the okay, walking laps around the ward with Oliver had been her nightly chance to get out of that godforsaken room without some sort of test or probe, and she'd looked forward to that nightly hour as if it were her wedding. Barely managed ten laps that first go-around. By the time they'd released her, she was up to fifty, almost half a mile, thrusting her hands above her head for a five-lap set, jetting them out to the sides like an airplane and making circles for another five (the ward physical therapist had told Alice the exercises would prevent her arms from atrophying). Next to her, Oliver did the same, or held on to the IV tower so it didn't wobble; he always counted out loud when they passed the nurses' station and completed a lap, tracking Alice's reps and pace. Every so often they broke into the chorus of that old Olivia Newton-John song. Nurses stared like these two aerobicizers were crazy, or made charmed cooing sounds, or else looked right through the two, just another day in paradise.

Using her body as leverage so the door stayed open, she rolled the battery tree out of her hospital room, and was surprised to find herself facing a different direction than when she left her New Hampshire room, the configuring of sink and supply nook different, too, more cramped, the shelves shorter, with supplies piled atop one another. The overhead lights were brighter, too, which seemed improbable, based on Alice's memory of that place, only here was the evidence, glaring down, reflecting even more harshly off the tiles. The hallway seemed to run forever, like one of those visual effects to convey eternity—an Escher effect. Alice tried to remember specifics, his various lithographs. She thought of a hallway from some Kubrick movie, but couldn't remember which.

Centered down in the distance on the other end, the outline of a person and an IV pole formed a small squiggle.

Expectations work against you, she remembered Eisenstatt saying. *You think you know what's coming.* It bothered Alice that Dr. Know-It-All was indeed correct. She wouldn't have believed that she'd gotten weaker since coming home, but walking fifty laps in this place seemed as possible as being named the queen of Spain. Her feet did not leave the floor; she shuffled forward, her old person's shuffle, in the direction of what looked like a barricade, a bunch of overflowing industrial clothing bins, gathered on the right side of the hall—the near door's sign read LINEN ROOM, and she made sure to give it a wide berth, navigating the rolling pole, a wide arc around the mess. Soon she was passing a stray metal stacking table, its shelves overflowing with uncovered trays of sloppy, half-eaten lunches and untouched dinners, Saran Wrap still clinging to the tops of their square trays. A bit farther down, beyond the door for the social services worker, sat a lab rack filled with blood vials. The hallway's near wall was lined with flyers and pamphlets: guides to various radiation treatments, how to deal with this or that chemotherapy, support group flyers, checklists for talking to your children about your disease.

Thank Goddess there was something else to look at. That little squiggle down the hall had taken the form of a person. A fully dressed man: loose blue-and-black lumberjack shirt, black jeans worn to dullness, the clothes hanging off his body in a manner she recognized all too well from Oliver and his friends. Would've been unassuming if he hadn't been pushing an IV stand. Alice immediately classified him: *Phylum: grad student who lives down the hallway; Class: odd and interesting, with hints of intensity.*

Moving parallel to Alice now, the man initiated eye contact. Gaunt, but not painfully so. Unwashed black hair splattered across his forehead, a boyish mess he was too old to pull off, but that held charm nonetheless. When Alice understood his brown eyes were trained on her, something inside her kicked up. She allowed a nod in his direction, kept on shuffling, the soles of her boots making scuffed sounds.

She'd made it down the hall, and completed a right turn, when he approached again—was it possible he'd lapped her?

His face almost alabaster in its paleness. A pronounced brow and pointed features made him look almost feral. Aquiline jaw muddled with a week of growth. "You need someone?" he asked. "To walk with you?"

She did not look at him.

"You sure?"

She wavered, but said, "Should be."

For reasons unknown to her, Alice kept talking. "My drugs haven't kicked in yet. And my counts are still high. The doctors felt I'd be okay—" She thought, laughed. "You know, I don't think this is a very good hospital."

His smirk was entertained, vaguely predatory. "I felt the same way when my doc asked if I needed to score."

"I suppose I could use the company. After all, what can happen, I'll catch cancer?"

He asked how she was doing. She gave him a tepid smile, and her fashion voice: "Let's change subjects, shall we?"

The man acquiesced, taking hold of her IV pole, assuming the responsibility for pushing both of them. He volunteered that it was his fifth day here. The story of him getting here was honestly *bizarre*. He played keyboards, mostly session work, but since he had a station wagon, cats figured they could ask him to sit in a set, get him to haul and store their gear. "I was playing with my friend's band at Brownies, you've been there, right?" He waited, checking if Alice had a reaction, continuing when there was none. "I'd had the flu, something. That shithole's a total hotbox, so going in I knew it was going to be a long night. But it's a gig, and, you know, playing is better than not playing. Anyway, behind the beat every song, head's all sludgy, just slogging through."

"You don't say."

"Carrying my gear outside afterward, arms were total noodles. I stopped to adjust my grip. Just looked up, like for a sec, up at the street. The old brownstones, snow hitting my face—"

Alice felt herself relating to and disappearing into the tale: the musician's legs *turned into buckling accordions;* the sound of his keyboards hitting the sidewalk; it registering upon him that this clatter had to mean hundreds of dollars in repairs. She didn't give in to the temptation to ask if he'd been under the weather beforehand. Alice was going to have to ask his name again.

He was explaining about a youngish woman who'd helped him

get to an emergency room. "We were getting to know each other, seemed like we had a little connection." So when this art school chick said she had to check her messages—"like the third time she'd said that, *at two in the morning*"—the musician should have guessed someone was waiting on her, or she was waiting on someone.

"My husband's been a saint." Alice felt happy to volunteer the information; saying the words was a relief. "The pressure Oliver must be under— Sometimes, I feel guilty for getting this. Ridiculous, I know."

He'd taken a few steps ahead, but stopped, and turned now, so he could watch her.

She kept on, dissembling: "I once heard that when you get past the honeymoon and the bliss, most marriages are one good fight away from being kaput. With us, the baby had already added a lot of strain. And all this dropped in Oliver's lap."

The keyboardist—"Mervyn? Merv? Thank you, Merv, I won't forget this time"—asked if Alice was doing all right, volunteered to slow down, and, after a bit, admitted that he hadn't added up all the signs with the girl, but "she must've taken her jacket with her, too. When you think about it, pretty big hint, right?"

"He's been better than anyone has a right to ask for," Alice murmured.

"Last thing she did: rubbed her hand on my cheek. Gave me this look, all soft and dewy. *You don't even know* is what she said."

Alice noticed him now, studied him, thinking. Her voice was sudden with amusement: "How could anyone have walked out on *you*?"

He laughed, a little.

"Really now?" She did her best to bat what was left of her lashes. "Who could say no to such a studiously and meticulously unkempt nature? That undernourished and malodorous body?"

Again he smirked. "That's me. Your generic, by-the-numbers, brooding antihero."

Alice's hand on her pole halted their progress. "I'll admit," she said, a bit winded, but sounding happy. "I'd stop you on the street."

"There we go."

"To settle a question about my income tax."

Hers was a mischievous yelp, score for her side. The musician felt at his jaw as if smarting from a slap. "You're right," he said. "I can't really blame her, leaving that freak-ass situation. Funny thing is, I *am* the responsible one. Rest of the band's out chasing tail, I'm the idiot hauling their gear." He stared at the floor, thrummed his fingers at the exposed knee in his jeans, as if for emphasis. "I mean, I'm old enough to understand how much of a cliché it is: *guy playing rock music.* Do this long enough, you better get some kind of comfort level with reality."

"So that's your angle?"

"Excuse me?"

"You're the smart sensitive one? The good man left behind?"

He considered this. "I got one for you. Singer I used to play with. His girlfriend told him, *I can't come over, I'm on my period.* Swear to God, Donovan goes back: *You're not bleeding out of your mouth, are you?*"

Alice snorted. "I might have gone out with that man."

"It's not even that he tells the story, you know? It's that *he likes* telling that story."

"But not you," Alice said.

Staring away, down, Merv seeming to concentrate on the wheels of the units. He tapped out the opening of an exercise for the piano, his fingers dancing in rapid, minor movements.

"Honest and revealing is your thing," Alice said.

"Dunno." His face stayed serious. "We'd have to discuss it over ice cream."

A current ran through her stomach.

"Oh, you're more into gelato?"

"Please, either way. . . . Wait—*that's* how you work?"

The deadpan gave way to mischief, a scraggly grin. "I'd ask you to get some with me."

A gasp, only with an upturn at the end, something near delight. "It sounds safe and nice."

"And innocent," he said. "Don't sleep on innocent."

"A creamy cool treat," Alice thought aloud.

"Only you've got licking."

She caught on: "Mouths and wetness."

"Throw in a daddy issue—"

"Well." Alice's voice made clear this discussion was completed. She looked at him for a time. "You may not look like much—"

"Yeah. But I'm actually less."

It was his turn to let loose, a full Cheshire smile. She laughed, leaned into him with her shoulder, nudging him just a bit. The musician flipped some kind of interior switch, became intensely alert, his arms extending, ready, just in case. After a moment he understood the nudge had been a form of approval, saw she was steady. Still he asked, "You okay?

"You know," he said. "It's good to vent to a stranger. I guess."

Moving into another right turn, a bit slower and more carefully this time, Merv concentrated on the rollers of each IV pole, guiding them in a wide arc, making sure all their wheels stayed on the linoleum. Once this had been negotiated, and it was clear Alice was not going to be giving in to his particular strangerness, that no venting would be forthcoming, he started again. "That ice cream line usually gets me in the door. Not that I'm Mr. Great Pickup Artist Bullshit Guy—back when I drank, I used to *really* be something. Only, it got to the point where I'd get a girl home, and I'd be thinking: *You fucking pig. I can't BELIEVE you fell for my shit. How can you be so stupid you'd let ME fuck YOU?*"

Merv grimaced, shook his head at the memory. "I couldn't *wait* to get away. Man hates himself that much, big mystery why I'm an alkey."

Realizing what he'd said, Merv gauged his companion's reaction, received nothing, Alice remaining inscrutable.

"Whaddaya think," he said. "Another go-around?"

Not another go-around. Another lap was too much, but she wasn't ready to get back to her depressing room, either. So he placed one hand on her shoulder, another on her hip, and eased her down into a metal folding chair. "Please assure me you haven't been roaming the halls to pick up chemotherapy patients," Alice said.

Some sort of timer must have gone off during their walk, because the overhead lights were blessedly dimmer, which furthered the hallway's already somber feel. Sneakers were squeaking around the near corner, some nurse laughing with another. "It's fine with me if you *are*," Alice continued. "At least that's original. It's actually the most warped, high-concept, black screwball comedy imaginable."

Mervyn's hair was in need of weeding and trimming. His flannel shirt was missing a button at its collar; its opening showed a concavity. He was looking down, and his smirk had transformed, more of a wince, as if he were sucking on a sour lozenge. Checking on her from the corners of his eyes, he began revealing information whose beats were all too familiar: nonexistent blood counts, an enlarged spleen, demands from the emergency room doctor that he be admitted to a hospital right pronto.

The emergency room doctor told him the two main candidates for his illness were lymphoma and AIDS. What does anyone do when you hear this, he recounted. He recalled the numbness. Pretty much in shock when they finally admitted him to this place, putting him in a private room. Two orderlies in blue protective outfits then erected a plastic bubble around him. He watched it go up. The next three days, his father basically sat vigil at the side of Merv's bed, staring with cloudy eyes and a hangdog face. Friends came by, and from the way they looked at Merv he understood they all assumed he was about to die, were trying to remember his face for future lyrics and songs and shit.

From around the corner, the squishy sneaker sound was again audible. Presently, Carmen said *There you are,* and asked if they were having a nice talk, if anyone needed some tea. Carmen laughed as if she'd delivered the funniest joke in the annals of stand-up, but also had a look on her face as if to say, *I ain't getting shit.* Alice asked how Carmen's night was going and Carmen answered that the Rangers had won, so she was fine. She then took Alice's vital signs, and made sure Alice's port and catheters were secure, and that there was no surrounding puffiness in her arm. Carmen let Alice know she shouldn't stay out in the hall for too long, and reminded her to keep her mask secure, and said more pills were ready back in her room. Alice nodded and waited for her to stop yapping and leave so Merv could pick back up with his series of blood tests, his biopsy, his numbers beginning to stabilize, the suspense he'd felt while waiting to find out which probably terminal disease he was going to lace up the gloves against.

Trying to get his mind straight, Merv had taken inspiration from sports figures at press conferences who answered questions about play-off scenarios by saying: *We can only focus on the game in front of us.* He'd also found solace because his probability for AIDS wasn't huge. Needles freaked him out. And he'd weaned himself off sex with guys for money back when he was a teenager, ha ha, so check that off the list. But he *did* generally dread having a stray puck of his slip past any woman's metaphorical goalie, and took steps to protect himself there. Although, granted, you still had that nightmare scenario: things having gone too far to head to the drugstore, and so you roll the dice and, atom bomb, lives blown straight to shit. In his head Merv had seen a slimy condom being pushed backward off his reddened member, and he'd wondered if that had been the one that had busted or leaked. He'd remembered being drunk, begging, *He hated those things, it was like fucking in a bag, he'd be careful, he promised.*

He acknowledged to Alice what anyone with half a cerebral cortex already knew: a *huge* reason any guy got involved with playing rock was to get laid, then insisted that it wasn't like he was the greatest cocksman of his era—and not for a second did he believe he had AIDS. Still, for three days, while he'd lain in that scratchy-ass hospital bed, he'd argued with himself. On the one hand, there were memories: the swell of a particularly full and round apple bottom uncovered by a sheet on a lazy morning; being ridden insanely hard and having a moment of eye contact and the two of them breaking out, laughing; a closed-lidded beauty in profile, the rictus of a smile forming along her pouty lips; his private stash; his most intimate carnal moments.

He didn't mean to be gross or sexist. He didn't want to come off to her as a pig. Probably some of those women had been promiscuous; Merv refused to believe, for even a blink, that any of them had been, you know, *dirty*. And still he hadn't been able to stop himself from zeroing in on likely candidates: the girl with beautiful jet-black hair down to the middle of her back who'd had the strange deal where even in ninety-five-degree heat she'd refused to go without tights (maybe that was why she never smelled fresh); the depressed, Rubenesque, screaming tiger in the sack who'd been training to be an opera singer, and who afterward had lain in bed, smoking a jay and rambling guiltily about her boyfriend in France (two nights later she'd answered her phone and spoken French in low sexy tones; an embarrassed Merv never called again).

Some part of him still clung to the idea that getting AIDS from a blowjob was impossible. But maybe that was one more piece of bullshit musicians told each other? And if it had been AIDS, then two days after the blood tests, wouldn't the doctors have come in and told him already?

In that hospital bed he'd regained enough energy to get squirmy, but at the same time being in bed for so long made anyone doze, so he'd be alternating between fading in and out of consciousness and feeling jittery, and starving. Now and again he'd wondered about what had happened to that goddamn art chick, if any of the guys had told her about him getting admitted and being at death's proverbial door. Eventually, Merv had started addressing the next logical issues: how to prepare himself for the confirming news, how bad his cancer was, what kind of road lay ahead.

But could he tell Alice something?

"Whole time, I never felt like something foreign was growing inside me. It just didn't."

"Mmmm hmmm," Alice said.

This morning, a few of his compadres had visited, started up this little jam session: Donovan with an acoustic, a flask making the rounds, popped beers frosting on the window ledge. Merv had been eyeing those beers something fierce: what better reason to get plowed than learning you have some spooky life-threatening shit? Except that if he *did* really have spooky life-threatening shit, he'd better make some good decisions, so maybe his head needed to be clear. The part of him in favor of being clearheaded had a slight lead on the part of him that was shouting, *BLOW YOUR FUCK-ING BRAINS OUT.* Then that warning knock that wasn't any kind of warning. Cue the white-coat fucknuts. Marching into the room like they were on fast-forward. Making a nice straight line across the wall right opposite Merv's bed. The attending took his place in front of them, goddamn marching band leader, and reported that Merv didn't have cancer, or AIDS. He had a disease so rare the oncologist never heard of the damn thing, was forced to research it.

Blechette's. Originated in Eastern Europe and Russia. Sourced in the inbreeding that Jews in shtetls had to do over generations, these inbred cells that over the decades kept being crossbred. About a thousand living people diagnosed, worldwide, and there were probably more except, as the doctor and Merv had learned, it was a tricky disease to identify. Some Blechette carriers could live their entire lives without knowing they had it; others would die early and nobody'd know the root cause. The telltale indicator being something you saw only if you knew to look, explained the doctor. But looking usually happened when you tested for other things, and those other things kept not showing up, and via the process of elimination, way toward the bottom of your list, you tested something called the chitotriosidase activity in blood cells—known as your chito count, which was how this Mensa society had solved this mystery.

Being afflicted with Blechette's meant being born without a minor, cell-producing enzyme in your bone marrow. The effects started early and increased as you got older, and once they accumulated, the lack of these helper cells in a bloodstream, as well as in key organs, could be, ah, *problematic*. This was known as a progressively degenerating disease. By the time most patients hit their twenties, their spleens had grown to at least eight times normal size, so one side of the stomach looked fatter. Other internal organs also could bulge, making you look pregnant or deformed. Scarring on your kidneys was an issue, and manifest in lots of night trips to the bathroom. An overactive spleen reduced your platelet count, made it harder for your blood to clot, so Blechetters bruised and bled—nosebleeds, bleeding gums, heavy menstrual flow, all that. The disease also lessened the number of white blood cells, meaning anemia was a problem. Bone disease became more likely, your bones turning brittle as they aged, osteoporosis going rampant, your spinal canal thickening with calcium deposits. One common result was losing control of your legs and sexual organs. They told Merv about one hulking guy—six feet five, exercised every day—whose spinal cord disintegrated to the point where if his car was tapped from behind, just a little fender bender, dude would be in a wheelchair for the rest of his life, so if there was anything he wanted to do with his life, doctors told the man to go and do it. Without any help, the average life span for the sufferer of Blechette's was forty-one years. Merv was twenty-eight.

"But fret not," Merv assured (as Alice stared in horror). The FDA approved a medicine, he told her, just under a year ago. Researchers culled it from the ovaries of striped Chinese hamsters. "Who even knew there were Chinese hamsters, let alone striped ones?" But those furry little bitches got drained into a two-thousand-liter bioreactor. They got synthesized, or bioreacted, some shit that Merv couldn't follow. Something happened to the ovaries in the bioreactor, and afterward this new stuff got filtered into this harvest tank, where it was fermented, or synthesized, some shit. What they ended up with was this pure, rare protein, and it was this stuff what got shaped into the medicine, this stuff what acted as a replacement for the enzyme. Taken long enough, this wondrous wonder drug didn't cure your Blechette's, per se, but it started fixing the scar tissue on kidneys, it stopped the growth of internal organs, even built up bones, some. Biggest thing, patients didn't get any worse. You got to live your life.

That's why Merv was still in hospital: staying overnight, being tested to find out whether his chito activity had grown to where he needed the drug.

So his conundrum was this: each intravenous treatment cost fifteen thousand dollars.

Alice gasped.

"Yup. Third most expensive drug on the planet."

All signs pointed to Merv going on it. His admittance chito numbers had been high enough. He was supposed to take some more advanced tests tomorrow to confirm.

Merv explained to Alice that patients took the drug intravenously every two weeks. So if he started treatment, he'd be responsible for fifteen thousand dollars a pop, every two weeks, basically for the rest of his life. Meaning he'd shatter the cap for his shitty musicians' union insurance plan in a heartbeat, and he didn't come close to making enough money to get on one of the higher-end plans—hell, he barely made enough each year to pay union dues.

Doctors said the drug company had a program to provide for patients who couldn't afford the drug, but doing that meant Merv dropping his policy and being uninsured.

Doctors also told him about the lady with the disease who'd had five hip replacement surgeries by the time she hit forty, so being uninsured was insanity.

But could he really give up being a musician and go be a drone with a real job, be some secretary in a cubicle or some shit?

He answered his own question: "Fuck that."

He shrugged. "I mean, what can they possibly be doing so that shit costs fifteen grand? That's a five-hundred-dollar-a-day heroin habit."

"You should be overjoyed."

"Five hundred a *day*."

One side of his mouth turned up, the crookedness of his smirk got more pronounced. "I guess that's one more scary problem about being sick. You're dependent on all these fuckers but for not one second do you believe they have your best interests at heart."

She couldn't even begin to tell him, couldn't imagine where to start. "What's money for, if not to pay for your health?"

"Know what? My old man went to the library. Turns out, the FDA developed the drug. *Public tax money* found that cure. Something called an orphan drug. Means the government has all kinds of rules on how to find cures for rare diseases. But some horseshit biotech company buys the patent. Turns out, the president of the company's one of those FDA researchers. The company tells *The Wall Street Journal* that promising a ninety percent markup for the drug price is the only way they could raise enough capital to bring this shit to market—the drug has to be so expensive that it becomes profitable to the investors."

"Believe me," Alice said. "Western medicine is more than welcome to kiss my ass."

"And since we lucky lemmings need them Chinese hamsters to live, the insurance companies have no choice. No biggie though.

Just raise premiums to cover the cost. Everyone gets paid, the medical-industrial complex marches onward."

"Maybe you should take a breath—"

He ignored her: "And it's not like I can ask my parents to float the insurance. I've put them through so much already—"

"I'm sorry for you." Alice cut him off, her tone polite, but forceful enough, snapping him back into the real world.

She waited until his body language softened.

"I'm still not sure you have the right to be mad," she said.

His eyes narrowed.

"This is saving your life? The processed hamster ovaries work? There's an organizational structure, however unjust, that's for paying for this. For a while anyway?"

He shrugged his shoulders.

"Maybe you could be thankful?"

"Right."

"Instead you want to refuse."

"I know," his voice acquiescent. "Every drug company's this way."

"So you can keep doing background tracking for scale? So hungover fools at the Sidewalk Cafe can hear your especially *ripping* version of 'Take the A Train'?"

His brow hardened. His eyes now dark pebbles.

"Believe me," Alice said. "I intimately understand clinging to every scrap of your creative life."

She waited for him to respond in some way, acknowledge her point. Though this response did not come, Alice proceeded, however gently: "Why can't you be like ninety-nine percent of the creative people in Manhattan who have to make their art in their spare time?" Then her patience was at an end. "You're being a spoiled child."

"Right—"

"Closing your eyes and having a tantrum."

"Here we go."

"Shouting: *I don't want to grow up.*"

"Woman's idea of being a man. Married. Boring-ass nine to five. Crying infant sucking every spare dime. Balls safe in wifey's purse."

Alice absorbed the blow. "It's a difficult thing to give your body to doctors," she admitted. "I know when I'm weak and ill and in pain, I become complicit. I almost feel like I'm my baby, looking up at me to take care of her. I *do* understand what it's like to be that helpless—"

A shrug of the shoulders. He kept staring to the right of her ear.

"I'm more than cogent enough to watch what the doctors and nurses do to me. I listen to their explanations. Believe me, honeysuckle, I'm not happy about . . . about *this*." She motioned with her hands. "Part of me that feels as if their medical work is separate—I'm watching a television show where doctors discuss my status."

"Right, it's so goddamn infantilizing."

"And it doesn't seem like I'm actually *doing* anything. I'm lying there, passive, letting them pump me with poisons. All I can do is hope that a donor match comes through. So I can go through some other horrible procedure that *might* save my life.

"I don't know you at all," Alice said. She felt herself tearing up. "But you're making me very angry at you."

He flinched.

Running a hand through his hair, sweeping his falling bangs back. Merv avoided eye contact, instead looking at the pamphlets on the wall behind her.

That stare of hers, still boring in.

"I sat in that forsaken bed for more than a month," Alice continued, "and believe me, the day's empty spaces, they grow until they become spectral. *Spectral.* I know all about silence expanding until you're sure it will never end. Every beep and knock swallowed, and you want to scream, *No, fuck it all, just fuck it*—"

Her eyes were unblinking, shining and gray and blue, not flinching.

"I'd trade with you in a heartbeat," she said.

Merv gathered the courage and looked at her. Her pert nose sniffed at its bridge. Her nostrils flared.

"Before Buddha was Buddha," Alice said, sniffing again, "he walked out on his wife and their baby. Being Buddha meant he had to be free, and freedom meant he could not have any commitments." She spoke through tears, her words blubbery, progressively more difficult to understand. "I've always wondered: What about the wife he left? What was she supposed to do?"

Alice's voice cracked. "It's disrespectful to challenge a teacher by asking, is what I've found. They go mystical and tell you the personal has to be sacrificed for the universal good. But for the good of the wife, they give no answer."

"There's no answer," Merv said.

"The most inclusive peaceful loving religion there's ever been, understand? So I hear you that you can't trust medicine. But it's not like the other choices are any better."

"Any God you want to pick," Merv said. "He's got to be one throbbing asshole." He seemed to mull this. "Or maybe it's that whole pay-attention-to-the-words-and-not-the-messenger deal? You know, like my high school gym teacher always said: *It ain't queer if you get paid for it.*"

"*Horrible.*" Alice's eyes were delighted. Her protective paper mask stretched, extending with her smile.

Some night nurse made her way down the hall, vanished.

"I've been telling myself *People get sick every day,*" Alice said. "But then I think: *They aren't me.*" She pantomimed a curtsy, as if to say, *See, I can feel sorry for myself, too.*

"None of the choices are worth a damn." His hand, pale, callused, moved atop her thin, gloved one. He asked, "Where does that leave you?"

"Oh." She waved him off. "What does anyone have? The people you love. The love you feel for others."

"Passion," Merv answered. "Living in the moment."

"I try to tell myself, I am my decency. In any given moment, I can embody my best humanity." She fingered the edge of her mask near her nose. "Sounds grand, anyway."

Awaiting a response that she assumed would shred her, half-wincing in anticipation, she was aware now of his eyes, this man examining her with such intensity it was as if he were looking inside of her, searching—but for what she did not know. It seemed there was some wildness dawning inside him. It made her self-conscious. She worried she might blush, that this man was just unhinged enough to lean in and kiss her; she was certain he was about to try.

But no. He was a counselor, accompanied by an imagined acoustic guitar, crooning to campers gathered around a crackling fire:

> *It's too late to complain*
> *Bad, bad timing*
> *Ugly saying*
> *FLAT-OUT FUCKED*
> *FLAT-OUT FUCKED*
> *FLAT-OUT FUCKED*

When Alice arrived back at her room, she still felt out of whack, unnerved by the scratch in his voice as it hit its pained, wailing apex. In the same way that his screaming had revealed the limits of his singing range, their conversation seemed to expose the outer limits of their respective sanities. Alice was sure this man was deranged. A part of her did not particularly mind, and even felt exhilarated by him. But she also felt relieved to be finished with this challenge, like a cat whose hair had stood along its back for too long.

Her room was dark, but she could make out the outline of her bed, propped up at a ninety-degree angle, her grandmother's quilt turned back, the exposed mess of tangled sheets. Alongside, the rolling tray was agog with plastic pitchers, half-filled cups of water, plastic hospital dish covers, and a cardboard take-out soup container. Scant light filtered in through the windows, while the furthest edges of a more potent source emanated from the high far corner, the flashing colors of the soundless newscast visible above the separating wall. In the room's stillness, she felt odd, almost contemplative, but also anxious. She wanted to call to see how things went with the child, say good night to Oliver, but knew better than to wake the baby.

It only took a few seconds before she realized something smelled foul. Worse even than the dry ice at home.

Mrs. Woo was moaning, and through her tube, her sounds were garbled, but obvious in their pain. Alice pushed her IV pole as quickly as she could, reaching the nurse bell. "Something's wrong. The other woman in here—please come. She needs help." Her hands felt clumsy, her legs heavy, but she managed her IV unit around the bed, toward the partition. Mrs. Woo sensed her presence. Before Alice could say anything, lights were hit; an orderly and a nurse were rushing around her.

"Damn." The orderly took a whiff, the pair now disappearing behind the partition. Alice heard rustling, the nurse telling Mrs. Woo they were going to take a look, instructing the orderly in turning the old woman on her side, telling Mrs. Woo not to worry, she was going to make sure the breathing tube was clear and remained in place. "We're going to take a look," the nurse said. "It's okay, dearie. You just had an accident. It happens to the best of us."

Two nursing assistants, both massively overweight, would soon arrive to clean and strip the sheets. The taller would say, "Always at night they do this." The nurse would promise Mrs. Woo that she'd check back with her and would order the assistants to stay with her, make sure that tube stayed clear. The nurse would take Mrs. Woo's hand for a moment and assure: "You'll be okay," and when she left, the assistants would grouse and bump and knock about, making jokes as they cleaned. Alice would wish she had made eye contact with Mrs. Woo, and finally she would not be able to take any more, and with what strength she had, Alice would say, "She's sick. Can't you respect that?"

And soon enough the eyes of the medical establishment would turn their attention onto Alice, for now it was *her* blood levels that needed to be checked, her vital statistics that again had to be measured, her IV bags rehung with new antibiotics, platelets, and steroids, her pills confirmed as having been ingested, and more than one of those catheters coming due for a change. Another urine sample was needed, and the morning nurse would have to rouse her again in six hours for another one after that, every six hours was the rule—although, before that happened, an assistant would come in, measure the exiting urine levels, change the toilet pans.

Throughout this night, Alice tried to be conscious and inhabit her best self. The smaller assistant—showing weak, gray teeth—asked if Alice had had a urine sample yet. The tall one made sure that the pitcher and plastic cup were filled with fresh water. Alice took care in lowering her head to the drinking straw. She asked each woman, separately, to say her name, then made comic guesses as to the origin countries of their accents. They listened to her inquiries about how long they had been on the night shift, her voice so worn that she might have been slurring.

Lon, the late-night nurse, the hard-faced woman with the gray teeth, told Alice she was doing great. All her signs suggested she'd be an early recoverer. She'd be out of here soon.

Her words might have been something all nurses said, something they knew that patients wanted to hear, and that would make the patients more compliant—would make following instructions that much easier. Still Alice thanked her.

It would be a while before she was entirely alone, in that darkened room, listening to the rhythms of that breathing tube, *long in, wheeze out.* By then Alice was exhausted. She had no strength to make sense of the events of the day. Instead she watched the night thin in the windows across the room, the impenetrable black lightening into slate gray. Thick waves of snow were coming down now, blankets of flakes. On Roosevelt Island, Alice could make out the fossil of an old factory—its three smokestacks sending white cotton plumes into the sky. The first colors of dawn were spreading in the far distance, yawning pink and orange, seeping at the edges, creeping over undefined, shabby warehouses. She watched the miniature trails of headlights from slow-moving freeway traffic, drivers getting a jump on the morning commute.

As the room lightened, she could pick out the pages and pictures of her wall collage: the superhumanly perfect limbs of Alvin Ailey dancers; Audrey Hepburn standing in front of Tiffany's, one cheek a little puffy from the donut she was chewing. How much time Alice spent staring at the rest of the wall collage she did not know, but the oncoming morning helped, and the gray shades kept thinning through the room, so that more pages and pictures became identifiable: the elephant head of the Hindu lord of beginnings, remover of obstacles; another goddess standing on a lotus flower, reborn from the swirling milky ocean. Slick magazine pages with gorgeous women in blouses Alice had helped create. Pages on which she'd written song lyrics. Inspiring aphorisms. Her eyeballs throbbed from so much concentration, but she wouldn't shut her eyes, for of this Alice Culvert was certain: if she fell asleep, she wouldn't wake up.

PART III

And what if he flinched

The first warm day of winter

ON THE SECOND Tuesday of March, winter finally blinked. Temperatures rose into the mid-fifties, territory that had become as mythical as a Knicks championship. Along the western end of Chelsea, it was as if a universal switch had been flicked, some mammalian, a priori urge activated. People actually *wanted* to be outside, free from their supremely ugly parachute jackets, the dragging weight of shearling or leather, coats whose linings were suffused with months of body sweat and smelled like cow carcass.

In the shadow of a brick housing project drab enough to be Soviet, along a courtyard of thawing mud, *abuelas* pushed wire carts packed with groceries and stuffed laundry sacks. Old men, sporty in panama hats and panama shirts, had busted out their lawn chairs and checkerboards and domino sets. For once no one was wearing gloves (so pesky and impossible to keep in pairs for more than a week at a time) or scarves (their annoying ends filthy with sauces and stains). Rather, as an unseen boom box blasted hip-hop jams, the fuzzy curls of hirsute chests were exposed by wifebeaters; teenagers talked shit and acted teenage crazy. One boy dribbled a basketball; his friend tried to steal it away; what they lacked in skill, they more than made up for in enthusiasm.

The town car containing the ragtag little family eased beyond the housing project and turned down a side street, passing a ru-mored crack house, a verifiable one, then a series of burnt-out cars, and a barren lot where the homeless congregated (for once, it was bereft of trash fires). Now a small triangular plot—one of the neighborhood's volunteer gardens. Flashes of brilliant yellow showed through its taut link fence. Spring's early arrivals. Admit-tedly gorgeous, but also oblivious, unaware of the concept of false spring, the irony that by opening their cups, these daffodils had doomed themselves. Nonetheless, instinct urged them: *Onward. Bloom. Live.*

Entering the Meatpacking District, the car slowed to a crawl, and pulled up in front of one of the block's slaughterhouses. When the rear driver's side door opened, Oliver emerged with a cleanly shaved head. Leaving his door open, he hurried around to the pas-senger side. He brought Alice out of the car, she was leaning into him—her pink wool winter cap had a puffball on top and long side flaps, and seemed far too large, nearly swallowing her head. Her silhouette was dwarfed inside her clothes. She had been frail, but this was something else—the effect of a second consolidation.

Presently her mother emerged from the passenger side. Holding a bundle close, she made mewling sounds, bounced the baby to her chest. Alice half-turned, thanked her mother, voice weak. A door slammed, the driver removing a series of travel suitcases from the trunk.

Once Alice and her mom and the baby were safely inside the warehouse, Oliver settled with the driver, and was halfway around the car, putting his wallet back in his pants, when he unclipped a small black block from his belt. He walked to a predetermined spot, a few steps off the sidewalk, and punched at that little device thing. Then he stopped. His body went alert, his head cocked. Concentration honed. Beneath the rusted elevated train tracks, he saw a homeless guy wrapped in a sleeping bag. But, beyond him, folded into the shadows, toward the back of the raised wooden platform that acted as a loading dock, something else. Someone. Leaning against the storefront's metal rolling gate.

Peekaboo, I see you. Alice hid her face, popped away the doors of her hands. She could not help but smile, and as she beamed, a prominent Y of veins split down the middle of her forehead. Home again, thank Goddess, still in remission. Yet even a glance showed that her skull had shrunken further, turned flat and boxy, with giant veins on each side of her temples forming squarish parameters, and her cheeks sweeping down into her jawline. All of her accursed extra baby weight had been shed, and then some. Indeed, for the first time since her teen years, hip bones were visible. Which would have been lovely, except her body had been sapped of its elasticity, her arms and legs robbed of their admittedly meager muscle tone.

None of it mattered to Doe, her little mouth open, chirping out birdie peeps of delight. "Are you happy to be with Mommy? What a gorgeous little gumdrop." Alice tickled the fat corners under Doe's arms, basked in her daughter's warmth, felt spent, leaned back—into her favorite chair, a seventies vintage recliner made by Scandinavian artisans.

The glare from the wall fixtures was brighter than she remembered. She kept blinking; in the few seconds it took for the brightness to make her wince, her mother figured out how to work the dimmers.

"Much better," Alice said. "Thank you."

She took in the large open space, the Japanese mural she knew so well, its succession of interconnected vertical screens lining a far wall, images hand-painted on long rectangles of rice paper: a lone traveler, waking tigers.

Behind her the front door shutting, creaks and weight, Oliver moving into the apartment's main room.

Alice called out, she never imagined their apartment could look so immaculate. She told Oliver how much she appreciated him getting it spotless for her.

"And did you see those nice smooth stones in the bathroom sink?" said her mom, coming out of the kitchen. "I love those."

Mom held a steaming cup of green tea on a small plate. She, too, looked the worse for wear, her face pale and drained, her shoulders slumped. The week of watching her only daughter had taken its toll, obviously, damage that had been exacerbated by an innate discomfort with the city's pace and noise. Alice accepted the ceramic offering, felt the steam clouds rising onto her chin and mouth and nose. Her mom smiled, touched Alice's shoulder.

Mom said she'd fix the bedtime bottles. She could never sit still.

Oliver was at the doorjamb to the entranceway, he was irritated, that much was obvious to her. And now she saw the room's dimness distracting him. Likely he was assuming that the darkness had something to do with Alice, and he'd find out more particulars soon enough.

She remained in that chair, in her robe, holding her daughter, who kept rubbing an impossibly soft cheek against Mommy's chin.

The first four days of her hospital stay had gone according to plan. No complications on the medical front, and when the nurse had wheeled Alice down to the ground floor, Oliver had already commandeered a conference room, and was waiting, with building blocks and stuffed animals spread all over the couch, pacifiers and a diaper-changing pad ready on the conference table. Alice was in a medical mask, lead smock, and protective gloves; her pole of IV medicines accompanied, looming above the festivities. Doe saw her mother and immediately bawled, absence backing up on her. Alice touched her daughter's tummy, lifted the child's little pink blouse, gave a big kiss through her mask. "Mommy loves this belly." She caressed Doe's knee. "Mommy loves this knee. Deep inside your heart, know I love this knee." Alice gave her daughter time to be sad, rubbed slow circles on her child's back. "Mommy loves your chin. Mommy loves your sternum. Mommy loves your thorax. I love every part of you, even when we are apart." Doe giggled, crawled, clung; though Alice tried to maximize their skin-to-skin contact (as the parenting books said you should do), doctors' orders made this almost impossible. "We will be together again soon—maybe in a few days," Alice said. "Until then, we will miss each other and be sad, but we will also both be okay." She and Oliver held hands, talked about logistics, about nothing, everyone enjoying this little created, artificial island of normalcy, right until the nurse arrived, and Oliver followed Alice's prearranged instructions: packing up and sweeping away the child as quickly as possible.

"You are in Mommy's heart," Alice had said, even as Doe, unable to understand, had started to bawl. "Mommy is in your heart."

The day before her scheduled release, Alice's fever had spiked and she'd been quarantined. Everything had become that much harder. Alice had been apoplectic, refusing to accept she had to be there any longer, she could not see her child. Her meetings with Eisenstatt became tense, full of impatience, willful misunderstandings. For the first time she was short to nurses. Then she had a blood clot in her arm, furthering her stay, and her cell counts started dropping, a result of the chemo. She remained an inpatient for a full week longer than they'd been expecting. At home Doe was inconsolable, bawling through the night, lashing out, kicking and hitting, even at Grandma.

Now that she was home, Oliver was getting ready to clean her port site—running warm water over washcloths in the bathroom—one red, one blue. He brought both with him, searched through the newly prescribed bottles of medicine, and brought a long tube of cream out to the sewing table, where he began loosening the collar on his wife's robe. Oliver kissed his wife's head, kneaded the back of her neck with the knuckles of his fist; Alice moaned approval.

Her eyes shut. "That feels nice." Oliver saw his wife's jugular: pressing up against the skin beneath her neck, a protruding root. Near Alice's left clavicle was that giant bandage, the reminder of her latest central line.

"Mother, do we have any green tea?"

"I brought you some already. On the table."

A laugh. "I guess this is what they call chemo brain. I overheard a nurse say it happens."

Oliver now set to the renewal of certain nightly rituals, dusting off the procedure for changing Alice's bandage and washing her wound. First step: running the damp red cloth over the transparent tape around the bandage. Next: he peeled a curdled strip of gauze from off her neck. Alice continued playing with Doe, feeding her child a thumb, enjoying the suckling sensation. Oliver finished taking off the last strip, reached for the soaked blue cloth. Alice felt his eyes studying the back of her neck, heard the undertones of his subdued breaths. She leaned backward, met his washcloth's circular motions. Both of them ignored the ringing phone. Besides, when her mom answered, whoever was calling hung up.

CASE STUDY # ⏐ *19*

North Shore Oncology, Long Island City, Suite 4

It was during her first week, working the front desk at an oncology office, that she felt a lump in her right breast. It wasn't imagined, that Patty Hearst syndrome thing. Quite the opposite: the lump was hard, and present, most definitely, a knob in her lower right quadrant. A person might think an oncology office would be the best place to work if you were going to feel a lump in your breast, but this wasn't the case. It was more complicated than that. The receptionist didn't have insurance before getting hired, for one thing, and the clinic didn't offer insurance until after three months on the job. The out-of-pocket costs of tests, consultations, diagnosis, therapies, treatments—all that would bankrupt her, that much was obvious. So without talking to her husband, ex-husband, or her grown children, without letting them know what she'd discovered or planned, she endured. Until her insurance kicked in, she'd just hope for the best.

And that's what she did. For three months: five days a week, eight thirty to six, the receptionist checked in patients who'd been diagnosed and were going to begin therapy and were plainly terrified. As a formality she made sure there had been no changes to the insurance policies of patients who were undergoing chemo. She relayed medications questions from patients who'd gone through the hell of chemo and thought they'd made it, only to have the cancer return. Patients with less than six months left spent hours of their lives in her waiting room. She kept her head down and bit her lip and tried to control her pounding heart so nobody could hear it. She did her job. There was one young woman the same age as the receptionist's daughter: suffering from ovarian cancer. Her uterus had been bombarded with so much radiation that putting on a seatbelt caused her pain. The receptionist overheard this and excused herself from her desk. She went into the ladies' room and hid in a stall and felt whether her lump was growing and sobbed until her body heaved.

Employees of the clinic received their insurance through a health management organization, whose contract contained a clause dictating that new members were only allowed to join on the first of the month. Therefore, the receptionist had to wait an extra three weeks before she could have any doctor's appointment that would be covered by her company's plan. Still she jumped through the requisite hoops and scheduled an appointment for the first day her insurance kicked in. Medical ethics forbade being treated by a doctor by whom she was employed. So, when the secretary finally confided her worries to a co-worker, the office referred her to a colleague.

From there things moved quickly. The receptionist was diagnosed with an aggressive stage two breast cancer. No word as to whether detecting it within the past four months would have kept it at an earlier phase—nobody wanted to think about that. A double mastectomy was scheduled, the first surgery date being available in mid-October.

Like any rational woman, she'd been aware that there was a month when all the pink ribbons appeared on blouses. But which month exactly? Not the kind of thing you paid attention to, until you had a reason. But in the weeks leading up to her double mastectomy, the receptionist noticed pink ribbons everywhere. Pinned to blouses. Adorning coats. One Saturday afternoon, while lounging on her couch and tuning in for the women's finals of the U.S. Open, she noticed pink tennis balls in the commercials. She and her husband ate chicken wings and watched *Monday Night Football,* and she took in the pink cleats worn by the quarterbacks and running backs and wide receivers. The overpriced pink teddy bears in the gift shop next to her clinic. The pink donuts at the donut place. Special-issue pink lipstick and nail polish. Designer breast cancer T-shirts. Gloves. Scarves. Winter hats with that pink ribbon sewn onto them. Jewel-encrusted earrings in the shape of pink ribbons. Breast cancer awareness necklaces. Pink zippered tote bags. Umbrellas. Car magnets. Moist towelettes. The receptionist felt even more isolated, as if her suffering were somehow an electricity source—being plugged into, taken advantage of. *Look, we are with you! Celebrate us for our support!* Everyone so great and informed and aware and together and so helpful. Meanwhile, she had to get both of her breasts sawed off.

As luck would have it, her double mastectomy was scheduled on the day of the Breast Cancer Awareness Walk for the Cure. Who schedules a double mastectomy for a weekend? Her doctors said they got more time to work, a quiet environment, it was better this way.

Naturally, York was blocked off. Throngs along the sidewalk made it all but impossible to cross over toward the hospital. After coming up from the subway, she had to hail a cab, which was forced into a long, circuitous route.

In years to come, every year when she had to come in for her annual tests—which were best done to the exact day—she'd have the same problem. She'd come to hate that damn walk.

But the surgery got everything, and, knock on wood, the cancer did not return.

I would search every cloud

THE WOMAN AT the door to the loft was cheery. Dirty blond hair, streaked with gray, cascaded down beyond her shoulders, overwhelming a face that was at once hard, and gentle, and pretty. Greeting Oliver, her eyes glowed with the kind of peace and clarity that, Alice knew, came from profound daily meditation. Most likely, Oliver would declare that same glow a sign of psychotic insanity (each privately admitting that both possibilities could be correct). Specializing in massage, trauma therapy, and holistic healing, based somewhere in the Northeast, Sparrow had been recommended to Tilda as having achieved *amazing* results with cancer patients, and had come to the city after Tilda's letters of unabashed pleading. Consecutive sessions during the early days of Alice's consolidation had been relaxing enough to leave Alice in a state of excitement and bliss. That was before her arm had reclotted, creating the quarantine.

As if she were viewing the scene through a thin haze, Alice watched Sparrow bow slightly to Oliver, and tell him the arrangement had worked out perfectly, she'd gotten his message, hopped on the 9 train, and just walked over. It was *such* a gorgeous evening. Now Sparrow handed over a bouquet.

The gaffe registered: a healer unaware that fresh flowers could compromise an immune system. Precisely the kind of thing that would get Oliver mocking Sparrow's legitimacy, Alice knew. But Oliver thanked her, asked if she could leave them outside. Speaking simultaneously to Sparrow and—Alice could tell—for her benefit, he said he knew how rough discharge days were, and he'd wanted to take care of Alice when she got home. Alice recognized the irony to his politesse, the hurt beneath his enthusiasm. But by then Sparrow had reached her, and was leaning in, all coconut oils and Eastern spices; Alice accepted the warmth of her embrace with as much appreciation as she could muster.

"It's time," Sparrow said. "Ready to begin?"

Alice blinked a few times, her eyes twinkling with kindness. Seconds passed before she gripped the edge of her sewing table. Forearm shaking, she pushed off, by which time Sparrow had managed to ease beneath Alice's pits, and was lifting with her.

The bedroom purifier soon shifted into second gear; a compact disc broadcast the chirping birds and babbling brooks and wind rustling through trees that constituted an Amazonian rainforest; votive candles were lit; incense sticks burned. Alice lay facedown, her head resting on a side. She was asked to close her eyes.

Sparrow lifted Alice's right foot off the bed and raised it. Hands that were hard and compact, powerful as a boxer's, gently pushed Alice's leg backward, testing. Sparrow similarly tested each of Alice's limbs and joints, found the limits of their flexibility. She ran her fingers down Alice's spine, kneaded the space between Alice's shoulder blades with closed, hard fists, her knuckles pressing. Raised indentations along Alice's back revealed the outline of her rib cage; Sparrow's fingers made soothing runs. She scooted and sat at the base of Alice's back, her weight pleasant on Alice. She pressed along Alice's scalp, finding those points along the bottom ridge where the neck gave way to skull. Through a delicious veil of sleep, Alice vaguely heard the healer: "You have a brave and strong body. What a boon and friend this body is to you."

. . .

If Alice died in her sleep, the way he figured it, Tilda would have to come and hustle the baby away, out to her apartment; although, if Tilda wasn't answering her beeper, or couldn't get downtown quickly, then it fell to Oliver's cousin and his wife to jet over. This had all been arranged. Alice's mom, if she was still in town, was a possibility, but Oliver assumed she'd be a wreck. He kept Tilda's beeper number at the ready, and had purchased a second clunky Motorola—one just like his—for Jonathan. Smaller and lighter and slightly better looking than those bricks from the eighties, the phones weren't going to win any kind of design contest, in fact were basically repulsive; people on the street universally gave Oliver shit looks when he used his, which was doubly humiliating, because reception was never better than spotty, anyway. But there was comfort in the theory that Oliver and his cousin—again, in theory—always could reach one another, that in a crisis he'd get ahold of *someone*. Only afterward would he contact a coroner. That was his plan. This way the baby would be protected: no chance the deepest part of her mind would get imprinted by the sight of Mommy being zippered.

Two in the morning. Alice and the child long asleep. Oliver imagined how it could go—the dilemma of simultaneously caring for what he imagined as Alice in emergency, spasming, in pain, body panicked and out of control, *plus* an infant. Game theory demanded Oliver plan for the worst. Meaning Doe awakening, sensing the chaos, then bawling her little head off. Similarly assume Tilda would be uptown, doing whatever the hell she did for rent, maybe plying some poor schlub with alcohol so she could drag him back to her lair. Figure Jonathan and his wife having complicated plans and important arrangements from which all kinds of disentangling would be required. Meaning Oliver had to plan for a good half an hour spent handling this crisis alone. Alice wouldn't be able to wait for the cavalry, would need help immediately—so Oliver was going to make sure each desktop had an instruction file, just in case the Brow might be at a terminal. Oliver was going to ask anyone who'd be around the apartment semiregularly to familiarize themselves with the instructions (they wouldn't; still he'd ask). He'd already been assured that select waiters at Florent had been through their share of AIDS tragedies and were more than capable in a crisis situation, Florent would even come himself if need be. Worst-case scenario, something happens at three in the morning, one of the transvestite hookers from the corner could take Doe into the bedroom; Oliver could put him or her on a retainer, have the pre-op hang with the baby, just watching, keeping Doe mollified and oblivious while paramedics attended to Alice in the main room. Shit might get stolen, but so be it; Oliver had to make sure the child did not scar from the sight of Mommy flailing and foaming, let alone the paramedics strapping Mommy onto a stretcher, carrying her away.

The apartment's large main area was dormant, just his desk lamp and screen light providing illumination. Printing out his list of emergency info from a gray laptop, Oliver taped a copy to the inside of the computer desk's top right drawer, so it would be easily available to him, but out of Alice's purview—yet another thing she didn't need to know about. When he finished he reclined in his rolling chair, staring out into nothing. It felt to him as if he were a little boy rising onto his tiptoes, reaching toward a shelf, his fingertips barely touching something, feeling smooth curves. That unseen object remained too large for him to fully comprehend.

It was fear. That their daughter would grow up without ever knowing her mother, that this void would dominate her life; that she wouldn't have a choice but to idealize her absent mother, and would blame her mother for her absence, and would curse her, as well as every woman her dad brought home (family friends who carved time in their schedules to try to assuage how sorry they felt; well-meaning girlfriends wanting to do good; all other sorts of potential stepmothers); she would curse her father; curse the world and, most of all, herself, herself, herself; that lonely teen years would be spent holed up in a corner with Mom's journals, reconstructing her own version of who this woman was—these were the broad strokes. And there were specifics as well. Even if he could not fully grasp them all, the imagining was endless.

The four-year-old ambles out of her prekindergarten classroom and into the hallway, where she sees all those different women, every one of them expectant, joyous, opening her arms. Every day she does this, ambles out of her class, into that hallway. Every day she watches mommies hug all the other children. Caribbean nannies are gathering kids, too, but his little girl sees those mommies, with their packages of fresh fruit, their baggies of newly steamed broccoli, their applesauce pouches and yogurt containers and Goldfish crackers. Her daddy is late again, out of breath, trying to figure out which of his coat pockets has that paltry-ass cheese stick.

He is up in the small hours, practicing on her Barbie, refining his technique for French twist braids. His thumbnails are slathered with pink sparkle polish, the result of an hour before bedtime when he needed to keep her occupied. His hands fumble, his manual dexterity light-years away from that of women who've been braiding hair since they were six. The next morning: he is woozy, but concentrating, making sure to follow each comb stroke so his daughter's hair falls according to the swirling part along the top, pulling and struggling to separate clumped ends, tangled strands. Fumbling with hairpins, Oliver gets surly, ordering: *Sit still already*. On cue, the girl pulls away, cries. Yet another school photo where stray thin hairs form around her head a backlit halo.

To honor his dead wife's wishes he won't let television raise his child, meaning that unless Oliver's paying for a sitter, cooking dinner's not a real option, at least not until Doe's like six or seven. The real-world translation: half-opened take-out containers, a fridge that wafts with strange smells, a kitchen sink piling with used dishes.

Relying on one or two distressingly attractive, semicompetent young women fresh out of art school who earn extra spending money through sitter work. Learning to have more sitters. To have a list of backups. To juggle their schedules. The girls are always looking for a real job, counting down the days to some internship, nurturing a relationship with his daughter but, as the job continues, showing up later and later. Doe wide-eyed, listening as Oliver explains still another departure; Doe's eyes not as wide, the child becoming accustomed to this whole attachment-abandonment cycle: you trust people, you believe in them, they leave, you have no control.

Another tantrum; constantly determined to show that her will is greater than his; overturning her chocolate milk. From the other booths around him come the stares, men who've brought *their* young children to this diner at nine o'clock on a Saturday morning—hoping to kill some clock this long weekend day. Faces entering the first pangs of middle age. As they watch Doe's meltdown, each man shows a certain sympathy, but also betrays something else. Coming from a place deeper than sympathy: a terror that is pure, whole.

But a learning curve can also work for adults, and Oliver moves from the overmatched griever, lashing back at the other diners with a look of vehemence (*What do you want? I had this thrust upon me. That's a different animal from your divorce*). He ferments into the panicky uptight dad who jerks across the table and lifts his daughter too hard, scaring her, *What did you do now? Look at this. Jesus, Doe.* He becomes the beaten man with his face in his hands, listening to his girl cry and wishing so hard that he could disappear. And then he survives, evolves: lifting his daughter out of the path of the pool of milk so her clothes don't get more muddied; pulling more napkins from the holder, telling her it is fine, and wiping away the mess.

And that name, yet again, always that name. The child falls and cries and says it. She doesn't get the desired amount of sprinkles on her donut and blubbers, *I want Mama.* She doesn't want to clean up her toys, *Mama.* Wants to stay in the playground longer, *I want Mama.* Wants to play yet another imaginative game with her classmates where they are the brothers and sisters, and who is she? *Mommy Mommy.*

And then he's survived until that sweet soft-ice-cream-pleasant and best time of the night, when they are in bed together and she is comfy under the comforter and flirty and loving toward him, gazing at him with what seems unabated love, paying attention to stories and pulling on his ear with affection. He's read two full stories and she's rubbing at her eyes with her little hands and it is time for lights-out, that part of the evening where he knows it will start.

I want Mama, she says.

The hope has been that each time Alice tells her daughter *Mommy is in your heart. You are in Mommy's heart,* Doe absorbs these words, they are lodged in her, somewhere.

Oliver tells his daughter to take a deep breath. He tells her to feel the warm syrup of Mommy's love spreading through her. He tells Doe to take another breath and start with the top of her head, now down into her forehead, the syrup of Mommy's love spreading behind her eyes.

The girl tries. Her lids open now. The whites of her eyes are large and liquid. Wide hazel irises focus on him. "Why can't I go to Mommy?

"I know Mommy is in the sky," she says.

Her voice is light, underdeveloped, committed. "We can take a plane."

He allows himself the time to blink, composing himself.

"The sky is so very big," he answers.

She is undeterred, promising: "I would search every cloud."

An immediate horizon

BUT THE DAILY grit of responsibilities took back over, their self-contained, hermetic little bubble resealing. Alice made sure she was on the phone first thing to schedule or confirm her follow-ups with Eisenstatt (Friday, the following Tuesday). She called nurses with questions about medicines, pharmacies to ask about dosages. She eventually got off the phone and into her day, usually with simple arm rotations and stretches, a basic tai chi routine if she was up to it. Then vitamin supplements, including one of Sparrow's warmed liquid packages of special Eastern herbs and blends. (It was supposed to fill Alice with vitality, but tasted like hot barf.) She might attempt a cursory bite of breakfast. She did her best to feed Doe spoonfuls of apple mush, made sure to clean her face with a warm wet cloth, even unhooked the baby from the high chair and brought her to the floor and let Doe use her pajamaed legs—along with the wooden sewing table leg—as leverage, the child still not yet walking, but happily in that place where she was trying to stand and move around. Alice still moved fairly well herself, although she had to be shrewd about just how much back-and-forth she could handle. Hot flashes intruded, six or seven a day, the most ridiculous side effect. She was freezing all the time and then— out of nowhere—felt her body flushing with fire? Alice compensated as best she could, with layers of ice compresses, occupying her mind, typing notes to herself on the cute new gray PowerBook Oliver had bought her, sometimes just running her hand over the trackball, enjoying its smoothness, the arrow cursor corresponding with zips and zags across the screen. She called friends, though conversations had to stay short. And Oliver helped on this front, not so much eavesdropping as checking in, he claimed, sussing out who she was talking with and how things were going. Alice could be overly generous, once even having some kind of counseling session with this weird guy she'd met in the hospital hallway, so Oliver had to keep the reins tight, especially considering how many friends wanted to be in touch with her. If the phone seemed slack to her ear, and Alice wasn't answering so much, and didn't seem engaged, Oliver would lean into the cordless and apologize as best he could. He'd explain she needed a break.

Writing thank-you notes also drained her. Even leafing through compact discs was a slog. On the plus side, Alice didn't mourn being done with changing Morrisey's litter (a corollary existed between proximity to cat litter and patients coming out of remission). Nor did she spend huge amounts of time bemoaning the loss of the private rituals involved with using a hand razor to shave her legs (the risk of bleeding out was too high; she'd have to make do with an electric razor). Her time went for more important matters, each day, all these wonderful friends, arriving into their hermetic and low-lit bubble: Susannah and Suzie and Sue, Christina, Jana, Julie, Karen, Mary Beth, Jess, Sarah Jay and her husband, Isidro, Marc and Marie, Crystal, Jynne, Fiona, Alison and Cindy, Sean and Daphne (with their little ones, Owen and Mira, in tow), and David, and Matt, Patty and Josh: core loved ones who'd been invited or volunteered, not just signing up for Tilda's schedule of visitations, but *adhering* to the crazy thing, never complaining about getting the required flu vaccine shot (single dose only, no clusters, mists, or live vaccines); who clearly understood they couldn't come up if suffering from the slightest cold, or if they'd recently been ill, or even recently had been hanging around someone sick. Sitting next to Alice at her sewing table; reclining on the couch beside her; knitting a scarf and talking about patterns; distracting and entertaining and charming her; providing opinions when she asked for them; volunteering thoughts when she did not; trying to hide any somber or worried looks, or not at all hiding their concern; getting philosophical and deep with her while joining in and doing those weird arm stretches; rubbing moisturizer into her skin; refilling that water cup; taking her into their confidence; idly gossiping; coming into the realization that she'd been sitting in that chair this long because she did not have the gas to get up and move—all of this while Alice slyly hustled them at pinochle. In this manner her days passed, divided into small portions of pleasant visits, right up until she needed a nap (a happening that, with any luck, coincided with Doe's sleep schedule), at which point most visitors offered to run errands, take the baby on a little adventure, do laundry, or perhaps didn't get the hint it was time to go, but instead sat and watched her sleeping body, taking in the enormity, just what was happening to this hollowed woman.

And her more mercurial friends—Golzi, Debb, and Annaka—the lightning bolt wild-childs who were allergic to plans, who weren't the type to *sign up* for, let alone adhere to, someone else's spreadsheet, and besides were busy getting fall lines ready for Fashion Week: calling, out of nowhere, asking if it was okay, zipping up with containers of freshly cooked high-protein food that met all of Alice's dietary standards, or maybe, since they didn't have the extra time, these were the ones who paid some Village restaurateur to run over a three-star meal. And the dear friend from her high school days who volunteered to come in from out of state (just for a few days, to hang out, run errands, take Doe to Washington Square, whatever Alice needed). And the guys from Oliver's grad school years, they tried, too, even though they hadn't been around that many kids and were basically scared of babies, and also had little idea how to cook, clean, or do anything practical. People came, they did what they could, whatever that may have been: hauling over loads of processed deli food that Alice couldn't eat, bottles of very good wine she was no longer allowed to ingest, baggies of hydroponic that whips and Rottweilers could not keep from her lips. They shot the breeze about television shows, they talked about nothing, enthusiastic and positive in a manner that did not begin to hide their worry, wanting to convey their goodwill, wanting so hard.

It melted Alice, even as a small seed inside couldn't help feeling resentful. All these people got to feel a little better about themselves, and feel sorry for her, and then leave and go on with their normal lives.

She'd castigate herself for her thoughts. Joke that her predicament wasn't so bad. She got to sit around and listen to music. She got to talk with these astonishing people. She got to nap and knit. Gratitude made it easier to forgive the few friends who *were* too freaked to visit. The ones like Winnie, who flaked and forgot and didn't show up for their scheduled day, did it once or twice, burned out, vanished.

To say nothing of the ones who walked in and saw Alice and just lost it.

Once, at the end of a catch-up coffee, Jeremy said he and his significant other were praying for Alice. Oliver answered with the same Grinchy statements he used when Blaine, breezing in with magazines, casually asked whether he needed anything. *"If you want to actually be helpful, contact the bone marrow donor registry."* Sometimes he launched into a public service lecture: *At the very least you'd increase the odds for someone out there.*

This day, Alice was unfortunate enough to be around. Placing her hand on Jeremy's arm, she did her best to short-circuit Oliver's vitriol.

"Thank you. Any good thoughts have to help."

. . .

Alice was still asleep; Oliver picked up the phone on the third ring. "Yo?" The line went dead. Later that afternoon, he was on hold to ask a question to an official at the small business department, and switched over to the call waiting, and promptly became a punch line yet again, hung up on once more.

When he checked their messages, he began noticing those quick clicks, the line going dead as soon as the answering machine started its greeting. Oliver checked the times of the calls—always that low middle of the afternoon, perfect for taking a break from your responsibilities, that dull stretch when you're just trying to get through.

Why don't your friends say anything to me? he asked Alice.

She assured him it wasn't them. She'd mentioned it. Nobody knew a thing.

"What about your little troubadour? From the hallway—weren't you counseling him on the phone for a while?"

Did she flinch? No. Her breathing stayed even. "I don't think so. He's harmless. It has to be a crank call," Alice continued. "Teenagers get a number and won't let up. Believe me, I'm annoyed, too."

Oliver nodded. He'd given this enough attention. And there were bigger fish already on his plate.

"Something I want to run past you, Ruggs, if that's all right."

Forgoing small talk, or even a greeting, Oliver started in.

"This lawyer who's been helping me, well, he pointed me to this city program. It offers small businesses employee health insurance. But get this, spouses are eligible. And in-network costs don't have a ceiling." Oliver waited. The silence implied consent. "Thing is, we switch Generii onto this plan, it's going to cost. Which is kind of why I'm calling. We have some money in reserve, but there's still a ways before the demo's up and running. Fucking who knows when we hit market. Meaning, you know, joining this plan? On the one hand, it gets Alice that policy and that's big. But for the business, purely from that perspective, ah—"

"Who do you need me to kill?" Ruggles answered.

When it was Jonathan's turn to hear the plea, he said, "It's nice of you to ask, Oli. But really?"

So the fax machine belched, pages curling out, dropped from off the tray, onto the floor.

CC: Oliver Culvert

Mr. Culvert, Attached is a bopy of my 2/27 conversation w/ Peachford. Please retain for your records. I hope this answers any questions you have. Do not hesitate to call i there is anything else.

Cleandra Sapir
Overseer
New York State Department of Small Business Services

Q: I have a person who is coming to Peachford Health Ins. from another plan, that had a low ceiling but was full coverage. Assuming no break in coverage, am I safe in stating there is no concern for preexisting conditions? We are discussing cancer care here. The member is understandably very concerned about cancelling his family's prior insurance plan, and wants to be very sure that Peachford will assume coverage for treatment that was started at DHMC and now continues at Whitman.

Cc: Oliver CulverT

Thank you for your inquiry and the enclosed information. The member will be covered fully on the Peachford plan.

Like that. The weight of a planet. **The member will be covered fully.**

They allowed themselves to breathe. He recounted for her the sequence of fax exchanges, suspense escalating through his progression, Alice clasping his hand in both of hers at the moment of truth. Cackling, she drew him to her, touched the front of her head to his, held her hand on the back of his neck.

He made copies of the fax, as Ruggles had said he should for important papers. Put these copies in separate safe places.

Of course there were more fires on the horizon—aside from just figuring out which bills could wait on for another month.

First was basic and unavoidable: the chief goddamn programmer behind this whole Generii thing remained indisposed, distracted, or missing in action for prolonged stretches.

Nobody with a heart would begrudge Oliver, or question his priorities, but it was still an issue, their original touchstone deadline long in the rearview.

Second problem: while Alice was getting her consolation, the Brow had taken over the workspace, programming round the clock, crashing on the couch. It hadn't reached the level of young Bill Gates—who, according to legend, used to fall asleep at the terminal when writing the first Windows code, then jolt awake and, without a hiccup, pick back up where he'd left off. But the Brow was basically chained to a desktop. And progress *was* being made; everyone remained hopeful. At the same time, Alice was home now, and her immune system wasn't safe around the floating biological circus of unwashed programmer detritus.

Meanwhile, every minute those terminals were vacant meant wasted time, the pissing away of definitively finite resources.

An afternoon's search uncovered a building around the corner. On the third floor, just above a storied meat locker, a small office was available. According to lore, twice a week for twenty-five years, a navy vet staggered up the death-trap stairwell and unpacked from his leather satchel needles, inks. Rumor had it he'd once beaten a murder rap in military court, which was why he called his three machines *kits* or *rigs,* as opposed to *guns,* growling to those who made the mistake: "Guns kill people. That's the diff." Cops, fire-fighters, and paramedics were foremost among his steady drip of visitors, who treated the city's ordinance against tattooing with as much regard as its laws against smoking dope on the sidewalk.

The space was cramped, dusty, hot as a furnace, its windows flooding with light from dawn to dusk. It smelled like an assigna-tion spot for hoboes. When Oliver asked, the realtor explained that the tattoo artist had passed away at his desk, and baked in the sun-light until his assistant finally came and discovered the corpse. Workers below had thought that one of their deliveries had been left out of the freezer.

So there was a new monthly rent, fumigation and cleaning costs, and new phone lines for a new Internet connection that would allow their computers to receive streams of information at an up-dated, previously unheard-of rate of 54,000 bits per second. He'd also need new secondary lines for faxes and calls so their fragile new state-of-the-art Internet connection didn't get interrupted. Electricity bills would spike. Throw in some new desks and ergo-nomic chairs because he employed a bunch of entitled, whining bitches. Clothespins for all offended noses.

"My fucking cousin wants to be an installation artist. What the fuck that is, I got no clue," Ruggles told him. "Kid got into RISD though. He's struggling but hanging in there. Know why?"

Oliver started to answer; Ruggles held up his finger.

"Kid lives on rice and air. Steals paper from Kinko's. The whole starving artist thing. Any baby bird, like our fledgling venture here, you need as little overhead as possible, capisce?"

Oliver apologized. "Right."

His friend's pupils widened: *Do you really?*

Ruggles had spent an afternoon during Alice's consolidation at her bedside, deftly goading her into a conversation about the up-coming Oscars. He had delivered, hands down, the best toast at Oliver's wedding.

Indeed, Elliot Ruggleschmierr had been key in Oliver's life since orientation weekend of their freshman year, a pair of mismatched majors joined together by their encyclopedic knowledge of Star Trek trivia. But as Oliver waited for his old roomie to render a verdict, he couldn't tell whether Ruggles might have taken umbrage at the possibility that all he cared about was money.

Maybe Ruggles had been touched by the fiscal concerns that Oliver was showing for the company, even in the middle of this ordeal? Was he simply calculating added costs?

"It's the worst possible time for this." Ruggles spoke slowly.

"What?" Oliver said.

As if making a decision, Ruggles seemed to shift into a different gear. "Okay, look. I really don't want to bring it up. I'm on your team, thick and thin. But this software thing is your baby. You're the point man. You had me go to bat for you with a lot of people. I'm talking hat in hand to every friend I have on the brokerage floor. That's a lot of good people, and some not so good people, too, putting hard-earned nickels and dimes into this on your word and name, because you made that presentation. Remember that?"

"I know."

" 'We get this thing in shape, show Microsoft and those other bastards that Generii can go in and out of their program like mice, take whatever we want, they have to pay us to protect their borders. Otherwise, their big Windows 95 rollout is worthless.' You were the one who stood up there, talked about free access and gatekeepers."

"I remember, Elliot." Oliver waited, stared; Ruggles downed a shot of Jameson, winced, pulled at his own tie.

"You fucking do what you got to, okay? Don't worry. We're all on board for the insurance. I already talked with everyone. Go with God. But, sahib, you got to make it right for us, too. Time to buckle down and kick shit into gear. Maybe it'll be a nice distraction, give you something else to focus on. I fucking hope so."

. . .

Alice's mother drew a small but decent pension for the two and a half decades she'd spent teaching New Hampshire farm children to avoid split infinitives. She'd kept herself busy in retirement with her dogs, her garden, art classes, reading group, cutthroat bridge, and three days a week working the receptionist's desk at a vet's office. Friends had been taking care of her Weimaraners. But the staff at the vet's office, for all their pledges of support, still needed someone to take calls and keep schedules. If Alice's mom was going to keep her dogs out of a kennel, and maintain her pleasant part-time employment—i.e., checks that weren't necessary but were far from unneeded—she had to get back to Putney. There wasn't any easy solution, so Alice's mother, in her measured and typical fashion, did the most reasonable thing she could come up with at that moment: change diapers. She doted on her grandchild. Replaced the filter in the air purifier, as she did not want that bedroom getting stagnant. She cleaned, dusted, sat bedside, held her daughter's hand. She rocked the baby and made goo-goo noises and recounted a story: Alice, six years old, falling off a horse and breaking her arm.

Hold your horses, Alice's mother said, as she padded across the apartment. *Hold on.* "Yes," she answered. "Hello?"

"I thought I'd never get you." The voice low, smooth.

"Do you want to talk with my daughter? Who should I say is calling?"

"Uh, I'm—"

"What number are you trying?" continued Alice's mother. "We've been getting a lot of wrong numbers."

Instead of an answer, the line clicked. Alice's mother placed the phone back in its cradle. She went into the kitchen, washed her hands, then headed for her daughter's bedroom, where she brought up the subject of white sugar.

. . .

The staff nutritionist in New Hampshire had been the first to mention the stuff. Sparrow, Tilda, Kate, and the rank-and-file of Alice's more health-conscious pals all had brought up the same worry: that cancer fed on processed sugar.

"Never again," Alice answered, raising her right hand toward Mom. "Scout's honor."

Dark chocolate, tiramisu, key lime pie, red velvet cake, all her favorite guilty pleasures. "Fallen to the wayside," she swore. "You'll see. A new regime."

Then the end of her next exam-room discussion. Alice volunteered her new eating habits to the medical staff, waiting for assent and approval. In fact, Eisenstatt was quick to answer. "With the chemo regimen we just put you through," he said, "sugar's not going to reactivate anything."

"Sorry?" Alice said.

"The disease isn't metabolically active right now in your case. Cancer cells aren't dividing in your bone marrow, the way cells divide in the gastrointestinal tract. Cycle tracts are different."

"You're saying there's no connection?"

"I'd say gaining weight is the priority. You want to eat *anything*. Whatever it might be, we need you eating."

Nonetheless, per her orders and preference, the fridge remained stocked with unsweetened soy milk, coconut milk, plain whole-milk yogurt and ice cream, agave nectar, really, really good cheeses. Oliver spent part of each day running around—on Alice's first day home he found a reasonably convenient lab that could turn around her blood counts, so that each night he could inject Alice with her proper Coumadin dosage (first wiping her lower belly with that brown antiseptic gel); he made copies each day for insurance appeals, double-checked things with his lawyers, handled Generii errands to get the new office in shape, juggled bullshit with the bank fools and credit card assholes. And always, before returning home, he'd follow orders, track down *Madame*'s every stated need: fresh mangoes and limes, tubs of weight-lifter protein powder, raw unpasteurized honey extracted straight from the rears of bees that had to be purchased on the black market because unpasteurized honey was one of the health hazards that had spread black plague and there were still laws against it. Each day brought news of a new special salve. A friend told Alice about it.

"While you are out," Alice wondered, "could you pick up some dark chocolate for me?"

Oliver stared. "So—"

"I'm giving in to Western medicine like you want." Alice crossed her arms, responding to his frustration before it had a chance to manifest. When one of his confounded looks followed, Alice snapped, adding, "If it was up to me I'd do it holistically."

"Candy's holistic now? I can grab you a Mountain Dew while I'm at it. I hear that's pretty organic, too."

"I've lost my hair. I get bombarded by radiation every month. I have all of three bites before a lid closes over my stomach anyway."

"Jesus," Oliver answered, rising. "I made a joke. Don't get so defensive. One second you want it this way, the next—"

"He *said* I could have sugar."

"So we're just cherry-picking the guidelines? This is the new regime?"

"I want a bite of key lime pie."

Implicit was her threat: if he did not get it, someone else would. Others already *were*.

Tilda's visit the following morning included a jaunt to the bagel place across the street. Presenting Alice with the small package—white butcher paper, a price scribbled in marker across the top—Tilda repeated familiar phrases. "That you even want to try is a good sign. Even a few bites will help."

Alice unwrapped the paper, stared. "Didn't I ask for strawberry cream cheese? I don't mean to be difficult."

Tilda was careful in her response. "It's pink, honey."

Alice squinted. "I can't see that."

In short order her support network was chugging on all cylinders, and had dutifully procured a saline solution. Dabbed eyes went teary; Alice blinked a lot. She and Tilda cautioned, making sure neither overreacted; they were rational and sober, and after some more discussion, came to a larger agreement: Alice had to search for new truths. This was the only helpful interpretation. "In the large scheme, what's pink? What's white?" Tilda sounded like a motivational speaker. "Who cares about a couple of locations on a spectrum? Use this as a chance to focus on what's *real*."

Alice smiled. Then her façade collapsed.

"A donor will come through," Tilda assured. She wrapped her arms around Alice's shoulders. "Oliver got the insurance taken care of, right? That was huge. Now they'll find this. It *will* get solved."

Alice sniffed, looked up at her friend.

"It's impossible to explain," said Alice. "How tired I am of being less than myself."

Both women considered her words. Soon, Oliver would as well, noticing that Alice had absorbed the sentence into her repartee, repeating it, verbatim, to at least four other guests.

Sparrow was the last of them. The healer listened, gave a slight nod, then searched inside her brightly beaded shoulder bag. A bronze figurine about the size of baseball. The healer placed it into Alice's palm. Cool to the touch, carrying a surprising weight. "A common misconception is that a bodhisattva is some kind of god," Sparrow said. "But a bodhisattva is just a mortal who has spiritually advanced into a being of enlightenment."

Alice examined the figurine, running her fingers along its grooves, into its nooks. A first glance could easily mistake it for a tree. With closer study, Alice realized it was something else: growing out of that stout, crooked trunk was a stout female figure. Her face showed large eyes, three of them. Arm after arm rose from out of her trunk like branches, or perhaps a peacock's fan.

"Guanyin is one of the four great bodhisattvas," Sparrow said. "Translated from Sankskrit, the name means: *observing the cries of the world*. She embodies pure compassion. But there were too many beings she couldn't save. She watched armies of souls stream into the gates of the underworld. She tried to reach for them, but was so disheartened, her arms shattered into a thousand pieces. Buddha Amitabha aided her, transforming those pieces into a thousand arms, that she might reach out to those in need."

Sparrow sat up, onto her knees, was directly across from Alice, facing her on the bed. "I have a meditation exercise."

She ordered Alice to sit up, helped her into a facsimile of a lotus.

"Trust me, this has very good results. I want you to look at the hands on the figure Guanyin. On the palm of each hand is an eye. See that? The plumage of a thousand arms each looks in a direction. Each arm takes in the suffering of others. When you are unhappy, when your lot is too unfair, or too hard for you, I want you to be an arm of Guanyin. Close your eyes and stare in the direction of suffering. Slow down. Back straight if you can. Imagine a young mother in sub-Saharan Africa. She has a family and is starving and is experiencing the same illness as you. Keep breathing now."

Alice opened her eyes and made contact, wanting to follow orders, but also skeptical.

"When you inhale," Sparrow continued, "I want you to take in the breadth of that mother's pain. Take in that family's pain. Now exhale, release, let all that pain go. Your sitting lotus is very strong. Excellent. And now we become another arm of Guanyin. Ready?"

Whitman Memorial, 1220 York Ave., Hematology/Oncology, Rm. 421A

Nearly eleven pounds, the size of a healthy baby on the plump side. Only this was lodged inside his face, encompassing nearly all of his jawbone. The tumor didn't respond to a number of treatments, so his final option was taking out the mandible joint and nearly all of his lower jawbone.

He was under the knife for more than sixteen hours and the surgery worked—the removal of the hinge helped the jaw to slide out—but the doctors also had to remove his tongue, and the membrane inside his cheek, and his lower lip. It took months before the wrappings and gauze came off, and more months before the swelling and bruising went down—and then his best friends and loved ones saw him. His sister struggled to keep a neutral expression, but he could tell she was horrified, fighting back tears. He couldn't say anything in return. That part of his life—the speaking part—was now behind him.

And chewing. No lower jaw meant he was done with chewing, too. A tube, surgically inserted into his esophagus, flowed liquid baby formula nutrition down past his stomach, into something called the jejunum. No more flavors—their savoring, their enjoyment. He wouldn't ever recoil from a jolt of unexpected bitterness. Not being hungry was about as good as he got. He was learning to make do with that, the pleasure of fullness. It was an adjustment. He was doing better at some parts than others. There were tastes and flavors out there that could not be satiated. Never again would he kiss his dog, let alone the proverbial cute girl he hadn't yet met, but who was out there, waiting for just him. Dating in the city had been hard enough with a full face. His life hadn't even started in a way that felt like it mattered. Young couples were always getting out of the city for a weekend, taking a weekend in Hudson at some quaint bed-and-breakfast. Lazy mornings in bed. Cozy brunch spots with bright yellow eggs, thick, sizzling bacon, all sourced from local farms. It sounded so simple, and it was impossible now.

He still could laugh, though, even if his laughter was different . . . *off.* He didn't make any sound, the way normal people did. Instead his whole body vibrated, and his breathing got clipped, the air coming out in short explosions. It could be kind of painful. His sister lived in the city. Sometimes she'd visit after a day of teaching pre-K, spend the night with him, correcting homework and doing lesson plans. She might tell him about something one of the squirts did, sitting all day learning his letters, jolly in heavy, soiled diaper. He'd start his laughing and shaking. That first time, she freaked out, tensing up, wanting to know what was wrong, if she should get a nurse. Nowadays she was used to it though. Now and then, his shakes even got her giggling. He'd laugh and shake and she'd laugh and her chest and cheeks might get red. She went and imitated him once, shaking on her own in her chair. The two of them laughing and shaking together and he couldn't even tell you why.

5:00 p.m., tuesday afternoon

THE ORIGINAL IDEA—JUST dump all the text from other word-processing programs into a blank field—had revealed itself as asinine. Dumping text sounded simple, but actually doing it meant incorporating every other programming code—lifting and carrying the words and symbols while still keeping intact all the formatting commands, something akin to transporting a body of water—a lake, say—into a larger body of water, one bucket at a time. Actually, it was worse—transporting the body of water, but then having to reconstruct it, putting every single drop in its prior location. Oliver had to do this inside the Generii field. The water wasn't going to stay in place. Not a chance.

Glitches and fuckery were perpetual: a minute typo sent the cursor careening, or created a second cursor, which went careening. Merging paragraphs from different programs demolished all margin settings, resulting in impossibly long vertical lines of language. No end was in sight, although it was also true, inside the reams of confusion, pockets of joy were available: solving the solvable, fixing the tedious. Five hours knocking items off your never-ending list of mistakes, that had its own perverse jolt. And there were worse feelings than ending the day with the sense that maybe, if you kept fixing, this thing could actually get done.

Oliver adjusted the angle of the desk light, called up his master file, stared at the green strings of data.

For as long as he cared to remember, *doing what he had to* meant being alone with his work. Being engaged with a project, mentally connected to the task at hand, allowed him to be civil around others. You reached that point where you'd spent yourself and needed to come up for air, and were actually *glad* to be around friends, willing to listen to their small talk, even *banter.* By the same token, quality time with Alice, or an easy night laughing with Jon or Ruggles, often unwound him enough to where he could strap in, head back down into the pit, alone, to settle in at his terminal, fully occupy and focus.

Over the radio Doris from Rego Park was coughing, saying the Knicks backcourt was too old, didn't value the ball.

Oliver saved his changes. Heading into his desk, he pulled out a folder of bills, placed them next to the keyboard. He now opened an older word-processing file. And began a new assault upon the keyboard:

```
. . . Calls to nearby New Hampshire and
Vermont hospitals confirm that no other area
hospitals have hematology/oncology divisions
(see enclosed list). In fact, under the
circumstances described, DHMC is the ONLY
hospital where my wife could have been
transported. Additionally, during her stay,
billing records show five different attending
physicians attended to my wife. The attached
registry shows seven physicians on the DHMC
hema/oncology department roster. It is
therefore statistically impossible for five of
seven physicians to charge above the area mean
```

at the only area hospital that could treat my
wife.

With this in mind, I formally appeal the
Unified billing department claim of denial for
the attached charges, and the illogical
justification that the billed pricing billed
is beyond *what is reasonable and customary.*

He corrected the typo, checked the clock in the screen's upper
corner.

And what if he flinched? Took a little break and slunk off to a
Washington Square hustler for a dime bag cut with oregano?
Bounced out for a night with the boys, as implicitly suggested by all
these people when they asked *How are you holding up?* Or tactfully nudged, *Make sure to take care of yourself.* Sentences filled
with goodwill and concern, the least painful way to address his
baggy red eyes and doughy second chin, his growing stomach pushing his belt and pants until they were halfway down his hips, his
stares of distance and incredulity, his quick temper and pissed-off
looks, a scowl that threatened to become permanent.

But what if he was indeed good to himself and accepted a joint
with a *thank you* and got so high that air traffic controllers had to
direct him to the nearest couch. If he let his friends buy him shots
all night. If a call arrived, once he'd done that. If something happened with Alice, something went wrong with the baby.

Like fuck he was going to let that happen.

Oliver's most responsible means of escape was employed rarely—
only at those moments when the planets were in their proper align-
ments, and he was feeling magnanimous, and had the energy to be
a good and upstanding daddy, and someone was around to keep an
eye on Alice besides. Lifting that papoose thing over his head, he'd

strap himself in, holster the little squiggler inside. He'd take Doe to the school yard on Horatio, lift her carefully from her papoose, fitting each leg into one of the plastic seats of those special baby swings. With the little one getting all excited and rocking in her seat, Oliver would push, not even close to hard, just enough. Once he'd gotten a decent rhythm going, he usually stared out into the basketball courts, watching men younger than him play three-on-three. He'd scan the playground, eyeing the young mothers in their sculpted jeans, the proudly displayed figures that had been worked back into shape.

Today that wasn't happening. Today was something else.

He'd withdrawn eighteen twenty-dollar bills from the company account. Fifteen sat neatly in an unsealed white mailing envelope, which Oliver now withdrew from a desk drawer and placed in the front left pocket of his corduroy pants. The other three were in his wallet, just in case. At the base of his keyboard lay a creased, lemon-yellow business card. He was supposed to call the number at 5:00 P.M. But he couldn't call from the office phone, as there could be no record of this call, and the people he needed did not talk to anybody on a cellular—twice Oliver had forgotten, been hung up on.

Just fuck it.

Rising from his desk, he glanced around, quickly checked his reflection in the terminal screen.

Heading eastward, passing the sneaker stores and boot stores and the health food place, his steps were making him a bit queasy, though Oliver still moved with speed. He didn't want to be late. He kept an eye out, cursed to himself because goddamn Giuliani still hadn't replaced any of the pay phone receivers or gutted wires. Moving to the other side of Broadway, nearing the triangle of busy avenues at Astor Place. And it was here that the old truism presented itself, the idea that you were only part of the city when your history here reached out for you. For Oliver it was a bulky line of bodies, ensnaring him in its meaty arm. Blocking half of the sidewalk and running along the base of the large commercial stone building that had been built back during the previous century. Bodies grouped in twos and threes, bunching up, leaning against, and blocking the large pictures that took up the windows of Astor Wines & Spirits; all these people killing time, shooting the shit with the neighboring stranger; standing and staring out at whatever. A blow-up doll was being batted like a beach ball.

Oliver hadn't realized it was Tuesday; but it had to be. Of course.

Every Tuesday afternoon, the better part of three years: this line, its untold bodies. That clichéd new arrival from the sticks with the hay straw in his mouth and dreams of making it big. The loser in a breakup who had to find a new place to pick up the pieces. You didn't have a friend who had a spare room or inside angle? You couldn't really afford to give fifteen percent of a year's rent to a real estate agent? Getting work in this city was so much easier than getting a pad; so, on Tuesday afternoon, it was in your best interest to leave work early, right around the time when the gray pages of *The Village Voice* were still warm from the printing press, and the recognizable royal-blue ink of the paper's logo was still seeping into its cover. Five thirty or so, the first bundled stacks of the famed leftist weekly came out on a rolling pulley, dragged from the headquarters near Cooper Union, onto the sidewalk of Fourth Avenue. The Astor Place newsstand—just a few hundred yards away—got them around 5:45 P.M. A solid hour earlier than anywhere else.

Even the Statue of Liberty knew that the *Voice*'s classifieds were the alpha and omega for halfway affordable places, so valuable that even the rag's most powerful editors, even its famed columnists, couldn't get advance access. The only early access was the front of that line. Every Tuesday afternoon, to supplement his meager grad school scholarship income, Oliver used to place business cards with the name Hudson Realty, as well as his phone extension, in each pay phone within a half mile of the Astor newsstand. Oliver then would offer a card to every person on line, chatting up those toward the middle and the back, explaining that if you weren't in the front third of that line, by the time you paid for your *Voice,* got to a pay phone that worked, and found a few ads that didn't sound like that much of a compromise, the numbers would already have been bombarded, and the dude who placed the ad would've given up on answering the phone, and even if this person's answering machine wasn't filled, you'd be like fifty-fifth on the list. No shot.

Once he let stragglers know that if the ads didn't net them anything, he'd be available to show them places, Oliver hightailed it back to a dusty office in an old Gramercy hotel, where he spent the evening answering calls. Next morning he was up at seven. On the half hour, lasting long into the evening, he met groups of six to eight strangers at designated corners of the Lower East Side, amid all those knish shops and *quinceañera* dressmakers and noodle places with dead plucked chickens hanging in windows. Listings generally were considered dogshit, where pretty much any agency could get keys, and commissions were up for grabs. Oliver always met his groups on the southeast corner—southeast was his. Other groups of prospective tenants would congregate around their entry-level real estate agents on the other three corners, all these clusters of nervous white people at once conspicuous and funny, a shaking little harbinger. Invariably, a grumbling super then led the *parado de blancos* up stairways thin and creaking and smelling of weird steamed vegetables, guiding them down dark hallways echoing with the cries of infants and the barks of ignored dogs. Always they ended up in front of some metal door festooned with half-ripped stickers—the Puerto Rican flag, some princesses, a purple dinosaur.

When the mom of a trench-coat-wearing graduate student complained that her family had spent fifty years working to get out of these low-ceilinged one-bedroom shoe box shtetls, Oliver would answer that she was totally right, this space *was* unacceptable. He'd also mention a bigger place his listing sheet said was nearby, a bit above their price range, but if she was interested, they could take a look. When the temp with ambitions of documentary filmmaking recoiled at splattered walls and a decapitated body outlined in chalk along the kitchen floor, Oliver agreed. *Totally unacceptable.* No reasonable person could be expected to make their breakfast at a murder site. *Except, you know, the floor's scheduled to be cleaned. And the walls will get a new coat of paint.*

His favorite had been a sous chef. Worn down from a nasty divorce, the inhumane hours she spent working at a trendy Village bistro, and months searching for an affordable place, she'd lost any ability to censor herself, and had screamed: *"You're not seriously trying to tell me this ABANDONED ELEVATOR SHAFT is a STUDIO? There's NO FLOOR. How can you EXPECT me to LIVE with NO FLOOR?"* Oliver had handed her a tissue and confessed he hadn't seen the place before. Obviously they should get out of there.

It was a kick to remember. The perfect part-time job for a grad student: juggling classes around the suck-hole of Tuesday afternoon through Thursday at noon; scheduling all his showings and contract signings during that busy stretch; then spending Friday evening through Sunday schlepping back and forth between computer labs and the Lower East Side. The job may have required attention and hustle, but not much mental energy, which helped on the school front, and he became an early adapter to laptops, switching his focus to swatches of programs while parked in a coffee shop, jumping in and out of assignments, working line by line through programming math and logic. Regular injections of commission money let him take Alice out for fancy meals, actually enjoy life. Friends wondered about the morality of the job, but Oliver was sanguine. Paying off doormen for tips on vacancies wasn't so bad, because everyone knew the deal and was kind of wink-wink about it. Cold-calling management companies for leads, sucking up to supers who already had their hands out, maybe that left him needing a shower, but again, this was the way of the world. And the verbal gymnastics that convinced a potential renter to give down-payment money weren't all that different from the raps a single guy in a club might use to ease women out of their underthings. You were just convincing them to do something they already wanted to do.

Oliver handed the newsstand guy a pair of quarters, grabbed a pack of fruit Chiclets. He felt sweat bubbling beneath his winter peacoat.

A friend of his cousin, this blond, classically northeastern, establishment-looking guy (with patches on the elbows of his jacket and the whole nine), had clued him in, handing him the yellow business card and explaining how things worked—clean breath wasn't just polite, it helped stop germs. It had been comforting that someone so prep school had been forthcoming about all this, a nice shot in the arm.

Oliver headed out from beneath the green awning. Side groups of angry young men had started to bulk in anticipation, waiting for the moment the newspaper vendor's X-Acto knife cut open that virginal bundle, so they could bum-rush the line and grab. In the intermittent distance, towheaded skate rats attempted tricks around the giant cube. A few stragglers headed from the subway toward the set-up beach umbrella across the street, where a guy sold old porn videotapes at a folding table.

At the nearest bank of pay phones, naturally, two people were lined up at each queue, waiting.

The realtor had wanted to hire him full-time, even pay for him to get his license, move into commercial properties. But the woman who'd stared at him with those big eyes in that shitty Williamsburg loft party, she'd asked. What did he really want?

Sugar clung, thick on his teeth.

Crossing Fourth brought him toward the delineation point of St. Marks Place, that famous stretch of sagging brownstones and their ground-level kitsch. Oliver ignored the video place where they had all the obscure subtitled shit; and the round-the-clock restaurant offering a perpetual special of fetid rice and a limp, tofu pita burger. Some crazed street artist had plastered, around a streetlamp, pieces of ceramic and mosaic tile segments and shards of mirrored glass, the effect funky and gaudy, signaling a thrum of creative energy—running beneath them, everywhere. Oliver tried not to think about the program that he wasn't working on. His head stayed down, huddled into his coat; he felt his neck going slick now, wished he had a mirror to check himself, didn't want to look like shit.

The famed fifties jazz spot whose bartenders routinely chased off an unknown, drunken Jack Kerouac had been turned into a Gap. The egg-cream counter and magazine stand still stood, though, and three fresh-faced foreign-exchange students were outside, replicating the cover photo of the first New York Dolls album.

Just for shits and giggles, he and Alice used to head into one of the music stores—Norman's, Venus, or Smash—any of them was guaranteed *slamming* at the right time of evening; tourists and locals, young and old alike, sifting through the racks, checking out jewel cases, album cover art, track listings. The cases were empty, a measure against shoplifting, and when you flipped beyond one, it made this plastic *click.* Oliver loved that sound, some store thrumming with minor *clicks,* like a busy typewriter class. Alice happily followed along—a secret music snob herself, she'd spent more than her share of teen hours in record shops. They'd tease each other with the worst covers they could find: a young pensive woman walking along the beach at sunset, her woodwind recorder raised near her lips. It was like a gauntlet thrown down: *Top this fat guy in his motorized wheelchair rocking the thumb cymbals.*

There'd never been any mystery about how important a kid was to her. She'd told him about it early on, in bed together one night, resting on his chest, the rattle and clank of a radiator in the background. Infants kinda creeped Oliver out, to be honest, always crying and shitting and helpless. But then he didn't come from a big family or have tons of exposure to little kids.

Still, if he hadn't said anything in return, he also didn't need to be told that no man could deny the woman he loved a baby.

Oliver hadn't wanted for anything: sneakers, ten-speed, home computer when he was thirteen, money for tickets to concerts in Sacramento, you name it—but through every suburban moment, he also understood that his bounty came from his old man's toil: six days a week, ten hours a day, pounding dents out of junkers, pickups, and off-road racers. His shop was called the Dent Doctor. Each morning the hulking slab would muss Oliver's hair at the breakfast table, scarf down eggs and sausage and provide a solid half hour of banter, then kiss Oliver's mom on the cheek and head off to swing his arsenal of sledgehammers. After sundown, his body dragging and smelling faintly of rye, the Doc would gather enough enthusiasm to enter the house with a hearty *hey hey*. He'd ask about Oliver's day at school, check that all homework had been completed, maybe shovel down whatever his wife had cobbled together for dinner. Then the Doc would disappear for a long soak. Later on, he might lumber in and read a bedtime story, ask if the kid wanted to sit next to him on the couch and watch the Giants for a few innings.

When Oliver had grown to where the Doc wasn't quite able to follow his math and chemistry assignments, the old man had nonetheless remained shrewd enough to understand grading marks, so that when ninth-grade Oliver phoned in one too many assignments, his dad noticed. Taking Oliver's hand in one of his hard, callused lumps, he'd pulled the boy close. Face red, breath hot and sour with whiskey, Dad insisted: *Don't you know? I'm doing this so you won't have to.*

Oliver had assumed it would be a variant of how he was raised, with Alice the primary caregiver, handling all the heavy lifting: the mommy. The kid in classes most of the day, running around to after-school activities and whatnot. Just like his dad, Oliver would muss hair and do the breakfast table thing. He'd show up for school plays, talk with teachers on parents' night, and sweep in late for bedtime stories, the occasional heart-to-heart.

Tragedy didn't follow any spreadsheets, did it? Tragedy had its own business plan.

Just this one time, he told himself. Get it out of my system.

According to lore, the street letter succession stood for *All right, Beware, Check yourself, Dead,* and it was well accepted that any visitor to Alphabet City was either looking for trouble or finding it. The Department of Transportation had long waved the white flag; they no longer fixed the streets out here, so sidewalks had gone uneven, thick roots pushing up, cracking and crumbling the cement. A bank of dirty curb snow still remained, thinning the walking path from the edges, plastic bags and soda containers and glass shards sticking out from the gray piles like remnants of some ancient civilization. At the same time, thin white magnolia trees *had* started sprouting. Oliver headed beneath the pink saucer buds, suspended and dazzling in the branches; past the abandoned storefront, its boarded picture window defaced by urban kudzu: layers of illegible graffiti scrawls, wheat-pasted posters for long-gone concerts.

Nearing the bank of pay phones, he heard whispered chants for that week's product: *body bag body bag.* Keeping his back to the corner homies, Oliver approached yet another bank of phone stalls. Just one possessed its receiver. Occupied, of course, this time by a robust turnip of a woman. *Don't give me none of that, Julio,* she harangued, pausing long enough to shoot a look, convey her intention to stay on the phone for the indefinite future.

Oliver kept his head down, and was past the phone bank when the laughter of the corner boys broke out, some joke that had to be at his expense. Overhead the sky was perfect and crystalline and darkening along its edges. The large building on the corner had been burnt out, and Oliver lingered, staring at its hull, every now and then checking back on the phone. A colorful handful of squatters was busy along the building's husk—one older guy violent in his adjustments of a roof antenna, two college-age women looking peaceful as they aired out a faded white cloth, the parachute sheet opening in slow motion, falling.

Oliver removed the lemon-yellow card. On the back he'd written these cross streets.

Below the curb ran the gutter river: runoff slush, three floating crack vials. Half-submerged, a needle casing bobbed.

One of the Jacksons from his wallet got rid of the turnip—*okay then, fool, DAMN*—and soon Oliver was spitting his gum onto the curb and feeling his pulse in his ears and waiting for the other end to pick up. He was giving his first name and apologizing for running late. He was breathless with anticipation, wrung out. A police siren was disappearing into the distance.

It took five minutes to find the given address, a pale yellow brownstone that had seen better days, iron bars crossing even its highest row of windows. The building buzzer must have malfunctioned and gotten stuck, because it didn't stop sounding until long after he was inside. No lights in the crumbling lobby, just a handwritten wall note offering a sign-up list, which apartments needed visits next month from the exterminator. Oliver descended to the basement apartment, but did not have to knock. The door was already ajar.

From out behind its crook, a head tilted. Dyed auburn locks obscured her face, though her smile had a hint of mischief. *"Hey there."*

Reaching, she took his hand and led him inside. It was as if he had passed over some sort of threshold. They entered a small, dark living room, where what little light existed was provided by a series of small, scented candles. His guide was short but not deal-breaker short. She wore only a faded tee, and it took Oliver a little effort to read the name on it, some obscure experimental theater group. He couldn't keep from looking down to her thighs: pale and luminous, their skin capturing and holding the flickering candlelight. Oliver admired their smoothness, their plumpness, full hips and roundness rustling against the bottom of that shirt.

Without warning she stopped, faced him, and grabbed his belt. Oliver's every nerve went electric. He had no idea what to do. She did, jerking at his zipper. Oliver moaned.

Pecker check, she explained, five seconds later. "You got a badge and I put your dick in my mouth, law says you got to identify yourself."

She must have registered his confusion. "Office says you canceled a few times. A girl can't be too careful with new customers."

Against a sparse wall of unvarnished red-clay brick was a blood-red couch. Its cushy leather gave easily under Oliver's weight. He looked across the room at the large framed print—the famous classic from Godard's *Breathless*. Below it, a blond wood table was empty except for a straw basket filled with pears. The woman introduced herself as Circe, asked if Oliver would like a glass of red. Had he come here straight from work?

She sat next to him now, tucking her small feet beneath that ample tush. Low lighting obscured how old she was or wasn't, though Oliver could see that her chest was flat. He could smell her lavender perfume. Circe picked up a lit cigarette from the lip of a Crystal Pepsi. She took a drag, exhaled streams of smoke through her nose. Oliver understood: the envelope should be on the table by now.

Circe giggled thanks. Asked if he needed to shower.

"I can't do this," he said.

It took her a second. "What?"

By then Oliver had pulled away, was rising from the couch. "I thought I could. But I can't. I'm sorry. I just can't."

Little Edie

TUESDAY EVENING, AN hour or so after dinner, Alice awoke from a nap and discovered white, hot brightness along the surfaces of her eyes. She let out a cry, slammed her lids shut, felt residual burning. By then, floorboards were rumbling. Oliver—who'd just gotten home—was rushing into the bedroom. "Why are they even on?" Alice cried. "They're off," he assured, trying to get up to speed, asking, "What? What's happening?" He again promised the lights were off, and by then Alice's mother had joined them, and was agreeing, in a soothing tone, *They're off, honey*. Now, from the depths of the apartment, the baby's upset was audible. Alice fluttered, tried again; even a sliver was too much, her eyes too sensitive. Oliver was searching through her desk, hunting down the ward's phone number, then thumping around, cursing each usual spot where he got reception. He gave up, used the house line, was put on hold. Finally a doctor told him that Alice's sight troubles were most likely a latent side effect of the chemo. Oliver was advised to keep washing out Alice's eyes with water, and that he should get an alcohol-free version of No More Tears. The ward was sending a prescription for stronger eyedrops to his pharmacy right now. If Alice did not improve, she *needed* to come into Whitman's emergency care center.

So long as everything remained covered in shadows—people appearing as dark forms against a thinner black veil—Alice was okay. Moving her head was fine. Entering a new room, though, being hit by some kind of light for which she wasn't braced, that she couldn't handle. Blinds were pulled, their bedroom transforming into a bat cave; Alice lay in bed, let herself go sedentary. If she had to be trapped, she was not going to feel sorry for herself; she would not wallow, fretting about the implications of this new twist. She kept running a hand over her small bronze figurine, familiarizing herself with Guanyin's grooves, her sudden points, her small indentations, that chip thing along her base, the rough ending to what Alice imagined as an elephant's winding trunk.

"I'll order a car service," Oliver pleaded. "We swoop into the care center, fix it, in and out."

"Can't we just wait?"

Alice was more than ready to be over and done with lying in bed. But she did not want to go back there.

Oliver couldn't say no to her request. He wasn't going to. Not after where he'd just been. Rather, he offered a papal procession of damp washcloths, made it idiot-easy for Alice to rinse her eyes, anytime she needed. They bought out all the Chelsea drugstores' No More Tears shipments, repeatedly flooded her pupils. A five-in-the-morning alarm waking the baby wasn't an option; instead Oliver showed initiative and nipped at Alice's lower lobe. The flesh was loose. His teeth applied just a bit more pressure, then he raised his mouth, nuzzled into her ear. "Time for your prescription drops." She stirred, emitting a sleepy but satisfied moan. Oliver further goaded, got into position, and without mercy used his fingertips to pry open her eyes.

These burned in a different manner than how light affected her, this burn more pulsing than it was painful, and going deeper, as if digging into the corneas, the irises, causing a weird tingle in those roots behind her eyes, those optic nerve things. Medicinal effects were immediate, her pain easing, some, so that if a room was mostly black, her eyes didn't hurt so bad. But even the weakest morning light—peeking in around the edges of the blinds—caused recoil. Her eyes were so sensitive that she could barely see anything, even in dimness. Her squinting became perpetual; Alice began staring down into her lap, hiding her eyes, squeezing her facial muscles to where her forehead cracked with lines of pain. Her shoulders perpetually curled, her body tensing. She placed gauze pads over her eyes, transforming herself into an Egyptian mummy. She had the awful thought of herself as a corpse, her bedroom a tomb. She kept rubbing at the gauze pads, patting them, exhausted but unable to nap, her eyes burning and pulsing. She felt thirsty, but couldn't pull herself upright to drink. She imagined that the throbbing could be scooped out from her sockets, like the meat from a melon. She concentrated on motionlessness, worked at stillness, daydreamed about sitting in a Korean nail shop, getting a pedi and reading a stupid magazine with advice about summer sandals. That dead-ice smell kept intruding.

One form of refuge arrived in the simplest of delights, flickering coolness on her tongue: rainbow sherbet. Alice indulged. The taste allowed her to imagine a very specific freedom: walking down the street, laughing and taking a lick from a waffle cone. Every so often she heard a song and let herself indulge further, imagining that he'd been in a studio for its creation. Alice saw him studying the sheet music, listening for his part and joining in, laying down tracks. She missed the humor of his calls, it was true. At the same time, she could not handle any more of the horror she'd felt those few times when Oliver had expected news from the hospital, and had picked up the phone.

How does Oliver see? The balloon floated through her clouded mind. *How does that happen?*

Past Alice's bedtime. Her mother in the kitchen nook, zoning, worn out. Another batch of that horrid tea brewing. "To watch my girl slowly disappear like this . . ."

She balled her hand into a fist, gave Oliver a hard stare.

"I know hippies. I raised my only girl in a hippie town. Lord knows, I don't have any problems with anyone having a spiritual center. But explain to me—not even *going* to the care center? Can she actually trust that statue more than her doctors?"

Oliver put an arm on her shoulder, brought himself down to her, and embraced her. In an even, sober voice, he promised: Katherine. He was staying on top of it all.

The next day, walking into the bedroom, Alice's mother saw her only daughter and granddaughter sleeping next to one another. Half on her side, the baby was leaning in so the crown of her skull almost touched the top of Mommy's, with Mommy's shoulder serving as Doe's pillow. Swathed by afternoon light, the sleeping infant had wrested free of the comforter and was nestled into her mother's side. Doll eyes were shut, doll lashes long and curving just like her mommy's had been. Doe's breaths were slight; the petals of her lips—so delicate they could have been painted on by a toymaker—puckered happily around her pacifier. To her gramma, Doe looked whole, content. Alice remained motionless next to her, asleep on her back like always, compliant to her child's clinging wishes, satiated by them, or maybe unconsciously oblivious. Alice's mother could not tell. The two of them, like this, was one of the more tender sights Alice's mother had witnessed, and one of the most horrifying. Her daughter's head was *so* diminished, so stripped down and smooth. Its resemblance to a skull was simply impossible to ignore. Indeed, her daughter's head was tilted backward, her mouth wasn't just open but gaping, so wide it might have been unhinged. There was no way around it: Alice looked like a corpse. Even when Doe's hand spasmed and came suddenly alive, dimpled chubby fingers clutching at Mommy's neck, Alice did not respond. Alice's mother dipped in, made sure she was breathing. Ten minutes later, she checked again.

Five minutes after that she still could not sit still. Could not be inside that apartment, could not do anything with her energy but convert it into action. She proceeded to go down the list that had been left for her, deciphered Oliver's chicken-scratch directions. She let Alice's friend know she'd be back.

Jefferson Market was acceptable enough, she guessed. Probably too in love with its pedigree for her tastes, and with prices that should have landed them in prison. Katherine loaded up, anyway. The store's color-coded grid of neighborhoods didn't include her daughter's, which meant they wouldn't deliver; but no matter, Alice's mother dutifully loaded her grocery bags into a wire rolling cart. Empty cabs zipped past her, and when one finally stopped, the driver asked if she was going uptown, then explained in broken English, *Shift over, have to get cab back, sorry.* No matter. She continued with the loaded cart, and for a time admired the city's hugeness, its teeming streets, even as she disliked and feared all . . . *this.* It took her some time. The pads of her feet got sore. Her right knee and hip ached. She stopped for bottled water.

Back at home, she turned stove burners on low and searched through cupboards for the right pans, until she remembered they were hanging above the nook. All the while she kept murmuring, continuing her indecipherable running monologue.

You are everything, I love you so much was what she used to tell her daughter when Alice was young.

Mouth accepted spoonful. The fluid, runny substance mashed between molars, onto her tongue, against her cheek's inner cavity.

Without any visual prompts to guide her, without expectations or ideas, she tasted what immediately became apparent as liquid, not water, almost viscous. Light enough, though, with a tang. It was hot. Alice savored a mouthful. Another.

"Sends me right back to being a little girl and coming home from school." She cooed. "Momma, I love your tomato soup."

During his evolution toward Buddhaness, Alice knew, the Buddha went through an ascetic phase, one in which he denied himself, each day, all food save one grain of rice and one drop of water. By this train of thinking, suffering could provide. Perhaps it did not provide enlightenment, but instead a means *toward* enlightenment. Alice figured she had this suffering thing down pat. Perhaps, she reasoned, the narrowing funnel of her visual capabilities could provide her with direction. By narrowing her own focus, maybe she could widen her capabilities, deepen and enrich every remaining sensory experience.

She slowed her thoughts, concentrated, focusing on the smallish grains resting in her soup. Oblong. Thick in texture.

"I get couscous," she said.

Another sip, a round solid substance, fibrous, with a give, her teeth sinking in. "And carrots. Mmm. Is that cumin?"

"A dash of harissa, too," her mother answered.

Alice nodded, the name providing access.

Her mother handed her what she said was challah bread. Mom stumbled over the rough *ch*, her effort game and respectful and a bit comic.

Alice dipped the spongy slice, soaking it; she took a bite, let out a groan of appreciation.

"The world can open in new ways."

"Sweetheart?"

Alice felt for and gripped and squeezed her mother's hands, enveloping their bony strength. She took a breath and exhaled.

"I can exist like this."

That afternoon, when Oliver came back from the other office, and entered the darkened bedroom, she was beneath Gramma's patchwork quilt, in a fetal curl.

"Get out while you can," she moaned.

Without delay he was on the move, heading right for the walk-in closet, in short order emerging with a sealed plastic bin. "I'm an idiot. Why I didn't think of this sooner?" Overturning the container, dumping out small black objects shaped like bats. "All these just stored away," Oliver said. He picked up a pair, checked the lenses. "How do you tell if one has lots of protection?"

She settled on a pair of oval couture Versaces that looked super-punkish, their arms crafted to look like steel safety pins. Today their appeal lay in their streamlined dark lenses, curving around the ridges of the eye like swimming goggles, sealing off all angles of light. Alice remembered them as a score, the primo takeaway item from a goodie bag given to her by a friend of a friend—a model turned trophy wife who'd decided to launch her own line during Fashion Week, hold her own, guerrilla-style show right on the side-walk outside Bryant Park's tents. Alice had pulled an all-nighter, alternately sewing and fixing like a banshee, holding the hand of this coked-up madwoman. Somehow, they'd managed to get the cocktail dresses close to wearable. The goodie bag had been Alice's payment, the sunglasses worn five times then lost in the bowels of her closet.

An aftershave she'd given Oliver for the holidays had a subtle combination—cloves and cinnamon and pepper. It reminded her of the pleasure of snuggling into his chest late at night. The con-nection between her senses and memories provided a small charge. A belief in her own abilities.

She could open her eyes, Oliver promised, it would be fine.

She ran her hand down the side of his face, appreciating the sandpapery feel of fledgling facial hair, as well as the lightly oiled flesh beneath. Bracing, she creaked her eyes a sliver.

The lenses did their job, layering the room in brown film. And it was indeed a pleasure to recognize features she well knew, the pa-tient concern in his brow, his widening smile.

He'd shaved recently, she noticed, which charmed her no end.

"Let me take you to the care center," he pleaded again.

"All I need is fresh air. Maybe we could take a little walk?"

Just around the block? A walk would give her some exercise. So her legs didn't atrophy? And it would give her mom a chance to change the sheets and air things out—this room was *so* claustro-phobic. Alice's pulse raced through each spoken phrase: she had the *perfect* floppy straw hat, the *hugest* brim. She'd put on a thick medical mask. Alice knew her blood levels were still low, she prom-ised Oliver she didn't want to make anything worse. It would be *so* good for her.

The ringing intruded, always at the worst moment. She could tell from Oliver's shift, his low *Jesus,* this could be a problem.

But no. She would not let it. Jeans that once had formed a sec-ond skin now were comically baggy, and Alice played this up, tak-ing a while to belt them a second time. Though her feet had inflated into small rafting devices, a pair of running sneakers could fit as long as she didn't wear socks. She completed the ensemble with a knee-length coat of distressed denim, its neckline fringed, white cotton shredded to look like feathers. "After all these years"—Alice laughed—"I've become Little Edie. *Finally.*"

She felt immediately ashamed, wallowing like that; nonetheless, momentum was flowing, the evening under way. "A respite from my own private Grey Gardens."

Oliver pressed on her shoulder, and joined in with the fun, kiss-ing her cheek, throwing his own idea into the soup.

Now Doe saw Daddy taking the harness from off the closet door. Recognizing that she, too, was going on an adventure, the baby drooled, spat with glee, little limbs flailing.

Alice reminded: Doe should face inward, toward him.

"Way ahead of you."

Out of the elevator, into the short hallway, overhead halogen sending crackles of fear through her ears, Alice tightly closed her eyes, said "Oliver." Her cornstalk legs trembled and her balance was unsteady, those ridiculous clown feet like sponges. Yet again, there he was: his arm a solid brick anchor around her waist, his prompts deliberate, his words soothing, his manner careful. "Small steps, all right, that's it, doing great." He propped open the front door, his body providing leverage, his hand guiding her forward.

"In three steps, you will have the first stair, we need to go down it to get to the street. Okay, one step and now, *step*. Now, again, *step*."

The false spring hadn't fully disappeared, but nights were getting cooler. Tonight's air was thick, sticky with the promise of rain. Streetlamp light was diffusive, the neon from stores carrying in small, thinning clouds. Alice shielded her eyes, looked away from brighter areas. With each step she measured and placed herself firmly on the uneven sidewalk. She also used each taken step as an exercise; first to acknowledge the fear in her, and then to gather resolve, continue onward. A few times she felt around Oliver's arm, tightening her grip, signaling he should slow. The residual stench of dry ice remained, even stronger out here. Still, being outside was a pleasure, the gloom of the Meatpacking District a treat. Even her developing sweat felt delicious, almost libidinous. Doe's neck was craned as well. Staring at Mommy, her eyes sparkled, that consciousness dawning, thinking what?

At the intersection of West Thirteenth, beneath the near edge of the elevated tracks, a pair of transvestite hookers were at their usual spot, one fixing her wig and applying mascara, the other scarfing popcorn. Donette and Michelle's thing: they dressed up as identical schoolgirl sisters. Alice had long grown accustomed to them coveting her boots, mangling pronunciation of the brand name of the pencil skirt they swore they'd cut her for. Tonight, however, their cattiness gave way to stone silence. What she must have looked like. She mentioned as much to Oliver.

He did not respond. Rather, she felt a different transition taking place inside him, his fingertips tensing, now gripping her hip, his posture going rigid.

She looked to him and saw his eyes squinting, his attention focused.

"Motherfuck," he said.

Alice tried to follow, to see what he saw; what met her were blurs, black streaks.

"What?" she asked, but knew, a horrible thrill. "Not again."

The anger consolidating through him was her answer. But he wouldn't, he *couldn't* abandon his blind cancerous wife on the street, just take off—not with their baby strapped to his chest? He *couldn't* make chase.

"Oliver?" she said.

"STOP BOTHERING HER."

From down the alley came the sounds of trash cans being overturned. Now a small dog, letting loose, pointed and angry yips.

Oliver radiated anger, screaming: *"STAY THE FUCK AWAY FROM US. I PROMISE. I FUCKING PROMISE—"*

The child was finally down and asleep, the two of them sitting together on the couch.

"Explain this to me," he said.

Alice felt his eyes on her face, heard the undertones of his subdued breaths. Now his voice was careful. "I still don't get how one random conversation in a hallway set this off. You bonded, okay. But . . ."

"He's going through something, Oliver."

Oliver's hands went wide, gesturing. "As opposed to the game of Parcheesi we've got here?"

"I don't know what you could possibly think happened?"

"On our list of problems, I know. I know."

Alice promised she had no idea why this man was following her. "We've had two conversations. That's all."

Oliver stared, as if studying something on her face. "I thought you said only one."

"The one in the hallway," Alice responded. "And he stopped by the next day, before he was discharged."

"So two," Oliver said.

Alice admitted, two. She admitted, it had been a mistake to give Merv her phone number. This had all gotten out of control, but—

her voice went shrill—she'd done nothing wrong. "This is insane. I can't even remember what he looks like."

Alice choked up, almost in tears. She caught herself. "Please," she told Oliver. "We're getting to a place in this argument where you can be right or we can be married. And I need so badly to be married to you."

She could sense his rage, but also could feel him working through this. He crossed his arms over his chest. He looked away, into space. He uncrossed his arms and did not move, and yet was not so stiff anymore, but internally seemed to sigh, or somehow deflate, as if some essential part of him were leaking out from a small hole. Again he seemed to sigh without sighing. He repositioned himself, scooting closer to her, reached for her thighs, picked up her legs, and placed them lengthwise across his body, so he could support her while she reclined. He said how proud he was of her for making it all the way to the end of their block. "We should do it every night."

Alice had small creases on the side of her head, little red indentations where the inside band of her hat had rested on her scalp. Through her tears she asked how she could have possibly done anything. "Why would I *want to*? Don't you see how absurd this whole thing is? You are my hero. Do you understand that?"

They talked deep into this night, unburdening, plowing forward, headfirst, through barriers, into confidence. Oliver told her he'd wanted to keep the money side from her, but finally had shared his relief when he'd understood the insurance deal *could* be a solution. He still worried that eight hundred things might go wrong. The worst and most negative part of him refused to exhale until Peachford had cashed that first check.

For the first time in how long Alice studied his face and recognized that his eyes had dark circles beneath them. He'd gained weight in his cheeks.

He kept on, sharing with Alice the pressure he felt to get the program finished. Whenever he looked at the Brow's code, it was sloppy, or rushed, incomplete, or just painstaking, lichen-like in its slowness.

Finding her husband's ear, she rubbed, enjoying the sensation of follicles just beginning to come in along the space behind his lobe.

"You always come through," Alice said.

Around his brows there was a tremor; in his eyes something appeared ready to shatter. He looked down, away.

Then Alice was admitting how much she missed Doe burrowing into her breast. She was feeling along her thighs, showing him the bruises from the last time the baby jumped on her. All Alice wanted from life was for Doe to take her for granted the way Alice took her mother for granted. But even that, having her mom here, working and worrying so hard and taking care of her, Alice hated it. She hated feeling helpless. She hadn't been sick ten days in her life. What, was she supposed to learn to embrace her growing sonar capabilities, like this was some good thing?

She did not know, she did not know, she did not know. But she was going to find out. "Honeysuckle," she said. "I am on a mission. I swear to you."

**Whitman Memorial, 1220 York Ave., 3d floor, Children's Oncology,
Rm. 323**

Sure, it made him feel low to watch other second graders run around the playground. But he'd made it up to three push-ups, was getting decent at fielding a tennis ball against a wall. He wanted to play T-ball that summer, wanted that team jersey, and to be in Cub Scouts, too. When you were eight years old, anything that meant you got to wear a uniform, he wanted to do. He was coming up on three years in remission, so he could still crash from a common cold, side effects from the Coumadin, whatever, but they'd gotten used to it, knew how to handle it.

This time seemed different, although maybe not so much, his mom couldn't tell for sure. But the boy's eyes were glassy, and, at dinner, she didn't like the way he held his fork, his grip limp like that. His forehead felt clammy. But the nodes around his neck didn't seem swollen. Now her hand along the side of his stomach, the way she'd been instructed. She kissed her son on the cheek as if blessing a rosary.

At the ER they did the boy a favor and let him venture out of his little cordoned area long enough to watch, on an elevated television in the corner, a report about that day's negotiations between the players' union and the owners. Handing over the case files to the desk nurse, his mother double-checked to make sure the boy's oncologist had been contacted. The boy's father had answered the message from his service and called the hospital: "Still at the office, leaving now." The boy's mother felt as if she knew something she did not want to know. The television was at a commercial, the report was over; she wheeled her compliant child back into his exam area, where he promptly zoned out. She watched him sleep for a while and headed over to the vending machine for their shitty coffee, and had an awful sensation, a kind of déjà vu. It wasn't so much that the boy's mother remembered all the times during the first go-around when she'd gotten coffee at this shitty vending machine, but *feeling* all of her exhaustion and terror during those months, what it was like to not know what was going to happen. She was already seeing a therapist twice a week. Taking Zoloft to get through the day, Valium to get to sleep. The boy's father had signed a lease on a small apartment two blocks from their home, a sign of his hopes for reconciliation, but also so he could be near in case of emergencies.

The next morning the oncologist performed a spinal tap. Grimly, he confirmed that the boy had come out of remission. The nurse-practitioner and the boy had become close as well—for his seventh birthday, she'd bought him a customized Yankees cap with a pinstriped brim. She teared up at the news. The large soft hands of the boy's father acted as a mitt, encompassing the boy's fingers. Mom rubbed his back. A course of action and treatment was laid out. Survival rates were reiterated. The boy listened with questioning eyes, seemed a bit shocked. He asked if any Yankees were going to visit the ward while he was there, or whether the baseball strike meant they weren't doing any more visits.

The exam room had no windows and nothing to look at and nowhere to go. The doctor was talking about checking him back in to the ward, new rounds of chemo, looking for a donor. His dad was blinking and nodding, staring straight ahead. There wasn't really any other direction, was there? You just had to strap up. He agreed to stay with his son. Later today he was going to take up smoking again. After he finished in midtown and got home to his empty, shitty little apartment, he usually had a beer or two. He told his son that whatever the ward offered they were going to milk the hell out of it. The mom gave him a look that conveyed unhappiness about the language he was using. She was about to head home to pack for a longer stay. (When she leaves the hospital, the mother will raise a hand in the air and flip off God, something she has not done since the last time the boy was ill.) Bring his Strat-O-Matic baseball set, the boy reminded her. He stressed the importance of the blue binder he used to keep the game summaries and statistics for his fantasy season. It should be on his desk but if not, under his bed. Sometimes during their afternoons together the boy and his dad played Strat-O-Matic and the boy made reference to one of their recent contests, in which he'd eked out an extra-inning victory. He asked if his mom could bring his lucky Air Jordans, the 3s.

Reinduction would start as soon as all the tests were done and his Hickman was back in. They'd start searching for a donor ASAP. The boy was pretty jazzed, actually, about being able to go back into the children's ward. His room was brightly painted, the walls luminescent with glow-in-the-dark planets and rockets and shooting stars. The boy wondered if any of his friends were around. He looked at the laminated menu and bit down on his bottom lip and made a long farting sound. Then the boy saw pizza tacos. He said those were new.

The ward may not have been a Ronald McDonald House, where kids were having fantasy wishes granted left and right, but it still housed children with cancer, and it was in New York City. It got more than its share of celebrity visitors. Every week the community service outreach lady and the public relations people brought in someone. Wrestlers Owen and Bret Hart stopped by and put everyone in headlocks. Mark Messier spent an afternoon and got choked up more than once. The boy took all offered hats and T-shirts, had Messier sign a puck with a silver Sharpie. Baseball players commonly visited the ward, the community relations lady promised. Logic held that they needed all the good press they could get, especially seeing how the All-Star Game had just been flushed down the tube. They'd be coming. But the schedule worked out so no baseball player was visiting until the boy's third week in the ward. Even then it was a member of the Mets, the deformed stepbrother of New York City baseball.

The boy turned away from the nurse, refused to get his temperature taken. His father raised his voice. Said this was unacceptable. Buddy. Come on now.

Dwight Gooden may not have been thirty years old, but he was a good half decade removed from the fireball-spewing heroics that had once captivated the city. Though his face was still smooth and bright, around the eyes there was some wear, some sorrow. Although he was known as Dr. K, it had been a while since Doc's last winning season, and the tabloids had taken a special glee in chronicling his most recent string of problems: his suspension for cocaine use, his Nike billboard taken down in Times Square. Doc had untold reasons to bail on his visit. He really didn't *need* to be there. He was wearing a collared cotton shirt that was open at the collar and had a thin band of gold around his neck. His smile was shy. When he spoke—*Hey, man, how you doing?*—it was low and quiet, just a few words. *Hanging in there is pretty good, I think.* He seemed friendly, but also reserved, as if a little embarrassed.

By then the boy was deep into reinduction. He'd lost all his hair. His pulse was weak. There had been complications. The easiest thing for him was to sleep. But he kept himself awake for this, asked Doc to sign his Yankees jersey.

Libertines

ISENSTATT FLASHED THE pointer at her eyes, promised he'd be quick. He made a sound that intoned recognition. "Chemical conjunctivitis. It's pretty much a standard side effect, especially in younger patients."

Alice kept blinking, her expression pained. As soon as the device clicked off, she looked down. She worked to focus, concentrated on that middle floor square, its inner flecked pattern. A single fleck. Feeling more centered, she grabbed for her Versaces.

"Three days," continued the doctor. "Admittedly that's atypical for conjunctivitis." Now Eisenstatt had the voice of a slightly vexed father. "And explain this again: why you didn't call the urgent care center."

The horrid hospital chill, the typical iced air of exam rooms. Once again Alice wrapped herself in the hospital blanket and shut her eyes—as if that would keep out the question.

"She didn't want to have to go back into the hospital." From his corner stool, Oliver blessedly bailed her out.

"Our goal is to get your wife to a transplant," Eisenstatt said. "Not to keep her out of the hospital." Speaking to Alice, he continued. "The marker for whether you call is *very* low."

"It wasn't getting worse," she managed. "Over the phone they told me to come in if it got any worse—"

"It wasn't getting any better, either."

Do you remember that part? She and Oliver searched out each other, his tinted confusion matching how she felt. For not the first time, Alice thought of the doctor via the same name that her husband used: Dickenstein.

"What was the point of going in?" She sighed. "What would you have done?"

"We could have increased your dosage. We could have changed your medicine. We definitely would have checked your eyes. Could have had you take an MRI."

"I certainly hope you'll be as thorough about my hot flashes." She laughed.

"Hot flashes?" Eisenstatt looked at his pad. Boyish lips pursed. "Yeah, we did that to you." He asked an unseen nurse to take a prescription down to the pharmacy once he was done: stronger drops for her eyes. "We're doing a lot to you," he continued. "But good things are happening as well. Your whites have started to come up, point seven. After bottoming out from the chemo, that's an encouraging start."

Eisenstatt continued, rattling off more numbers. Down the list: hemoglobin eleven, platelet count fifteen.

Here his lips pursed, a child considering a fish. "This is something to talk about."

Brightness somehow penetrated her sunglass protection, she felt the room's chill, her blanket itching.

"It's nothing monumental," the doctor assured. "Red counts are always the last to rise. But in our situation, we don't want to wait. These numbers—see here—put you right on the border for a transfusion. The safe answer is to give you plasma today. Fresh blood will shore up your platelets for a while." Eisenstatt asked the nurse to call right now and see about a transfusion, if any slots were available after this consultation.

"They take how long?" Oliver asked.

"A few hours."

"I can call your mom," Oliver said. "We should be fine. And I'll get ahold of Tilda just in case."

Alice reached toward him, a gesture of thanks. He ducked his head, searching through a backpack for that obnoxious brick of a phone.

"If your numbers don't stay up, if your marrow gets to where it's not producing blood, we might start giving you transfusions when you come in for your consultations. This would be every couple of days."

"And I'd be doing this until the transplant?"

Her heart crashing five floors.

Eisenstatt acknowledged her question with quietude, perhaps considering the phrasing of his response. "The U.S. registry hasn't hit any perfect matches yet."

He admitted this, and Alice felt light-headed, and had to grip the railing alongside the bed.

The doctor was firm: "I don't want you to go there." His hands went out in front of him. "We still have plenty of moves to play. There are always new donors. Every day. And we're starting on other possibilities, including whether we can find a donor with enough key matching categories that we might proceed. Until that comes in, blood can get you jump-started, give you the energy we need you to have."

"The hardest part is waiting." This came from some other part of the room. Alice recognized her mincing voice. "But when it happens it all happens very fast."

"Oh, Dr. Bhakti," she said. "I hadn't even realized you were here."

"And rooms on the transplant floor are the best in the hospital," Bhakti assured. "Even better than those private suites up on obstetrics."

With a glance, Alice cut her off. "Thank you, Doctor. You are always a help."

. . .

Returning from the little Indian place on the other side of Sixty-seventh, juggling overloaded bags whose scents were causing havoc with his saliva glands, Oliver was a few yards from his intended elevator bank when he heard a mangled version of his name—called as a question, uncertain in its pronunciation.

It had come from the business office. A woman stood there looking like a preteen girl, only done up to look like a secretary in her school play: hair pulled back. Oversize plastic glasses. Black polka dot blouse, pencil skirt, clompy shoes. Nearing, she struggled with a stack of manila folders that were about to capsize. "I *thought* it was you. Looks like we both got our hands full."

Now he recognized her: Miss Culpepper. She shifted back and forth on her heels. She had a chance to catch something before it slipped out from beneath her elbow, but instead watched the pages spill to the floor. Eyes Oliver often swore to be dead had grown some kind of inner life. Her face—pretty, if naïve—betrayed exhaustion. It took a second for Oliver to realize she was waiting for him to make conversation.

"I was really glad to see you all got that insurance problem handled," she said. "Make sure you give my best— Tell Alice my prayers are with her."

Adjacent to the mighty Connecticut River, nestled near the picturesque joining point of Vermont, New Hampshire, and Massachusetts, downtown Brattleboro was full of handsome old brick: a food co-op, gourmet coffee, old-town diners, and high-end bistros. It had head shops and tattoo parlors, as well as a number of bookstores (both new and used), furniture stores (antiques mostly), video and record shops, a classic art deco hotel and adjacent theater that showed new releases and hosted community theater. Former academics gravitated for retirement; college-educated, white-collar hippies found the town a safe place to raise kids. It was civilized without being urban, rural without being *too* rural, a hub where burnouts and townies and foodies and barbecue aficionados could coexist with old-time country folk and ski bums, and everyone tolerated the healthy flow of weekend warriors: the leaf watchers and motorcycle-riding types.

It was ideal backdrop scenery for a precocious teenager: rehearsing for her high school drama productions and pulling all-nighters so she was ready for the rhetoric sectionals; replicating the best styles and patterns from classic movies and fashion magazines, studying their cooler cousins, *Paper* and *Interview,* for missives from Manhattan's downtown scene.

When Alice looked back, she remembered adolescence as a string of nights twisting herself with longing into a phone cord as she spoke in hushed tones to a best friend, yakking deep into the cold night about boys who barely knew she was alive. It had been endless drives down back roads with the leaves turning above her while Alice and her clique lit clove cigarettes, ate magic mushrooms, and adjusted the dial to get reception on the nearby college's radio station. Alice relished those sun-dappled summer afternoons at swimming holes, rubbing high-SPF lotions on herself and lying out on rocks high above the falls. She remembered the winter storms she'd survived by holing up with a Ouija board and a stolen bottle of Mom's sauvignon, steering her dead father toward one absurd question after another: *Do you miss me? How hot is it down there?*

How many daddy figures had she chased—in books, in movies? How many corner booths in ethnic and world restaurants had she appropriated, she and the rest of that self-proclaimed deadbeat club of friends, cherishing every townie's glance at her blue hair, their secondhand ensembles? On prom night she'd sat on the steps of the city hall and passed a bottle back and forth and watched the sun rise over the mountains, her head firmly lodged on her best friend's shoulder. From a few trips a year to real cities, Toronto, Boston, Manhattan, she'd gotten enough sophistication—what she'd thought of as sophistication—to realize, *totally,* she needed more.

When she arrived in Manhattan for college, she gravitated—inevitably, insistently—toward the East Village, the concentric circles of its colliding worlds. She trolled art gallery openings for free liquor, bluffing and nodding her way through conversations about the pieces; she missed a friend's horrid band when they finally made their drunken, two-in-the-morning CBGB debut, instead occupying the abattoir that passed as that club's bathroom, doing a bump off the end of an apartment key held by a lanky boy with perfectly feathered hair. The status quo: flailing to hold a pose at Integral Yoga; struggling to keep the beat to live drummers at a Saturday afternoon Afro-Brazilian dance class; grinding her hips all night at Pyramid, or Save the Robots, or Area, or Limelight; scraping together, in change, at three in the morning, the five dollars necessary for one of Yaffa's sunshine veggie burgers ("side of quinoa thanks"). One New Year's Day, green-gilled and still hungover, she'd sat for hours, until she seriously could not feel her ass, atop one of the side-row pews in St. Mark's in-the-Bowery, watching the Poetry Project's marathon fundraiser with her gay friend, and had gotten what she'd waited for: Jim Carroll, mop-headed and junkie-thin (just how you wanted him to be), had read a short story, and, after him, downtown goddess Patti Smith had scratched out a gravelly, goddessy chant of a song, and then, to top it off, a wonderfully round and cheery Allen Ginsberg had ambled up and, to the holy hush of the packed, breathless church, read a half-assed, dashed-off excuse for a poem. Afterward, in the church's back room, she'd felt privileged and joyous when Ginsberg had slicked down his famous bushy eyebrows and—showing far more grace and charm and effort than he had onstage—unabashedly hit on her friend.

Discovering just who you were, refining who you wanted to be, choosing to root that life below Fourteenth, on streets free of franchises, amid a small teeming outpost that stood against the white-bread homogeneity that Reaganism kept jamming down your throat; for Alice, this included an added bonus: sightings—all of the other spectacular one-of-a-kind freaks; club kids coming back from a bodega with some veggie juice while in full night-crawling regalia (hair conically spiked, faces shining with glitter, wearing only high-heeled combat boots and newspaper-made bikinis); dreadlocked girls in geisha robes and corsets of body latex busily hauling bongos from rehearsal. That so many others were making their own explorations—grabbing, discarding, combining, without any kind of map, purposefully throwing away all instructions— excited her. So Alice hosted sushi-rolling parties where her girl-friends chanted rap lyrics; she attended seminars on Transcendental Meditation, staffed a tent that did free Wigstock touch-ups and fixes. Between slurps of borscht from the all-night Polish diner, Alice argued about foreign film with modern dancers, volunteered to sew the costumes for underground theater troupes who had no choice but to be unwatchable. She let herself be drawn in the nude, photographed in bondage gear, doing it for friends, for love, for art, for the hell of it; yes, even that de rigueur, eyeball-bleeding stretch where she fell under the seductive spell of the death of the author. And still kept winding herself in phone cords, despite her hang-overs and cotton mouth, trying always to get to the other side of yet another cute, selfish, shitty, unreliable boy. She studied her patterns and color schemes, made skirts gratis for friends, haggled for a sec-ondhand mannequin at the Chelsea Flea Market, used the flimsy dummy to model outfits that she re-created from film stills. She cried and delivered food, both for and with God's Love, marched and chanted and raged against the police protest barriers with other ACT UP protesters until her hands were frozen and her throat was raw. Alice mourned the gorgeous lanky boy Ginsberg had hit on. She celebrated the man he had been. She was a woman now, indulging, absorbing, borrowing, embracing, pushing against, piecing together.

Now she was here. The fourth floor's rectangular maze funneled to a dimmed back area. Half-submerged in a worn comfy chair, swimming inside her pink ski hat and punkish sunglasses and pink fuzzy robe, Alice looked like alternative rock royalty, sullen, a bass-playing legend nodded out in her dressing room. A swollen baggie hovered over her, its catsup-thick plasma dripping into her veins. When she saw Oliver pulling at the blue separating curtain, her dormant form animated, a corner of her mouth rising. The arm that was not hooked up welcomed—a weak floppy wave that turned into request, as she reached for the Styrofoam cup.

"You have it," she managed. "Goodie."

Mango lassi. Sweet and thick and bubbling with foam, that tangy kick to cap its smoothness. How many times had she ordered it over the years? She couldn't estimate. You don't keep track. You sip, taste, feel its kick, appreciate, sip again.

Now a protracted sip left a thin, fizzy mustache. She leaned back into the chair, made a contented sound. Oliver pulled out a Styrofoam container, unveiled some sort of black lentil tandoori mess. He kissed her on the cheek, reported how amazing the puree smelled. After she did her damage, he told her he was going to devour the rest. He plopped down his can of soda, her bottles of water; he started ripping open plasticware.

He was about midway through a just-savory-enough chicken tikka when a voice pretended to knock on the curtain. Eisenstatt ducked sideways, entering almost in segments, slicked coif and head and neck not moving, torso lurching. The doctor took in the food. "That really smells good."

"Would you like some?" Alice dipped an untouched piece of naan into her sauce. "Or are we in trouble again?"

Eisenstatt stared down at the offered flatbread. His expression contained amusement. "I came by to see how everything was going. Also to chat about parts of your treatment. Having said this, you're right. I'm not pleased to see what you're eating."

"They knew I was going to lunch." Oliver gestured toward the hallway. "I asked if it was okay to bring food back. I talked to the nurse."

"She may have figured you meant the cafeteria."

Alice slurped her straw, purposefully drawing out the sound. "I'm just a sick and weak, blind invalid. But I'm confused, Doctor. Why would anyone choose of their own volition to eat at the hospital cafeteria?"

Eisenstatt refused to give. "My concern is how well cooked the restaurant food might be, and what would come of that."

"Oh, I can see you think we're daft." Humor provided energy; she rode its charge, shifting into Fashion Voice: *"Spend your weekend at the urgent care center when you could stay home? Procure food from somewhere besides our lovely hospital cafeteria?"* Alice lifted the Styrofoam cup, an imaginary toast. "We're just a couple of bon vivants. Libertines, is what they call us."

"If I didn't give a fuck about her well-being," Oliver said, "I *would* have gotten food from the cafeteria."

"Yes. Very entertaining, as always. But you know the deal: eating has been a problem. We have concerns about your nutrition. Your husband has been asking whether an endoscopy can diagnose if there's a problem in your stomach."

"Another whodunit for you to solve," Alice said, bone dry. "Hurrah."

"The way this hospital works." Eisenstatt again refused the bait; his voice and manners remained restrained, even as he gripped the table ledge behind him. "An endoscopy gets scheduled six months in advance. *Then* your doctor calls and makes an official request to move it, and it gets moved to the same week. We are talking about a serious procedure. If endoscopies were innocuous, I'd say let's try it. All I am asking: watch what you eat. Please. I'm also writing you a refill for Cthulesta."

From behind a curtain somebody was laughing at his own joke. A loudspeaker crackled, went silent.

"Cthulesta," Oliver repeated. "Again?"

"Same routine. Take the nightly shot with a fatty meal. The fat allows the medicine to get digested and be absorbed. With any luck we'll spur some white blood cell growth, increase production of your neutrophils, decrease odds of fungal infection—all good stuff."

"Ginseng is an antifungal preventative," Alice said.

"I don't know if you knew this," Oliver said, rubbing his chin, looking down, "but after her first consolidation, the bill for that same prescription was five grand. Our plan only covered fifty percent. Of course insurance denied the claim."

"Didn't we submit a form?" Eisenstatt asked.

"After I called two times. Then you got the payment codes backward."

"With a little luck, this will keep you out of the hospital," Eisenstatt answered. "That's what you want. It's what I want."

"But you said my numbers are going up? I'm doing so well? Maybe I don't need it?"

Leaning against the wall behind him, the doctor crossed his right leg in front of his left, putting himself in an odd position, especially considering the man's bulk. Now he tapped his pen against his opposite arm's lab jacket sleeve, watching the flick and rebound. In certain moments, he seemed young, reminding Alice of an alone child.

"Logically, what you're saying is reasonable," he began. "A normal person recovering conceivably would not be at risk. But it's normally not someone walking down the street who's battling leukemia and is likely to get a fungal infection. When you're neutropenic, or coming out of this state, it's comparatively common to have fungal pneumonia as a side effect."

Oliver waited for the doctor to finish, raised his hand. "When we went into the emergency room that first time, Alice"—he hesitated—"they diagnosed you with pneumonia. Could that have been—"

"We don't know that it was fungal pneumonia," she said.

"Do we know it wasn't?"

"That's how every single thing is going to be from now on?" Alice's voice simmered, but did not boil. "We can't say anything with certainty, but you should still do every single thing we tell you? Then afterward, you hand me a business card, tell me to go wait in the corner like a good little girl. I still die, but this way I die knowing I did everything I was supposed to?"

Finishing, she exhaled and looked down, inward, and if there was a bit of smugness to her—as if she did not need their responses, was not interested in their answers—then there was also satisfaction: a woman who had answers of her own.

The end of print party

D URING JUNIOR YEAR, a professor turned mentor needed help on some sample pieces. She made a simple request after class, and invited Alice to join that proud lineage of Competent Students More Than Eager to Be Worked to the Bone. It was a new world for her, and during those first weeks, as she hunched over a design table in an immaculate Chelsea studio, Alice felt as if she'd been given keys to a special castle wing, heretofore off-limits, that she'd long dreamed of entering. Soon enough, however, she learned that these keys opened doors to oddly quiet rooms, where her weekends would pass, working back-to-back ten-hour days, all but chained to those designing tables and sewing machines. Still, her temp gig evolved, becoming a full-fledged apprenticeship. Alice fleshed out lines for struggling and overextended houses. She figured out the logistics of a knockoff version of a trendy pantsuit that *everyone* needed. She learned to find the poetry in silhouettes and lines and draped patterns. For her efforts, she received next to nothing—though the day rate, to a twenty-year-old, seemed as extravagant as those gilded buildings alongside Central Park West.

But the way her industry worked was a lot like the city itself: either you owned or you kept renting; either you moved up the food chain—impressing a creative director, getting a shot as a designer yourself, gathering commissions and backers and starting your own line—or you hit your apex and started down the other side. The assignments stacked up, and at some point in between all those deli salads, Alice turned twenty-seven. Her love of clothing and fashion was no longer so glowy, her creative energies too often felt summoned from her body like those last bits of toothpaste, rolled from the tube. She was still working the same brutal hours for that same day rate. It no longer felt glamorous. She still didn't have any insurance or benefits, still felt herself sprinting to keep from being crushed beneath the hamster wheel of city life. All the while, over her shoulder, in her rearview, newly hatched and eager former hers kept coming, more than ready to push the present her aside. Alice found herself feeling a nostalgic closeness toward her mother. Passing any child opened an ache in the pit of her stomach.

Coming off a string of first dates so astonishingly banal they weren't even worth relaying to friends, she was working some freelance job or another, taking smoking breaks with Kira, a youngish, also-going-nowhere designer from Milan. There hadn't been any reason *not* to bond, not to drink together after work. Sometimes this meant spending time with Kira's friends—journalists from Uzbekistan with disdainful sneers, grad students from Paris who enjoyed dancing around the highest flames of their parents' stacks of burning money. Kira invited Alice to a "kind of theme party." She couldn't quite articulate the theme, but that hardly mattered. Tilda was supposed to be Alice's sidekick, but at the last minute booked extra work on some kind of slasher flick. If Alice wasn't turning cartwheels about going alone, she figured that if pretentious expats were good for anything, it would be a house party.

She was rocking a pixie cut at the time, her dirty blond hair a swirling patchwork ragbag, all firehouse streaks and lollipop highlights, a look she liked to think of as both psychedelic and elfin. That fall was slow in arriving, caught in that amalgam stretch where walking in the shade caused chilliness, but the bright sky was warm enough for a girl to get away with her favorite sleeveless black sweater—especially if she'd inlaid its scooping collar with ceramic pears and strawberries. Alice had run with her instincts, piling her neck with junk necklaces: beads sized like lug nuts and elephant eyes. The common complaint of friends was that she tried too hard, made her tastes too obvious. Why not make it work for her? She put on a few mobster pinkie rings, squeezed on a pair of velvet pants of fairy-tale purple. Giving herself her final once-over examination in the full-length, she saw the shiny fabric hugging her tush and thighs in a way that, huzzah huzzah, did not make her want to vomit. The curved ingress of her skin, robust and pure, flashed in that space just beneath the bottom of her sweater.

Kira's handwriting had been perfect as a polite child's, and Alice followed her directions to an almost inhabitable stretch of Williamsburg, civilization only in the sense that it boasted its own twenty-four-hour deli. After she'd been buzzed in to the Uzbek funeral home, but before entering the mourners' lobby, Alice took the instructed hard left and entered a long rectangular room, the first section of what would show itself to be a railroad flat.

Maybe ten people standing around, fig-leaf groups, their buzzing energetic, even hopeful. The only illumination was across the otherwise dark room, a blue glow from a pair of large terminal consoles—the types of screens you consulted in airports to find out whether you were going to make a connecting flight. Near the consoles, people were leaning over, writing. Soon it became apparent that to head into the railroad flat's larger living space—where the real party was under way—you needed some sort of name tag. Maybe that was what people were writing? Alice started searching for a sticker when Kira shouted her name, and rushed over with her flatmate, a louche woman whose name Alice never remembered.

House music drifted in from the other room, the real party.

Someone was showing his friends a name tag, receiving a scrum of laughter or applause. Though Alice was a bit intimidated by them, both women looked genuinely happy to see her: Kira's arms opening for a big hug, the French woman following up, swooping in with an air kiss.

Maybe it was simple relief: Alice knew someone here. Maybe it was receiving any shred of kindness. But likely there was something else. These weren't her best friends, but their openness made her glad to be here, glad to see them.

In the voice of a Vichy collaborator, the louche woman turned, shouting an order to someone: *"Oh, do her. You must."*

Alice saw a stout man responding, approaching dutifully. Trailing behind him, not looking happy at all to be there, was another boy.

"You have a name tag?" Kira asked her. "If you're not into doing the code, it's fine. Just write a number."

Before Alice had time to ask what she meant, Kira and the louche girl and the first guy were bantering in French, back and forth at a speed that Alice's broken command of the language couldn't follow.

"They're supposed to ask if you want to learn to write your name in code."

The other one. A bush of brown curly hair. He continued, "That's the grand theme."

"You mean an even better theme than keeping all the alcohol in the back room until your guests fill out applications?"

He took her in, seeming surprised by her wit. Eyes with an intense depth calculated, and their math added up to losing a fight against his oncoming smile. Now he sidled next to her. Digging through his pocket, he pulled out a ballpoint. "Enjoy. Don't let me keep you."

A cursory search discovered there weren't any nearby stickers or name tags to write on. But what Alice did turn up was equally interesting: the counter was covered with pages of textbooks, novels, paperback romances, different book sizes, crazy languages. They'd been lacquered, shellacked, or maybe varnished. Alice showed this to her new compadre. He refused to be amused.

"Oh, give it up," she goaded.

Running her hand over the counter, she felt roughness, bumps, creased edges, different layers of hardened paper. "Don't they look like musty relics? All just found in Granddad's library. I think the reflection of screen glow's an especially nice touch."

"That's kind of the idea, right?"

Alice followed his lead, looked through the jumbled bodies, saw the large font, scrolling wide letters: RINT PARTY END OF PRINT PARTY END . . .

She didn't get its meaning; meanwhile the boy had started talking again, but in a new way, faster and more invested—as if Alice had met some kind of standard, one that released his internal spigot. Alice wondered if he was going to provide his name. Unlike everyone in the fashion world, Bushytop definitely gave off a hetero vibe, and was not in any way *un*cute.

He was apologizing, saying this whole thing was his fault, in a way. His buddy Ruggles—the dapper asshole with his arm around that French harpy—had been on him to take a break from work and school. Dragged him to some poker night with the Expats. Which, honestly, had been a trip: great smells from the pots atop the stove distracting you from your middling hands; different spendy crackers and good cheese making the rounds; more than a few glasses of a nice red to boot. Seven-card stud was the game, but with showers of wild cards, crazy amounts, like where you passed the second and fourth cards of your hand to the immediate right. During one of the snack breaks, he'd answered a question about what one in graduate school for computer science *did*.

Alice looked doubtful, but encouraged him to go on.

The boy answered the Expats with an explanation of virtual realities, the possibility of creating—inside one's computer—a reality and life and system that you kind of *lived*, but simultaneously, along with your life in the outside world. Oliver told Alice this virtual life could *also* be three-dimensional, meaning it would include commerce, entertainment, and sex, of course. A complete parallel reality. Or at least a supplementary one. "Like, it can filter into the real one. You'd start to pay your bills through computers, who knows, even go shopping on them—"

"I could certainly do without salespeople." Alice laughed. "But buying a dress without seeing it on?" Her eyes rolled. "Let me know how that turns out for you."

"Right." He looked chagrined. "The thing, nobody knows what they'll come up with. But it *is* going to become more ingrained. And what I do—"

"That's the coding?" Alice asked.

"Yeah."

"Meaning you what?"

"Okay, so, if you want the computer to do the shit we're talking about, you better be able to communicate with it, right? So think of the codes as languages. English. Urdu. I was telling your friends here, there's not even a question that speaking these languages, having conversations where you can direct the computer and create the programs it runs, it's more important to our future than anything on some fucking page." He waited. "Yeah. Your buddies bought it as much as you. So much they decided, *Hey, why not celebrate the end of the written word?*"

His arms opened up, toward the rest of the room. "This is their celebration. A bunch of papers with codes are floating around. I guess you write out your name. On the key, each letter corresponds to a number. So you can convert your name to BASIC, binaries. Then you're supposed to go around the party, introducing yourself to everyone with your code. Since it's my bright idea, I'm kinda obligated to be here."

New papers had been brought out onto the counters. Alice grabbed one, bounced a bit in place. She read the code keys, thought for a second.

Immaculate, scripted capital letters followed:

ONE.

The invention of fire

TODAY'S AIR-PUFFED MANILA envelopes included one state-of-the-art multimedia magazine from a group of upstart culture peddlers, and two samplers with the first level of a different three-dimensional role player game. Each mailer represented millions of lines of code—written over months, perhaps years—burnt onto compact discs, and sent out by other hungry young programmers with ambition and dreams and hustle to spare. It was a little depressing, when Oliver thought of it. So Oliver didn't. He separated the mailers from Alice's fashion glossies, ignored whatever subscription cards fell loose.

The hidden, smaller envelopes were where the action was. Hospital billing departments sent out statements starting on the twentieth, he knew. Usually the queasy feeling began in his stomach around the twenty-third, kicking up a few notches whenever he got near the mailbox. Especially dreadful was the sight of an official-looking, sky-blue envelope, stuffed fat with pages of billing procedures. Today had none of those. The only hospital bill was a thin envelope, even lighter blue, a type he'd grown accustomed to. This one contained a short payment request: seven hundred dollars, for Alice's visit of April 11. Across the page, red letters warned: if this amount remained unpaid, the balance would be forwarded to a collection agency.

Oliver paid minimal attention, sorted through today's avalanche of communications from the insurance companies. Among them, the monthly statement for April; a small packet listing procedures that had been covered for the April 11 visit; some one-page quickies explaining why certain payments for the April 11 visit had been adjusted upward, thereby reducing Oliver's responsibility; some other quickies explaining why certain payments for the April 11 hospital visit had been reduced, thereby increasing his responsibility. . . .

And a new thing. This envelope lemon yellow. The same shade as the florist's business card. Oliver's knees went weak.

But no. It was just from some medical place he didn't recognize.

Entering the apartment, the first thing he saw was that Doe had applesauce all over her face and her bib. She'd turned her tray into a giant shining swamp. Her bright eyes gleamed; she smiled big and wide at Daddy, rocking back and forth in her high chair, then doing little jumps, and Oliver's fury abated, a tad. He was about to shout *hello hello,* the way his father always used to. But the kid started making an even *bigger* mess now, flinging *more* applesauce.

Next to the high chair, globs dripping off her curls, Alice's mother looked exhausted and miserable. Someone else was there as well, someone new: brunette, young, Oliver didn't recognize her.

"This is Samantha," Alice's mom said, trying to sound pleasant. "She'll be helping after I head back."

Not bad looking: severe bangs, a nose maybe a bit too long, but eager eyes, a well-meaning smile. She held a spoon and the tin. Her efforts had also been rewarded with applesauce: her chin, hands, sleeves coated in it.

Oliver welcomed the girl into his home, but his smile felt odd, and he knew it must have looked halfhearted, and he needed to move, forward, respectfully, but still hurrying, that crumpled letter dangling from his hand.

. . .

Comforting chimes and wind instruments—soft harmonic sounds came from the other side of the bedroom door, and this irritated him. He pushed in, ready for the usual deal: low lights, a few votive candles along the sill. But not this whole scene: Tilda on the yoga mat, in a beige leotard and caramel-colored sweatpants—kneeling on one knee, reaching upward with both hands, toward the sky. Skin was everywhere exposed, flushed and clammy, and the image brought to mind some ancient wildebeest, heaving and covered with morning dew.

Beyond her, Oliver saw his wife dangling off the bed's front corner. Wearing her shades, Alice had one of his baseball caps on backward. She was working to keep her arms raised, as if trying to signal a touchdown. She'd gotten both hands above her shoulders, but her elbows were bent, her biceps trembling.

"Seven," Sparrow said.

From the front of the bed the healer kept modeling a perfect warrior pose. "Breathe. Keep holding it. And exhale. Okay, eight . . ."

Now Oliver became aware of an aroma, familiar, certainly not incense. Did he really want to believe they were in here baked, doing yoga?

"Remember how that goddamn ER doc wouldn't let you go with me?" He couldn't wait any longer. "Well, get your clown shoes on and join the circus."

Alice remained focused, mouth rigid with concentration.

"Your policy didn't cover the ambulance ride. Just got the bill. Guess how much."

She held her pose. Exhaled.

"Twelve hundred dollars. Clown shoes, right?"

The lenses of her sunglasses black, blank.

"I mean, in the large scheme it's nothing. Only you'd think—"

"I can't worry about that right now."

"—the sheer balls—"

"Oliver," she said.

Don't overreact, he reminded himself, though his face was hot. *Sure.* Let them invade every room. Let them have their rituals, their clucking *empathy.* He retreated from the new age coffee klatch, their baked stares of disapproval. Storming past Alice's mom, he registered the concern in her expression. Oliver surged with the desire to bark her away, rid himself of all these goddamn women.

Out of the apartment, he jabbed at the button, bounced on his feet, and punched his hands in his coat pockets, discovering that he was constitutionally unable to stay in this hallway for the thirty seconds it would take that rickety *bitch* elevator to creak up.

The Brow was in the other office, in front of his terminal, shoulders hunched forward, neck jutting. From behind he looked like a shaggy, concentrating turtle.

Had to be a good sign. Maybe even a breakthrough.

Oliver started toward the closest terminal. Low sounds met him. The stanza was rhythmic, short, and muddled—a series of low chords repeating in a manner both monotonous and propulsive. White conical speakers, each located on a side of the terminal screen, further muddled the sound. Still, Oliver recognized that short finger-tapping riff—straight from the eighties with its cheese factor.

And on the monitor, visible around the Brow's body, that abandoned space station—its industrial background, its darkened caverns—was every bit as familiar.

Angles went jittery, red orbs flying past and lighting up the screen.

That goddamn centered hand, returning Taser rounds of fire.

"Enough with fucking Doomguy," Oliver said.

He asked the Brow to email him files of the previous day's work. It wasn't a request.

He withdrew from his pocket the small pad that served as the repository for his scribbled coding changes—each note purposeful, just two or three keywords, as few symbols and numbers as possible, the hope being that concision would engage him, force his mind to re-create the bulk of his old work, trampoline him into a strong workday.

He learned nobody had called from the house.

He lay lengthwise on the couch, unfolded his laptop.

Of course it was a given Alice shouldn't be dealing with money stuff—he was completely wrong to even bring it up. But was he supposed to just stuff every concern inside him? He takes care of her and she gets to decide his worries are of no concern? Meanwhile, if she's always crying how that kid's so important, then why is some nobody shoving applesauce down Doe's yap while Mommy's getting high in the drum circle?

He grabbed a soda from the fridge, paced the office, unscrambled his headphone cord.

In the notebook, besides his scribbled notations and ideas, were pages of columns: the costs of the taxis he and Alice took to and from hospitals on appointment days, untold amounts of money that had been set on fire. Plus totals for however much they still owed New Hampshire. And were still trying to get a final tally on the out-of-network costs from the old policy at Whitman. Two grand a month going up in smoke for the new family policy. Another six hundred for rent on the new office. In addition to his regular monthly nut. And the fifteen an hour he was paying that idiot to play videogames. Plus a hundred a session, plus expenses, for that fucking healer. Whatever that tight little tush of a nanny was going to pull, also full-time.

Then again, more than a few friends owed six figures from college and grad school.

And pretty much the whole goddamn nation lived with debt, no?

They'd find a way. The immediate answer was to get Generii to market.

. . .

More than a few afternoons he'd moseyed past those workrooms. Cavernous spaces, usually, with naked lightbulbs hanging from overhead wires, minimalist style to the desks and lamps. Alice was inevitably working on some garment, her hair messy and in a scrunchie, that lovely mouth holding a swatch of pinned fabric. Even in splattered designing overalls and a little tee beneath, she'd look astonishing, good enough that deliverymen and sales reps would hang around, searching for excuses to chat her up. But whenever a member of the species *Modelus dramaticus* arrived—for a fitting; for a shoot; to get sized, pinned, or altered; to drop off whatever garment needed to be returned—their ethereal natures were obvious, as was their growing cynicism, blasé attitudes acting as both protective wall and mask. Every bit as apparent to Oliver were Alice's earthbound and worldly curves, her face's open nature. Oliver not only found humor but took joy in how little Alice cared for the implicit pecking order between freelancer and model, whether it was Alice volunteering her thoughts about the lines of a dress she was hemming while one of the swans lingered around her table, or asking about the mass-market paperback that happened to be peeking out of some teen's three-thousand-dollar shoulder bag, or complimenting the ballet flats this girl was wearing around town. Oliver would watch her engage with and draw out these children, and the difference between her—this almost-plump, thoroughly decent woman—and those spoiled, fawnlike babies made him swell. He felt a clumsy pride, being the guy who was dating her, the man whom *she* chose to hang around, whom she undressed with and shuddered for and collapsed on and then looked at with such intimate wonder, that intense purity.

Her affection elevated him as well, turned him toward those better angels. Through the power of her smile, he became less confrontational toward others. Enabled by the faith of Alice's goodwill, he was able to make small talk at a social event. Oliver still could jam his foot into his mouth; he still had a propensity for saying the exact wrong thing. At least now he would be aware; now he'd apologize. And the more time he spent with Alice, the more Oliver realized he needed to up his game even further. Become that much more attentive to personal grooming. Be solicitous toward others. At least pretend to be attuned to the world and culture at large. If he wanted to keep this amazing woman looking at him like that, to somehow make this luminous creature *his,* he had to become kinder.

It would be the greatest trick of all time.

Twilight was spreading its desultory magic as he crossed West Tenth. Grayness and barrenness everywhere, just too much; he wished someone would unleash a high-pressure hose, blasting away the neighborhood's grime and brokenness. How had this shithole seduced him? How much emotional capital had he invested, convincing Alice this was the best place for them? All the money and sweat he'd devoted to being here. *Here?*

Oliver's head swiveled; he checked in each direction. Any asshole lurking in those side streets? All that turned up were a pair of undernourished teenagers spraying complicated graffiti onto the side of an eighteen-wheeler. Their jokes did not pause when Oliver passed, and this furthered his rage, his body knifing through air that was unseasonably sticky.

Maybe halfway down crumpled and forsaken Gansevoort, a distinguished couple emerged from a small saloon. Possibly they'd visited the son they were supporting at the bar where he worked part-time. Holding hands, they walked toward the lone working streetlamp, underneath which, it was apparent, the front headlights of their Cadillac had been destroyed, its bumper half-hanging. The aged man stomped his right foot in place. His wife looked at him in horror, said his name out loud. As if on cue, a police car approached, slowed, cruised onward.

Oliver didn't know where he was going, had no specific purpose. Maybe he'd head for the comfy nooks and cramped sidewalks of the West Village, lose himself gazing through the windows of tasteful boutiques where doctors purchased brocaded knickknacks for mistresses.

But if he was to survive this next half hour, he had to get away from the stench. The frozen death.

He smelled the smoky aroma of roasting peanuts from across the street. He could see the vendor scoping the teenybopper bridge-and-tunnel girls coming out of the PATH station, passing the minutes until he could push his cart toward its nightly storage facility.

On the side of a bus stop a poster showed a black woman adorned in a headdress, dashiki, and multicolored earth-tone pattern, looking so stereotypically African it almost hurt the soul. She offered relief, 900-737-3225, the Psychic Friends Network, $3.89 a minute.

Muscled young men in T-shirts from a corporate basketball league were tossing a basketball and quoting hip-hop lyrics. Coming from the opposite direction, an elderly woman wrapped her basset hound's shit in a plastic bag.

Oliver let himself be distracted by all this: classical white American southern Protestants and preening goths and carefully put together burnouts, all of them without any awareness other than their own concerns. A particularly civilized and gorgeous and sophisticated couple caught his eye. They sauntered at a leisurely pace, motioned toward one another with their hands, made warmly funny comments. Their subject? Where to go for dinner.

Oliver marveled. Like he was witnessing the invention of fire.

He was heading back home when he noticed two women exiting a discount wig shop. Minuscule skirts and long legs, shapely in fishnets, made them impossible to ignore. One woman was pulling at the other's plastic bag. The second was slapping back, laughing, telling her not to play.

"What you looking at? Oh, it's sweet hubby." A smack of gum. "Hey there, sweet hubby."

The second one joined in. "Yo, sugar." Her Adam's apple throbbed.

"Oh," said Oliver. "*Oh.*"

"Don't act like you ain't know."

"Hey, Donette—" Oliver said. "Michelle."

"Yeah, I know you seen this good stuff, baby." Extending the gum from her mouth, the first teased out a long slick line, sucked it back in. "How that lovely wife of yours holding up?"

What could he say? What was there to say?

There was this to say

"I LOVE YOU MORE than life."

Oliver watched her compose herself: cap off, sunglasses off. Bare head. Her eyebrows gone so that the ridge of her forehead was apparent, patches of dried skin patterned like small scallops at her nearest temple. She was wincing, etched grooves at the corners of her eyes, gunky and glistening, lashes fluttering.

Still she focused across the room, finding the camera.

"Your birth was without a doubt the greatest thing I've experienced," she continued. "I'm so grateful I had support: my doula, Oliver, all my friends. They allowed me to go without any pain meds. I'm so grateful. I was lucky enough to receive the gift of feeling you exit my body. That sound and feeling, *lump, thump, bump*." She laughed. "I thought it would go on forever. There was *so much* baby. So much of you."

Her hand rose, long fingers caressing her cheek. Alice's voice was winsome. "Seeing your face for the first time, that was the single best moment of my life. Finding out you were a girl . . . I fell so deeply in love. . . . I couldn't sleep that night, after you were born. . . . I just kept marveling at you, holding you."

It seemed she might cry. Instead she said, "I am so blessed to have had that experience."

Her concentration broke, and she emerged from what might

have been a trance, bald head gradually rising. Looking reedish and mystic, she spent a moment taking in the chaos around her on the bed: note cards scattered atop the throw quilt's ragged panels, a small brass statue—some kind of mutant elephant—knocked on its side. Directly in front of the covered lumps that had to be her legs, a yellow pad with bullet points was propped on a throw pillow.

"I had an order to what I wanted to say," she thought out loud. "But I don't think, what feels organic—"

"You're doing fine," Sparrow replied, without looking up from the viewfinder, the video camera mounted on a tripod.

Alice covered her eyes with a cupped hand, checked with Tilda.

"What you said was beautiful." Her voice came from behind the light source. "Go on, honey."

She understood, looked at nothing, inward perhaps—opening a drawer in her mental desk, peering at its contents. Eyelids lowered, stayed shut. Now a thin smile widened her lips, chapped and blistered.

"When you are asleep, my Doe dear, I watch how trusting you are. I just bask in your breathing, that face I love more than life, that face that is life to me, it's . . . it . . ." Alice sniffed, crinkled her nose. Lids opened onto black diamonds, wet and sparkling. "It means so much to me." She directed her attention toward the camera now.

"Since falling ill, I have kissed you so many times. I have always known that the moment would come when I can't kiss you anymore. If I look for too long it becomes impossible to appreciate the sight of you. I can't enjoy the moment. But, my dear sweet girl, please know what I am saying. The pain of your face is not your face, just the fact I have to be away from it."

From the doorwell, not meant for the world's ears: "*Jesus.*"

Oliver, exhausted and shabby, arms folded across his chest. His eyes were soft and open, his cheeks still ruddy from the cold air. He felt at once stunned, touched, and horrified.

"You weren't supposed to see."

Her eyes red—more hashish? Crying?

"Isn't giving up, isn't this the opposite of what we should be doing?"

"I thought this might be the right time."

"Believe me, it's not like I'm in love with that hospital. But lots of smart people are devoting their lives to fighting this horrible shit and helping you get better—"

"I can't eat. I can barely see. We don't have a donor. What should I be doing?"

The bedroom blinds had been raised, presumably to give them light while filming, but night had taken over, spreading shadows through the room's edges. Out of the window the elevated railroad tracks were blackened husks.

A new voice interrupted: "She's not giving up."

Sparrow had uprighted herself, was placing herself between Oliver and his wife. "I've been meaning to tell you," she told Alice, "I asked about Siddhartha leaving his wife to become Buddha."

"Right, your treatments," Oliver said. "You have a history of amazing results. That's what I've heard?"

"Come on already," Tilda said, off to the side.

"Why—" Alice complained.

"I get it," he cut them off. "I just want to learn. *Really.*" To Sparrow: "Your treatments have cured cancer?"

"I've had successes."

"You've put people in remission?"

"At the ashram we've—"

"And where's this ashram at?"

"Western Massachusetts, just north of the Berkshires."

"And in that ashram just north of the Berkshires, you cured how many people of cancer?"

"Oliver, this is not the place or time—"

"I'm a big girl, Alice."

Sparrow remained fixed on him, that weirdly intense gaze of hers, holding him, searching out his vulnerability. For an instant, Oliver felt himself drawn in, buckling, wanting to trust her. And it was in that moment—as he felt himself waver—that Sparrow unleashed her smile. The kindness bloomed in her voice: "With care and help and the proper meditation and chanting, we've been blessed with a ninety-five percent success rate. And before you ask, more than half of those who come with us *do* stay in remission."

"Ninety-five percent? Wow. From yoga and herbal packets?"

"There is science beyond Western science. Coffee enemas purify a bloodstream. Broccoli and other fresh, steamed greens—"

"Really impressive. *Really.* But here's what I'm curious about. If ninety-five percent of the cancer patients you gave broccoli enemas went into remission, why aren't you on the *Today* show? Why aren't you consulting with doctors everywhere?"

Oliver paused long enough for the point to impact. "This disease is the worst fucking scourge in history," he continued. "The single *worst*. At Whitman, they capture cells at the fucking moment they split, so they can learn whether the new cells are *potentially* cancerous. You're telling me the medical-industrial complex can't figure out if something inside *broccoli* might contain a cure? Come on. Pfizer'd have fucking stormtroopers marching through that ashram. They'd be rushing those packets through clinical trials like shit through a chicken, monetizing like *fuck*."

Oliver's stare challenged. But rather than meet her eyes this time, he looked slightly higher, to the little gulley, the planted field of gray hairs down the separating groove where her hair parted. She'd probably been the smartest secretary in her department, passed over too many times for promotion, maybe. Or maybe some deep family trauma had caused mental collapse? Whatever it was, she'd risen from the ashes, this grande mystic of the Berkshires, passing her days in careful meditation while bilking sick people desperately grasping for hope.

"It took years before Buddha returned to the castle."

Sparrow's voice was not loud but placid, a fall breeze.

"The baby was much older by then, naturally. Buddha's wife was also older. Though she had not seen her husband for long years filled with hardship, she accepted him into the castle without complaint. And still, another three weeks passed before the Buddha visited her quarters."

"Women can't even *be* Buddhists."

"*Oliver—*"

"I read it on the Net. They have to be reincarnated as men. *Then* they can."

Sparrow waited, the etched time lines of her forehead remaining flat. "The first thing Buddha's wife said to him was 'Did you have to leave?' Buddha answered, 'No. *But I could not know this without leaving.*'"

The skin of her cheeks was hard and smooth as carved wood. She let her story sink in, then told Oliver, "I'm not taking money for anything."

"You fucking shouldn't."

Behind him there was a misstep, a bump—the light source flickered, the room's balance of light and weird shadows recalibrating.

"I think Oliver and I need to talk." Alice's hand was steady, moving to her heart.

Sparrow understood, broke from her duel, and hugged Alice. She held both of Alice's hands even as she backed away, and now their arms improvised a circle. Sparrow whispered; Alice nodded.

As the healer began gathering her bags and books, Tilda and Alice now shared a look, communicating in their own exclusive language. Alice assured Tilda she'd be fine, told them to leave the equipment, though it would be nice if Tilda could turn off the light, please.

Alice motioned to Oliver, patting the adjacent space.

He didn't sit. He loomed.

She asked if he could hand her the water.

During each of her two gulps, her Adam's apple seemed inordinately large for her neck.

From the other side of the drywall they could hear the sounds of the women retreating, clumps and whispers, Alice's mom warning, the baby was asleep.

"If I die in the next little while," Alice said, "I'm afraid you'll let your darkness take over."

His eyes were whirlwinds.

"I'm saying this to help," she continued, "you shouldn't take it personally."

"Just the kind of qualifier that ensures—"

Her raised hand halted his sarcasm. Looking up, she tried to focus on his face, but it proved too difficult. Instead her eyelids landed with force, remained closed.

"I just want you to know. I hope with all my heart that you will fight the darkness and not stay there."

"I'm not giving up, Alice—"

"You can have a wonderful life without me. You can meet someone else who can be a good partner for you, a good mother to Doe. But that will only work if you open yourself to that possibility."

"I'm not giving up. If that means someone's got to be King Dick around here, fine, I'll take the mantle. But—"

She bit her lip, placed a hand on his knee, felt his tension, the solidity of his resistance.

"I know how hard this is on you. I feel the pressure you're under. But it's poisoning you, Oliver. You bring me so much joy. I want to spend years with you. I even want to keep going through this hell with you. I want to be a parent with you. But if I don't get to do that, I don't want you to do it alone."

"Yeah well," he said, "I can't worry about that right now."

"Be open to love, Oliver."

"Christ—"

"Be open to goodness."

She took extra care with each word. "I guess I'm just trying to figure out how I want to live with what I have left."

He looked away, felt himself choking up. "And that's what Joey Keyboard was about?"

A flinch. Then her mouth rounded, forming the word *oh*. No sound escaped. Her hand rose, as if she might insert her fingernails and eat them. Her forehead and cheeks reddened, pupils shimmering.

She forced herself to keep eye contact—thinking, studying.

"I need to do something for you," she finally said. "Come here. Sit."

She did not wait but reached out, touching the bottom of his jacket, which she lifted, reaching for his belt buckle.

"What," said Oliver. *"Hey."*

Clumsy, careful—still fumbling, for she was out of practice—she unlooped his belt, in a workmanlike manner, and ignored his rumpled shirttails. His extra flesh and flab must have registered, for he had never been heavy like this, but she did not acknowledge as much. Oliver remained tense, unnerved, mildly alarmed. But he wasn't stopping her from handling his jeans' top button, lowering his zipper, reaching in.

A musky scent rose into the room. He was warm, sweaty, oddly red, not limp but far from stiff. His jeans and boxers down now to the middle of his pasty thighs. He'd stopped breathing, still was shocked by the happening. When Alice's hand closed around him, he moaned. Her pace increased and she worked as best she could; he gasped and stared at her hand on him. And now he was looking toward the corner of the bedroom, that spot between the drywall and the weird angle of the roof, where that sliver of space still let in sound and smells. He moaned again, throaty, approving.

It was not long before he could tell her arm was tired. But she wasn't deterred, and didn't hesitate in leaning forward and planting a kiss on his bulbous, crimson head, licking awkwardly, like a hesitant cat, around its ridge. Enveloping him, her mouth was warm, wet. His shoulders hunched and he let out an involuntary, high sound; his head leaned back and he shut his eyes; his right hand went onto the back of her head. Oliver felt the barren desert of her skin. The air in the room warmer, her breaths coming at shorter intervals. She went at him, gallant and resolute, going faster, her eyes shut, cheeks pulsing.

But he was not close.

He was careful in lifting her off him, and he brought her to his face, and kissed her with all the tenderness in him, and on her lips tasted his own heat and salt.

Oliver pulled Alice's bird-frail body to him. He took her face into his shoulder, caressed the back of her head, and laughed, amazed, holding her to him.

She was sobbing by now, and her sobs continued for a time, their force increasing, sending her body into racked, great heaves.

"*Favorito,*" he said. "*Favorito.*"

PART IV

Enlightenment

YOU WORK NOT to gawk at the man with no jaw, the one standing by the plants. That poor man with the back hump and the marble eyes wants you to focus, though, wants you to see him. As you pass some helpless pile of bones on a stretcher, it takes all the discipline you've got not to stare at those sarcoma lesions, dark and purple. You sit on some couch, waiting for your appointment. You try not to be disturbed by the row of future corpses hooked up to oxygen tubes, try not to think about the random nature of illness, the absence of reason as to who recovers and why. No, instead you come into contact with these unfortunates for fleeting seconds, and you cannot help but look, and it goes without saying, your heart goes out to them. But also: *At least I'm not that bad.*

And then you are the one in the waiting area beyond your usual waiting area, and you feel eyes checking *you* out, recoiling, afraid.

I am at a juncture where I must summon my inner warrior goddess to stare at a mirror. It still brings tears. My hair has started growing back from this last consolidation, but it is mossy, fuzzy, almost translucently thin. Gray fills in more of the front than last time. My face is now a skull, dug up after thousands of years, my skin brittle and dry. As a girl I always wanted those large, anime puppy eyes. Now I have them. They're trapped inside hollow sockets, searching for a way out. Drugs have swollen my cheeks like a botched face-lift. I used to pout about my extra baby weight, now I'm nostalgic for it, for those excesses of meat on my hips and thighs (my whole life I hated my fat thighs). My hip bones jut in jagged peaks that make me think of all those teen models I used to fit, though I look nothing like them.

I look more like a prisoner in a concentration camp; I hate to say it, but it's the unavoidable association.

Included in this diminishing is what is happening with my thin, gorgeous band of simple gold. Six months after my wedding, my ring finger had expanded to the degree that, there was no question, the band was never again coming off. This thought—*No way that's coming off*—always ignited a satisfaction inside me. In the middle of some long manual stitching job, I'd look down and see my ring, that quick gleam, and I'd think: *I have more than just fashion.*

But now, if I even point down, that band slips off.

The cusp of autumn. Chill infuses the air, night's dominion coming earlier and earlier. I try and focus on the task at hand. We've received the call. We've been promoted. This new waiting area has different artwork—those familiar Impressionist retrospectives replaced by Lichtenstein. Each bank of chairs retains the same dull layout, the same dusty plants and ancient magazines. Still, when I recognize my favorite nurse-practitioner, I feel a charge: something like hope.

My hands grip, pushing against the cushioned metal armrest. I plant and propel, and manage myself, somewhat, upward, into a squat. Still, the wheelchair is too low. My thighs can't push my body into the standing position.

"Usually I can get it," I tell Requita.

"I know," she says.

"Just not this time." I smile.

Watching, Oliver twists in place. I know he's irritated, why do I insist on expending unnecessary energy? He ducks in, reaches beneath my pits, holds me lightly. "Ready," he says, "steady, and—"

We ease upward; he makes sure I'm balanced.

"One more," he says. "Ready?"

Steady never makes it from his mouth. I'm already sliding over, onto the exam table, doing it on my own.

Easy mannerisms and lanky height, bouncy hair feathered down the middle, the doctor immediately makes me think of some tennis star or surfer from the nineteen seventies. "Sergio Blasco," he says. His accent is European Spanish—obviously cultivated through decades of boarding school education. "I'll be taking over your treatment. I'll still consult with Eisenstatt, *naturalmente* But from this point forward, through the transplant and then afterward, consider me your physician."

The hint of dismissal when he says *Eisenstatt*—what might even be disdain—endears him to me that much more.

I cough approval; he halts, his brow knitting.

"How long, that cough?"

Oliver answers: "A few days."

Blasco stays focused on me, thin brows crumpling together. "Two days? Five days?"

"She had it last Friday for her appointment," says Requita. "It sounds deeper now."

"May I?" Blasco approaches with his stethoscope.

A nurse comes from the side and wraps a warm thin blanket around my shoulders so it hangs like a poncho. She puts a cup of water to my lips. I nod, whisper thanks, and keep the cup. Blasco presses to my chest, listens, does not move. Taking the instrument buds out of his ears, he heads back to his chart. He reads, flips. "Right," he reads: "History of stomach virus."

I can see he's considering what he's heard from inside me, what he's read, cross-referencing . . .

"Nose and throat," he tells Requita. "We need cultures. Make sure to have that today."

His small gray eyes dart, back and forth, taking in as much as possible, yet they remain calm. When he fixes on my face, I feel humanity—not just doctor training and generic sympathy. I feel my shoulders and neck going rigid—this also may have to do with the attention of a handsome man on me. Probably that is too simple. Something more is taking place. For all his easygoing athleticism, Blasco is a thinker, delving, measuring. How can his calculations do anything but put me on edge?

"All notes here point to what an impressive woman you are. This is very good for our purposes. You have held on through induction and—*four?*—four consolidations. Quite a gauntlet. And finally a donor has come through. This is tremendous news. You have had very bad breaks and a very hard slog. But to have this donor come through this way—getting marrow withdrawn so soon after discovery—we are fortunate."

I nod.

Without warning, he claps his hands, creating a small dry explosion of sound, a signal for attention. "This procedure we hope to perform. *Allogenic bone marrow transplant. Allo,* Latin, *from the outside.* Practical terms. The donor has surgery on the lower back. The marrow is harvested over five days and taken from the spine. We use these stem cells to grow you new bone marrow."

He waits, making sure I am following. "A very complex procedure. Many factors are involved. But we have reasons to believe it can be successful."

"That's all we need to know," says Oliver.

We need to know quite a bit more than that, I want to say; instead I feel Oliver's eyes moving to me, searching.

"You're not going to draw on a whiteboard, are you?"

My first words to the doctor; naturally, my voice has the chirp of a baby bird.

The doctor freezes, doesn't understand.

"Private joke. Go ahead."

Half-embarrassed, Blasco raises his hands from his lap. He places a large knuckle on the bottom of his chin. Now his eyes go steely. I smell a faint residue, something I cannot place.

"Your bone marrow, as you know, is producing the leukemic cells. We therefore hope to replace that marrow. We hope to do this using the healthy marrow from your donor. But replacement means something unfortunate. We must first remove, or eliminate, your cancer-producing marrow."

My eyes shut. I perform a quick visualization, embrace darkness. "Release me from my suffering," I say. "And from the cause of my suffering."

The room goes silent, as if no one knows how to take this remark, let alone respond. Then the doctor clears his throat. "Mrs. Culvert, what lies ahead of you is not an easy task."

My eyes open. Blasco is waiting, patient. "You have been through very much, I know. But this is a species unto itself. You are undergoing a marathon of sprints. Have been sprinting and sprinting. Now there is a new separate marathon of sprints. This will require its own fortitudes and endurances. I want you as strong as you can be. I want us all prepared."

My mouth is a desert road. I cannot manage enough moisture to swallow.

"Our first step"—Blasco speaks with caution—"high-dose radiation therapy. Three days is usual. Two doses a day. Sometimes we do three. It depends on how you are doing. If you are having problems, and need to go slow, we add the fourth day."

"The rooms are much nicer on the transplant floor," volunteers Requita. "It's a good place to recover."

"So we've heard." Oliver doesn't look up from his notepad.

"After radiation, the next step is a high-dose chemotherapy regimen. Thyatemper. Cytoxan. Daunorubicin. Other drugs and steroids to help with the effects. Four days of this. Then you rest a day."

Oliver is writing as fast as he can; however, I am trying to unclench my knotted innards. I feel fear leaking through my eyes. I try to exhale, remember how to breathe.

Blasco's concern is apparent. "You are all right?" Once I nod, he continues. "Following rest, we give you the stem cells. This part is not bad. The stem cells are delivered into your bloodstream intravenously, usually through a central catheter. Very similar to the blood transfusions you already have. The stem cells travel through the blood into the bone marrow, where they take root. We wait while you recover and the marrow takes hold, so it can start growing inside your bones. Usual stay, four to six weeks."

A ballpoint is removed: the doctor's large thumb clicks and unclicks and clicks again, an obvious tic. "I am not one for sugarcoating. How thin you are is a very large concern. I worry your body will not be able to withstand the rigors of the transplant. I worry your heart will not be able to take the stress. This is not a reason to not try. We will run you through tests. Either you handle it or you can't."

It is hard to know which direction to turn, where to focus. I notice that Blasco's long legs are out in front of him, crossed at the ankles. His shoes have been cobbled at the toes and heels.

Requita hands the doctor a new clipboard, which he takes without a thank-you or acknowledgment, explaining to me there are perfunctory questions before we can start moving forward. While Oliver squirms, we cover the usual greatest hits: family history, how I was diagnosed, have I used recreational drugs, any huffing? Then: "Have you had unprotected sex with a prostitute in the past five years?"

"Ha. I wish."

"Your sexual history in the past five years has been—"

I feel myself swallow, my throat clenching. "Monogamous, yes."

When I'd finished visiting with my friends or completed meditating; once I'd completed my relaxation techniques, or was roused from my nap, and the coast was clear; Oliver would enter, sometimes bringing our Doe with him, or lifting the Blueberry away from the sitter and eating her nose. "Daa," she would say, our big girl, talking now, giggling, and he would swing her as if she was a rag doll, swooping and carrying her, finally, with a happy splash, depositing her onto the pillow next to me. Other times she was already on the bed and he'd crash whatever little game we were playing, capsizing whatever book I was reading to her, inserting himself into our revelry. "Hello, my beauty," he'd say, or "Good afternoon, my heart," unless he did not say a word and instead made a beeline, kissing me, melted butter on my barbed-wire lips. (When he was feeling optimistic I would know, for his kiss would start out with force, then become more sensual.) Tucking himself inside the comforter; collapsing atop it; careful not to land on me; making sure not to hit my leg; snuggling into my side; taking my hand inside his as if he were clasping a peanut. He'd sag and merge into the mattress, shutting his eyes and letting out a breath, lying still for a moment, unless he could not be still, had to stroke my head, had to turn toward me, plant petal-soft baby butterfly kisses on my closed eyelids. His body was typically stale with sweat, radiating heat and exhaustion and twitchy follow-up thoughts, his eyes often red, so many hours of meticulous logic, staring into his screen. We'd lie together until it was time to address dinner, or my pill schedule, whatever was next.

If you think of a blessing as something you need, but do not know that you need, or do not know to ask for—then my afternoons with him were blessings.

But there was something else. Since my bout of blindness, or perhaps because of my meditation techniques, my senses had become sharper, more attuned. There were odd afternoons in that summer, not many of them, but a few, when Oliver would lie next to me and lean in and snuggle, he would hold my hand and stroke my hair, and from his skin, I would smell—what? Not nothing, not quite, but a chemical variant of nothing, an antiseptic freshness—radiating from his body, lingering in his scalp.

From a shampoo? A body wash? The scent appeared, what, maybe every two weeks. I can't say it was even as regular as that. But I'd smell it.

The third, maybe fourth time, I asked Oliver if he'd worked out.

"I guess you shower at the gym?"

Motionless.

"I ask because you've never mentioned a shower at the rental office. I'm assuming you'd use it more if it was there."

I could sense him groping, could tell he was unmoored.

An apologetic shake of his head. A slight smile. Hadn't he mentioned it? The Brow had guest passes at Crunch. He'd been trying to deal with all the stress. He thought he'd told me.

I never smelled that antiseptic cleanliness again. Not from his hair, or off his skin. That smell vanished. Those few cameos remained unexplained, anomalies. If anything, Oliver was even better toward me. Impossibly better: waking me each morning with a kiss, arranging my pills and administering my treatments and warming my herbal teas. He sat and read to me, brought me iced water, fed me soft scrambled eggs. He went to the medical supply store in Chelsea and bought me a walker and worked with me to use the blasted thing. He made sure it was bedside in the morning and then helped me upward out of bed. Oliver scheduled the car service trips to the hospital and aided me getting my walker into the car and checked me in with the receptionists. Then he came back and sat by my side and held my hand. In the absent empty hours I would lie in our marital bed and still could not help myself, returning to those few clean whiffs, what to make of them, whether my mind was doing this to me.

The sitter was with Doe, he'd made sure of it, and now he'd casually closed the bedroom door, was sitting at the side of the bed. By magic, my hand had become clasped inside his. "So this thing."

Silly as it may sound, my first thought was that his favorite jeans got shrunk in the dryer, that I had made a costly mistake on his computer. I had a flash of guilt: *Whatever it is I didn't do it.*

Then, I thought: *Oh.*

He met my eyes, then stared past me, fighting through something.

It wasn't as if he wanted intimacy, he said. He didn't want any kind of emotional connection. Not a mistress. Not to cheat. He wasn't going to bang the babysitter. I was his everything.

I understood the meaning of each word, but their arrangement, the things he was saying, they didn't apply to my life.

Yet he kept dissembling, circling and landing on the subject for just the briefest instant. It's not like I'm betraying you. Hell, I've mortgaged my company. My life is committed to getting you better, taking care of Doe. I just— All I want is relief. Get the animal urge off my back. It's anonymous. It disappears. I go back to being kind and taking care of you. I'm here in all ways.

I felt my eyes wide, my hand shaking. He was holding my hand and it was shaking and he let it go. I couldn't make noise. Couldn't breathe.

Oliver removed from his wallet a business card. It was the yellow of faded sunlight, with hard creases to it. ALEXA'S FLOWERS, it read. EXQUISITE FLOWERS FROM THE WORLD ALL OVER was beneath, a smaller, black script. There was a phone number. My eyes went blurry, the numbers and letters now going smudged.

Since the summer. Months of this.

He always made sure he was safe. He wanted me to know. This mess has been hanging over him, it had him wrecked. He couldn't lie to me anymore, he said. He didn't want this. He never saw the same woman twice. It didn't mean anything.

It was as if a gloved hand were slipping through the cage of my ribs. I felt its icy grip, clutching at my heart.

One of our last date nights before I fell ill. We'd prepped the sitter, then made our getaway to a small, busy tapas bar on a Chelsea side street. Plied with good sangria (just enough fruit to taste, but not get in the way of the alcohol), we waited for small hot plates: braised chorizo, herbed baby potatoes, a warmed asparagus dip. On our right, a table erupted, the woman throwing down her napkin, the man jerking away, reaching for his wallet. They were impossible to ignore: getting their coats in haste, their faces stone with anger, each maneuvering down the crowded aisle. Once they were safely outside, every other couple in the restaurant, including Oliver and me, let out sighs of relief, as if to say: *It wasn't us.*

Amid the low lights, over scallops ceviche, I reminded Oliver of our first major fight, and told him that, afterward, I'd called my mother and she'd relayed this message: in every good relationship, every strong marriage, there came a point where no matter how much you loved one another, you also knew too much about each other—your strengths, your weak areas. "The two of you are human, you're frayed."

On the night of my blind walk around the block, when Oliver pressed me about Merv, my mother's words were stones on me. I'd answered that he could be right or we could be married. I'd told him I needed to be married to him. This new bombshell returned me to these memories, those spoken words. In the weeks that followed Oliver's whore bombshell, my Whitman Memorial hallway thoughts—*Thank God I'm not that bad*—transformed into *Well, now I know the other side.* But my mother's words remained. And I stewed in them, boiling in anger and indignation, my sop sweat and humiliation, my naked heartsickness.

Funny that you should ask, Doctor. As it happens, my husband routinely rendezvouses with whores.

The truth means insurers have an excuse to not spend ungodly amounts of money on this procedure. It gives the out that ends my life.

Oliver doesn't hesitate in answering Blasco, lying like the hall of fame, heavyweight champion liar that he is.

"Of course she hasn't."

Blasco checks off something, not so much as looking up. "Very good."

Presently the doctor takes his time. "After the transplant," he says, as if explaining a tricky lock to his houseguest, "you will have a little worse immune system than a newborn. All of the questions that a mother needs to ask about her newborn will apply to you. *Would you take a newborn here? Would you let a newborn do X?* A huge issue becomes who will be your primary caregiver." Blasco's eyes dart between Oliver and me. "This is by your side each day at the hospital, in charge of your care. Is a round-the-clock job. Seven days a week."

Again Oliver does not hesitate. "I'm her primary. Have been. Will be."

Contrariness swirls through me. I want to shout, *No.* Then catch myself.

My mom has to take care of Doe. Tilda just started her new gig as an editorial assistant. Other friends may want to help, but can't give up their lives. Oliver's the only one who can see this through. I stare ahead at the doctor. Oliver's jaw clenches, his tendons flexing in a manner that means he knows I'm watching. The dent of his Adam's apple bobs.

And so it has come to this: I am to give myself to a culture of medicine and procedures in which I neither trust nor have faith. That I might be mother to my child, I must abandon my child. Essentially helpless, I must trust in Oliver when I can't even look at him, can't even think straight around him. I don't know if we have a marriage. I don't know if we have a life anymore.

The First Noble Truth is the Truth of Suffering: "You are born. You live. You suffer and get sick. You die." But of course nothing is so simple.

"What can I do?" I say. "I have to do it so I'm going to." My hands are shaking in front of me, I can't control them. "She's on the verge of walking. She's saying her first words. I don't want her to miss me. I have to do it, *but how can I abandon her?*"

Oliver doesn't dare move, but he doesn't need to. Requita is next to me, rubbing wide circles on my back. "She won't remember a thing. It's going to be harder on you."

"You're a bit traumatized," says Dr. Blasco.

"Falling apart in these exam rooms again." I sniff. "So humiliating. I guess some things don't change. But this is the last time. Believe you me."

Oliver helps me with my coat. He places down the flats on my wheelchair and secures my feet. Leaving the exam room, he takes his time rolling me to the elevator. When we emerge into the rain, Oliver makes sure I am dry underneath the ancient metal awning, and runs to the curb to see if the town car is where it is supposed to be. No. He tries to run down a cab, lets an elderly couple take the first available one. The rain has let up a bit since our arrival, but is still coming down at a steady pace. I see his hair going sticky, his face and ears turning slick.

Our ride home is a muted slog, with thickets of afternoon traffic, and the silence settling into the backseat more nebulous than the standard silence that has taken over between us. Oliver asks if I am hungry. He tries to engage me about who is coming over tonight. My shut eyes block him out; I start my visualizations, trying to accept, or escape. For his part, Oliver accepts. He says he'll wake me when we get home.

At the apartment, he is especially careful in helping me into the elevator, and then to my desk, and then he ushers the sitter and Doe toward Mommy. As I embrace my girl, she begins repeating her first and most favorite word, *"Mommy."* When Oliver prepares a fruit smoothie with protein powder, I make sure to thank him. When he puts his hand on my shoulder, I do not move away. Do these decencies indicate a thaw? He may choose to believe so. He does make sure to give me space, but also hovers, keeping an eye on me.

"Believe me, Oliver, I understand what it is to feel your heart pounding between your legs." I can take no more, and lash out. "I know all about wanting to escape. But if you think you deserve a lollipop for telling me you fuck prostitutes while I'm decaying in bed with cancer? If you think you can convince me you have a *right*? What do you want, Oliver? Absolution? *Permission?*"

Without trust, your shit was through. Maybe it happened in a slow circling of the drain. Some trial separations, efforts at reparations, couples therapy, all that garbage. But after you attempted to bang away the dents, if your *belief* in that other person couldn't be banged back into place, couldn't be welded back together, your marriage was done.

And if you were the idiot who inflicted the damage, the way things worked, you couldn't be the one who made it better. You didn't get to fix it.

But someone had to get that transplant precertified. Someone had to get the ballast of tests precertified. The radiation treatments. Plus, the hospital needed copies of Alice's last Pap smear. All of it had to get in gear tomorrow, because in two days they were scheduled to start showing up at Whitman between eight thirty and nine. Alice's sneezing, or cold, or whatever, was enough of a concern that she'd been prescribed five hundred milligrams of Levaquin per day—doctors wanted that cough under control as quickly as possible. So Oliver was supposed to make sure she took her scripts. He was under orders to keep her away from echinacea, and any other natural healing remedies—the doctors didn't know what kinds of effects would be released into her system, what might happen.

So no. Distance wasn't an option. Not for him.

I am tattooed! The most insane thing!

When I was in high school tattoos were dangerous. I pined for one, but never had the guts.

Now I have a pair. It happened first thing this morning. I was told not to eat or drink anything after midnight, and am a bit piqued by this. In a large cold room I lie on a long table. "Okay, down with the smock, please," says the attendant. I suffer a moment of confused modesty, so she helps, lowering the smock edges below my shoulders, halfway down my arms. Not happy with this, she tells me we need to lose it. I embrace the order. *Take a look.* Evidence of what I've been through: my breastbone all but breaking through my skin, the pattern of a butterfly skeleton along my chest. They measure the breadth. Then down my sides. Then I'm turned over, measurements taken down my back. The attendant washes and sterilizes my chest.

It happens so fast, it's shocking, just a few moments, an electric charge that leaves me rushed with adrenaline and wanting more. But here I am, inked with a pair of dots, each the size of a ballpoint stain on a pillow. One is high on my chest, in the middle of my breastbone, just above where my cleavage used to start. The other at the equivalent point on my back. They mark where my lungs begin, so the hospital can customize lead guards.

The orderly who wheels me up to the sixth floor, Donnay, is massive as a linebacker. Though his orders say he has to get me to Cardiology ASAP, he saunters with an easy rhythm, and his words have a similar flow. "They got you on lockdown, huh? You gonna be all right, though, I see it." I smile back, attempting to plug into his good nature. But when we arrive at Cardiology, the waiting room is distressingly full, and this turns me dizzy, weak as a washrag. Oliver is already at the front desk, bent over, talking low with a receptionist. Donnay rolls me up, pounds his fist against my hand. "Stay black," he says. "Stay strong."

His retreat is a slow, almost guilty strut, and it's not long before the thrill of his goodbye phrase gives way to bureaucratic cinder blocks.

"Unfortunately," I am told, "this office is on a tight schedule."

Since I was late, they had to bump me to the next slot, which created a logistical nightmare. After this test I'm supposed to have chest X-rays, an EKG, and a meeting with a dentist, who will need to take care of any cavities. While I was being wheeled up here, the receptionist and Oliver were juggling my next three days, whether I can move my bone marrow biopsy, my meeting with the hospital psychiatrist (who's supposed to assess my mental state and, more important, prescribe anxiety medicines), my group consultation with Eisenstatt and Blasco to talk about the first rounds of test results.

It's enough to make a girl swoon. But the secretary is promising it will get taken care of. And Oliver, who wouldn't spit on a hospital bureaucrat to save her from burning, assures me: "We're straightening it out."

"Can I bother you for some orange juice?" I ask.

"I'm sorry," says the receptionist. "You aren't supposed to eat or drink for four hours before the heart stress test."

"I haven't had anything all day. You ordered me not to eat or drink before—"

"It's horrible. I know. Please hang in as best you can. We'll get you in as soon as possible."

How long do I lie on a waiting room couch, wrapped in my family quilt, with Oliver holding me, brushing lightly at my temples, sheltering me? His pulse throbs in my ear. His care is at once horrible and tender, but I can't break away, don't know if I want to.

During the first month of our courtship, he came down with a flu. I spent an afternoon in my impossibly small kitchen with all the burners going. It was so important to show him what I could do, let him know I could take care of him. I remember sweating rivers, second-guessing myself over a recipe I'd made countless times. I hauled that huge vat of lentil soup to him, which meant a subway transfer at Times Square, walking about eight miles through its underground tunnels. Just a mess of a haul. Of course he had two bowls and chucked the rest, assuring me he ate every delicious morsel. I miss being able to take care of him that way. I miss being able to take care of myself. I miss taking an early afternoon dance class—following the pounding, ecstatic drum rhythms, the tribal syncopations and flails and stomps and gyrations, me and the rest of the room, so many similarly concentrating, sweating, glorious women. Those rare mornings—a month at a time of them—when I was motivated and somehow rose early and jogged along the Hudson. The bliss of fully occupying my body. I miss just standing in my kitchen, losing myself in the slow meditations that come with making tea. Me and my simple, stupid rituals. My unspectacular, operating body, that wonder.

Oliver wouldn't show me the kitchen until he'd finished every last installation. When he finally brought me up the elevator and removed his hands from my eyes, it took me a second to take it all in—he'd made so many promises, and I'd known it would be impressive, sure. Still I squealed and hopped in place. Then I started laughing. I couldn't believe it, what he'd made for me. Right now I'm not sure there will be another time that he sidles up behind me and puts his hands beneath my hem and caresses. It's hard to believe I'll ever again grab on to the counter edges and widen my stance. I don't know if I'll ever have the chance, if I even want it. This realization sends tremors through me; I'm repulsed and turned on at once.

I think about the two of us on the couch after a dinner party. We've finished gossiping and tied up loose ends, and are at once wired and weary. I think about the joy of his alcohol-soaked kisses, about that combination of desire and exhaustion, when you are teasing, wanting to play, while also wanting nothing more than to sleep. He's the only person in the world who knows my longtime fantasies: old fat men of power taking me, using me, their little slut.

Right now, my desire has me ashamed. Worse than my shame is fear. Will I ever stand in our kitchen and make a big Sunday breakfast for Doe? Will we ever lick the frosting from the side of a bowl?

"The transplant is very stressful on a heart," explains a new, stooping doctor. "Let's make sure your heart is strong enough." He speaks as a nurse grasps and kneads the long muscles in my arm, my biceps going squishy, giving way as if she were squeezing a tube of warm whipped potatoes. After an excruciating amount of time, she summons a vein. Hurrying so she can keep it, she punctures my arm. When I am not wincing, I notice the syringe is odd looking, lined with a slate-gray metal.

The IV withdraws my blood; I'm told it will get mixed with radioactive isotopes, then shot back into my body. The nurse secures the line, helps wrap my feet in paper footies, leads me to a stationary bike in the room's corner. A technician enters from the other side of a glass wall and starts adjusting the bike seat. He guides my still-tender chest against a special camera. I'm supposed to place one arm on the bike for balance, while the syringed arm must hug the camera, keeping it close. As best I can understand, the camera will track the radioactive isotopes through my bloodstream.

"We'll do the bike at three levels of resistance," the doctor says. "Twenty miles per hour at first level. Then thirty. Then the most difficult. We want you pedaling harder and harder so the cameras can check the different chambers of your heart."

I start out okay, eager to show that I can do this. But holding the camera to my chest is awkward, and not easy, especially with the technician telling me, "Keep it still." Before long the pedals start feeling weighed down: getting them to roll over to each next rotation is a slog, as if I'm pushing through thick mud. I start breathing hard, but manage to finish the second level. The third is too much, I can't do two pedal rotations.

When the doctor comes in, I am bent over the bicycle, sucking for air. I look at him and feel the desperation in my eyes.

"All righty." The doctor watches me, hunched over the bicycle, watching him. I see his concern, that familiar pity.

He turns to the technician, behind the glass in an adjacent room. "Do the second level again. Maybe that will get it."

They salvage eight decent photos; twenty would be ideal. I traipse around cones, drink radioactive dye, sit under scanners. Results are inconclusive. No one's pumping a fist and shouting *You can do it,* but then we don't need bells and whistles. Ambiguity is solid. The powers don't have a clear case for pulling the plug, and not stopping us is more than enough. It's astonishing, the relief. *This is going to happen.* And an all but hysterical panic. *This is happening.*

My mom comes back down for the weekend, energetic and helpful as always, wanting to get everything, pack everything, take care of me. I feel her love for me. Just as obvious is how excited she is to take the baby back to Vermont. Her *anticipation.* Being a parent is supposed to give you a true appreciation for what your parents went through for you. Maybe I need to try to concentrate on appreciating my mother more. But I am small. I feel so jealous, robbed yet again, in yet another way.

I remember my own girlhood, surviving snowy afternoons playing dress-up in Mom's closet. I remember leafing through her magazines, admiring pretty ladies, their spectacular frocks. I so clearly remember playing Mommy, pretending to be a grown-up. That I might not get to see my own daughter do these things, that I might not get to *model* the grown-up, the mommy, for my girl, it is too much. If I start to think about my Doe, lonely, forced to occupy the same rooms I was in, without me . . .

I know these thoughts aren't good for anyone.

So here I am, suffering through yet another Last Night Before I Go Back In. Tonight, I'm wishing I had a lobotomy—if they'd scooped out my frontal lobe, I wouldn't have to be present for what they're going to do to me.

This last weekend has been impossibly beautiful, and it has been slow-drip torture. The specter of one of those hospital beds, the beeping IV tower, the fluorescent light—it's all coming. I watched Doe sleep this morning: she kept snuggling closer to me, her face an inch away from mine, slack and soft, pacifier hanging half out of her mouth. She reaches for my hand; hers is so tiny in mine, so trusting. She takes me for granted; I want her to be able to take me for granted. But I wonder if she's clingy because she understands things better than I give her credit for. I watched her this morning, tried to soak in her breaths. Nothing is more important than feeling her, hearing her, smelling her baby smell, melting next to her, knowing this peace. At the same time, the pressure I feel to enjoy these moments, it crushes me.

If I really believed all the chants I repeat, if the lessons and meditations had actually stuck, then not having a guarantee could become beautiful.

I know I don't want to die. I'm not ready for that—to not see her or put her down for bed or change her diaper or eat her toes.

But I have to let go of when we will see each other again. I have to trust that it will be when we are both healthy enough to enjoy each other.

I can still taste the blood running inside my mouth, damage from the mouth guard I had to wear during my EKG test. I had to get a drug for my throat that makes my tongue hard, and also makes it feel too large for the inside of my mouth. My fingers keep tingling, and seem dense to me, not the numbness that comes from sleeping on your hand, but an impenetrable, unworkable density, peanut brittle that's been left on a counter for days. I am under orders to wash my chest tonight. I have to stop eating and drinking at midnight. I need to learn the words to prayers I am afraid to speak.

She's in my arms, heavy-lidded, eyes unfocused and gunked. I rock her into my bosom, inhale her slightly sour scent. I transfer everything I have through my eyes—all my love, lifetimes of love—through my pressed hand on her chest, through my pounding and suspect heart. Oliver pays the driver, instructs him to take my mother and Doe back to the apartment. He asks if my mother has the spare keys. I barely acknowledge him, and say nothing about his newly shaved scalp.

. . .

That dead-stretch stillness before the dawn. Whitman's church façade looks even more ancient when coated with shadows. The lobby is a mausoleum, everything muted and somber.

Waiting at the admissions desk, I see another version of myself: a wraith of a woman, diminished in her sweatpants. She already has on the same protective mask and rubber gloves that I'll be wearing. I recognize, from behind the desk, those familiar and gorgeous braids; today they've been knotted in an intricate pile of tight cornrows. Flesh spills over from kitty-cat scrubs, Yolanda is doing her thing, growling throaty denials into the phone. Now she grabs the phone from out of her neck's crook. She pounds it onto the desk, then shouts back into the phone's speaker end: "Gertie, why the fuck you think this woman coming up in here at the ass crack of dawn? You gonna get this woman to surgery *fore* doctors go they rounds, *fore* them patients is up and wanting breakfast. I ain't playing now."

Oliver wheels me toward the desk. Brows rise; chocolate irises go cartoon large.

"Listen, Mrs. Culvert, we backed up to shit. I'm doing what I can, but you gonna have a wait."

"May we go outside?" I answer. "To get some air?"

Without help, I shuffle through the automatic opening doors and embrace the morning dew soft and light on my face. Frost comes into my lungs, spreads out a solid chill like a picnic blanket. The sky is still in prelude to dawn's silver hours, a royal and depthless blue. I head southward, toward the towering Queensboro as it trails off. Beside me, Oliver's concern radiates like heat. He's right; I need to be careful.

"Walking feels good," I say. "The air is refreshing."

Two men have finished pushing their bagel cart into place at the corner. They're breathing heavily as they unlock the stand. Though my orders do not allow me any liquids, a bottled water sounds deeply satisfying, and we get in line behind two people. I find myself ravenous for that first sip, and stare at a picture taped to the cart's smudged glass—the freckle rash of poppy seeds on the bagel's dough, the paste-thick schmear of cream cheese. Cars whoosh down the FDR. I imagine starched hospital sheets against my skin, that stale air recirculating.

A month, if I am lucky.

We sit on a bench, the air sharply cold, the damp wood soaking into my jacket and sweatpants. I remember staring out the window, as a girl, while the sun rose over green mountains. I remember looking up into the night sky from that stretcher and seeing the snow come down. I stick out my tongue again, this time licking condensation from chapped lips. Chewing at his roll, Oliver watches. I know he wants to comfort me; but he doesn't, allowing me these moments. Dawn has started in double time now, the sky lightening in a way that to me seems layered and spectacular and wholly indescribable.

Then the hospital beeper goes off. Then Oliver looks at me, his eyes hurried, questioning. I see that he's afraid, but also pressing. I recognize his utter investment, *his belief,* in what is about to happen. I brace, start to get up, then think, *No.* Releasing my grip from the side of the bench, I lean back and look up, toward the gloaming, and give my face to the morning dew. Oliver moves to help me upright, then lets me be, and I keep looking. It is all so plain; it is all so beautiful.

Powdered plastic gloves snap around wrists: low-dosage morphine drips. I hear background murmurs, exchanged remarks. Above me are a trio of masked and scrubbed bodies. They are concerned with how frail I look. A looming nurse is aware enough to distract me with small talk. Casual as a dowager discussing a Broadway play, she asks if I am ready for my transplant month. She uses rubbing alcohol to coat a nozzle, which is attached to the end of a plastic tube. The tube seems oddly large: "Like something frat boys suck beer through," I slur. Someone is slathering brown cleaning goop on a cotton swab stick: in three widening rotations, the goop is swabbed around that bruised juncture, right before jugular meets clavicle.

"It's going to be a long month," the nurse tsk-tsks. "I just hope you're ready."

What's wrong with you? I want to respond. *Why would you say that?* Except some sort of honeyed light is spreading through me. It's nice enough, and I start to fade, feel my eyes flutter. Then a sensation hits, sharp pain, more concentrated, more focused, than any I have experienced during any central line installation. I wince, and moan, and shut my eyes so tight that I can feel the sides of my face cracking. The pain corkscrews further, boring in deeper. I hear myself, an animal in distress. *"More morphine. Give me more morphine."*

"There there," says the scrub nurse. "Why the central is bigger, and it hurts so much. If you had a thinner line, the stem cells could break."

My next awareness is a pulsing. At the base of my neck.

My mind is dull, packed in cotton; my body feels fragile, every outer layer peeled away. I check the throb. Near my clavicle, gauze and plastic tape pile; a series of butterfly stitches keep the tube embedded in my skin. I follow the plastic line and discover I've been connected to an IV, they already have something pumping. I'm in a room that is all shadows, not much natural light, these weirdly angled walls jutting together like the sides of a huge, three-dimensional pizza. It's a small room, though. Small and triangular. Now, someone is stroking the side of my face.

I'm not used to seeing Tilda like this, in a fitted coffee-colored jacket. The satin blouse beneath is the color of a cinnamon stick, and flashes as she moves. Tilda's hair has been styled into a layered bob, the bangs cut straight across the middle of her forehead.

"Vision of loveliness," I say. "Gorgeous woman."

Tilda smiles. "This old schmatta? Part of the gig. I took a few hours off. *Schlepped* over from the magazine." Her bellow brings me joy. "I never get tired of that joke," she says.

Now the nurse wheels in a sturdy IV stand, its base visibly wider than the regular ones, its pole more broad. Branches extend for extra bags. Four battery packs are attached. Now the glow of level monitors imbues the room in radioactive green.

"All that talk about the rooms on the transplant floor being nice and big," Tilda says, pretending to speak to me. "The only window is actually *behind* your bed. You don't even get a view."

The nurse pauses from plugging in the final pack. "I checked like you wanted. Ward's in capacity. There are six people ahead of Mrs. Culbert for the other rooms."

I ask Tilda if my backpack is near. She hands it over, and I withdraw a small journal, its pink suede cover still pristine. My newest Receiving Journal; I made Oliver take a special trip to get it. Flipping to the first page, I ask the nurse for her name. Half a page is scribbled with dates, corresponding names, and a note, including, I quickly see, *Donnay, Orderly, "stay black stay strong."* On the first unused line, I write. *Maggie.* I write *vitals. Will run my first day itinerary.* This is part of my plan. Whenever somebody is going to do something for me, take me somewhere, give me anything, I am going to make a note. A series of short, sweet anchors. This is how I will survive.

Not five minutes in and we've got beeping, one of the battery consoles blinking red. Maggie rolls her eyes. Checking, she resets the battery, doubles back to get my blood pressure sleeve and start my vital signs. She scans my chart and says my name, but this time with a question. Am I the one friends with Yolanda?

A smile. "Girl, Yolanda put the word out. We supposed to keep an eye peeled on how you doing."

I thank her again. Maggie opens up, embracing me as one of her own. In short order, she confirms what I'd begun to suspect—that my radiation will not begin today, which makes sense, but still disappoints. Maggie commiserates, lets me know that Dr. Blasco also will not be in today, but is monitoring my numbers and test results. Maggie has procedural forms for me to sign and initial. She has guidelines. She has a sheet that asks if scraps from my biopsies can be used in teaching labs.

"If you want visits from a minister or rabbi, I'll sign you up. Social worker comes by on Mondays if you want a session. We got art therapy, light yoga, massage, you can even learn to play the guitar."

"It all sounds wonderful," I say. "Like I'm going away for a vacation."

"I know the music therapy dude was around earlier. He mighta left for the day. Kinda weird, that boy. Supposed to be on schedule two days a week. The fool here way more."

"I do have a request," I say. "When the treatments start, I will be trapped in this room, correct?"

"They'll take you back and forth for radiation, but pretty much—"

"Could I walk the hallway? While I still can?"

Maggie looks uncertain.

"My friend will go with me."

"Let me call the attending."

Within minutes, a put-together woman knocks on the door. Hair in a bun, with similarly tense bearing, she introduces herself, shakes my hand, and firmly advises against a walk.

"Is there is a patient's bill of rights?"

"There is."

"Can I see it?"

"Alice?"

"I'm okay, Tilda. I just want to know."

"Mrs. Culvert, if you go for a walk, obviously, we are not going to call security. You'd be back in the room before they got up here. But a lot of people come through the hallways. You could have someone sneeze on you and, who knows? Once I had a patient who had the flu when he came in here. He didn't tell us, and died two days after the transplant."

"How many people haven't died?" Tilda snaps. "Bring that up."

The woman shoots Tilda a sobering look. "What if I told you I was that patient's doctor? Or maybe that's just one more scary story we use to keep the halls clear. Either way"—a polite smile—"I'd advise against that walk."

Having lugged her suitcases and bags into a messy pile outside her room, Oliver found the area with a patient pantry, where he went to work, labeling and dating the Tupperware bins—TURKEY LOAF, BAKED CHICKEN, STEAMED BROCCOLI. Making sure Alice's name and room number were legible on the strips of masking tape, he wrote down the next day's date, buying more time before the food got cleared out. He prepped Alice's protein shake, nuked her turkey dinner, did the same for her lentil soup. He backed the food tray into her room. Conversation went dead. Tilda fixed him with a stare.

Why wouldn't she know? Who else would Alice tell?

Oliver put down the food. He started hauling in luggage, asked if Alice wanted anything else. Then he told her that a wall of the break room was filled with pictures of people who'd had successful transplants and went on to live normal lives. He told Alice that at Christmastime the ward had an anniversary party for survivors, and that the break room wall had a giant photo record from the party, showing all the survivors who came back. Everyone looked so happy. One really caught Oliver's eye, this beaming black guy, head perched next to his daughter and above his two granddaughters. "They have photos up of people who've survived four, six, nine years. They're all still going."

Swollen cheeks went rich, the crimson shade spreading until appreciation swallowed her face. Arranging her meal on the rolling tray, Oliver was close enough that she could easily touch him. But her hands remained clasped atop her bedsheet. Oliver finished prepping. Avoiding any possibility of eye contact, he walked away from the bed, unzipped the smallest suitcase, and withdrew familiar trappings: their framed wedding photo; Alice holding the newborn, seconds into Doe's life; six weeks; nine weeks. He took out inspirational sayings from their other stays—they didn't have the energy or time to start over—along with that unfolding, giant, taped-together sheet: CANCER SCHMANCER. Tilda let out a little whoop and grabbed one end, which made Oliver feel even more alone. Grim determination had him. He didn't ask what the deal was with this cramped little room but instead walked around the length of the bed and examined the small, plaid lounger. He pulled and lifted its seat, folding out the sections, into the long cot he would sleep on. The end of the cot kept bumping the bedside table. By the time Oliver successfully repositioned it, Tilda was rubbing moisturizing cream onto Alice's forehead.

With a knock, Blasco entered, the attending physician and Bhakti following right behind. The doctor looked around, winced, and ordered Bhakti to work on getting Alice a new room. He washed his hands, checked Alice's port, mentioned the skin was red, asked the nurse to get a cleaning kit and saline. The room's natural light was on the wane. Blasco scooted a chair next to Alice and plopped down, setting his hands in his lap. He wanted to know how she was feeling. First days were horrid, he agreed. He also told her she couldn't shower for the next twenty-four hours. "But," Blasco added. "Wash off your skin cream in the morning. Having skin cream on before getting radiation? Do you put on tanning oil before walking on the sun?"

Lights go on and I am dragged out of sleep. The clock says five. The nurse is a short Asian woman; she moves and talks with an alacrity that overwhelms me, checking my face. "Already the drugs are working," she says. "Red cheeks and forehead are one of the effects." She asks if I still get my period. When was the last time? I guess: "Maybe two weeks before I was diagnosed?" The nurse has me fill out a breakfast card, reminds me to pick from low-micro-meal selections, calls in the order, says it should be delivered between seven and nine. She has me push my arms against hers to check my strength. She does the same with my legs. Helping me up, she again lets me know I can't shower for twenty-four hours. She weighs me; just over one ten. Oliver is stirring as the nurse is putting my mask on for me. Donnay—my favorite—enters with a wheelchair. In what I have come to recognize as his no-sweat fashion, he unplugs the IV battery packs. I am deposited into my chair.

"So here you go." Oliver clasps my hand.

"Marathon of sprints," I say. "Here I go."

When Oliver leans in to kiss me, I offer my masked cheek. He holds my hand for an extra beat. Then my nurse drops, into my lap—*boink*—a large blue three-ring binder containing my case file. I shoot a pained look. *What's wrong with you?*

Halfway up the IV pole, thin metal branches stretch vertically to hold a second layer of fluids. The second layer makes the pole trickier to move, its balance uncertain. Donnay takes his time making sure no lines or plugs get tangled beneath the heavy rollers. We move slowly down, through the second floor. I get distracted by a series of windows, thin branches on the other side, blue sky peeking through random spaces. We head down another corridor, into what seems a different zone. The walls are painted in thick, primary colors; a glass window looks into a separate, brightly lit, and also happily-colored area. Here kids are playing. Some have patchy heads, others pates clean as pool balls. They chase each other across the giant, fuzzy map of carpet. They climb on beanbags, play with dolls and blocks, just sit on couches, reading, working on puzzles. Some have IVs. I see a child spring to a corner, bend over, and vomit into a bucket. Without pause, he comes back and rejoins a chase.

Leading up to the radiation waiting room, the hallways begin to line with the unwell. Right outside of the radiation room, a man stands out: upright in his slate-gray, three-piece suit, head so bald it looks spanking clean, his health is obvious. Some part of me thinks I've seen him before, but I can't place where. I notice his meaty right hand has a tasteful gold wedding band. Now the door to the radiation room opens. A bald boy is wheeled out. Can't be more than seven. The suited man's smile is enormous. "Hey, buddy."

I would happily give myself to him right here and now.

Door hinges groan, heavy with reinforced weight. Inside, the walls are thick with lead. I am wheeled to some sort of mechanism: a metal stand with a bunch of levers, pipes, and padded handlebars. All the pipes are at different levels and locations, and, as I near, I see that each pipe has measurement markings. Below them all is a bicycle seat. One of the orderlies starts positioning me, helping me toward the stand.

Maybe five yards away, the radiation machine waits, dormant. It looks like alien weaponry, a space cannon, eight or nine feet tall. At the end of what seems to be the weapon barrel, a chrome eye is angled, looking down unblinking. I can't take my eyes off it, either, which makes me less sturdy than anyone's happy with.

Once the orderly has guided me to the stand, two techs approach and split off, each heading to a side. They start applying these, these *things,* I don't know what, but they're foamy and big. Half-spherical, they go onto my shoulders with a *clomp.* Apparently they are clamps. Their purpose is to keep me in place.

The second orderly starts arranging my custom-made lead shields over my lungs and kidneys and internal organs. Using the few small holes in the lung guard to check on where the tattoo is, he makes sure everything's properly lined up.

So long as I breathe, I will be all right.

Now black straps go over my breasts, making an X, belting me in. They're looped through the poles and pulled, and it's so tight I can't move, can't so much as twitch. The first orderly positions the bicycle seat directly beneath my bottom.

"Just in case," he says.

I'm told if I pass out, the straps will keep me in place until the session is over.

So okay, Goddess, the first day wasn't so bad.

I need to keep letting go. Maybe I just need to sleep. Here is not so bad. Here is where I am. Just keep focusing on what I can do in here—I can write, I can read, I can meditate, I can draw, I can knit, I can paint in my limited, clumsy fashion. I know that I want to be a clear channel. The truth is, I'm not miserable. This little part of me nags, a dog nipping at heels, yipping, wanting me to be sad, to worry. *Remember, you're miserable! Remember, this is terrible!* But haven't I lived with the black box on my chest for so long? When I'm at my best—which is not often but sometimes—I know I don't have to live inside my fear, but can carry its weight. I wonder what happens if I open the ribbon to my black box and pull off the lid? What happens if I put soil inside, plant seeds, add water and regular light?

Look at how life has surprised me today. Look at all the ways I was taken care of, all the ways I had fun.

After the second treatment blast, after I was wheeled back to my room, I was greeted by the wondrous surprise of Jynne, Susannah, and Patty, as well as a double shock of a treat—Geeyan, straight here after flying all night from the coast. I hadn't been able to finish my second round of radiation without sitting on the bicycle seat, and was tuckered out, but it felt so good to see them. Geeyan was a glamorous and wonderful mess after her red-eye, and had finagled a screener that even out-of-the-loop me knows is the hottest movie in years, something ridiculously violent and cutting-edgy that won everything at Cannes.

"The director's supposed to be some geeky savant. He uses pop culture in a way that's both low and high. Dude's got all of Los Angeles repeating lines about what you call a Quarter Pounder with cheese in France."

In another life I'd have been beyond interested. In truth, I *did* feel tinges, that familiar desire not just to know but to be inside, not just to see this film but to *have seen* it. And I could tell that my friends—all of them plugged in—were excited. Geeyan wanted to get a video machine and watch the film all together. She promised insider gossip about the district attorney's preparations for the Simpson trial.

"Give it up," said Susannah.

"Everything," said Jynne.

"What's taken you this long?" said Patty. "Spill."

They continued with the third degree, but I felt myself shrinking, and started playing with the letters on the magnet board—one of the presents that Susannah brought me. Soon enough Jynne noticed. She'd brought poetry, took out a paperback, read out loud to us. It was wondrous, and if I could not keep my attention through parts about a grasshopper—I think, washing her face, snapping open her wings—we still took some of the poet's lovely phrases, made affirmations on the whiteboard ("I do know how to pay attention! I do know how to be idle and blessed!"). We also tried some drawing and painting exercises. I still can draw, *quel relief,* but have never been great with a brush, and was surprised that making thin straight lines had such a powerful effect on me. "It's funny," I said. "I'm having such a hard time painting while trying to address my fear of imperfection. I think it brings up my desire to be perfect. But also a counterinstinct, the feeling that it's okay, I don't have to be perfect."

I laughed. "This is the perfect medium for me."

I want to paint small pictures for Sue and Susannah and Julie for Christmas. That's my project for this week. Who else? Tilda? Debb? On small pages, I can draw a little heart or flower in pen, then paint it. It might take practice. But this afternoon was a joy. My friends talked about their problems, their lives, and I got to escape myself a bit, fluttering in and out, my naps and fugues. My friends gave me loving looks. They whispered around me, their fixed gazes and quiet words acting as my blanket. I heard them updating one another: Jynne's promotion, Geeyan closing on her new house, weather, omelets.

And Patty is so good! Coming back from the pantry with something to munch on, she asked, "What's the guy in the next room have?" She didn't know this ward's for cancer patients only.

"I know," I said. "Depressing, right?"

Jynne told me the same thing: everyone else here looks like they've given up.

I get these incredible women every day! These incredible visits each afternoon!

Let Oliver be miserable. I hope his conscience *is* eating him alive. I'm more than fine each afternoon when he sulks away, I guess to his office, who knows? Maybe this is just our personalities. He's tortured and miserable a lot. I often am not. He should be miserable for what he's doing to me. I'm not large enough to be at a place where I feel anything but fury and humiliation. I just can't let these feelings sink me.

Jynne also read us some Thoreau, and I wrote down the line: "as if I were mere flesh and blood and bones." *Yes,* I said. *That's how every doctor sees me.* Thoreau also wrote of his prison: "I did not for a moment feel confined." I also felt that today. If I died, would it really be so bad for my consciousness to be released into the universe? I feel myself closer to making peace with this, even while I plan on keeping going, staying here, and raising my Doegirl. It's a contradiction, I know. The other times I've been in here, I wanted pictures of other people's strength; now I'm grooving on my own. I want to go into the mountains and have someone take pictures of me naked, posing on a rock, a pillar of strength.

The big specter looming is the transplant. But that is not today. That is not today.

Each time he picked up the phone and called the number on the card and spoke carefully in terms of what kind of flower he might like—a little bouquet from the Far East; something busty and Russian—Oliver knew he was breaking a covenant. Still, he placed his orders, and made sure to avoid asking for a Friday appointment, for they were always fully booked, filled by jacked-up businessmen from out of town, or bosses emptying and readying themselves for that long weekend at home. (Just thinking of what a full schedule meant made Oliver squirm, especially when you were offered a later time.) The booker always talked in terms of *flowers.* Delicate Asian flower, very young, full on top, very special, in bloom for just next week. Only three hundred flowers.

If Oliver didn't ruin himself by getting too excited and jacking off the night before, or didn't chicken out—canceling with some obvious excuse, emphatically busying himself with some task—then he'd begin that dreary set of rituals: placing withdrawn company cash into a plain white envelope; calling back for the location; spitting out his gum and entering that saloon at the appointed hour; setting eyes upon the tastefully dressed woman alone at the end of the bar. And still. Every time he was buzzed inside some designated building and headed up or down a stairwell while his heart raced; every time an apartment door was opened ever so slightly, beckoning; whenever he went through with all these small moments and kept heading forward, doing all the ridiculous work of scheduling and running around, through every passing second, he understood the magnitude of his betrayal. Oliver understood he was failing her.

He also understood that he was failing his own idea of himself: the decent and upstanding husband doing right by his woman, the best person he'd ever known.

Although, again, she had insurance. The transplant was happening, wasn't it? The child was more than cared for. And he was here each day, destroying his spine and throwing his company in the crapper, all to take care of her. Whether he was having sex behind her back or owning up to it, how did that measure against being by her side, devoted to getting her better?

Except he *felt* his dishonesty. Because he hadn't given her a choice. He'd deceived her until it was too late for her to do anything. She was already helpless.

He couldn't talk about this—not to Ruggles, not to Jonathan, certainly not to his poor father (halfway across the country, barely conscious at the crack of dawn, working just to follow along with each medical update). He couldn't live with them knowing. So, Oliver admitted his feelings to the prostitutes. Afterward, when they were sweaty and lying on the bed and still breathing hard, Oliver unburdened himself. The women listened, usually: lying on their sides and staring at him, or with backs flat while looking at the ceiling, or with their eyes shut, their faces ruminative and placid. Some didn't understand enough English to follow along. At least one said her mother went through something similar not all that long ago.

Then it was just after dawn. Once again he'd compartmental-ized, was back at Whitman, stumbling through the corridors, tak-

ing a right, getting himself reaccustomed to not using the bathroom
in their room.

Oliver flushed, washed his hands. Returning down the hallway,
he garbed and masked once again. When he entered, Alice was motioning for him.

She awoke to a feeling. "Pushing."

Mumbling, her voice a flutter. "At my jaw."

She had him place his hand on her throat. The nodes, glands,
whatever.

"Swollen," Oliver confirmed.

"I feel like a chipmunk." Her eyes glistening, her expression
pained.

Nurse Hwan responded to the buzz and promptly examined
Alice. Without alarm, she explained this was a common side effect
of the radiation. "We have a mouth rinse that usually works for
this."

"Also my kitty feels a bit itchy."

The practitioner stared over the top of her eyewear.

"It burns when you urinate?"

"No."

"Any discharge?"

"No."

"Discomfort?"

"Just what I said."

"A bit itchy?"

"A bit itchy."

When the doctors on rounds made their way to the room, Alice
played her role to perfection, answering the questions of the attending (old man; trim gray beard), correcting his facts, then making new admissions: her ears were filled with fluid; she'd had two
attacks of dry heaves during the night, felt a seasick sort of stomach pain. Her thermometer check revealed fever. Examining her
mouth revealed blood clotted along the inside of her cheek, the inside gums.

The doctor prescribed a few drugs, as well as a couple of tests.

Nurse Hwan took the samples, and the breakfast tray arrived. "I'm famished," Alice said, but Oliver noticed she took only two bites of her bagel. Then her hand stretched toward her stomach. Her legs rose. She cringed.

Nurse Hwan reached for the house phone, told the floor operator to page the attending.

"So easy to be positive when you aren't feeling horrendous," Alice whispered. "The pain melts all of it."

Oliver started toward her. She winced again. Nurse Hwan told them she was still on hold.

And knocking. A thin orderly, his smock reaching toward his knees, pants bunched in folds and creases around what looked to be hunting boots. He pushed a wheelchair inside. "Transport here. Up to radiation—we ready to bounce?"

Alice studied him, her face twisted, a dawning horror. "Oh no. I'm so stupid. My lotion."

"Lotion?" Oliver asked.

She staggered, rose to the side of the bed, and unplugged the Christmas tree of IV bags and batteries. Alice was a soldier with orders now, wheeling the tree to the bathroom. She stood over the sink; water ran. She raised a wet cloth and soap to her face, began a vigorous rubbing.

"Yes," Nurse Hwan was saying, into the phone. "Correct."

A new nausea medicine was ordered from the pharmacy, and the doctor was explicit in his desire for it to be humming through Alice's veins before she went down to radiation. But this was not Oliver's trigger. Rather, it was that skinny homeboy, the orderly. Homie heard the news about the new infusion bag, he looked down. Dude sort of shifted his weight from one mosquito leg to the other, cursed under his breath—Oliver saw that he was irritated by the wait, and this is what got him.

Oliver estimated how long it would take for the medicine to arrive, then for the IV bag to empty. He guessed at the waiting time in a backed-up radiation center, plus two hours for the physical procedure. It all but guaranteed that today's coffee klatch would be here by the time Alice got back. He needed to survive a little longer. Make it that long, freedom was his: the city streets, their clutter and hassles; skies full of bus exhaust, a train pulling into the station while he waited to buy a token. Oliver went to Alice's laundry bag and checked its contents. He tightened its strings, checked her drawer, made a mental note to himself to buy her new underwear, so she would not have to wear the hospital's mesh ones before this load came back. He asked through the bathroom door if she had a preferred or favorite place.

He grabbed the 9 heading downtown—best thing he could do was get to the office.

Basically, Generii was done. The graphics, interface, and layout all worked: a grayish white field, a minimal ruler setting off page dimensions. You could import paragraphs, even whole files. True, the goddamn cursor kept going loopy when it ran over the bottom quadrant, meaning Oliver still had to track down that erroneous line of code. And any extra spaces, colons where semicolons should be, or slight typos resulted in all kinds of weird shit. There was still a laundry list, thousands of fixes.

He'd also done what he could to hold off the oncoming financial disaster, subletting out the new office space for a few months, moving the base of operations back into the apartment until Alice came home. But the Brow only came around one night a week to code, and even that was for a few hours at best, claiming he had no spare time, was back in graduate school.

Worst of all, Ruggles had started leaving messages on the apartment machine. *Hey, bud. Hope all is great with the wife. Hope you're hanging in. Sending much much love. Okay. Yo, my man.*

Just checking to see how Alice is doing. I've been meaning to get up there and see her. Maybe Friday. Give me a call, we'll set that up. (Whether or not Oliver felt guilty about his suspicions, he didn't return those calls.)

His subway car was jammed; he grabbed the nearest pole to keep from lurching when the train started. On instinct, Oliver felt around in his coat, made sure he had his little hand sanitizer bottle. In front of him a young woman with platinum dyed hair and bangs was listening to her Discman. The bright yellow strands of her headphones ran down the sides of her neck, and the front of her leather jacket, into her lap. He noticed her sniffles, how she dabbed at her nostril with a Kleenex.

Letting go of the beam, Oliver started toward the car's opposite end.

I plant myself in that bicycle seat without pride, do not even think of standing. Behind the protective wall of glass, they press their buttons. That giant machine hums. Presently everything on my skin gets so warm. I am dried out beneath this heat lamp. I sit there so long, being bombarded, that I lose track of what's happening, where I am. When they finally unstrap me, I practically pour from the chair, so worn down that I'm thankful an orderly is waiting, and don't care that it's the slim, sullen one. He wheels me down the hallway; I tell him of my gratitude. He responds by letting me know, "I get paid to wait through patient treatment."

We pass an elderly woman on the hall pay phone. She's explaining the horrible smell from whatever medicine they're putting into her husband's catheter. "I can't take it anymore," she says.

I know how you feel, I want to tell her.

But then catch myself. Because I don't.

Waiting for the elevator, the orderly at my side. Just the two of us now, neon fritzing above. "We all have jobs," he says. He's looking straight and forward into the thick metal doors. "Doctors do they jobs. Technicians do they jobs. Nurses sometimes do they job. My job, I get graded on pushing you where you need. I makes my bonus on how I keep that schedule. They keep you waiting, I don't get paid. You feel me?"

"I feel you," I manage. "But I don't understand what you expect me to do."

He shifts his weight, stares forward.

"Doctors ordered the drip," I say.

Not blinking. Hands behind his back as if cuffed.

"Now that you mention it," I continue. "After the surgery for my central line, I spent three hours drugged in a hallway, waiting for *anybody* to take me to my room. Who gets the bonus on *that*?"

A sounding chime; a green arrow points downward. I surprise myself again, rising, of my own power, from out of the wheelchair.

"Hey," said the orderly, "You can't—"

"Watch me."

With one hand I hold my giant binder to my chest. With my other I grab my Christmas tree.

"Come on," I say. Thighs trembling, I step inside. My voice is a melody: "We *must* get upstairs. Have to keep the schedule, *don't you know*."

What I am doing is *wrong*, this is clear: heading back to my room, standing on my own accord, refusing to make eye contact with the orderly—causing problems for *him*. Tattoos swirl on his forearms and alight on his wrists, can't be twenty-two. It's hard to believe he's pushing me around so he can sock his minimum-wage salary away for graduate school. I'd take that bet, anyway. Most of my nursing assistants seem recent arrivals to this country, probably they commute an hour and back from their nether-boroughs each day, then spend interminable shifts changing my sheets and empty-ing my pisspots, only to have their employment agency take a nice cut of their checks.

The elevator slows, descending back to my floor. I'm reminded that our mayor—whom I did not vote for—got elected in no small part by demonizing untold people of color, and that he did this to prey on the fears of a demographic that's undeniably my own. I'm suddenly chagrined, ashamed of having added, however fleetingly, to the cultural hostility in our smoggy air—especially as my well-being, indeed, *my life,* to no small extent depends on these all-but-indentured servants, waiting on me, literally with hand and foot.

Still, I feel so alive.

Almost soaring. Riding this righteous wave of anger.

And it is here that I realize—maybe the right word is *appreciate*—just how much I enjoy my own voice.

Stillness has taken over, the resonant quiet before my friends arrive. I'm determined to not let this quiet crush me. I have to use it, head deeper inside. Back in my bed, I take three spoonfuls of chicken soup—all I can handle. I feel myself being sapped, all adrenaline dissipating, the price of my insolence. I'm heated, my face damp. I lie back, shut my eyes, but the room keeps spinning. Thoughts drift, collide—not quite a fever blur, but not lucidity, either, my states of consciousness like a series of possible outfit choices for an important date. I keep slipping in and out of them, am only aware of them in retrospect, seeing the eyesore of dresses all over the floor, the stray thoughts of my naps and half dreams.

I don't know whether to feel relief when knocking intrudes—recognizable and catchy rhythms, a light metal song, all over the radio ten years ago.

"Music therapy?"

I raise my head, am still in a fugue state, groggy—not quite awake, not asleep—half-wincing at the overhead lights.

"They said at the desk you might—"

Peeking into the room—his sculpted hair, that stubble.

"Whoa," he says. "Funny running into you here."

Still gaunt, that beaten air to him. His leather jacket fits well. He stops in the doorway, starts putting on a mask. The way his eyes inhale me is unmistakable. I feel myself panicked, breathless.

I say, "I hoped we wouldn't see each other again."

"I know. I'm sorry."

His body lurches to the left as he enters the room. His limp is pronounced, each step of his right leg a test of its ability to carry weight. It's almost painful to watch. A beaten black case drags down his strong side. His other hand holds a small amp.

"What happened? Your leg—"

"This? Just a flesh wound."

"How can you be here?"

"I got carried away. I know."

"You're not still—"

Navigating his gear around the bed is a struggle, but he manages, reaching the far side of the room, in front of the lounger. "No," he says. He leans over, unlocks the case, removes his electric keyboard. Turning, he spots an outlet in the corner, bends to plug in. "Honest, I'm just here to provide you therapeutic release from your ailments."

I wait a beat. "I'm surprised you didn't bring ice cream."

He turns, facing me. "I got carried away."

On my right hand, in the space between my thumb and longest finger, I notice a long sun spot. My hands are dappled with them, whiskey stains on a tablecloth. "They warn you the radiation does it," I tell him. "But when it happens it's shocking." I know he's watching me, keep examining my hands.

"What songs do you play?" I ask. Because he has not left. Because something has to happen. "Come on. Give the sick woman a show."

He keeps staring. "Enough of soft-eyed male pleading," I say. "Enough with the apologies. I'd like some music therapy, please."

He plinks a key, as if testing it. Two more in quick succession.

His attention moves to his amp, some knob—twisting, checking a plug.

When his head rises I recognize fragility, someone trying to catch what he wants to say. He leans forward, puts his hands on his knees. He starts tapping, his fingers dancing in practiced syncopation, maybe one of his exercises. Bushy eyebrows rumple into his concentrating face. "You know what, remember when—" He stops, put a fist on his mouth. "Okay. Do over."

"During the summer I busted my leg, yeah, can you tell? Fucking thing—just the way doctors warned. *Don't watch where you're going, you'll step wrong and wham*. Did my stupid ass listen? One clunky step on an uneven sidewalk. I heard the snap, felt a jolt, *wham*."

"Bad?" I ask.

"Busted femur. They're telling me I might not ever walk normal again, might never run again, even after all the therapy."

"Mervyn—"

"Yeah. Thigh cast all June. Had to move back in with my dad in Jersey. At least I found a subletter so I can keep my pad. But a big wake-up. No more denial."

When I nod, I feel a tightness in my jaw, a twinge.

"I'm taking courses at NYU, working toward grad school. Music is what I can do, so music therapy. Maybe I can do something for other people. That's the plan anyway."

"I remember you being more cynical." I catch myself, wait. "You're not the musical therapist then?"

"They have one on staff. She's great, actually. But only two days a week. And they've got all these patients just sitting around, waiting for what? There's a demand. I saw the flyer on the department board at school, so here I am, volunteer intern. I do some requests, a few classics, or just play along, you know, listening to them and adding background noise."

He looks at me, says: "It was that horrible?"

Those eyes. Their desire. Their hangdog sadness.

"Not so bad," I answer. "It wasn't anything."

And then I say, "Do you know what you caused?"

"What? Wanting to live a little?"

"My husband—"

"Innocent pecking? That's so wrong?"

"Like I said, it wasn't anything."

"*I* know."

"Nothing happened that mattered."

"I know," he says, softer this time.

"What could have happened?"

Orderlies wheel a food tray past the room. Their heads turn.

"Nothing could happen. Nothing."

The strain burns, cords flaring through my throat. I cough; pain rises up my jawbone, my vocal cords tightening. I reach for my neck. With silence the hurt withdraws a bit. My eyes are shut; I hear him, feel his energy—he wants to help. I chance it and twist my neck as much as I can, motioning, side to side. *No.*

Oliver returned to Alice on her side, zigzagged beneath her quilt, motionless, her eyes shut, her mouth wide open. The stillness of the room was eerie to him. He noticed that the lounger where he slept had been moved closer to the bed. He noticed that much of the hospital lunch had been eaten. Oliver spent some time throwing out the remains of the morning's untouched Ensure drink. He poured a fresh glass of ice water. When Alice begin to stir, he approached, wanting to kiss her on the near cheek. She sensed something, was startled to attention, her eyes going wide. Oliver watched her take him in, uncertain about who he was.

But in one, two blinks, she had her bearings, and was recognizing that it was him.

Oliver knew what his shaved face meant to her, how she interpreted his washed and combed hair. Immediately, he felt exposed. But before he could respond, her eyes went moon large. She was trying to speak, looking to him for help. Moaning; low, pained sounds. Her panic radiated outward now, contagious. Oliver asked, "What's wrong?" even as he saw that her jaw had locked, rigid indentations of their hinges and gears flexing down her left side.

Mm tttttttngggg mmmm tnhhgg.

She moaned, unable to open her mouth, sounding pained, pointing now: *Ccnnnn tllka. EEyy Ccnnn tttlllk.*

"*Get someone here,*" he told the squawk box, blunt as a hammer. Then he spoke with a resolution that was precise. "*Room six. Oh. Eight. Jay. NOW.*"

Taking Alice's hand, he told her it was okay. He told her to breathe. "Let it go. In and release." Maybe they could do a breathing exercise? The rhythms from her birthing?

He could see her mind racing, sizing up the possibilities. She gave in, tried breathing out, releasing through her nose. Her posture became that much better, back straightening, shoulders going wide. When she inhaled again, her eyes had cleared of panic. Alice nodded at him, released another breath. Her face now held the shrewdness of composure. She mumbled once again, could not be understood, and this started to vex her. Now she thought, waited, pressed her tongue against her locked jaw. Tapping a hand to the other side of her face, she motioned.

"Tongue, too?"

The night resident, a youngish man with short brown hair and a long nose, was not surprised. He eased his gloved hand against Alice's jaw, helped open her mouth, shone his penlight inside.

"Plus a swollen tongue, check. Listing and to the right."

She moaned assent.

"Yeah," he responded. "Radiation does weird things to salivary glands."

Lemon drops were the answer, the doctor reported. Alice needed to generate saliva and her problems would subside. "Drink more water. Lots more. Eat and suck on lemon drops. And don't talk so much."

Oliver rushed down five flights of stairs and dropped eight dollars on a bag at the gift shop. The drops worked—unclenching Alice's jaw, loosening her tongue. When she finally spoke, her words came slowly—*thnnk yuuuu*—and it sounded as if she had marbles in her mouth. An hour later, when the attending stopped by again, Alice volunteered, with more than a little defensiveness: she thought she'd been drinking a lot.

How many cups had she finished today? the attending wanted to know.

A guilty motion. "That's my first." She saw the liquid along the bottom. "I'm still working on it."

The attending did not seem impressed. He looked around, told the nurse, "We've got to get her a bigger room."

A snapshot: my hair long, unwashed and piled into a scrunchie, my face still plump in a way that embarrassed me at the time. I beam in her direction. She stares with a dumbfounded look, big ears protruding, the cutest little yellow headband across that bald moonchild head. You can see a chubby segment of her hand, the bitten red star on one of her teething bubbles.

I open the orange envelope with the name of a drugstore that is no longer in business, flip through the snapshots, check if there is a duplicate, take out a negative. I raise the small strip of hard plastic film toward the ceiling. The practice is second nature to me, carried over from the fashion world: checking on the originals from a shoot, checking head shots. "Get a duplicate of the teething one," I say. "Maybe blow it up to eleven by fourteen."

I keep moving through the album; I'll have him do the same for the one where I'm holding Doe and she's adorned in floaties, in the pool behind my cousin's house. And the one of her twisted baby face, intense in its fervor, biting down on my thumb.

As I keep flipping, however, I notice something odd. A gradual shift: from photos of the two of us together to photos of Doe alone. Instead of Oliver taking photos of her and me, I'd taken most of these pictures of her; in them she was alone. This infuriates me, sends a baseball bat of doubt crashing through our happiness. Where had he been? I wonder if he'd ever been all that happy. I wonder how deep the fissures ran through the life we'd built together. It makes me doubt the wife I was, the happiness I trusted. It's all I can do to not scream.

Then I think: *What if these photos are all he'll have to show Doe of the two of us, mother and daughter, together?*

Glendora, the name of tonight's night nurse, gets written in my Moleskine notebook, though it isn't necessary, for her impression already is made. A Caribbean woman in her fifties, Glendora is mother to a litter of children, gramma to tons more. Her hair is piled high in a black block, like a tower of chocolate cake, and she has a penchant for unusually-colored eye makeup—bronze shimmery liner with blue mascara, both of which are shocking on her dark brown face. As if this is not enough, she's drawn dramatic half-moons for her eyebrows. A large woman, she seems even larger because of how she lumbers around this little closet, wheezing through her nostrils as she checks the levels of an IV battery, clears a clogged line, takes my blood and vitals, makes sure my medicines are correct, helps me to and from the bathroom, answers questions from my friends and relatives, asks me questions for the doctors, and writes down answers in my file. She always tries to be pleasant. Looking at the bedside photos, she says my daughter is a blessing. She says that having Oliver look after me is a blessing. My temperature being around normal before heading off for my third radiation blast today? Also a blessing.

Presently, her rear end knocks a photo off the bedside table.

Glendora apologizes and picks up the picture—a framed snapshot of Doe and me in a different hospital bed, the child bright red and mushed in the face, not minutes after she was born.

"What a blessing," Glendora says.

"Thank you."

"Honey, you gonna get through this."

"Of course," I mumble. "That's not up for debate."

She smiles. "You have to think like that."

Oliver's eyes are already with me, and for a moment—*because otherwise death is waiting? That's why we have to think like that?*—we are united in our irritation. But the moment doesn't last; his clean face again ignites me, and he recognizes this, and goes back to whatever he's doing on his laptop.

How much of life is regret, fretting over mistakes, wishing you'd had that perfect comeback to your ex, trying to make good for a turn from which there was no returning; reckoning with errors made from pride, desire, need, or defensiveness. Making mistakes because you were afraid. It's a necessary pain: understanding there are fissures that cannot be healed, our time here is messy.

I've seen weight lifters in the free-weight area of my gym pump each other up before a massive bench press. "No pain, no gain," they shout. This also happens to be one of the teachings of Satchidananda. Well, here is my pain: my swollen jaw, my muddled mind, my torn heart.

All the nurses are busy; Oliver is in his chair, still doing his thing with his laptop; the room is quiet. It's moments like this I feel most alone, most scared of what's ahead. I wish I had Tilda here, feeding me, caring for me, reminding me to eat every two hours.

But this is the wrong way to look at things, I know. So I ask myself: *What stands in the way of me fully taking care of my physical body?* The answer isn't comfortable. I get food delivered to my bedside, but let it sit out and spoil. I don't drink enough water or eat enough ice. I don't brush my teeth at night. I am too much in love with the idea of Tilda, a nurse, or some old Indian woman caring for me, bringing me soup, changing the blankets I've soaked with sweat.

What happens if *I* become that Indian woman caring for me? I can isolate the pain in my jaw and mouth, reducing it to one small throbbing blip in the vast blackness. I can place the absurdity of Oliver's appetites into a closet, shut the door, and let blackness wash over him as well. I can turn my back on the horror and fear that arrived this afternoon—my own absurd brush with appetite— when desire manifested from the ether and walked into this room to sit at my bedside. But it also walked away, didn't it? I can stay in the moment of now. But it's so hard to detach from her.

Finally, a good half an hour later than had been arranged, the room phone rings. I want to get it, but Oliver's already picked up the receiver, is bringing the phone to me.

"She had a big day," says my mother. "She did so good at the children's museum. I got a disposable camera and took pictures. I'll send them off like you want, every day. More than a year old—my precious girl is getting so big. We had mac and cheese for dinner, then *rub a dub* in the bath. She's a tired tomato right now. *Yes you are.*"

My mother describes the face that my daughter makes when she is trying to figure something out. "Right now she's scrunching her nose and tossing her head to the side a bit. Like what is happening is *yucky*. Anything she doesn't want to do is *yucky*."

I hear Doe's laughter and my mother fussing over her. My heart is gray coals, its embers burning.

"Your laugh is the greatest thing." I say. "You light up when you laugh." I am thinking of her when she is uncertain, holding her arms out to her sides, palms up. I whisper to Doe that I love her. "Today I am missing you very much. I wish I could have you in my room and we could play together."

There is static on the other end. Fumbling sounds. Now a wail.

"I'm sad, too," I say. "I'm sad, too, Blueberry."

The crying increasing, becoming oppressive. "Every minute of the day I am loving you," I continue.

"She's tired," my mother says. "She doesn't have the attention span right now."

"Then why call so late?"

My voice wavers; I'm on the brink. But Oliver steps in. Interjecting, speaking over me, he calls Doe little macaroon. He sings to her, the first letter of the alphabet. The second.

The other end stops futzing.

"Tell her she is in Mommy's heart," he says to me.

My vocal cords strain: "MOMMY'S IN YOUR HEART."

The other end softens, goes silent. I hear a garble.

A questioning "Maa?"

And then "Daa?"

And, "Haa?"

"Mommy, Daddy, heart?" I ask.

"Maa daa haa."

The Second Noble Truth of Suffering, or *dukkha*, seeks to determine the origins of craving. I might crave fine silk sheets, the pleasures of a Dolce handbag, but these cravings are transitory, a thirst—*tanha*—that might be allayed but never quenched. Buddha teaches that *tanha* grows from a lack of personal awareness, that grabbing wildly for one thing after another is an illusion. Says Buddha: "If, in the world, you overcome this uncouth craving, hard to escape, sorrows roll off you, like water beads off a lotus."

Maybe I could accept rough, starched sheets. Maybe I can stop desiring to watch *Pulp Fiction*. But I will shout, straight into Buddha's face: You *listen to that baby who came from your womb*, you *give up your desire to be with her*.

The other end of the phone is silent, but my heart is jammed in my throat, my pulse racing through my jawline. I am aware of Oliver's hand on my shoulder. My face is a blubbery wash.

I am here. Possessed. In this moment Fully alive.

"It is true," I say, carefully enunciating, working against the swelling. "Mommy and Daddy are in your heart. You are in our hearts, too. So we're really not apart. Our desire lifts us. It delivers us."

From the extended lounger, he says, "I guess the whole thing was a success."

The events behind us, the room finally black.

"It was nice," I manage.

"I think we're doing this well, so far."

The walls black and lighter black.

"The night nurse is a piece of work, right? With those eyebrows?"

"Glendora?"

"That's her name? Were those tattooed on?"

"Those are drawn."

"*Drawn?*"

"Mmmm. You shave your eyebrows and draw in more dramatic ones. A lot of women do it."

"Yeah?"

"I'm wise to the ways of women, Oliver. I know these things."

The air conditioner kicks into a different gear, a slight shift.

"Do you want to talk about it?" he says.

"I want to sleep."

"Because I'm willing. I want to make things—"

"It's been a long day, Oliver."

He waits.

"I need to sleep," I say.

His resignation is palpable. I hear him shifting on the lounger. "Right."

. . .

Dawn, or five minutes after. Whatever awful time it is. I am roused from depth and drool. The young nursing assistant, Noelle, tells me the doctors want samples—"Stool sample. Urine sample." My throat remains tender, as if I'd spent the evening chewing on shoe leather; and this is an improvement. It's possible I can string together a few sentences. I am careful, slow. "Bad enough pooping and peeing into hats," I begin. "Trying to do it in *separate* hats."

Noelle doesn't break from her plastic smile.

I keep going. "Especially when those pills cause diarrhea. My poo is liquid as my pee. They both come out at the same time. Getting them into separate hats? You're asking me to perform ass gymnastics."

Noelle looks at the pictures on the bedside, says how beautiful my baby is.

Usually I fall back to sleep after vitals, but this time I'm too worked up. And now Nurse Hwan makes an appearance. She wants to know about my jaw. "How's it doing?"

She walks me through the previous day: my medicine regimen when I woke, the trip to the radiation room. That afternoon. Before I went to sleep, did I feel any symptoms? Swelling in my tongue, pain in my jaw? Were these immediate when I woke after the midday radiation treatment? She tells me she wants to be my advocate.

"Advocate for what?" I ask. She does not answer.

An hour later, Blasco comes in, along with my radiation doctor. Familiar with what I've told the nurse, they ask more follow-ups, trying to fill in the time line: step by step, what side effects took place starting here, what drugs I was taking beforehand, how long beforehand. "We want to know as much as we can," Blasco says. "Any tips or hints can be helpful."

He asks how the lemon drops are working. I nod and say they've helped. Dr. Blasco looks relieved, and proceeds to my bowel movements. "Records show you haven't had one since checking in."

"That's not true," I say.

"You're on Zofran, and that causes constipation," Blasco continues. "Let's start you on a pill regimen that will soften your stool."

"No."

"It should loosen things up."

"You don't understand."

The radiation doctor nods at Blasco. They look to me to make it unanimous.

"Is it my turn?" I ask.

It will be the last time out of my room, at least for a while. We get to the second floor and start down the corridor with the row of windows. I pay extra attention to the pale white sky, the blustery day, the highest branches of trees passing the ward's windows, swaying back and forth in thickets. Their remaining leaves, all the reds and oranges and pale yellow shades that define fall, seem ready to fly off into the wind. But right now they are hanging on, the branches swaying closer to the building, so close that a few leaves actually press against the windows, and then spring away. Watching the syncopations, I feel a violence in my stomach, as if I could vomit.

"I will give you a hundred dollars," I tell the orderly, "if we can play hooky and go outside for five minutes."

Emaciated, with a junkie's shrunken-apple face, jailhouse tattoos on his neck.

"What happens when I get caught taking you outside?" he says. "Hazard a guess."

"Two thousand dollars."

He clucks his tongue.

"Come on," I say. "Let's go get high."

He goes inward, studies me, taking in my rabidness.

"*Sheeeeeiiit.*" He laughs.

I laugh back, stick out my swollen tongue at him.

I've got an easy dialogue with Paul, the radiation guy, though it's not quite a rapport. The most revealing thing I've learned is that he's friends with Dr. Eisenstatt; but when I asked how old Eisenstatt is, Paul got flustered, as if I'm not supposed to know human information about the man, am not supposed to think about him as anything other than my doctor.

Today, however, I can't keep up my end of the banter. My head is pulsing, my breaths labored. When I move in any direction, I get a rush, must hold on to the sides of the bicycle seat. Paul tells me to take as much time as I need. I stare ahead, hoping to find an object to focus on. A vomit bucket—in actuality it looks like a bedpan—has been tied to one of the nearest handles; however, these handles are immovable, and there's no way my head can reach. My breaths are not coming any easier. The air in the room has a slight chill. I have goosebumps. All around me is that constant machine hum. I think of telling Paul I can't keep going. I imagine being unstrapped, the port gently withdrawn, getting disconnected from all these tubes, waiting outside for the car service. But it doesn't feel true.

This is what people go through.

Now is my turn.

I catch my breath, brace myself, grit my teeth, feel the tightness in my jaw, less than it's been, but still tight—an odd relief. I ready myself; nod.

All right, I tell myself. *I never have to go through that again.*

My pajamas and undergarments lie on the floor next to the bed. Since I am now approved to shower, it has been impressed upon me that cleanliness is very important to my health. There are no words for how ready I am to wash away the bed grime, the sour stench of my own self. I use the intercom to let them know I'm going to shower. "You can come in and change the sheets."

A chipper answer: *"All righty."*

The water is a refreshing assault; I let it wash over my skull, my shoulders, turn and lift my head, let the water batter the front of my neck. I hold on to the steel pole for support, stand under the blast for as long as my legs allow. Afterward, still soaking wet, I defy fate and manage a bowel movement. The plastic lid is sealed, the small container gets placed as instructed, atop the toilet.

Back in my freshly cleaned bed, settling on the spanking white sheets, I again call the nurses' station, report that I have a sample.

Another *"All righty,"* just as chipper as the first.

Feeling a measure of competence, I shut my eyes, let myself drift.

Across the street from Penn Station, a dusty office building from the era of brimmed fedoras and three martini lunches: Oliver ignored the rental cop at the counter and headed straight to the groaning elevator. He traversed the dusty maze of deco hallways with their obsolete bronze mailboxes, their ornate eagles—eyes still alert, watching. Then he was at his destination: that dark room, its door creaking ajar. Illuminated by the usual series of scented candles, she emerged: small, curvy, fitting the description he'd heard over the phone, her body fully packed into that matching bra and panties. Perla, this one's name. Attractive enough, but older than promised, her nose long and Baltic and red and veined at its rounded nostrils. The wear of life around her eyes. Mouth pinched at the corners. She purred his name, held out her hand for his picture ID.

This moment remained a stomach churner, a test of his most paranoid self: Who needed to get caught in the middle of a sting? Or what if something went wrong and his identification got taken, or fell onto the floor and was left behind? Along with his appointment record, this could be an evidence trail, a way to track him, expose him to the world. (Thank hell, nobody had done that pecker check since the first time.)

Perla handed back his card.

And so here he was, in yet another nondescript bedroom. And this wasn't even that, just a bare office space with gothic moldings and a queen-size in its middle—far enough away from walls that the headboard would not thump. Oliver stepped inside, moving onto the industrial carpet and past the line of canvas sneakers and platform shoes, all of them in small sizes, almost like children's shoes. The closet door was open, a travel suitcase on the floor, overflowing with tangled tops and jeans. Next to it sat a small pile of goodies (logic suggested they'd been purchased from nearby Koreatown wholesalers): perfume boxes still in cellophane wrappers, toy stuffed bears, samplers of dark chocolate.

Putting the envelope on the small bedside table, he turned to her, expectant, experienced enough now to know the deal—for these rates, he wasn't getting street whores. One had worn a sleek evening dress. Another, at Oliver's request, had been in casual wear, like she was the girl next door. They poured tasteful wines, asked his feelings on the market, made an easy segue into whether he wanted a massage; they rubbed breasts up and down his back, nibbled at his ear.

"You want shower?" Perla motioned.

Thin white towels stacked atop the toilet. The above shelf held a pink gallon jug of Vagisil, an economy supersizer of Listerine. Mouthwash killed germs, made blowjobs safe. Before penetration, your more experienced girls worked the condom application into their routine, putting it on with a sexy handjob or the mouth. Once, Oliver had been with a gorgeous but nervous African girl— new to the biz, barely out of her teens, she'd refused to start until he'd washed his genitals with antibacterial lotion. *Do NOT*, she'd demanded, *touch your dick*. Still he'd gripped (*Force of habit, sorry*). She'd ordered: *Go back to the toilet, do it again.*

Fragrance-free shampoo by Vidal Sassoon. Oliver flinched, stayed the hell away.

Patting himself down, he wrapped a towel around his pudge, and tried not to think about his expanding belly, let alone the mess of used towels filling the hamper. In the main room, the stereo was already playing, shitty pop like always. The envelope had disappeared from the table. Perla's bra and panties were also gone. Burnt-orange tan, melons huge and juicy, midriff showing a cesarean scar. Smiling at him, her face became soft and young. She motioned him onto the bed. In a manner that a man might let himself believe was genuine, she whispered: *"I will take care of you."*

The lie he'd told himself was: one time. *Just to get it out of his system.* It wasn't so easy. Though they barely kissed him, or kissed with a grudging stiffness. Though they only got wet from douche. They licked, bobbed, gagged, grinded, pressed, moved from missionary to doggy-style, bodies pliable, up for any position, any act that you could pay for, but only that much. That constant distance. Sex for the john to bust his load and feel satisfied. Oliver might come—might come really hard—but he always left those apartments unfulfilled. Depressed about sinking so low in the first place, and then paying for *that*? He'd feel taken advantage of. A failure in every way a man could fail. There was only one possible answer: another appointment. And on those rare occasions he staggered away with his head woozy and his knees weak, need also gnawed at him—another really good fuck, soon as he could.

He was in a different universe than the one where he'd been looked at with abject love. This much was certain.

And yet, female skin remained its own miracle.

Perla's eyes went heavy lidded.

She moaned, bit her bottom lip. Her nub of clit glowed red and full of blood. Oliver felt the deeper muscles in her vagina contract around him.

No matter if there was professional distance, no matter the emotional barriers, reminders seeped through: the human body's higher capacities. Had he made her come? Made her feel anything real? He was ashamed it mattered to him, and chose to believe anyway.

Afterward Perla smoked in the small walk-in kitchenette. While Oliver dressed, she made a call and talked briefly in Russian. She paid him the requisite, above-the-marquee compliments—that was *sensational,* he had a *sensational* cock. Then she gave him the usual sell, telling him *he* was *sensational,* and that she wanted him to become her regular visitor. Once again, she asked if he wanted to use the shower, checked through the peephole to make sure nobody was in the hallway.

How long he's been at the side of the bed, I don't know. His irises deep with relief, his face concerned. If I possessed the energy, I would reach out and stroke his cheek. "How you doing?" he asks, only the words are garbled, something in his mouth. "Hanging in?"

Too worn to smile, I keep looking at him. His hair flops down in front of his face, and he concentrates on the keyboard, hits a few soft notes. My bag of lemon drops rests on the furthest keys. There's something he's been working on, he says. Can he share with me?

Pensive notes in a middle register. They build, but not quickly. He hums along. The played notes may be diffuse, but a rhythm forms from them, and the sound moves, higher, coming quicker. I shut my eyes and listen. I let myself float.

I feel the radiation sunburn pulse across my forehead.

The song drifts like leaves. Soon I understand that its melody is a form of flight, and choose to ignore the clumsy parts. It is nice to have something surprise me like this. To not worry about consequences.

"Lovely," I tell him, "that you wanted to take me away."

"Work in progress." His grin is thankful, mischievous. "Want to hear another one?" Instead of waiting for permission, he acts like a college boy with an acoustic guitar at a kegger, anxious to show that flock of coeds what he can do. His new song kicks off with a jaunty rhythm, one that could lead a parade down Main Street.

Then it happens. Oliver enters the room. He's already speaking, loudly congratulating me for getting through my radiation, saying he's so proud of me. Here the melody stops; the closing door knocks into Oliver's back; I see the scene register on his face: Oliver first digesting, then figuring out who this keyboardist is, absorbing the manner in which this man is looking at me—and perhaps how I am looking at Merv. How *have* I been looking at Merv? My immediate reaction is terror. We've been caught. Then I think, *What is there to catch?*

Oliver's eyes are liquid pools. He looks as if he's taken a blow that's buckled his knees, rocked him back onto his heels. Now I see him registering the open bag of candy on Merv's keyboard.

For an instant I worry I am watching a man being broken. But I also want to shout: *See how it feels. You aren't the only one.*

And now I see that Oliver is taking me in: my diminished body wrapped in so many bedsheets, nearly mummified; my sunburned, grotesque face; my expression at once terrified and wired.

He is silent. He is still. Like a layer of protective skin and marrow has been stripped away, revealing a more naked, essential being.

I have a beat of worry that Merv will say some asshole thing.

"Keep playing."

The flat dagger of Oliver's words. He takes two steps toward me, looks me in the eye, kisses my cheek.

Reaching for a metal folding chair, he is resigned, reflective. I see his hurt.

He shrugs. "More the merrier, right?"

Merv is glancing between my husband and me, looking worried, considering what to do. An upper corner of his lip rises. A twisted smile. Now he looks down, devotes his attention to the keyboard.

He launches into what sounds like cabaret styling, only it somehow seems bouncier, jaunty. It takes me a few seconds, but then, before I even know what I'm doing, I squeal. *" 'Show me, show me, show me how you do that trick.' "* Oliver looks at me with obvious dismay. Still, I blurt out the next lyric, *" 'The one that makes me scream,' she said,"* diving into that radio standard from years ago.

We go on for a while, four, maybe five songs: blasphemous rumors as espoused by pale Germans in a competitive world; patient boys simmering in untold waiting rooms; a lovelorn question delivered from some early-morning barstool into an answering machine. Each song is not just recognizable but a jewel, culled from how many nights spent fiddling with a radio knob, stretching out an antenna, hoping to coax forth middling reception, that favorite, faraway college radio station. Oliver's being polite—I can even sense his appreciation—but I can also tell that he's measuring, wondering what Merv's presence in this room means. Merv meanwhile has a performer's studied immersion. With practiced and nonchalant one-upmanship, he goes out of his way to concentrate on that keyboard, as if everything that matters is located there. Every now and then he looks up, glances toward me. I keep that beatific smile plastered on my face.

Bless Glendora! She shows not one care for our little triangle, only for her responsibilities. Plodding to the side of my bed, she stoops— her head, neck, and shoulders lowering as if worked by a rusty crank. Her lower torso follows, then her waist. In this groaning manner she manages toward the floor. An excess of old syringes and runaway tubing lies around the overflowing red plastic container. Glendora sighs. "They ain't cleaning none of this?" She starts gathering the excess. "Some cock and bull—" she begins.

"*Bullshit,*" Oliver interrupts. "Straight-up *bullshit.*

"I could tell you wanted to say that," he adds.

I feel myself wanting to apologize. Merv meanwhile has stopped playing, is laughing into his shirt collar.

Glendora seems uncertain whether the white people are having a laugh at her expense. Then she shakes her head, calls us a bunch of silly crackers. I hear the rest of the room's appreciative yelps. My relief allows me to join. Now Glendora places the tubing in the trash bin outside, comes back, opens the bathroom door. "You got that stool sample for me?"

"I gave a sample this morning."

Purple-shaded eyes blink repeatedly. She puckers her mouth. "Blasco just asked."

"It's not on top of the toilet?"

She looks around. "Not in here."

"I promise I left it."

"Ain't on the chart, honey. Ain't on the chart, we ain't got it."

Don't ask me how, but I manage yet another accomplishment: an unheard-of second gold medal in ass gymnastics; yes, another clean sample, achieved in a single day. The nursing desk does not answer. A second call brings no response.

Finally, at almost nine in the evening, an hour and ten minutes after my first call, someone answers.

"I need help with something," I say. "And I still need someone to pick up this sample."

Within minutes, another Caribbean woman arrives—I believe her name is Shanti, but don't have time to check my notes. She says there's an emergency on the floor. Glendora's busy dealing with that. "What can I do?"

"Thank you, if you could clear away my tray. But really, I called for the sample to be picked up."

I see she's hurried, and clearly annoyed, presumably *with me*. She goes into the bathroom. I hear her say, "Sweet Jesus." A splashing sound: the toilet flushes.

"Shanti, did you just flush my sample?"

"What?"

Oliver is up, starting toward the bathroom. "The stool sample we asked to be picked up *more than an hour ago*?"

"I didn't know it was a sample." Shanti folds her arms over her breasts. I feel myself warming, want to stay calm, am not doing a very good job. "I can't believe you did that," I say. "I called three times for that to be picked up."

"I didn't know," she repeats, stiffening. "Nobody told me."

"When you walked in the door she told you," Oliver says. "I heard her."

I am hotly aware of not wanting to look like a bully, let alone like a racist.

"Oliver, thank you," I say, "I really don't—"

Shanti is just standing there, numb, waiting to absorb whatever abuse, and this makes me a bit sick. Seeing I've finished, she apologizes once more, but it's apparent she doesn't mean a word. In the quick motions of a hurt girl, she turns and leaves.

More knocking now: a supervisor enters, followed by Glendora. The supervisor is short and Asian—younger than me, lively with her greeting. She likely makes more money than I did on my best freelancing days. Her front teeth are ragged fence posts beaten down by too much time and bad weather, and they don't seem to faze her at all. She's odd and distinctive, and was likely discriminated against in her lifetime—certainly she caught some hell about those chompers, but odds suggest she doesn't get abuse like Shanti, or Glendora. The class dynamics seem different; the power dynamic between her and me is obviously separate from the dynamic I have with the other nurses. She asks what's been going on. Something in me opens. "I'm not blaming Shanti," I say, "because it clearly wasn't her fault, but something's obviously wrong. I keep being told I'm supposed to deliver the doctors a stool sample. Meanwhile nobody knows they're supposed to pick up that same goddamn sample."

"Oh, she knew," Glendora volunteers.

"She knew?" I feel a horrible relief.

"Shanti came on shift. I told her I needed your sample."

"I can't believe this—"

"You clearly have a lot going on right now," the nurse-practitioner says. "I hear that you are upset."

"I appreciate you trying to validate my experience," I answer. "But it doesn't change that I'm trying to do what I'm supposed to do, and people are throwing it away."

"What can I do to make things better?"

"Okay. One thing. How about you tell the guy answering the call bell that his job actually matters? He's like, *all righty, okay,* sounding all efficient, then doing nothing. Tell Shanti that her job *actually matters*. People around here need to do their jobs. They're *actually important*. And I'd really like to get some sleep tonight, so I'd appreciate it if my vitals were taken as late as possible."

"I'll tell her to do you last."

Oliver breaks in: "Is there anyone besides Shanti who could do them?"

Immediately I am grateful, look for the answer.

"I'm on it."

"Thank you, Glendora," I say.

"I got you, honey. No problem."

It feels very late. The room is basically blackened, light beeps and blips of machines sounding out every so often, intruding on the quiet. I feel wholly alone, stuck in this horrid place, unable to sleep, aware of the cancer and nuclear radiation both teeming through me, my cheating husband asleep next to me on the pullout bed.

Then why am I almost deliriously happy?

I finished a major part of this procedure today. I ate enough protein. I spent an hour knitting. I listened to music that, at moments, made me happy. I felt loved today, even if that love was misguided, coming from an odd half stranger. But when he sang to me, he tried to take me away, or make me feel better, or give me hope. I felt that. It mattered.

Today I let myself rant. I knew I was being *bad,* knew I was doing *wrong.* But I did it anyway, I let my own voice thrill me—its quickness, its agility, my own contrary surges. Since my illness, I've felt a kind of lightning through me—stripping something away, peeling off layers.

The Third Noble Truth of Suffering involves the cessation of *dukkha,* meaning the cessation of suffering. Reason extends this to cessation of the causes of suffering. To ease our cravings we must eliminate the causes of craving. Our wants, desires, delusions, appetites. I don't think it's possible. I know it is not. Not totally. But since I have been ill there has been a kind of lightening. My body has been husked away, reduced to its essentials. And today, for a little while, maybe I found a path to my essential self.

Argh argh argh, I just found out I'm clearly having an allergic reaction to whatever cream they are using at my entry site, and I'm yelling now—somewhat good-naturedly, with love, yes, with love—to my lovely overnight nurse, Tara:

"Clown-shoe motherfuckers!"

Breakfast: nuked oatmeal with agave nectar; I can't manage two bites. On my fifth sip of Ensure, Dr. Blasco enters, adjusting the strings on a paper mask. My eyes gravitate to his protective smock. Made of something that seems like a space-age yellow chiffon, it is semitransparent, clingy, and lined with lead. Tied around the doctor's neck, it otherwise hangs free and open. He approaches, pleasant as a bird greeting the sunrise: "You are ready for the next marathon?"

The way the smock hangs seems poignant—its spreading breadth, its loose yellowness. I think of a barbecue apron worn by a friendly and preoccupied father, eager to begin his yearly backyard grilling adventure—he has no idea that it can only end with his children crying, his wife disgusted, everyone still hungry and angry at him.

But what is this? What's happening inside my head? How can I be getting maudlin? How did I become this swinging pendulum, my moods reversing course so quickly, all confidence draining?

"More than ready," I tell the doctor. "Let's get this party started."

The steps are familiar by now, though each still sends creepers through my stomach: nurses entering with their horror movie get-ups, everyone in paper mask and powdered gloves, trying to move their arms in a way human arms aren't meant to move so they can knot the strings behind their necks; Oliver flushed, sweating like a pig in his garb, grousing that the gloves make it impossible to use his laptop.

"We want a clean slate," Blasco says, meaning blood cells without cancer. Now he gets to the specific, final steps that must be taken before the transplant. Two drugs will enter my system during this first round of chemo: Cytoxan, which will aggravate the bladder, and Thyatemper, which I'll receive over four hours. "You take a shower an hour after getting it," says Blasco. "This will help your lungs with breathing, it can help to prevent clotting and dyspnea. Another shower six hours after that. You should not drink the shower water."

Here is the part where my hands grasp the pregnant and transparent bottles, moving them back and forth as if weighing them. Here is where I grip their sides (my hands go flat, I press). Here I thank and welcome each concoction, loving it, praying for that poison's effectiveness, embracing it with all of my warrior spirit energy. *"Let's do this!"* I say, but I feel myself manufacturing the enthusiasm. I tell myself the medicine is making me better in its way, and I am making myself better in mine. However, my mantras do not feel so sacred anymore. It's more like I feel some part of myself separating, a distance opening. I can't stay in the moment but instead hear a voice inside me, ordering: *Stay in the moment.*

There's nothing enjoyable about being nuked until you are a glowing and bloated and scabrous kumquat, but at least radiation got me out of the room. Not anymore. I'm trapped inside this vulgar little triangle of space, I have to make my peace with that.

My catheter continues its disco throb, but I'm told I must deal. Any painkillers might inhibit my ability to recognize pain, alert proper authorities to larger problems, which is important for me right now. Bless Blasco for prescribing Ativan. When it hits, the drowsy sensations are like that satisfaction you feel after a second bowl of excellent soup. Still, when I'm awake, I'm lucid, which every nurse says is a good sign. Furthermore, the familiarity is helpful, not a comfort but at least known. I keep my journal updated when nurses add a bladder protectant called Kenzlo to the Christmas tree. My mouth has gotten cotton dry. I try to drink more water, but sometimes I forget. There's so much to track; some things slip past. I am allowing myself the luxury of more naps, especially when chemo bags are up.

Apparently Tilda has found a niche at *Schlep*—its editors are more than happy to exploit her to the hilt; but here she is, still forcing herself not to crumble at the sight of my face. She spends time looking at the backs of my hands: how orange they are, their burnt hue, their texture hard and rough as mussel shells. Cleaning the clutter from my tray, Tilda calls and tells the desk to bring a new pitcher of ice water. She unwraps steaming edamame and grilled lemon chicken from Tupperware containers, a new tube of moisturizer lifted from the magazine's makeup room. She wants to know how I am, meaning she wants a medical update. Even this kind of talk sends us back into our old dorm, college roomies— easy and familiar—again commiserating about impossible boys.

I let her know about the return of the musician—keeping it coy, roundabout. She's suspicious and delighted. Then an actual gasp. Tilda's gloved hand rises in front of her masked mouth. "I would have paid to see that."

"To his credit, he didn't break that keyboard over the guy's face."

"Oh, he had to be pissed. Was he pissed?"

"Tilda, I have a real dilemma. If you could see how devastated—"

"Please. That dog doesn't have a leg to stand on."

"Other than finding the insurance, you mean, and paying my premiums, and running around dry cleaning my underwear—"

"Where was he all afternoon?" Her voice is knowing.

"Can't exactly blame him, can you?"

Before she can correct me, I am correcting myself. "Right, I *do*. But I understand, I think. The pressure he's under. The man's been by my side for everything. Part of me wants to say, Go. I have to live in this every second, who else should have to? Get fucked. Some piece of *ass,* who cares?"

"You care, though—don't you?"

"It *is* a betrayal. I mean, we grow up knowing men cheat. You worry so much about finding someone and getting married. And then you spend your marriage with the hovering possibility; every woman lives in fear of it. All the perfect couples that don't make it. People get divorced. Life goes on."

She provides her rubber yellow hand, clasps my dry-bone knuckles.

"Even with this rupture," I continue, "there's still our *depth*. I think that's why it hurts more. I *do* need him. It just burns at me, Til. But, maybe, I mean—"

Tilda blinks, trying to follow.

"I'm confused, too." I squeeze her fingers. "Yesterday was *horrible*. Sitting there and looking at one another and not trusting *anything*."

"Ugh."

"*Ugh*. But, but somehow, when Oliver backed down and let Merv stay, he must have put his faith in, what—the idea of *what was best for me*? What was *larger*?"

My throat feels rough. I motion for the pitcher, pour what remains into a glass, sip at tepid water.

"One consolation," I continue. "I don't need to do anything about it. I guess I'll figure it out after. If I survive."

"When," Tilda says.

"When," I say.

"How's that keyboardist's tushie?" Tilda asks.

We make eye contact. I wave her off.

"You're talking about a man who can only find an audience in the bedridden."

"So then, *my type*."

"When I got mad at that nurse, the terror on his face. *So* in over his head. But there's a charm. An eagerness. It's sweet. I like him coming, making me feel a little alive."

"I don't think it's the worst thing for O to remember what a catch you are." She squeezes my hand again.

I thank her, lie back. "Sometimes, I think about what his life will be like without me."

Tilda's face goes rigid. I motion, *Let me continue.*

"He might be able to finish his program, if he was able to give it the attention he has to give me. He can hire sitters. He's young. With the violin and sob story he'll be able to wheel out, soon enough there'd be another woman. But even when this transplant works, it's going to take me time to get better, if I ever do."

"Alice—"

"I'm not having a pity party, just admitting it. He might be better off—"

"You're strong enough to have these feelings," Tilda says. "And I'm strong enough to sit with you while you have them."

I squeeze, thank her with my eyes, take and suck an ice chip.

"The thing that gets me—is my daughter's life without me. I can't."

"I know, honey."

"I can't imagine it," I repeat.

"So don't."

I recognize an exhaustion in her voice. She's been through this dance enough.

She says, again: "So don't."

He hadn't been able to sleep, work, eat, think of anything else, anyone else. That he might lose her to cancer was already unthinkable; that he might lose her heart to another man was what: Repulsive? Emasculating? It was impossible. It was his fault.

He managed, at best, two hours of lackluster troubleshooting before saving the file, shutting things down, and heading by her magazine place, where he grabbed anything he hadn't already seen in Alice's room: *WWD* (cover: drop-dead pouty blonde with bangs), *Italian Vogue* (pouty blonde; long hair spraying everywhere), and *Cosmo* (famous amazon, pouty mole). With his every step, an instinct said he should check over his shoulder. In the middle of the sidewalk he envisioned seeing that limpy motherfucker, that bouncy mess of hair.

He picked up her laundry from the dry cleaner across the street from Whitman. He stopped at a pharmacy and bought a few tubes of ChapStick. He might not get any decent work done with his mind like this; but he could still take care of her. He could protect what was his.

Three hours before his usual time, Oliver arrived in front of her hospital room and stopped at the supply counter.

The only gloves were midget-size. Their plastic barely reached over his fingers, cracking and popping and going no farther. He was putting on his mask when he became aware: someone approaching, slowly, behind him. Leather jacket. Stubble.

The interloper arrived, put down his amp and keyboard case; he avoided eye contact, waiting for his turn.

"Can't you see what's happening to her?" Oliver said.

The musician looked down and away, seemed to suck on a thought. His hands went to his hips. His elbows jutted. Now he'd scraped together his answer. "I do." He pursed his lips. "There's nothing between us. Okay at first, I, but—she had an effect on me, is all."

"Please. Whatever bullshit—"

"Dude, I'm just trying to do something good here."

The guy raised his gaze and looked Oliver in the eye, and Oliver felt himself go rigid, felt the need for some kind of response.

"We can't be at war," he finally said. "Not now."

Merv blinked, stared.

Imagine my surprise when they file in, Oliver sheepish, leading the way, laden with today's offering of grocery bags and a bunch of magazines stuffed under his armpit; then Merv, a few workmanlike steps behind, his head and shoulders hanging, arms dragging in his long black case and speaker casing. Oliver kisses me on the cheek, wants to know how I am doing. Merv cleans off a flat surface, asks about refilling the water.

Maybe I'm reading too much into things, but after this moment, I swear, during the remaining day or so of my chemo, something inside that room changes. The mood, yes, but more. I'm convinced my rash is lighter along my forearms. And my voice grows stronger. Even the natural light from the window behind me feels different, warmer; I know it sounds ridiculous, but I swear it's thicker, hues like the early afternoon light from some Parisian painter's garret. This when there's already *so much*—any time I awaken from sleep, or come out of a hallucination, friends surround me: Jynne with the cassette mixes that accompanied our cooking forays back when we lived together, or Mary Beth with swatches and slides, as well as a duffel of this season's winter sweaters. I am content listening to their gossip, watching them eat fudge. Then we all take a break and do some meditations.

And yes, Merv is here, hanging out around the edges, playing background melodies to accompany the mixtape offerings. He smiles at my friends as if to flirt, breaking in now and then with an anecdote from his days on the road. Oliver often volunteers to run down to the gift shop, or to the break room for supplies. Every so often someone exits the room just to take off their scrubs and cool down. A nurse ducks in, we get worried she's going to scold us for the noise. Instead of telling us to turn it down, she sings along, faking it when she doesn't know a lyric.

However long this stretch runs, hours or days, it reaches some kind of apex when Tilda again stops by. Oliver kisses her masked cheek. Extending his arm, he introduces her to "our house musician." (I *so* wish I had a picture of Tilda's dumbfoundment.)

This momentum sweeps me forward, into the next leg of this blessed marathon, when Blasco enters, bookended by his usual phalanx of residents and nurses. Seeing so many people in the room obviously jars him, but he smiles. He is focused in a manner that suggests something serious. "I want to ask how you are doing this morning." He puts a hand to my throat, listens to my pulse, examines the backs of my hands, squints. "But it is apparent you are doing very well."

Each of the two nurses is holding a bottle, I notice, each one

about the size of a child's football—dense, smooth glass. One nurse
has a mucousy-looking syrup, the dark mixed color of bourbon
and blood. The other liquid is clear. Blasco tells me these two drugs
are the last step before the stem cells, but they are a big one. I take
a deep breath, exhale.

"Do you need us to clear the room?" Mary Beth asks.

Blasco studies the source of the question. "Policy doesn't allow
more than two visitors at a time. But everyone is already in here.
And so today policy shouldn't be a problem." He refocuses on me,
saying the drugs will be given simultaneously. He refers to the
darker concoction by the letters ATG. It is some kind of globulin,
will work as an antibody, fighting something in the T cells that can
hurt me. Apparently, the clear stuff used to be some kind of horse
serum.

I admit, when he starts explaining about severe allergic reactions, low blood pressure, and problems breathing, I tune out some,
and even get a bit testy, for I've heard every possible side effect by
now, and the truth is, *I have to do this anyway.* I pout some, and let
myself be distracted by the knocking resident, late to the room:
he's busy tying the knot behind his neck, doesn't seem to care what
the doctor is saying, instead gawks at my wall murals and slogans.
One more minor victory for me.

The nurses are adding another tier of hangers to the Christmas
tree, for the new drugs, and then an assistant interrupts, peeking
her head around the doorframe—she starts to ask if she can clean.
I watch her take in all the doctors and nurses. She grunts, closes the
door. Oliver smirks; head still down, he goes back to taking notes.

I'll be even more tired, I'm told, but will be getting very little
sleep because I need to protect my bladder, and I'll be peeing every
two hours. "Wonderful," I mumble; dear, alert Mary Beth asks me
to repeat myself. I demur.

"Who is to say?" Blasco continues, as always upbeat. "Your appetite might even come back."

I nod, but am visualizing that new tier of the Christmas tree filling up; I'm seeing even more of those thin tubes running down from the new bags and bottles, all that tubing connecting to the central line, small streams flowing into a mighty river, into my port, into my body.

I feel my heart slamming repeatedly against my chest, trying to escape for the next room. My eyes wander, and I watch as two battery packs are added to each side of the tree, bringing the total to eight batteries that are keeping my drugs flowing and regulated, four thick plugs going into the wall sockets. My Lord. One of those tubes is always going to be getting clogged. One of those batteries will always be blinking red.

What happens when I go to the bathroom? Will I be able to unplug all of them in time? *Every two hours.*

"When I was a little girl I used to play a game."

I say this to the room, but my friends do not hear, they are focused on Blasco, attentive students to his lecture. Then Merv asks if I said something. This causes Jynne and Mary Beth to turn my way. Blasco pauses. I can see Oliver looking at Merv, irritated.

"The floor was an ocean," I say. "My bed was a boat. I had to stay in the boat and navigate the seas."

They are pretending to follow me. I let them pretend. I keep going. "It always was so much more fun when there were friends to be on the boat with me. I'm so lucky. All of you are around to be on my boat."

I hear Jynne's voice: *We're right here.* I see blurry motions of their nodding in my peripheral vision. The nurses, meanwhile, have not stopped working, are hooking up the bottles. Glendora checks and replaces a vented spike. Friends turn back toward Blasco.

"I have a secret voice inside that thinks I am going to live."

There is applause. Whooping. A thumb rolls on the catheter; the drip rate adjusts. A coolness enters.

I am lurching. My jaws unhinge. From inside comes bile and yellow and fluid. Each heave causes shock waves through my entire body; they feel like they last forever. The flow is more than makes sense—there's not enough food in my stomach to come up like this. I feel Blasco's hand on my back, helping me. I vaguely hear my husband's voice saying my name. More comes up. All over my new sweater. My scrubs. Even my family quilt.

And now Oliver is wiping clean my face, dabbing at my eyes with his sleeve. Glendora is matter-of-factly unfolding new bedsheets. Speaking over my apologies, with as much decency as I have ever heard, she says: "Don't you worry about it, sweetheart. You can't control these things."

Just as the wave crested, the wave ebbed, the shock to her system abated. One of the battery alarms was always going red; one of the lines was constantly clogging. But the drugs continued their drip; the doctors threw their smocks into the trash bin; nurses came and went, their usual fixes and schedules. Alice's heart rate normalized. She calmed, drifted off to sleep, for two hours, anyway, until the clock alarm sounded, at which point Oliver roused her, helped her to the bathroom, tucked her in, dealt cards, was caught holding embarrassing amounts of points. Waves of friends arrived, filling more shifts, twelve to three, four to six, bringing knitting and books and meals and sweets and newspapers. Alice napped and woke and napped some more. The soldiers on Oliver's wall of defenses had been on full alert for a while now; instinct said they could relax some. He also knew the chemotherapy she'd just received was something from the nineteen fifties, a carpet bomb, supremely punishing; it made the previous induction and consolidation concoctions seem sophisticated and subtle. The horse serum was its own form of death. The other one, the one with the letters, if you took it too much, actually *caused* leukemia. There was no reason to tell Alice, any of it, no reason to let even Tilda know.

Every time he left that room he was aware of the clock, the possibility of limited time, knew he was turning his back on this time when he left; so he tried to stay in that room, he tried to stay put. And still she was asleep, and Jynne was there, and Julie was arriving soon enough. Oliver had decided that sitting there for too long while she was asleep was like waiting around for disaster. He wasn't going to consider morbid shit like that.

Perla had been the only availability on short notice. Oliver's clothes were still on, his shoes still tied. She sat next to him on the upscale hotel bed. Oliver could not stop talking. Perla, all but busting out of a silky peach baby-doll, stroked his shoulder.

"It would be one thing if she's going to survive, if she's going to *live*," he said. "Three years. Compromised state, professional patient—whatever. It's worthwhile. There's a purpose."

"What she is going through, so she can raise child," Perla finally answered. "Her suffering is biblical, no?"

His bedrock belief—which had made his assignations possible, and had made his betrayals more absurd—was that these women were not worth the sweat on Alice's brow. They couldn't be.

He couldn't answer her, didn't undress, just left the envelope on the bed, didn't look back.

"And for her to suffer through all this, for her to jump through these goddamn hoops, I mean, fucking *days* away from the transplant—for her to get this close, and *die*?"

Ruggles bit into the burger, appeared oblivious to the meat juice dripping onto his chin.

"It goes into this other realm," Oliver continued. "It's impossible to even call something just, or unjust, right, or wrong, merciful or cruel."

"Brah, food's getting cold."

"I can't even put my head around it."

"Beyond fucking reason." Ruggles picked at a fry, sinking his teeth into its lukewarm density.

Oliver hadn't been keen on getting in touch, but he needed to speak to someone, and when they finally did touch base, Ruggles must have recognized something in his voice, because he'd responded immediately, not just asking about Alice but wanting to know where Oliver was right then, and pushing. They should meet up, grab a bite.

Now he said it outright. "We got a cease and desist from Word-Perfect."

Oliver raised his eyes.

"I'm sorry to bring it up, especially—I know it's the worst timing ever, but I don't see much choice." A sip at his beer. Ruggles wiped away the foam mustache, dipped into Oliver's fries.

"We could just obey the order and fold up and that's it, ball game. But I think we're all in agreement: *Fuck that*. Another way, we go to court. This route, they're funded like sonsabitches, lawyers up the yang. They draw it out, bleed us into the goddamn poorhouse."

Ruggles chewed, waited.

"What I think, we scrounge up whatever we have, use it for distribution, throw our baby into the world. Let's show we can go into any writing program they got. Do our damage, eat into their business, give these fucks some real reasons to buy us out, make us disappear. This way, we survive from the rubble, who knows, maybe even more?"

"What about reaching out?" Oliver said. "Maybe we ask for a meeting?"

"I thought of that, too," Ruggles said. "Show what we have. Let's scare them enough, they pay us to go away."

"Maybe Microsoft while we're at it?" Oliver thought out loud. "We might catch a break, play the two against each other."

Ruggles grimaced at the idea, as if the possibility was too much to hope for. He fiddled with his napkin, and now leaned in, over his plate, crowding the table, shortening the distance between them.

Oliver felt his hot, meaty breath. "This is what it gets down to," Ruggles said. "You got that program for me or what?"

Oliver arrived back at the hospital with three new pajama sets from her favorite West Village lingerie boutique and discovered, right outside her room, a huge orange tackle box, large red cross on its side, oxygen tanks along the lower level. What hospital people referred to as the crash kit.

Snapping on the mask, he ignored the sting atop his ears and got on the gloves and did not worry about tying the back and opened the door and his wife was propped up on the bed. She was so pale, her profile reflecting light in a way that made her look ghostly, one of those transparent apparitions in a carnival spookhouse. She tried to smile.

"I'm so glad to see you."

"She hasn't been doing so great." Merv was on the other side of the bed, those fucking ivories in his lap.

She'd needed to go to the bathroom. Only Jynne had left to make her three o'clock. And Julie was supposed to be here but wasn't. Nobody was with her. It was disconcerting but not unusual, these things happened, she'd been fine with it, and had gotten up to use the bathroom, then, about halfway through, started feeling unsteady, sapped of strength. She barely made it to the chair and rested there for a while and waited and still the room was spinny, and she rested, and waited, and was too far from the emergency call button. Even making it back to her bed felt impossible. Then she'd soiled herself.

Oliver cradled the back of her neck, lowered his head so the growth on the top of his skull rubbed against the fuzz atop hers. For the first time during this admission, he noticed, her arms were trembling, and this struck him as a kind of marker. He stared at the yellow plastic bracelet hung around her wrist. On it large black letters: FALL PRECAUTION.

Oliver passed his hand over her forehead, felt its furnace of heat, the indentations of the veins where the ridge of her cranium jutted over her temple and sloped. Small and protruding, heading down the sides of her face, veins split in little patterns that were reminiscent of the spine of a leaf, arteries on a subway map. Sun spots littered her forehead, dappled the sides of her face, running toward her jaw. Her rash was back with a bright vengeance, her cheeks badly swollen—her skin sunburned red in some places, orange in others, in still others she looked pasty, chalky, had turned so pale she'd taken on a greenish hue. She was flaking everywhere. Her lips had severe cracks in them, dry white crud in their corners.

She'd finished recounting her tale, and had nestled into his shoulder, resting, eyes shut. Only with a short pained sound, she now pushed away. The cords in her neck strained into dock ropes; her head jutted forward. Like she was some kind of mystic animal, her mouth came unhinged. She strained; her face went this grotesquely deep red shade; nothing came out. She barely finished, then heaved again, more violently this time, this unstoppable wave, moving from her stomach and up through her body.

Oliver had grabbed the puke basin by then, and caught most of the bile. A third retching followed, this one impossibly violent, bringing only a thin string, yellow mucus.

And then he was in the bed alongside her and she was nestled beneath his chin, looking up at him. She'd passed her large eyes down to their daughter.

Oliver felt as terrified as he had ever been, but he gathered her frailness in his arms.

Alice sniffed mucus from her nose, said: "It's getting a little bad now."

. . .

They bring in a portable commode and place it next to my bed. "If you can't make it to the toilet," says Nurse Hwan. I appreciate her gentle discretion, implying I have some sort of choice, as if I could even begin to rise in time to get to the bathroom. Any urge now prompts me to call for a nurse. And the basin is used for another purpose. When mucus gets caught in my throat, and I vomit it back up, for example. Or when I don't eat enough, because I have no appetite—and my stomach revolts. Or when I give in and nibble a horrid bite of white bread, and even this feels aggressive, and within half an hour, those chewed foamy particles are reversed, bringing with them strips of flesh from the top of my mouth. Or when the room is too hot, and up comes yellow bile. Later I am curled into a ball, I am trying to sleep, and overhear the nurse telling Oliver it was not really phlegm but my decomposing stomach lining.

The night is long; I soil myself twice. Two more times I vomit into the basin. Choking my tears, I apologize.

"You're doing great," Oliver says.

He again holds the plastic yellow basin to my mouth. He again lies on the side of the bed with me. He once again wraps his arms around me, strokes the side of my head, feels my thin little invisible hairs.

Once, in my twenties, I started working on a men's collection inspired by early twentieth-century modernism, tweed vests and the like. For context, I tried to read *Ulysses*. Though I didn't make it even halfway through, I remember being struck by its boldness, the idea of trying to capture every stray thought and digression that might run across a human consciousness. While preparing for my transplant, I thought I could will myself into that same heightened consciousness. It hasn't worked so well. I follow lines of association like some tagalong friend, ambling behind, constantly trying to catch up. But I trip, the bond breaks, the thought muddles, all colors dull. Or maybe pain flares and whitewashes every thought. Or I vomit and it's gone. The truth is, I am simply less.

But every now and then, I still can find that scant line—a memory, an idea. However long it might take, I find where I left that line, gather myself and pick back up that line and lick its frayed end, making it usable to thread a needle. There is satisfaction there, stitching, following some little notion.

I assume it is morning when Blasco enters. The doctor is pleasant but serious, checking on me, going over my night's troubles. "Overall, it doesn't look horrible," he says. Then he asks whether I want to go on a PCA. "Patient-controlled analgesia," he says after realizing that I am waiting. "One press or squeeze will give you a hit of morphine—although we don't give enough that you can go numb. You also won't be allowed to go nuts. No real parties."

I nod. I want it. Of course I do.

Keyboard music drifts without weight through the background, and it takes me a bit to realize where it's coming from. There is a spoken promise, someone vowing to be present when they put in my stem cells. I want to thank Merv, but am aware of Oliver telling me I should not talk so much, I need my rest, the next days are biggies. I respond by rambling about my lonely childhood, admitting to Oliver news he already knows—my longtime desire for brothers and sisters. "I kept holding out hope that I could've had more children."

"Alice."

"I know what they said about the procedure, but I was praying there was a way. I wouldn't be barren and maybe a few years down the road, you'd be enjoying Doe so much, you'd be excited for another one."

He strokes my stubble. Through his eyes, I recognize what is happening to me.

After the nurse changes the dressing around my port, she takes my vital signs, then buzzes the desk. Soon the shift nurse arrives, takes my blood pressure, and buzzes the desk. When the resident arrives,

Oliver repeatedly asks what's wrong. The resident checks my eyes, has me open my mouth. My blood pressure's very low, he says. I ask him how low but do not get an answer, which means it's serious. My eyes flutter and I let them shut—having this doctor work on me without so much as addressing me grants a form of permission. I focus on my breathing, filling my stomach as if it were a balloon, letting air expand through my chest. I feel a cold pack on my cheek, pressing, then on my neck. I release my tensions in a breath outward, hear Oliver ask if I can feel this, and indeed feel a new cold pack pressing into my stomach. "Soothing," I mumble. I assure him I am not in pain, very little feels rushed, or wrong. Someone is speaking to me now, a voice I half-recognize, and though I am familiar with his words, for some strange reason, I cannot respond. I feel my body moving, the bed churning behind me, pushing my torso forward; I feel people taking me under my arms, forcing me to sit upright. A small disc presses against one side for a bit, then another. Blasco says that my lungs sound good. He listens to my belly. It's a bit of a nuisance, but I let him do his business. My body feels comfortably distant from me now, an arm's reach away.

"My worry is she's decompensating." Blasco's forehead was light with perspiration, his breath hot in Oliver's face. "It could be that all the stress we've put on her heart has registered. It could be kidney failure, dehydration, or some infection that we don't yet know about. She's neutropenic."

"She's been neutropenic before—"

"Correct. But this time she has neutropenic fever. And the radiation we gave her is starting to kick in."

Oliver remained focused on her, the outsides of her eyelids busy with small red veins. Bone-white rings beneath her eyes.

"What I am going to do now," Blasco continued, "I am going to widen the spectrum of her antibiotics. She's on a lot. We're going to do more."

"How does that affect today?" Oliver asked.

"My hope is this will at least tamp down on the fever. I'm also starting her on an IV for nutrition. We'll give her platelets—"

"And the stem cells?"

"Also a wide spectrum of blood tests. These should narrow the possibilities of what has caused this blood pressure drop. When the tests find the right germ, I'll give a more thorough and focused antibiotic."

Oliver held the doctor by the elbow, as if keeping him in place, as if Blasco were going anywhere. "She's so close."

"The stem cells are here." Blasco waited for a reaction, continued. "Ideally you want them in a patient as soon as possible. Your wife's weakened state is a concern. But some of that might have to do with painkillers. Myself, I feel better about getting the cells in my patient than having them in deep freeze."

A sound. Alice twitched; her eyes blinked, batting, opening, unfocused. She looked toward Oliver.

"Thank you for everything," she said.

He studied her, leaning forward. "Do you remember that first night?" he said, every feeling he had ever known rushing upward through him. "It's still true. I could fuck you right here and now."

Blasco had one gloved hand around her propped shoulder. He held a basting syringe of comic proportions—large enough to squeeze thick streams of icing out onto an institutionally large birthday cake. Made of plastic, the holding tube was long and transparent. Visible inside was a cloudy, cream-thick concoction, a weak pink.

Alice managed something resembling a smile. From the way Blasco's cheeks rose and his mask jiggled, it seemed like he was smiling, too. Oliver had gotten pretty decent at reading expressions from brows and facial movements. The doctor held the bolus between himself and the patient as if he were displaying a prized trout. Oliver snapped the photo, and another—just in case, at which point the doctor nodded formally. Back to business, he changed out of his gloves, putting on a new set.

Presently, Bhakti arrived, her boots clicking across the floor, dark hair lustrous behind her, her skin the hue of whiskey—all but glowing in health. As she apologized for her lateness, her beauty appeared that much more striking against her ridiculous protective garb. Next to Carmen, Nurse Hwan was pumping hand sanitizer onto the baster, making sure every area that had been touched, gloves be damned, was disinfected. Now she was going over the syringe's entire surface.

"You've come so far," Hwan said. "Let's keep it going. Let's bring it home."

"Home." Alice's eyes shone.

Blasco motioned toward the line. Bhakti took a moment, recognized her own name being spoken, pointed to herself to make sure. She moved forward, a bit hesitant, as if her usual assured manner were a façade, and a window had exposed her true, insecure self: that thin schoolgirl with wild hair and glasses, intent on impressing teachers, not letting anyone see her terror in the hallways of her new public school. Tentative, taking the bolus from the nurse, she held the instrument by a corner, almost as if it were a full diaper. Blasco continued his instructions, easing her toward the next step. With only the slightest shake in her biceps, Bhakti connected the syringe's front spout into the port's barrel, checked the connection was secure, would not leak.

All morning Oliver had felt so jittery he could barely stand in place, could not sit still.

"Blood pressure ninety over fifty-three," called out Glendora.

"That's what we want," Blasco said. "Ready?"

"Three," said Bhakti. "Two—"

Oliver did not make eye contact; Alice transmitted no unsaid messages. Each remained silent, attentive, focused.

"They're here," Alice said.

Then, "It's very cold."

"A new life." Glendora's booming declaration, almost childlike in its excitement, caught the doctor's attention. He grinned. Then reached for Bhakti's wrist, steadying her, directing the bolus angle, the liquid flow.

"What time did the platelets go in?" Blasco asked.

"We haven't got them," answered Nurse Hwan.

"On their way?"

"What they're saying."

Vibrations along Hwan's waist; she checked her beeper. "Just nonstop today."

Alice's face was glowing, tears running freely, making her cheeks and chin slick. She didn't lift her arms to stop them. She said, "I'm ashamed to cry."

"Cry," said Oliver.

"Is no shame," agreed Blasco.

During the next minutes, Oliver could barely hold still. Instinct, *nature,* said he should be next to his wife, in bed embracing her, at least holding her hand. But the bedside was too crowded. The last thing he wanted was to accidentally infect her. He stood on the periphery and beamed at Alice. At moments she felt him watching, paused from her meditative breathings, and met his gaze. For once her eyes were not glassy from the drugs but sunshine bright; indeed, her damp face all but glowed, the tears seeming to have smoothed out the discolorations and wrinkles, providing her with an extraterrestrial elegance. On their wedding day she'd worn her hair pulled away from her face, and flowers had pinned the bun. She'd designed the pink slip of a dress herself, had smoked cigarettes and dieted for months. The result was as beautiful a woman as he ever hoped to see, the happiest day of his life. The memory threatened to break him. He kept watching.

At one point, he actually thought, *This would be a perfect place for some music,* and felt entertained by this, and irritated, and wondered where Merv was. Not that he missed him, but Oliver remembered him wanting to be present.

The stem cells must have been about finished, because Blasco tipped the syringe to a downward angle, shook the tube as if prepping a martini. "We want to make sure you get every final drop of new marrow."

Oliver's hand formed a fist; he shook it at his side. Then a motioning nod. "Can we have that?"

Blasco shook his head. "When we finish, it goes off to the microtics lab. Those last dregs get cultured."

Two days after the transplant, a larger room becomes available. It doesn't feel like such a gift. My white blood cell counts have started crashing, and asking me to get in a wheelchair and take a trip, even if it's just down the hallway, seems as realistic right now as undertaking astronaut training. "If you don't change," a nurse tells Oliver, "you'll lose the room to another patient." He gathers up my fall coat, the shoes I wore in here, books I haven't touched during my stay, my Discman. He spends a good ten minutes taking the pictures from the wall across from my bed, gathers my stray clothes into one pillowcase, my laundry into another.

Arriving with all his gear, Merv sees the half-dismantled room, Oliver sweating. He's confused, then catches up, and says he's glad he didn't show up after I moved. "See that room empty, man, I'd have freaked something fierce."

I don't have the heart to tell him that he missed the transplant, and Oliver keeps zipped as well, although it isn't as if Merv is waiting for an update, rather, he is stripping off his bib and gloves, heading out of the room. Soon enough he returns, dragging a number of wheelchairs. Oliver remains inside the room but lugs my travel suitcases toward the doorway. Though Merv's limp is pronounced, and it's not easy for him to haul things around, he takes each suitcase, creates a neat stack on the first chair. He and Oliver form a decent team. Both sweat freely, but when Merv takes an album, he looks perturbed. I can sense his impatience. He enters the room now and starts stacking items. Oliver grabs the side of his head and begins pulling at his own scalp, loudly recounting the rules about protective gear—"*Come on, hoss.*" I feel myself looking at Merv, pleading. *Please.*

But Merv is oblivious. He grabs one of the trash bags the nurse brought in, places the stacks of posters and pictures and yearbooks inside, and then, in quick, disciplined movements, wraps the rest of the bag, in circular layers, around them. "I've wasted more time moving gear than you even know," he says.

My new room, in comparison to the dungeon closet, is a palace—it could be a large studio apartment—and the far-side wall is essentially a window, with afternoon light filling the large rectangular space, and a view that extends beyond the nearest buildings and water towers. I ask the orderlies to let me sit for a bit on the sunny side, shades drawn. I look out onto the urban sprawl: small old apartment buildings and bigger ones behind them, rooftops and blocked views, spires and towers stacked like toy blocks, juxtaposed, elbowing, sprawling for as far as the eye can see.

Eventually the nurses do their sorry jobs and ease me into bed; the second orderly tends to the Christmas tree. Oliver keeps bringing packed trash bags into the room. He's sweating freely but will not take a break. Why he's decided to nail himself to the cross and martyr himself, whether there's some inner competitive thing he has, I don't need to figure it out. Merv has seated himself beside my bed, legs extended, and he's watching my husband with more than a little amusement, now even putting his hands behind his head and stretching out. Honestly, his amusement is infectious. My system is stressed from the room change. I'm happy to have the company. Happier to share moments of absurdity.

"So," he says, once Oliver is safely out of the room. "You holding up?"

The look I give must suggest he's insane, stupid as moss. Then I understand. I take my time in smiling at him, doing so without opening my mouth, a fooled Cheshire grin. I feel myself eyeing him, and keep examining him. I am implacable, mysterious.

"Why do you keep coming around?" I ask.

He shifts in his seat, rubs the back of his neck. "Well well then."

"I don't mean to offend you."

"It's a problem?" He smirks. "I can see he's wrapped tight—"

"I've asked you before, haven't I? I'm just not sure I understand."

Is it adrenaline that makes me feel this lucid? I have no answer, but I do feel more alert, much better than earlier. Still, it's a strain to talk this much; I start coughing. He hurries, offering ice chips, water. My coughing ends, and I thank him, take the glass, sip, feel the cold against the back of my throat.

Right, Merv says. If his only motivation was to help people, why wasn't he volunteering in a hospital closer to his dad's place? Why doesn't he play music for patients on other floors or in other wards?

"Don't," I say.

"You need a transplant, you're getting treated at this hospital, so if there was a pissing chance you were in this ward, I wanted to be here for you."

My skin crawling, my innards curl.

"Wait." Now his voice carries a level of authority. "I know you're not, what, *available*?" He visibly enjoys his joke. "Yeah, bedridden, the radiation, the chemo, that plus the body-wrecking high-end medical procedure—they might have tipped me off. Honest, I'm ashamed of before. When I was laid up in my cast, I kept thinking about the way I'd followed you. *Stalked* you, I guess. The last thing you needed."

Different thoughts flash across his face. Now his fingers move of their own accord, tapping out the rhythms of some exercise or another.

"A hard cold wind was blowing inside me for a long time," Merv says. "I knew it, and still let it take me. Told myself whatever, couldn't stop myself. It was fucked up. I know. Still, even before I was in that cast, this is the truth, when I thought about how you were doing, what you were going through—"

"Mervyn."

"I took it one way, I know, ran down the wrong road. Maybe I'm on the right one now. A lot of that has to do with you. Lady, I think about your will. Your life force. Reaching out like that?"

He doesn't have a chance to continue, and I don't have a chance to answer, for Oliver, with his usual impeccable timing, has returned with another loaded wheelchair. Merv starts to rise, as if ready to help, but Oliver makes a point to proceed as if he does not see him: unstacking the suitcases, leaving the pile just inside the doorway. He wonders whether he should leave some sort of sign at my old room, inform other visitors.

And then he's leaving again. Merv and I look at each other. We don't even try to keep from chuckling. I study his perpetually unwashed hair, always falling down in front of his eyes, his unplucked, full brows. Merv again stretches out that lame leg, feels at his thigh. He bends his knee and extends again, almost as if testing the joint, its working stability.

"It's sweet," I say. "A very romantic thought."

"*Insane,* you mean."

My knee touched his, if we are being honest. This was our first contact. While I recovered from my walking laps, we sat and talked in that antiseptic hallway, and our knees touched, and I did not pull away, but allowed my knee to keep touching his. I took my mask down, so it rested around my neck. I tilted my head and moved forward, toward this man—this man I did not know, had not met, until that night. Numb unreality had me, the feeling of entering a new dimension, a place where there were no rules. I pressed my lips against his; he gave nothing in return, a statue, causing me to pull back just a bit. I allowed him a moment. And then my gloved hand cupped the underside of his stubbly chin; I came in for more, and felt him pressing back, acquiescing. His breath was warm and musky, his lips thick, with a supple strength. I took his bottom lip in between my teeth, sucked in its rubbery substance, teasing, gently chewing, and now opened myself, though only a bit, to his tongue. I was the one, directing his hand: taking it from off my cheek, moving it downward, to my breast. I was the one, moving his hand further downward, past the cinched, knotted cord of my bathrobe. Long seconds there. My eyes glassy. I let out a little sound, the fear recognizable in my purr. "That's enough, I think," I said, and then took my time, putting my mask back in place, straightening my robe. Me, the demure schoolgirl, without the slightest ambiguity, rising, starting back down the hallway.

We are grinning like conspirators. We *are* conspirators. And here is my dear husband, back once again, He Whom Is Conspired Against, on the other side of it all, huffing for breath, his adrenaline receding. However suspicious he might be, the flat truth is, he also is back up, out of his chair, forming a rickety sort of tandem with Merv, the two of them working with a quiet efficiency, putting up half of the wall of pictures. Similarly, they set my clothing into the bureau drawers, hang my coat in the new closet. It is immediately after this last task that Oliver pauses long enough to appreciate the light and space of this new room. He laughs about how tired all this zipping has made him, and says he feels like spending the day in bed, and wants to know can he get in with me, and we do lie together, snuggled in a bed that has been built for one, and the three of us find the cards and play gin rummy. And Oliver stays within striking distance of my point total, and Merv is actually an amateur at cards, which is a bit hard for me to believe—"isn't there supposed to be all that downtime in the studio?" I ask him—and

Merv laughs at himself, and he hangs in as best he can, trying to learn the game, and if Oliver does not join in the laughter, he doesn't try to trump the guppy straight down the drain, either. And then Tilda surprises us with chocolates and noisemakers, she can't believe she missed the big event!

Every night a messenger service delivers vials of my blood to a lab in New Jersey, whose scientists examine it and check the numbers themselves and see what I need, and they make up a special mixture of chemicals and medicinal gunk, which gets delivery-serviced to me for the following day. Nurses replace my intravenous tubing every day to make sure there's no bacteria growth. One nurse absently tells me she wishes she'd bought stock in medical tape. All of them encourage: I should hang in, I should keep hanging in. Friends keep arriving, sitting bedside, strapping themselves in: even Lani, who's canceled on so many plans, bailed early on so many visits. Face soft and stricken, she presents me with a signed poster from the virtuoso singer-songwriter whose yearly concerts at Town Hall we used to faithfully attend. Underneath the struck, muscular pose the dreadlocked rock star has scribbled my name and *Hang in there*.

And my hair is falling out again, in clumps and balls, also short little gray or black strands, pretty steadily now, floating away and resting on my shoulders, the little clippings that must be dusted off after you get cut and blown and styled, and I can't pretend this doesn't send me plummeting, and I suspect something must have happened with my most recent platelet infusion, because I'm itching something fierce, my rash morphing into armies of ants up and down my forearms, and the vise has similarly tightened around my throat, and my feet have swollen into cinder blocks (doctors constantly asking if I feel tingling sensations in my hands and feet; I don't know what to say, don't know what answer I'm supposed to give); and, if this isn't humiliating enough, I've started getting the runs, again, really bad, and it's horrible, unmerciful—I can't really get anywhere, already I'm so weak that a nursing assistant is supposed to accompany me on all trips to the bathroom—as soon as I feel that little rush inside of me, I'm supposed to buzz, and sometimes the nurse makes it in time to help, but mostly I have to use the basin, and there are the times it doesn't work out, when the assistant has to scrub my bottom clean, and my sheets have to be changed as well, and it's infantilizing, I am as helpless as a baby, and I weep at this, I weep so much, can't help myself, and on top of all this, they have me taking that stupid stool softener more frequently, which doesn't quite make sense, given that I am shitting the bed three times a day. I write a note to Oliver: *When does it get easier?*

Vaginal spotting is just another way of saying *bleeding*. At least I'm down to two pads a day. Still, I'm constantly telling Simone and Requita and Alvarez that I need more pads, please. I taste blood on the inside of my mouth, and only get the taste out when I swish the special mouthwash to prevent sores or infections. There's an air pick next to my bed that sucks away phlegm and blood and dead skin. My face and neck bloat further, my cheeks droop around my mouth. I get more estrogen. I get this protein mixture that looks like a big bag of urine. My skin is still sunburned and swollen, only now there are cracks and I'm being told it's not good to have lots of cracks like that in my face, it means my skin is breaking down, I need to apply a lot of lotions. I have store aisles' worth of lotions, oceans of lotions, and need to apply more. The remaining strands of hair on my head look like stray feathers on a baby chicken. My hands shake and shake and I can't stop them. An older physician who shows up for rounds—very neat, with straight up-and-down posture—asks me, Isn't this view astounding? "If only someone would wash the windows every once in a while," he says. A nursing assistant is outside my room on watch, sitting on a chair around the clock—in order to help get me to the bathroom, that's how I choose to think of it. Julie reads the day's gossip from "Page Six." I hold her hand and laugh with her and stare at her gorgeous face, and from her expression I know she feels my love for her. When I listen to my mother's updates about Doe, with every gurgle and noise the deepest well of love opens inside of me. When a resident tells me it's been six days since I've had food or water, I want to ask how she thinks this is supportive, and then I try to remember the last time I could speak for myself, but can't do it, and just can't worry about it, either. I can feel my heartbeat through my ears. Machines are being plugged and unplugged around me. The Christmas tree is towering now, its battery packs and level monitors giving off a green glow that filters through the bags and reflects off the windows, imbuing this side of the room with an eerie radioactive hue. Over the hospital intercom, someone says, *Mary Kate, eighteen, needs something for nausea,* and this loops through my head: *Mary Kate, eighteen, needs something for nausea. Mary Kate, eighteen, needs something for nausea.* I grip my husband's hand.

The Fourth Noble Truth of Enlightenment is the truth of the path that frees us from suffering. Humans aren't meant to have our desires satisfied, or to achieve personal satisfaction. This is a false road. The true quest is for *bodhi:* to be awakened, to be aware. In this search, a doctrine of activity is demanded. Diligence. Manner. Process. Utility. Habit. The path to *bodhi,* therefore, cultivates concentration, develops character, and nurtures inner wisdom, showing the way to live a virtuous life, so that, finally, one blossoms, becoming compassionate, becoming wise. An enlightened being. I feel myself separating from the physical world, slipping into something else, and very much doubt that I need to worry about walking whichever path, living any doctrine. There is no pain.

When I was eighteen, before I went away to college, I was deeply in love with a boy, and one weekend I lied to my mother and we went away to Burlington and I ended up pregnant. I know termination was the right thing, but I have always thought of that little baby, it stays with you, and maybe that fueled the desire in me to get it right someday. I don't know. I do wish I'd had the chance to really get it right, to raise and love my little girl, to know her and to let her know me. I know I did get a chance to love her, that is one thing I believe is infinite.

On the morning of my wedding, Tilda and Julie and my mother and my other dearest women friends surprise me in my hotel room with breakfast and all join me, crowding into bed. During the ceremony Oliver and I embrace one another, and our gay Unitarian minister wraps us in a prayer shawl, and as he recites the final benediction Oliver and I hug each other so tightly, I feel the world whirling around us. We spend the next day driving through Vermont in his cousin's old station wagon, feeding one another remains of our wedding cake. On my lips I can still taste the buttercream icing, the cake's moistness.

I am alone in my bedroom with scissors cutting up fashion magazines for my wall collage. I am rushing home so that I can be on the phone with the same friends I spent the entire day with at the high school. On the final night of our goodbye trip before we head off to different colleges, we're sitting on the steps of Sacré-Coeur, staring at Paris spread out below us. All around us cute European boys party and dance; immigrants rush to try to sell us single Heinekens out of their six-packs. My friends have spread a map of the city and try to reconstruct our path tonight, figure out where Jill might have left her wallet. Jill is half-hysterical. We are buzzed, slurring. I stare out into the black night, more than ready for life to move forward.

It is 4:00 A.M. and the day is just getting light and down the corridors of the city streets there is not much traffic and I am heading home from that party in Williamsburg, holding my heels in one hand, and I have a bit of a buzz, and am biting into an apple and feeling a sense of possibility, a weird inevitability, as if a key had been discovered to a lock I didn't know was inside of me. The city feels like it's mine.

My dad drives us out to Putney and the biker barbecue place that is our special secret getaway-together spot, and we sit on the picnic benches and swat away bees and share a big plate of ribs and get lemonade and after, he helps me clean my face with Wet-Naps and lets me have a black and white milkshake.

How much I love shopping for baby clothes—little girls' clothing makes me so jealous; I would wear so many of those little outfits if they came for adults. Why didn't I ever design a line of little girls' clothing for grown women?

If and when there is a memorial for me, it would be a nice thing if they play my favorite Stevie Wonder song, and let it be known that it is for my beloved friends. Maybe use the chorus, where Stevie is happier than the morning sun, and that lovely refrain, thanking friends for being allowed inside their lives.

Waiting to get my first period and waiting for it to happen and it will never happen ever—then that afternoon I am lined up with the other girls doing jumping jacks for Miss Rutman and there it is.

Mother loading bags of candy in her purse before we head into the gorgeous old art deco theater downtown and watch a matinee.

The joy of finding that compact changing kit that I could travel with, unsnap and lay the baby onto. The utilitarian pride I feel whenever I whip out that kit, I am a soldier mommy, able, taking care of business.

They *should* have a memorial for me. I deserve that.

Oliver and I are on the couch and it has been a long day; he is squeezing and massaging my feet; I finish rolling the joint, light up, release the smoke toward him.

I stroke a few lines with my L square as a guide, and complete a drawing of an empire skirt, and the garment seems so simple and perfect and elegant, as if it were the shape that my body had been waiting for, all this time and all these struggles to get it right, but look how easy it is.

People should not get too sad. I just hope they remember how much I loved them.

The blue stripe on the tester. It is staying blue.

Those long moments not knowing whether my baby is a boy or a girl but just holding, appreciating, feeling relief and panic, her body so small and wrinkled and red, holding this little bundle of weight, the tears flowing, finally I give in and say, *Okay, tell me*.

Those walnut-large eyes looking up at me, that little potato of a face, delighted.

I don't believe that I am going silent. I am joining everything that's ever been alive. If my vision of the universe is right, I will be helping from the other side.

But I enjoy my voice. I think I might miss it.

How the game worked: nurses and orderlies on a floor each ponied up ten bucks every pay cycle. From the desk, they got the bowl. You pick a slip with some random number. Payday comes, the attending physician goes down to the cafeteria, gets a coffee, brings back a dollar bill, a five-spot, whatever piece of paper money. Last two numbers on the serial. Whoever has the lucky number wins the pot. Anywhere between four and seven hundred dollars. You didn't miss ten bucks from any check, but, baby, when your number hit, you felt that win.

Glendora had cut deals with her friends who worked on other floors. If their kids got sick or some emergency happened, the nurse agreed to cover shifts; in exchange, her friends agreed to enter Glendora in their lotteries. On four different floors, she was in lotteries. With her winnings she'd gotten dental work, paid off the fuckos from Internal Revenue, she'd bought herself little getaways to South Beach and Puerto Rico and Costa Rica. She'd gotten her new couch off a win. She'd also learned that, on other floors, patients didn't hold back, complaining about all kinds of nonsense, pitchers being out of water, room temperatures, batteries in the remote controls being on low power so it was difficult to flip around—that was a biggie. Glendora would think: *You have no idea*. What her stem cell transplants went through was living hell.

With the rare exception, her transplant patients were so nice. So grateful and polite. Glendora had been working this ward for twelve years now and was sure she could never work anywhere else.

Devanshi Bhakti had devoted her doctoral thesis and three post-doctorate fellowships to researching the specifics of genotype and phenotype relationships in nucleotide cells—so why was she here serving backup on this patient consultation? It made no sense. She should have been back in the lab. Any resident could have been standing here instead, and she was three times smarter than the specialist anyway; she'd solved simple division problems at the age of three, read chapter books out loud by the time she was five; the smartest living thing to ever escape from her back-roads village; the most brilliant student in her London preparatory school. Valedic-torian, Fulbright; ninety-seven percent on her graduate school exams; nearly perfect on her med exams; she'd come so far, had worked so hard, even eventually accepting that it was okay for her to be ambitious, it was okay to desire attention, to want to match her wits against the unsolvable, to take on Manhattan and cancer and every big challenge. There were larger reasons she slept in sto-len two-hour stretches on a cot in the doctors' lounge. There was a greater good behind her social life of reruns and movie rentals and reheated lasagna, all that shitty 3:00 A.M. take-out from diners. She was of prime childbearing age (her mother reminded her of this every single time they spoke). She had curves and hips that turned *her* on, just looking at them. She kept finding herself in this or that trendy bar, accepting a drink from another man with an expensive haircut and a name-brand suit; on the phone and apologizing for having to reschedule dinner at another three-star restaurant; hav-ing some version of a conversation in which this hedge funder swore he wasn't like the other hedge funders but was really a nice guy, possessed a soul and everything, and could handle her weird schedule, he worked long hours, too. High points like a rock-climbing weekend getaway. Gifts of pendants and earrings. Bhakti always got to discover, usually inside of four months, that this hedge funder actually couldn't handle it, was just like the others. The inevitable rebound rut followed; zipless, sloppy, partaken with that same sweet, boring, but mostly inoffensive resident, held in a romantic locale like some empty patient bed, or—once—the test cylinder of a magnetic resonance imaging machine (after which she at least got to check out what a scan of two bodies fucking looked like). Devanshi Bhakti saw males, doctors and patients and orderlies alike, stare at her. She knew the nurses called her princess. Jokes circulated about the smell of her privates. She kept reminding herself of the greater good. She stood without emotion in the back of the exam room and thought about the experiments she'd get done later. She caught herself playing with a strand of her hair and halted—remembering one of the photos on the bureau; how this patient's hair had once been long, too.

Sergio Blasco wished he could just explain, step by step, the science of what was happening to the man's wife. The obvious stuff he'd already said: she was in a delicate place, it could go either way, she needs time so the marrow can take hold, the big question is whether her body can hold out. The husband understood all these things but right now was looking for something else, saying, *I just don't see how you can take this every day.* The husband seemed to expect an answer. *It's much easier on me than on the patients and family* was what Blasco said, followed by *The truth is, you never get used to it.* These sentences were his twin stalwarts, though Blasco's mood also could change things. Sometimes when his eyes were bleary and he was coming off a marathon twelve-hour shift, he just started spouting and had no idea what he told the family members. He knew his answers deflected the real question, the thing family members really wanted to know: *How am I supposed to deal with death?*

In fifteen years of practice, your database racked up a lot of names. Your case folders filled more than a few back-room file cabinets. But you never got used to a patient going into a spiral. Never. Blasco also had a marriage to keep afloat. He had kids to raise. He was a scratch golfer, a collector of expensive cigars. Every Thanksgiving he took his family and worked at a soup kitchen. He'd built his wall of defenses.

Still, he couldn't pass a certain block on the Upper West Side without thinking of Mikhael Bishop. Sometimes just heading to the Upper West Side made him think of that night: he'd ducked into a sports bar to grab a beer and watch the Yankees, had received the page about Mikhael. There also were mornings he looked into his bowl of krispy flakes and saw the reflection of Joy Washington staring back at him. Miss Washington had been in her early twenties when she'd gone through the transplant, and, nearing the one-year anniversary, she was throwing this big party to celebrate the milestone and her recovery. Blasco had gone so far as to send in his RSVP card. Then her stomach began having problems. She'd started feeling really not so well, that's what she said, *really not so well*. He'd had her come in for a blood test and a biopsy.

He'd forgotten other names, but the tilt of a head on a subway might rush one back. He'd be sitting, sipping tea, and would see the liquid brightness of a set of eyes. The infinite would open.

He tried to keep a lid on his drinking. Some nights were better than others.

No movement or food or responses from her for days now. He didn't leave the room. Then he had to leave. For this. The second Oliver was off the floor, he felt the gravity of his mistake, the pull of centrifugal force back toward her orbit. If anything happened, he needed to be there. It bothered him to think it was possible he wouldn't be.

Ruggles was already at Blauner's office, confabbing with the lawyer who had helped Oliver with medical insurance, as well as Jonathan, the three of them forming a small group. Ruggles greeted Oliver with a strong handshake, acknowledging how Oliver looked, asking in a serious voice how she was hanging in. Oliver answered that he was hoping for the best, and needed to get back as soon as possible. All the men understood. The contracts were unveiled.

"I wouldn't be pressing this if we didn't have to," Ruggles insisted, apologetic but firm. He explained to Oliver that a finished project was the only hope. "I talked to the Brow. I guess he's on board," Ruggles said. "Whatever. I know it doesn't really matter in comparison."

Blauner stepped in and explained the terms. Without much fuss, Oliver signed over his controlling interest of the company to Ruggles for a named sum that, given the circumstances, was more than generous. Items including the computer terminals were included in the price. As the lease to the apartment was a commercial one, with the company name on the document, Ruggles would assume control of the space, but clauses ensured that Oliver's family would have no deadlines to move.

"Buddy, the last thing I want to do is hurt anybody," Ruggles said.

Oliver declined the offer of lunch, even as the request made him aware of his hunger. Waiting for the hospital elevator, he stood beside a well-groomed man in a perfectly tailored camel-hair coat—Alice would have recognized its design. The man held a briefcase in front of him, below his waist, with two hands. Oliver figured him for some sort of heavy hitter, a hospital exec most likely. He had a small pin on the lapel of his coat—it looked like one of the AIDS ribbons, only this one was green instead of pink.

When the elevator arrived they both got on, and were alone in the box. Oliver pressed for the sixth floor; the guy asked for eight. Brief eye contact. "How are you today?" asked the man.

"Hanging in, you?"

"The same."

"What's the pin for?"

"Organ donation."

Oliver stared at the guy. His hunger gnawed. The elevator hummed and the two rode in silence. At the sixth floor a bell chimed and Oliver couldn't step out quickly enough.

"Good luck to you," said the man.

As the doors closed, Oliver answered, "God bless you, too."

He started into the familiar hallway, with its cellophaned lunch trays stacked on rolling carts, its orderlies in a small group shooting the shit, middle-afternoon languor, its everyday plainness. At this point, doctors were prepping him for the endgame; when Alice's mother updated him on the baby's nightly activities and health (*Today we picked apples and played in the leaves*), he was trying to figure out whether he should tell her to come back down. His head felt as if it could split open at any moment. He felt coils inside him tightening, ready to spring at anyone who so much as looked in his direction.

He thought about what that whore had said: *Her suffering is biblical.* People wanted suffering to be biblical because they wanted it to make sense, wanted it to have a purpose—just like they wanted to believe in guardian angels, spirits with a purpose after death, some kind of cosmic system that let the dead stay close to what they'd lost. But if you had to lose this much, wouldn't it be better to forget? To be allowed to let go?

That's what you ended up with, no matter what: The brick wall. The void.

He washed up and put on all the gear while the nursing assistant snored. He didn't care if anyone else was in the room, and immediately homed in on his wife: laid out, neatly tucked in, her thin body causing only the slightest raised outline beneath the covers. Alice's face was pale as a bone, her eyes shut, her mouth just a bit open, as if words were poised, ready to escape. So smooth, this sight, so minimal. Its horrid beauty made him shiver. Oliver's weight collapsed onto the little chair. He leaned into the bed and stretched his arms toward her, laying his head down, his cheek pressing on the scratchy sheet. From this vantage point he could see the slight movements of her throat. She was breathing. Barely. He gulped, and watched those slight, almost imperceptible breaths. "If you have to go," he managed, "you go. It's fine. No matter what, *tu esta mi favorito*. So if you have to leave us all, leave. Don't worry about me. Don't worry about any of us. It's going to be good. You do what you have to."

On the sixth day after the transplant, she was down to one pad a day. Blasco guessed it was simply time. Her body was ready. She no longer needed platelet transplants. For the first time in a while, they took a bag off the Christmas tree. The heparin drip remained, of course, and the saline, and the liquid nutrition, and more than a few antibiotics. All of her hair was gone, and her skull was smooth in the manner of clichés (cue balls, eggs), and when there was a wrinkle in her brow from a bad dream or inner tremor, it made a line that ran all the way back into her scalp. She had no eyebrows. They still had the patch behind her ear to deal with nausea, and were still putting the suction stick into her mouth to get rid of buildup—and Oliver still couldn't get a straight answer whether it was mucus they were sucking out of her mouth or strips of her flesh. But her liver counts had dropped, which was encouraging as well. Best of all was her white blood cell count: .4. Hospital staffers were impressed and reticent, as if they were scared of getting too hopeful. But the bounce had arrived one or two days before the best-case scenario time lines, and that was exciting. Alice celebrated by sleeping through the day.

The next day her white blood cells had jumped to 37, and her platelets were at an astonishing 8,000. The swelling in her feet had receded; now bones in her feet were actually visible, for the first time in who knew how long. When Alice managed to get her eyes open, they remained unfocused, or vacant; she stared at a person but really seemed to be looking into some faraway universe. Oliver said her name, received no response. Tilda did the same, and got something more: a glint. A smile imbued with a hint of crazy. The resident on rounds found it unsurprising. "She's on a lot of different painkillers."

The first thing she was able to eat was an orange Tic Tac. Hours later she felt game and managed two sips of tea, though her throat almost closed up during the second sip. She gagged. Her face went open with panic, but Oliver remained calm. "Close your mouth. Hold it in your cheeks. Okay. Tip your head back. On three, ready?" Her shock gave way to agreement; her focus narrowed into a grave understanding. Oliver was ready to take her and physically tilt her back, but there was no need: the tea went down. Later that evening she managed two sips of water. She followed this up by nibbling from the corner of a cracker. The next morning, three sips of Ensure.

She was still sleeping a great deal, working her way toward sitting up without the mechanical bed, but also greeted friends with lucid eyes, managing short sentences of thanks and affection: "It's great to see you." "I'm so blessed you stuck with me." Blasco wanted to start switching some of her medicines to pill form, wean her off so many intravenous drips. The second pill she tried came back up, meaning the antinausea drip would take its place back on the Christmas tree. Throughout her days, her hand was often in Oliver's. "Eating is very important for you now," Blasco said. "High protein. High calories. Lots of liquids and fluids. We want a thousand calories a day." Alice nodded, a vigorous up and down.

As if it were her turn in a script, Nurse Hwan stepped in and took over. "We had a patient who had to get his weight up; we told him if he eats a thousand calories a day, he gets out of here. This man had his wife get him boxes of Oreos and some milk. A box a day, he dipped them Oreos in milk and ate. After five days, they let him out."

Alice squeezed Oliver's hand. This marked the first mention, the first raised possibility of release. The words were electrifying, and their hope spread. Friends now had license, a directed purpose, their love arrived as food: visitors donning the hazmat and presenting Tupperware dishes, at once nervous and eager, as if they were supplicants from the outer provinces and Alice were the fickle empress: her beloved key lime pie, homemade and still warm from the oven; chocolate babka from Zabar's; layered lemon cakes; fluffy almond croissants. Tilda schlepped over a blender, set it up in the pantry, and mixed protein shakes with 200 calories a pop. One of Alice's notebooks got appropriated as a daily calorie ledger. A Xerox with a list of different items and their counts was pasted in. Blasco was supportive, he wanted to get her off liquid nutrition as soon as possible, it would be the best thing for her. But the 450 calories in a single slice of key lime pie remained a fantasy. Same for a Krispy Kreme glazed donut (210 calories). Even half of a single serving of Rice Krispies (child's box = 130 calories) was impossible. Three sips of apple juice (one glass = 120 calories) was an accomplishment. Just eating toast brought back the runs. "It's expected," explained Nurse Hwan. "Your body has to adjust to eating food again. You will get lots of stomach cramps."

With generous scoring, rounding up, she managed 150 calories that day. The next, her total shot up another hundred.

Two more bags came off the Christmas tree; the first battery pack was detached, unplugged, and taken away, along with the chaired assistant, removed from deathwatch in front of the room. She just stopped being there at some point. Also apparent: the rest of the nursing staff was taking longer to respond, checking in more sporadically. Oliver realized this was because other patients were in the critical stages of *their* transplants. Alice, by contrast, was getting better.

. . .

I look like a molting lizard. Maybe I shouldn't have asked for a mirror. But I wanted to see myself, after all this time.

I wish I could provide a window about where I was. But I have no insights, could not tell you if I left: so there is nothing, really, to report. I am choosing to view a good sign in the scabs that have formed over the sores at the corners of my mouth, a better one that these scabs have started peeling. I am hoping that the burn of red will fade from my face and even out with my ivory scalp—for now, however, I am two-toned. I am concentrating on performing the tasks asked of me: standing for minutes at a time, doing my little arm rotations, raising one leg at a time in sets of ten. Nurses come by to motivate me, passing along what sounds like both a rumor and a challenge: if I am strong and eating enough by the end of the week, I can go home. They want me to stuff myself, urge me onward. My whole life I've wished for this: being told I'm *supposed* to binge on desserts. Now I have a parade of beloved friends delivering them up, and of course, I can't eat more than a few bites. That will change, I am sure. I couldn't be more motivated. I even have my own soundtrack. Whenever Merv comes in, he starts his playlist off with a ludicrous rap that includes these words: *I'm hungry, I'm in the mood, plain and simple, I need food.*

His visits aren't every day. Not anymore. "Just keeping you honest," he tells me. "Thought I'd do something nutty. Actually, you know, follow the schedule they set for me."

"I see."

"Honestly?" I see the romance of what could have been. "Classes," he says.

Perhaps Oliver said something about him to the higher-ups in Social Services; perhaps more happened between them. I'm not willing to find out. The two seem comfortable enough that Oliver doesn't mind walloping him at cards. That's plenty.

"Of course," I say.

The rules: I cannot be in crowds; I cannot take public transportation; I cannot be in places with dust; I should not be around a construction site. What about a newly renovated apartment? "No newly renovated apartments," Blasco responds. "Nothing with dust still settling." I know my husband enough to see him processing the answer.

Then I realize: "We need to call my mother." I address Oliver, rousing him from whatever he'd been mulling. "I want Doe home as soon as I am."

Oliver takes his time. "Are you sure we can take care of her?" He asks me to hear him out, tells me he misses the baby, too. He wonders if it would be wise to wait a week or so. "Just until you get stronger?"

He wonders if my mother can come for a little while, whether she can take off any more days from work.

"I'm recovering early," I protest. "I'm already ahead of schedule."

"Everyone is pleased with how you are progressing." Blasco smiles, patient as always. "What we don't want, is for your baby to come back and give you a cold. Then, four days, you are right back here with me."

"This whole thing bites us right in the ass," Oliver says.

They are nervous Nellies, says my mother. She'll get everything packed. She can load it into the car and drive down in an afternoon. Just give her the word. And so we continue riding on so much goodwill and radiant love. It's humbling, how many people continue to go out of their way for me, how much effort has been lavished upon me. Oliver agrees. Blasco nods and seems a bit choked up and tells me again how impressed he is, but that we have to be very careful. When the doctor and nurses are gone, Oliver and I are alone, and I tell him that I know he's taken good care of me. I know it hasn't been easy on him. I have a lot of feelings about him right now, I say, but I would be wrong to not thank him for this. His eyes are wide, his face half-contorted.

"I was thinking. Williamsburg has those big lofts. What if we buy another rattrap and fix it up? I liked doing that. We could wait until you are good to go and it's safe to move. It's one of those hoods your übercool friends love, right? We find a building with an elevator. Stay there long enough for you to figure out what's next. Let Doe get a little bigger. See if the neighborhood develops."

He's aged so much. Through his brow and tired, baggy eyes, here is a boy, pleading.

"I just want to get out of here," I answer.

"Yeah," he says.

"We'll figure the rest."

"Yeah?" he asks.

"We will," I say. "We'll try."

This is as much as I can give right now, and he must understand, because his hand grips mine. Soon he will be cleaning the room, carefully removing the pictures and cards from the wall, then removing the tape, then folding the posters, and putting them away, placing them in a shoulder bag I long ago received for working some show. He stacks the cards. He starts folding my clothes. Soon he will go downstairs and pick up my many prescriptions from the pharmacy.

One thing I am going to have to learn to do for myself is change the dressings that surround my central line. It needs to stay in for a while after I am discharged, insurance against something going wrong, so I must be responsible for it staying clean. Nurse Hwan puts the sealed plastic kit in front of me and gives me instructions: put on gloves, put down a sterile tarp, put on a mask. Always have a box of extra gloves nearby. When the kit is open, put on a new pair. Wipe with the sponge to help the tape come off. Cap your dressings in the same order every time: red, white, blue.

I watch. I try to learn. I am going to have to learn so much again.

The physical therapist—younger than me, tall and dark-haired, hatefully skinny—knocks and peeks her masked head inside. Justine asks if I feel like getting out of the room. "One time around the floor. Let's get you walking." I am stunned, a bit worried, but at the same time, the possibility is exciting, and Justine makes it easy to get swept up, her positive attitude contagious. I am stronger, but it still takes me time to rise, don the proper garb. Justine is patient and competent and grounded, and between us we figure out that this is the first time I will be out of a hospital room in twenty-five days. This time I am not doing the rounds with Oliver. I am not walking with Merv. It's me and the therapist. I am learning to do it by myself.

My steps are painfully slow: short, tentative shuffles. Once I'm home, well-meaning acquaintances will ask how I'm doing, and hear that I am doing well, and often will get the wrong idea, which is understandable—people think of doing well as having recovered, reverting to normal, with deadlines to meet, crosswalks to rush through as the light switches to red. But for me doing well is being able to hold down a sip of soup, take bites of a cracker. I can't eat anything that's been reheated, am stuck eating mostly frozen dinners. Reheated rice will get me puking like a fountain. Not losing weight during a given week is a success.

With time my hair and eyebrows and pubes will grow back in, but curly, and in a much darker shade, a chestnut brunette. I also have a different blood type. My fingernails broke off and are starting anew. There are weird scars on my tummy. All sorts of challenges await me at home—I have no energy, no appetite; I've lost muscle mass and muscle tone, have all sorts of problems with cramping and muscle locks. I will spend aeons sitting in my desk chair, holding my child, while watching friends carry out the most basic household activities for me. I will be reading to her in bed and will fall asleep well before she does and Oliver will wake me when she's crying and worried. We will become obsessives about hand washing, small bottles of Purell resting on every flat surface, always within grasping distance. Twice a week, on Tuesday and Friday, like clockwork, I will visit the hospital for blood draws, plasma transfusions, breathing treatments, for medicines to deal with bizarre side effects, for medicines to deal with the side effects of the medicines that dealt with the side effects. The constant scourge of graft-versus-host threatens, with feints and jabs, landing, or perhaps not; the bad meal that sets me back a month; the living hell of a Saturday afternoon spent waiting to see someone in the cancer center emergency room. As much as I hate the hospital right now, I will grow to despise it even more, feeling disgusted and terrified each time Oliver wheels or walks me through those sliding doors. I concentrate, clear my mind, meditate, chant; all revolving around the idea that my cancer is gone, I am healthy. Yet constant is the fear: this thing remains a part of who I am, deep inside, dormant, waiting to start all over again and take another, more serious run. I know I'm not alone in this fear. Any foul mood or stray cough jerks Oliver to attention. A single sneeze or blemish, any body fluid looking even slightly out of the ordinary, jerks the entire ward into action. Should my body temperature creep to triple digits: more blood draws, yet another biopsy.

Yet I am in the top ten percent of respondents and recoveries. This is one of Dr. Blasco's frequent refrains. He's been upstanding no end, a prince in this city of heathens. Oftentimes, he wears open-collared tennis shirts, sometimes sweaters appropriate for ski resorts. Our appointments usually begin with him volunteering small details about his children. I know he uses his kids to underscore his points. Whenever I'm frustrated by restrictions, he'll say, "As you know, I have two small boys, so I do understand a bit."

There's no way to brace myself for the amount of effort it will take before I can walk to the corner of my street. Over and over, I tell myself I do not need to be better all at once, I just need to do better than yesterday. I need to trust in my improvement, whether I can see it or not. Four weeks and three days after I am released from Whitman, the sky will be filled with lazy, fat clouds, the cold bone-chilling. I will walk for twenty minutes and only take two breaks to lean on metal garbage cans, and when I make it all the way around my block and back to my front door, it is a major victory—if I had the energy, I would raise my hands over my head like Rocky. In another four months, I will have even more stamina. I will be doing tai chi in my room, will be antsy for action, ready to eat in restaurants and push my child in her stroller. When I am tested, my T-cell count is 170, still in the range of a patient with full-blown AIDS.

Somewhere in the midst of all this, Oliver and I will try to have sex. We will use an ocean of lubricant and the pain will be significant, not the shocked discomfort that came while losing my virginity at fifteen in the back of an old Subaru, or the intensity I felt when I pushed my child out. But a quake nonetheless. Still, my body will start to lubricate. I feel electricity where I haven't felt it in ages. We will not go for long before I turn sore, ask to stop, and Oliver withdraws. I handle him for a bit, and soon he asks me to squeeze his balls, something he's never done before, not in all our years. I can't help but wonder where this came from. Still, I fulfill his request; he finishes, his voice going high for a slight grunt, his body shuddering, contracting, and then collapsing. We hold one another. The electric sensations continue for a while through me. I wish I knew what to think about this. I know that I don't need to.

I am luckier than I can ever express. I know this is true. It takes two hours for the orderly to arrive at my room with the wheelchair that will guide me to the special elevators, and down to the hospital exit. The sun is low by this time, the sky has a silver glow that coats everything below—buildings and cars and pedestrians. The autumn breeze on my face is thrilling: the first natural weather I've felt in so long, it hits me like a song that I once adored but haven't heard for a decade. Oliver is already filling the trunk of a cab with my suitcases. The orderly makes sure to position my wheelchair at a horizontal angle, as close as possible to the open yellow door, so that I don't have to do much more than rise a bit and fall into the backseat. It is fantastic and foreign and unfolding so plainly. "I can't believe this is happening," I say. Oliver's arm is wrapped around me. He is saying sweet things, how proud of me he is, and while I hear the words, they don't quite register. After all this time, the black box finally lifted off my chest. Only the sensation that has filled in its void is not lightness but one I scarcely recognize: something foreign, almost hollow.

Tones of pink and light blue and a purplish orange fill in the spaces between the spikes of midtown's towers and creep along the vanishing line of the horizon. Clouds are gathering in the south, the high sky darkening, a steel gray that promises rain. We pass the giant naval destroyer, covered in shadows, dormant, parked in the dock. The waters of the Hudson appear choppy and gray, white crests and dirty metal. Cars move slowly toward the logjam for the Lincoln Tunnel. The oncoming evening, the glittering urban panorama, its chilled beauty, its hugeness, life unfolding and all that awaits, chokes me up. I remind myself to breathe, let myself exhale. I see her large hazel eyes. Her joyous face. I see her and at the same time cannot see her, cannot imagine how much she has grown, how her face has evolved. But I don't need to, do I? I don't need to know the answers. I don't need to know more than the next breath. All of this is happening. And when my child arrives home, my arms will be open, waiting.

EPILOGUE

2010

May, Third Wednesday, Early Afternoon

TOUCHING HER FINGER to the rectangle of glass swept away one image, brought forward the next. In this new one she was sucking in her cheeks, blooming her lips outward, as if mocking, or offering the prospect of a kiss. Her dirty hair was slicked back into a bun so hard that it pulled the skin of her forehead. Her face was dominant: saucer eyes focused, those pursed cheeks. No morgue-red lipstick today, no morbid crypt-black eyeliner—*tasteful* and *appropriate* she'd been ordered, and it was one of those orders she could not blow off. The photo showed her holding her phone at the distance of an arm's length, toward the large-scale bathroom mirror. The sleeves of her respectful, oversize black blazer had been rolled back into cuffs, whose white lining dwarfed her fingerless gloves and all but enveloped her gripped iPhone. The subtle pattern of her dress—red cherry blossoms and orange lilies—was all but invisible, blending into the blackish blur. In the small slit of space where her dress parted, however, there *was* a flash of thigh, the muted pattern in the webbing of her tights, large flowers sewn in outline. Couldn't get more tasteful than that. The photo provided confirmation, the reflection she wanted: sophisticated, sexy, untouchable. Maybe could pass for early twenties.

One thing about School of Performing Arts, everyone had some kind of project. Two other sophomores had started their own fashion line—out of one of their mom's basement, naturally—and they'd paid her two hundred to model clothes on their website. For whatever reason part of the photo shoot had been on the High Line, the old elevated rail system that had been transformed into a seriously *gorgeous* walking park. Tourists had gawked while she'd done classic ballerina poses in hip-hop garb designed by rich white kids. The shoot had held up all the foot traffic and the park rangers had made them leave and they'd done the rest nearby, on side streets of the Meatpacking District. It was gritty, with hints of danger and street art—kinda like Bed-Stuy and Bushwick—but at the same time classy, upscale. Ever since, she and her girls had started to come down for adventures. She was against people having too much unnecessary crap, but you didn't need to be a materialist to appreciate the couture in stores like Alexander McQueen and Comme des Garçons, plus Stella McCartney's first U.S. store was straight up *banging*. Grab some lattes, a cupcake, maybe the newest thing, a mash-up between a cake and croissant and donut (off the charts on the calorie front, *someone* would say, eyes flashing with delight). Maybe head over to Ninth Ave to buy some single loose cigs from one of the remaining Mexican delis, bounce over to the Apple Store. The High Line was lamer now that redevelopment people had gotten all graffiti off the neighboring buildings, but the Meatpacking District was still flush with trendy glass hotels, gorgeous restaurants, wine bars, and rooftop nightclubs where bouncers had to pick you out of a line. Maybe one night she'd wear this outfit, try out her new fake ID. Sometimes, hearing about her sojourns, her dad would get all back in the day, especially if he had a few drinks in him, unrolling his grumpish, dreamy, we-used-to-have-to-walk-five-miles-in-the-snow tales about transvestite hookers on the corners. It was hard to imagine. She had *no* memories of being a baby, or ever living down here, let alone what her mom must have gone through.

Gawd. Today was an all but guaranteed drag.

Her phone was vibrating off the hook, texts doubtless asking where she was. Doe did not answer them but booked it through the reception lobby, into the brightly lit bullpen of partitioned work areas and cubicle spaces, its always rotating staff of stylized and slightly haggard men and women, most seeming just a bit older than her. Down the farthest row, steel desks guarded doors to corridors of power: Corporate Slave Janice was chained to her desk like always, this time eating some sort of curry. She got passed with perfunctory mumbling—*Hey, Janice, running late, I've got to*—and a wave that fell somewhere between perfunctory and embarrassed. No slowing, no knocking, defense shields powered up, more than ready to catch whatever hell was coming her way, she sort of burst and stumbled at the same time.

"It needs to be better. Much better. The interface has to take on more responsibilities."

On the other side of the office, behind a desk of polished steel, the large woman broke away from her smartphone long enough for her mushroom of hair to shake. As she made the universally accepted motion for *just a sec,* her blouse caught the light. What at first glance appeared to be a black fabric instead revealed itself as deep, roasted chestnut.

"Right," said Tilda, speaking into her boy-band headset. "Only you're not talking about the most technologically savvy group in the history of time."

Doe had been visiting this oblong building of cool, dark blue glass as long as she could remember—ever since she stayed up late trying to decide whether she liked princesses or fairies better. Through all of it: problems holding her pencil, playground dynamics, growing-pain leg cramps, her first menstrual stuff, anything she couldn't go to anybody else about, she ended up looking at the backdrop of floor-to-ceiling windows, their meeting-point power corner, the endless and waiting sky. *Schlep* had been that rarest of magazines: not only surviving but adapting to the electronic age, transforming itself into "the centralized Internet lifestyle resource for Jewish seniors on the go." Auntie Tee had survived as well: her grumbling and malcontent earthiness serving her well, her persistent pigheadedness (as well as the lack of a significant other) giving her license to stay late after work, make sure shit got carried out and done right. Freelancer to associate to senior editor, she'd become indispensable. Senior vice president, complete with profit sharing. Even the long-standing joke about her brown outfits worked for her, now something of a personal brand: flowing chocolate shawls, suit and skirt sets in decadent russet shades.

Doe pantomimed apology and softly stepped into the large, minimal office. Clean lines and muted colors, with small towers of books stacked along white shag, floating racks of imperfectly hung clothes. Reaching the table of thick glass, she eyed the ceramic bowl of jelly beans, then passed it, instead sitting on the edge of Tilda's desk. She picked up and put down the doorstop masquerading as *Vogue*'s September issue, then opened her auntie's purse, looking for a floating twenty or whatever.

Tilda's eyes went wide. *"Hey you."* A flurry of motions, as if Doe were a bee that needed knocking away.

"Just joking."

Sounds forced Auntie's attention back to her conversation. "Right," Tilda said. "Listen, I have another appointment, I gotta go. . . . Yeah. . . . I know. . . . I gotta—Sorry, we'll talk tomorrow." She pressed a button, waved the device away from her body. "Motherfuckers."

Motioning for the purse, she took the heavy bag from Doe, dug around, handed Doe money. "I told you we're putting the *Schlep* name on an app, calling it the Schlapp. Ridiculous, right? But cute. Thing is, it's not just for seniors. I mean, it is, but these are *Jewish seniors*. The Schlapp has to do *everything for them*. Buy their plane tickets, confirm and check them in, dress those bubbies on the morning of their flight, deliver them to their gates, fasten their seatbelts, even gather their luggage onto the cart afterward. Our programmers don't seem to get it."

Doe casually reached for the jelly beans. "Oy."

Auntie's face delighted, then went contemplative, and Doe was sure she'd reminded Tilda of the past—something she always tried not to do.

"Well, you definitely got your mom's eye." It took a sec to understand Auntie was talking about her outfit. "Very respectful. Still you."

An electronic chime. Before Tilda could decipher Corporate Slave Janice's loudspeaker garblings, the door was open. Doe's father. His hair was receding from the temples in twin incursions, so a small widow's peak of tight curls had settled atop his forehead, and gray was encroaching around the sides. He wore his perpetual expression, at once rigid and haggard. Still, her father cut a pronounced figure, a strong profile, especially wearing this three-quarter-length topcoat and dark suit. One of his common refrains was that he kept himself in shape because someone needed to be around to take care of things. He also told Doe this was why he'd traded in his T-shirts for collars and button-downs. Why he religiously shaved each morning. He wanted her to see that he was together and alert and correct. He wanted to be a model for her.

Today his body language was oddly unwound, absent the aggression he often had when running late, or when any other human being had somehow affected his idea of how something should be. Instead he seemed patient. Doe already had a sense of what that meant.

No small talk between her father and Tilda. They just waited for the Icon Herself.

Nothing new here: her mother, slow and measured enough in movements that her presence entered before her; slim enough to cause any female (Doe included) to go nutsy with insecurities about herself, as well as concern about what this poor woman had been through. And yes, it went without saying, her mom always dressed to within an inch of perfection. Better than perfect, marked by some odd little switch or flourish, something inevitably unexpected and tantalizing. Today her mom was dwarfed by black straw whose oversize brim ensured her face would not get any sun. A creamy blouse flowed as if from a hanger, was plumed at the waist, and cinched with a black velvet bow. Midthigh the layering ended and her blouse gave way to a black chiffon skirt whose hem grazed the floor. Mom always rocked the best boots, and these patent leather bangers were no exception. She looked elegant, hip to the point of ridiculousness, a cross between a nun and a flower girl and maybe some sort of undead wraith. Small wonder that, in the insular world of fashion, she was considered a muse. Hell, one glance and anyone on the sidewalk would be tempted to sacrifice a goat for her.

Her mom was always late; Doe had gotten her chronic tardiness from her. Even that had its twist, naturally. Mom had that bona fide trump card of her history, and if that made *you* late for something, or impatient with her, then *you* were the asshole. Doe, by contrast, was always getting hassled and busted and reprimanded and taken aside for talks. Just how shit went down. Mom was sick. Mom was bedridden. Recovering from some surgery or battling, limited in activities, able to play dolls on the floor for a bit but then needing help up onto the couch, where she watched. Before play-dates or first visits, Doe prepped her middle and grade school friends, summarizing the ordeal that she herself did not quite understand—*My mom had cancer and still has a lot of fallout;* going over rules about hand washing and surface areas, emphasizing that they shouldn't be weirded out at how frail her mom could be. She and Cyrus—founder of the basement fashion company, her worshipful and polite and (at Doe's behest) rigidly platonic best friend—had bonded during those marathon weeks when an unquantifiable bug had come to life inside Doe's mom's stomach, and all the doctors had been worried, everyone terrified they were going to lose her. And what about that horrid stretch—as awful a four-day stretch as Doe could imagine—when low white counts hinted at a relapse, and Cyrus had started dating class starlet Mindy

Wilsey, so Doe's besties had been forced to hold her up through both rounds of tests? This was how life had been. Doe had never known otherwise. And while she knew that Mom's limitations had nothing to do with love, sometimes her dad still had to remind her, taking her aside in the study of their brownstone, or embarking upon one of their long walks where they really, you know, *cut the shit*. Take on more responsibilities, he asked her. Be *more* patient, be that much better a person. *Rise to the challenge*. This is what her father wanted from Doe, and it was no exaggeration to report that Doe *tried:* indeed, she helped with whatever shots or IVs or medicines her mom needed, did whatever chores were required. Doe felt a depthless love for her mother, she wholly appreciated how unique and funny and honestly amazing her mother could be.

But she'd sort of tired of her mom's limitations, if you wanted to know the truth. Was pretty much over rising.

"I'm still not sure why I'm going to this."

Her dad muttered something like *You and me both*.

Then he said, "You're going because your mother wants you with us."

Then he corrected himself once more. "Both of us want you to go."

"I said I'm going. I'm just not sure why."

"We're going to honor someone." Her mother's voice was its usual soft monotone. "A long time ago he was . . ." She trailed off, still as a statue. Overly large sunglasses gave her an intractable veneer. No way her mom would have arranged for her to get out of classes early if this didn't matter. Doe felt a moment of guilt, but still defiant. "Maybe the best answer's just for you to come and have the experience," her mom said.

Slave Janice knew to bring in bottled waters, and her mom thanked Janice and smiled. She asked for a moment to collect herself. The car downstairs was waiting, but it wouldn't matter if they were a little late. Tilda sat next to Doc's mom on the couch and kissed her cheek. Doe's mom thanked her for letting them congregate here, and for maybe the billionth time Doe was reminded how much older, how much more ravaged, her mom looked than her aunt, her mother's former roomie and best friend, and this made Doe uncomfortable, so she looked away from them, to her dad— who seemed lost in his own internal mechanisms.

Having turned toward the window, he was looking toward the High Line, in the direction of a boutique hotel, the twenty-four-hour concierge out in front. He didn't like coming down here, Doe knew that. Whenever he wasn't able to turn down the fee, and his consulting company got hired to retrofit one of the old slaughter-houses, he spent months grumbling, more testy than his usual grouchy state. After a few drinks, with his face red and blotchy, he sometimes opened up, but the stories were unfocused, vague. Doe knew he'd been bought out of his own software company—before he did construction, before he could finish his own program. She knew the program never made it to market. A big company had bought it out, though, just so they could bury it. Everyone but her dad had made buttloads.

He put the point of a finger against the glass, seemed to trace something.

"I know, Dad."

Immediately Doe understood she was intruding.

"I can still smell dry ice."

Her mom's voice hung in the air. She'd taken off her glasses and was looking at Doe's father. Dad came over, stood behind his wife, and draped his arm around her shoulders.

"I guess you can miss anything," he said.

He leaned over the brim of her hat and kissed her on the fore-head. Doe's mom clutched his hand in hers and they were quiet for a little bit. Doe wondered if maybe she should come over and join the vibe. She was already giving enough this afternoon.

Moving ahead, she asked were they ever going to this memorial or what? For emphasis she swished her little dancer's caboose, did a few chevals, and sashayed out of the office, heading down the hallway of cubicles, with any luck catching the eyes of a few cute nerd boys, especially that odd one with the medieval red beard. Mousy women with buds in their ears were eating lunch at their desks and revising their dating profiles. She could hear her father a ways behind, joking about digging up his Sub Pop Singles of the Month collection, whatever that meant.

Their driver was a genial man from Central America. Doe's mother had requested he take them across town via St. Marks Place, and the driver had some trouble programming this into his console, as it was not the satellite system's preferred route. Doe's mother politely insisted, saying it would be appropriate for today. She responded to Doe's eye rolling by asking why Doe could be so lovely to everyone else and take out all her troubles on her. Doe answered by staring out the window. She felt at the hairpins in her bun, thought about jabbing them into her own eyes.

The car passed an American Apparel, an Insomnia Cookies, a Crumbs, Johnny Rockets, and competing banks on opposite corners of an intersection. Her father wondered out loud who had air rights on the little places. Her mother did not acknowledge him, but finished using her hand sanitizer and now shut her eyes, running away to that private happy nirvana place where she pretty much lived these days. Everyone else in the car was staring at a screen, the driver using one to guide him, her father now checking email, Tilda thumbing out an answer to a text. Doe began flipping back through photos of herself, deleting away the uggos. It was quiet in the car, except for Tilda cursing her programmers every time she read a response, then attacking her little screen. Doe noticed her father being distracted by Tilda's conversation, paying attention to words like *specifications* and *platform*.

"Who's organizing this thing anyway?" Tilda asked, now speaking toward the backseat. "How come they contacted you and not me? I dated him. Five months. That's not chopped liver."

Doe's mother seemed to be reminded of something, and responded by looking into that depthless shoulder bag of hers, and extracting a single folded page of typing paper. Now she took off her sunglasses and moved her attention to the lines of neat laser printing. Her lips began moving slightly but no sound came out. She found a pen, began making quick marks.

"I'm not saying you shouldn't be involved," Tilda continued.

"Money and time. Disease and cures." Apropos of nothing, her father had started—though whether he was talking to Doe, or the rest of the car, she could not tell. Preoccupied, like he was still engaged with some previous conversation, whatever ideas were in his head. "I used to think money and rational decisions and technology could be medicine, they could fight against time. For the city I mean. Time is the blight and this is the cure." He motioned out the window. "Well . . ."

The driver was muttering that it made no sense for St. Marks in-the-Bowery to be located two numerical streets away from St. Marks Place, and he was displaying enough irritation with traffic that Doe's father quieted down and let the driver concentrate, following the screen instructions, turning off Astor, then executing a series of quick maneuvers down a pair of small, residential side streets.

The large, stately stone spire acted as a guiding point, and they gradually came closer. White tents of a farmers' market littered the large gray courtyard. Blond ponytailed women strode past teenaged buskers, oblivious to their twangy little songs, talking instead on phones. Toward the stately columns a few men and women in dark clothes were making their way into the large old church.

Doe's father helped her mother, and Tilda took the other side, making Doe the proverbial fifth wheel, on the far side of their little chain, the group entering the lip of the chapel, being greeted by a pair of middle-aged women—a short pudgy one and a taller pudgy one, each in simple black—the short woman had straight white hair to her linebacker shoulders, a small, golden septum ring, and, between her black-laced bosoms, a clunky silver cross pendant; the taller one boasted long black dreads, colorful rosary beads, and, at the end of dragon-patterned hose, high black platform shoes. Each nodded respectfully, offering a folded, light blue paper.

Doe recognized, vaguely, the man in the picture. An older version of him used to drop by and collapse on their couch, where he'd complain about not knowing his way around Brooklyn Heights, and lament missing his shot to move out here before prices got nuts. Like once or twice a year. Doe's mom always beamed, laughing at everything he said, loading him down with food when he left. At least once Mom had gone into her purse for him, emerged with a checkbook. Doe asked, low, the deal with this guy again? Instead of an answer, she heard acoustic guitars, loudspeakers playing Pink Floyd, the annual swimming adventures of two lost souls in a fishbowl.

The lights in the chapel had dimmed, a slide show already under way, projected against the back wall, this latest slide showing a smoldering young man in a weird jacket with padded shoulders. Exhausted, drenched with sweat, he was hoisting a beer with other similarly exhausted-looking musicians. His eyes were dark with chaos, and brought forth slight responsive sounds, audience members laughing, someone sniffling. Probably half of the pews were unfilled, but the crowd seemed sort of large, not that Doe had any expectations. Her dad funneled them into a back pew; Mom stayed on the aisle. She reached into that depthless shoulder bag, emerged with cushions for her back and bottom.

The event honoring Mervyn "Merv" Goldin was more absorbing than she would have guessed, and Doe found herself relating as childhood friends recounted the funny young man who spent a lot of his spare time reading science fiction, and who seemed to push back against every fact or stated truth he heard. When somebody talked about Merv leaving college and pursuing dreams on the road with a band, her father gave Doe a look and whispered, *Don't even think of it*. When an older guy—really nice hair, crags in his face like he'd had a rough go—reminisced about the hours they'd spent on a couch getting baked and brainstorming their now famous ploy—asking a girl you wanted to make if she wanted to go get ice cream—Doe could not help but smile and whisper, *Pretty good*. She decided she definitely wanted to wear her mother's glasses with her outfit when she tried to get into the rooftop bar at the Standard, which *definitely* was going to happen. Her phone buzzed. Across the top of her screen, she read the first words of a text that appeared to be from Cyrus. Her mother put a hand on Doe's wrist. Away went the phone.

Mostly the crowd was made up of the kinds of middle-aged men who played pinball in bars during the middle of the day, or congregated at classic car conventions on the open streets of Vermont towns, or maybe sold clocks made out of old records along some beach boulevard: aging hedonists and bohemians, potbellied, with consumptive faces and gray-streaked hair gelled back into ponytails; the women usually *juuust* too old, too heavy, to get away with those fluorescent dye jobs, those nose rings, those worn-ass tattoos. Today, however, among the pews, standing around the periphery, rumples had been smoothed away, collared shirts ironed, bodies squeezed into corsets and respectful office dresses and Sunday finery and what could best be described as *tasteful whore on the prowl*. A few air-kissed. Others nodded, let out warm *heys*. Doe's mother was spending a lot of time scanning the pews—and here she let out a gasp, whispered, *Carmen. Is that really?* Doe's mom clutched her husband by the hand, then motioned, waved. Doe could not make out the intended target.

Never married, Merv had been engaged twice, one fiancée loving him when he was a raging alkie, the other when he'd dried out. Each of the goth-attired women who'd been handing out flyers agreed: he was funny, quirky, soulful, saw things his own way, and couldn't be convinced otherwise. Once the pain of their prospective marriages had subsided, each had stayed friends with Merv, and to this day wished things could have worked out. There had been one or two other serious girlfriends as well, and a few bar chicks, some lady friends who through the years obviously had shared benefits with him, maybe a handful of musicians he'd gigged or laid down studio tracks with, plus honeys he'd met at twelve-step meetings, one or two he'd taken graduate school classes with or just sort of somehow came across, and more than a few of these women confirmed the effectiveness of his ice cream line. Tilda stared numbly ahead, once or twice squirming in place. She grumbled and let Doe's mom hand her a tissue, wiped her eyes, and whispered to Doe's mom: he'd been a fuck-up, but a harmless one, a really fun guy.

Doe thought maybe she'd ask Cyrus if he wanted to get ice cream sometime.

Tributes ranged from first-date awkward to show-business smooth, solemn to bawdy, but were always touching, occasionally suffused with blubbering—from both speakers and the crowd. The composite figure who emerged was difficult, cranky, charming, thoughtful, sensitive, someone who'd gone out of his way to show up for people he cared about, in a way that suggested not just thoughtfulness, but also loneliness; a hothead full of bluster who was perpetually caught holding the bag, letting himself be talked into storing band equipment, returning a van to the rental agency; a guy who'd been bitter about never making it big, but who never had any problem playing a simple duet with a sick patient, though that graduate degree in music therapy hadn't been the guarantee of employment he'd thought it would (this line drawing laughs from the crowd); a Tuesdays-at-eleven meeting regular who took his sobriety as seriously as his friendships, and good thing, too, because it helped him manage the diagnosis when it came, right out of the blue, and changed his life.

Doe's mother was holding her typed page again. Frail hands shook slightly; a dried and properly lipsticked mouth made small movements. On the stage four men with acoustic guitars who sat in a half circle finished performing their collaged interpretation of the deceased's original music. A young man was waiting for them to clear, and now was nervous, stumbling into a story about his mother-in-law, a secretary, meeting Merv when her breast cancer had returned. Doe watched, surprised and interested in the intensity of her mother's preparations.

A friend remembered smoking cigarettes deep into the night on Merv's fire escape, talking about generic drugs, patent law, and his crazy-expensive hamster-ovary infusions. He remembered another fall that messed up Merv's elbow and wrist, Merv's body going on a spiral from which he was never able to fully recover. He'd seem to be doing good, but then would bloat, or might cut himself and bleed crazy amounts. He'd fall out of touch and you might forget about him for a bit and then out of nowhere he'd post something insane and funny on your Facebook page and remind you all over again how much you dug him.

Doe's mother handed Doe the sunglasses and took her time in rising. Her father followed her into the aisle and took her by the elbow. Once behind the podium, Doe's mother spent a moment adjusting the microphone, a bit lower now. She tapped into it, and Tilda's voice was clear in calling back, "We're good." Her mother took off her hat and revealed a short shell of candy-pink hair. The crowd murmured approval. Her mother smiled and her eyes were bright. She looked so tiny up there. So old. She began to speak and then choked up and stopped and her face crumpled a bit and she did a half wave, as if dismissing the microphone.

"The first time I met Mervyn he tried to seduce me in a hospital while I was having chemotherapy." She waited through the group laugh and then said, "That's true. That happened. And I totally fell for him. It was brief and it was spectacular.

"The second phase of our relationship, I was recovering from a different bout of chemotherapy and he staked out my house and all but stalked me." People laughed again and Doe knew her mother was being charming, but also felt the intensity of truth in her mother's words, and while she was accustomed to her mother speaking truth, and being serious, this was different. Doe did not know how, but it was.

"Then the next phase. I was helpless. That man came to my room every day and sang his songs to me." Her face crumpled. "I often was not in a condition where I could hear. He sang them anyway."

Her father had lowered his head and was holding his eyes. Doe could not remember seeing him cry before, yet he looked pleased somehow.

"He was a friend, and he came and sang those songs and tried to help me to recover. That is an amazing thing. He came into my life in such a strange way and we had this wonderful arc."

She cleared her throat, seemed to consider something.

Alice closed her eyes, took a breath, exhaled. "I did not know Mervyn very well. Nor was he the most important person I've ever met. But at a very hard time, he was special. He tried his best, for me."

Through the crowd and pews, the murmur passed, a low, cresting wave, approval but something more as well. Doe kept her eyes trained on her mother: her turtle-skull lowered, a hand wiping away tears, purposefully heading away from the podium, into the open arms of her husband; Doe's father helping her down the three steps from the stage. There, they stood to the side and looked at each other. The next speaker was saying something nice to them and heading up to the podium. Tilda was blowing her nose with force into a Kleenex. Doe knew her parents loved her and she knew they once had been in love, but she often wondered about whether they loved each other. Now she watched them staring at one another with a clarity and intimacy that she recognized as laden with tenderness, and history, and more than that, too.

The right thing for her to do was to rise from the pew. The right thing was to head toward the aisle, embrace her parents. Of course, she'd heard her mother's cancer stories a zillion times. She had emails and texts to answer, exercises on the barre to complete— a host of other things she could do with this afternoon. But maybe it was worth talking to Mom anyway? Maybe there were stories she hadn't heard yet. A restlessness, so familiar as to be eternal, swelled inside of Doe. She didn't know what to do, didn't have any answers, not any good ones, anyway. She stretched her arms over her head and toward the domed sky. Presently the confused young woman did something that, to be honest, she rarely did anymore: following one of her mother's common pieces of advice, she took a deep breath and exhaled.

Acknowledgments

In the summer of 2009, my late wife, Diana Joy Colbert, was diagnosed with leukemia; our daughter was six months old. Diana was sick for two and a half years, and passed away three days before our daughter's third birthday. During those years, more people than I could ever document went out of their way to help our family. You tried and you made our lot easier. A thank-you doesn't begin to convey my gratitude. Know you have my unending love and thanks. I hope these feelings have been conveyed in person. Again, you mean the world to me.

I similarly cannot begin to list or thank the many people who helped try to put me back together after Diana passed. There are just too many for these meager pages. We are the sum of our friendships, and this makes me very lucky.

Diana kept a journal during parts of her ordeal, in the hope that she would write a memoir and that her experience would help others. What she left was raw and in its early stages, far from finished, let alone publishable. But it was important to me to try and share Diana's spirit and heart. With this in mind, portions of this book—specifically, its fourth section ("Enlightenment"), although also in the extended videotape scene near the end of section three ("And what if he flinched")—have been inspired by select passages from that journal. In these and a few other instances, I created scenes based on journal passages, or fit sentences (or ideas) from those passages into necessary existing scenes. Sometimes this required rewriting Diana's words, changing Diana's voice to fit Alice's, and/or editing down those journal passages. My goal was always to stay true to Diana's feelings and respectful of her privacy; simultaneously, I wanted to keep the novel true to Alice's arc and the book's own life. I hope these many things have been accomplished, and that Diana's love of life and will to live were properly conveyed. If they were not, it is because of my own artistic limitations.

Logistics: It's important to thank New York University for the teaching gig; Paragraph Workspace (a.k.a. "Cubicle") for the writing space and the support; the HALD Hovedgaard Danish-American Writers' Retreat for some time away when I was a mess; the Civitella Ranieri Foundation, specifically Tina Summerlin and Dana Prescott, for embracing me during another horrid period; Candace Wait, Elaina Richardson, and the Corporation of Yaddo, for everything; and the Authors Guild and Alice Rubin at TEIGIT, who worked to get us a new insurance plan when life quite literally depended on it.

Special thanks to the wonderful women who've helped care for my kid: Sam Miller, Nina Namthip, Liza Reytblat, Jen Hyde, Joyce Sotter, Michelle Marisola, Lauren Piven, Jess Prestia. Lindsey Kennedy has been a tremendous friend.

Leigh Newman, Fiona Maazel, and Mary Beth Hughes organized and put on a fundraiser that was invaluable in help defraying some of the medical costs—this and many other generosities put me in your debt. Richard Price, Rick Moody, Jonathan Franzen, George Saunders, Jon Foer, Sean Wilsey: I can't pay you back, any of you, not a cent, but maybe I'll be able to pass your kindnesses forward, somehow.

Andrew Ginsburg. Gina Grimaldi. Hannah Tinti, Jaime Clarke, Nicole Krauss, Alison Smith, Sarah Jay, Sheri Fink, Will Lychack. Evan (The Rooster) Hughes and Adelle Waldman for every Saturday night for three years. Josh Ferris and Eliza Kennedy. Julie Seabaugh. Mark Roberts, who almost kept me sane.

I was supposed to deliver a manuscript to Random House years ago. The powers that be easily could have terminated my contract and saved themselves a lot of headaches; instead, under the direction of Gina Centrello, they sent my daughter a giant pink stuffed animal, helped me find sitters, were patient and supportive, and worked to turn this manuscript into a gorgeous book. Every writer should have a publishing house as supportive and smart. Thank you so much, Gina, for your care and attention. Thank you, Rodrigo Corral, for staying with it and nailing this amazing cover. Simon Sullivan, for the perfect interior design and art. Beth Pearson, for the unblinking eye and the gentle hand. Michelle Jasmine—master of the art of public relations. Andrea Walker, for stepping into a difficult spot and handling all matters like the champion you are. (I am so very excited to see what we can do together.) Caitlin McKenna, for your good spirit, efficiency, and keen advice. And my editor emeritus, David Ebershoff, is all class; he is a genius, and, moreover, he is kind. I am choked up writing this. Thank you, my friend, for holding my hand through this entire journey. No one could do better.

Jim Rutman knocks down shots whether you put a hand in his face or not; I am so proud to be his client and backcourt partner.

Howard Axelrod and Matthew Thomas answered every call, every time—a man could not ask for better friends.

Diamond, Jhanine, and Yale. TJ and Declain and Isadora. Crystal Kenneally, who is everything I could want in a sister, plus a side of guacamole. Caryl and Howard Bock, whose support and love are just endless.

David Colbert, Susannah Maurer, and Peggy Taylor. I am sorry we could not keep her. We all miss her, separately and deeply. Know that you are heroes. Know that I adore you all. More important, know that Lily loves you.

Leslie Jamison returned me to the living, made me whole again, and makes every day worthwhile. Each day I try to show my thanks, my love.

Lily is my bright and shining star.

About the Author

CHARLES BOCK is the author of the novels *Alice & Oliver* and *Beautiful Children,* which was a *New York Times* bestseller and Notable Book, and won the Sue Kaufman Prize for First Fiction from the American Academy of Arts and Letters. His fiction and nonfiction have appeared in *Harper's, The New York Times,* the *Los Angeles Times,* and *Slate,* as well as in numerous anthologies. He lives with his wife, Leslie Jamison, and his daughter in New York City.

About the Type

This book was set in Sabon, a typeface designed by the well-known German typographer Jan Tschichold (1902–74). Sabon's design is based upon the original letterforms of sixteenth-century French type designer Claude Garamond and was created specifically to be used for three sources: foundry type for hand composition, Linotype, and Monotype. Tschichold named his typeface for the famous Frankfurt typefounder Jacques Sabon (c. 1520–80).